The Kingdom of Greed
The Kingdom of Fear
The Kingdom of Hope

Every European who ventured into the land of the Mayans
and experienced the power of the Mayans' alien gods
lived inwardly in one of those kingdoms. Many, many of
them died almost unimaginable deaths in them, too,
because in the brutal clash between European and
Indian, the arrow and the ax sometimes worked better
than gunpowder.

But slowly, after nearly two centuries of Spanish aggression
and disease, the Mayan empire fell into ruins . . . except
for one proud city called Tayasal, in what is now
Guatemala.

Tayasal still stood proud, challenging the foreigners,
dangerous in the extreme to those who took the challenge.

THESE KINGDOMS

A novel based on the facts of history and the passions of
the human heart.

THESE KINGDOMS

KENNETH McKENNEY

BALLANTINE BOOKS • NEW YORK

Library of Congress Catalog Card Number: 87-91139

ISBN 0-345-34109-0

Manufactured in the United States of America

First Edition: August 1987

Cover photo: © Hamlyn Publishing

Don Luis nodded.

"How much time do we have?" Cazaux called down to the longboat.

"Less than half an hour, sir." A duty boy held up the hour glass he carried. "It has turned for the last time."

"Then you are fortunate," Cazaux told Don Luis. "You have made a better bargain than you thought."

Don Luis sighed. "This had been planned well," he admitted. "Make your signal."

Cazaux smiled. He turned and lifted a hand. Three sailors in the prow of the longboat raised their muskets and, one after the other, fired into the air, shattering the outward peace of the morning. Immediately a flock of gulls rose from along the foreshore and wheeled into the sun, their cries extending the disruption.

D'Avila was considering his moment to fire when the sound of the muskets came up to the fort, confusing him with their suddenness. He turned his startled eyes toward the gunners, then nodded abruptly.

CHAPTER 3

STONE TURNED TO VAN STAAL AS THEY HEARD THE MUSKETS and the cries of the gulls that followed. Then the sound of cannon shattered the air about them, and from somewhere below came the screams of wounded men.

"Sweet Christ," whispered van Staal, his face suddenly grim. "Three muskets were to say that all was well."

"The cannon were from the fort." Stone also spoke softly, as if they might be overheard. "The Spaniards have fired back."

"The fart-suckers," the Dutchman cursed. "What do they intend?"

Stone spat on the limestone. He lifted his head clear of the outcrop and stared openly at the sight below.

Of the four cannon, three had discharged successfully. The fourth burst, killing its two gunners, throwing others to the ground. Capitán d'Avila was struck in the eye by a piece of flying metal. He reeled by a parapet, pawing at the blood that ran down his face.

Two of the cannon missed *La Petite*, but roundshot from the third crashed into the forepeak, shattering timbers, breaking in two the figurehead: a nubile woman

In the eight years I spent with this book, many friends helped me with research materials, criticism, and simple encouragement. I should like to thank them all wherever they may be, but in particular Luis Madariaga, who was thoughtful enough to hunt down and present me with a copy of *Campeche Durante el Período Colonial,* which I found invaluable. Also, I feel a great regard for the enthusiasm Bob Wyatt of Ballantine showed when he accepted the novel for publication. And I was especially heartened by the painstaking editing Julie Garriott provided. Without all these good people, this book would not be.

For my children:
Sarah, Kathryn, and Michael.

A hard time we had of it.

With an alien people clutching their gods.

—T. S. Eliot
Journey of the Magi

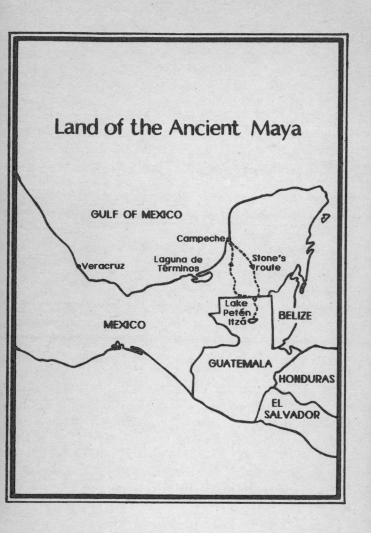

Land of the Ancient Maya

Many of the events on which this novel is based occurred, in one form or another, in the colorful history of Central America. Between 1661 and 1663, the port of Campeche was attacked at least four times by pirates. Yet in 1667, a certain Robert Chevalier, after looting the Laguna de Términos, arrived in Campeche and married the daughter of the sergeant major of the town. The city of Tayasal existed on Lake Petén Itzá, in what is now Guatemala—there all the kings bore the name of Canek. In Tayasal, the Maya lived with their gruesome gods for one hundred and seventy-eight years after the arrival of Cortez. They remained intact, though greatly reduced in number—mainly because of the diseases introduced by the Spanish invaders—until 1697. Then they were overcome by tactics, albeit on a grander scale, similar to those related here. A galley was built, other boats accompanied it, and gunfire destroyed the Maya warriors. When the carnage was over, and the temples destroyed, among the brown-skinned, black-haired citizens, a red-headed man was discovered. His presence has never been satisfactorily explained.

PART ONE

THE KINGDOM OF GREED

CHAPTER 1

THE PLAN HAD BEEN JEAN-MARC CAZAUX'S. THEY WOULD intercept the Spanish fleet, seeking stragglers among the twenty-three Spanish ships that sailed each February out of Veracruz. They would come with the wind and swoop on the lame, those whose hulls were thickest with seagrass, whose planking was deepest bored by teredo worm, whose sails had had most of their strength bleached from them in the long winter wait in Veracruz.

They searched the Spanish fleet for three days and found nothing—no trace of the treasure-laden galleons beating the resisting trades, bellies deep in the Gulf of Mexico, hammering toward Havana. The bullion that Spain depended on and they intended to pirate was seen on no horizon.

Then the wind changed. It sprang from the north like an uncaged beast to fling them downcoast toward Campeche. It tore at the frigates, the *Courage* and *La Petite*, as though bent on their destruction. The last Stone glimpsed of Cazaux before *La Petite* disappeared behind a wall of spray was the Frenchman's embattled figure on the quarterdeck, calling to his men.

As the storm roared, Christopher Stone, the English captain, mightily regretted his decision to join the persuasive Frenchman in this foray. As water bucketed

3

4 KENNETH McKENNEY

across the gunnels and the wheel tore at his hands, he cursed Cazaux—and the gold that had escaped them. Beside him, Rolf van Staal, mate of the *Courage,* bore the same bitterness in mind.

They contrasted strangely, the men who fought the bucking wheel of the *Courage.* Stone was tall and gaunt, his face skeletal. His eyes, peering from their red-rimmed sockets, held a look of furious intensity. He would be thirty this April, yet in the height of the storm he appeared ancient; weatherbeaten and timeless. Van Staal was forty-three, shorter, thicker in body than his captain. His round head, bronzed by sunlight, was almost bald; in the pale, sickly light of the storm, it gleamed with his movements.

The sea heaved, and the *Courage* rose. The masts came upright, the wet ropes cracked. Wind tore, and suddenly—where there had been six struggling figures locked in the ratlines, only five remained.

"Man overboard." The cry was hurled in the wind.

"Who is it?" shouted Cramer the Black, a six-foot Negro with a missing left ear. "Who's gone?"

Beside him appeared Percy Flanders. "It were Mc-Brice," he said in his soft Cornish accent. "I saw him go."

"Turn her," shouted Stone.

Wheel spokes ran through slippery hands. Sailless, the wind in the shrouds howling, timbers creaking, poles humming in the storm, the *Courage* came broadside to the weather. She hung a moment, swirled in a trough, lifted, her weight in the stern, then plunged down the leeward of a wave; running sideways before everything, she was loose and drowning.

"Keep her," Stone shouted to drive himself. "Keep her coming."

"Aye." Van Staal's cloak lay open to the wind, his powerful arms were bulging. "Give her more."

They fought until it seemed they would surrender. They held the frigate until she came to the end of her broadside. They struggled as she settled in another trough, and then she was round, her stern to the wind, running before, safe for the moment.

"We have her," Stone cried.

Van Staal grunted his affirmation, breathing deeply.

For twenty hours the storm continued, then it began to die. The sea steadied. The wind blew out. The wake of the weather's passing left long trails of cloud bending to the horizon; their edges were tinted salmon pink in the evening sun.

The day dawned clear and hard. A brass sun hung in a washed blue sky; a dry wind spun in over the mirror of the sea. In the town of Campeche on the Gulf of Mexico, Indians, bright with serapes, began to fill the Plaza Principal. They gathered in the shaded side of the square and laid out their produce: pyramids of lime-green avocadoes, polished so that they shone; multioranged mangoes with their myriad scents; dun-brown mamme cut to show a sliver of sweet vermilion flesh. As they spread their wares the traders chattered, their children clinging to them, mole-eyed and cautious.

A sudden sound of hooves heralded the arrival of a Spanish officer in a tight red doublet. He rode through the square, the tattoo of his progress ringing in its corners. The Indians fell silent. Behind the horseman marched the guard on its uneven way to the fort. A soldier scratched his unshaven cheek, another whistled to a girl; their presence took some of the simplicity from the morning.

From the balcony of his house overlooking the waterfront, Don Luis de Córdoba, mayor of Campeche, stared at the smooth expanse of the sea. Apart from three shrimpboats netting the morning tide, there was no vessel to be seen. Don Luis sniffed the air, then hurried down the stairwell, wondering if there was any substance to the rumors he had heard the evening before.

There were foreign ships off the coast, watermen had reported; it had been suggested that they might be corsarios waiting to attack. No one had been sure how many there were, but against the setting sun the shapes of distant sails had been seen.

Don Luis hoped the rumors were unfounded. Campeche was growing, even prospering. It was the main port of all New Spain, and no one wished to see it destroyed. Burned as it had been burned by Mansvelt in 1663, with the survivors huddled in the church of Guadalupe waiting for a ransom to be raised; women in the hands of the pirates. The dead had lain unburied in the bloodstained streets, and the sound of foreign voices had been everywhere.

Don Luis shook his head vigorously—he would not let it happen again. He crossed the freshly swept courtyard and entered the high-beamed dining room, where coffee and hot sweet breads stood on the long colonial table. He sat and beckoned urgently to his majordomo, who waited stiffly at the far end of the room. The man, a mestizo who wore tight hose and a striped jerkin, approached Don Luis with great formality.

"*Sí*, señor," he enquired. "How may I serve you?"

"Where is Angela, Manuel?"

"She will still be asleep, Your Worship."

"Wake her. I wish to speak to her now. And"—Don Luis indicated his untasted coffee—"heat this. It is cold, as usual."

"Of course, señor."

Don Luis waited impatiently, his fingers idly pulling apart a soft sugared bun. He was a thickset, portly man in his early fifties whose doublet did not seem to fit and whose hose was always wrinkled. But his appearance belied his fierce ambition.

He had come to New Spain in 1657 through family connections with the conde de Baños, the twenty-third viceroy to that Central American dominion. Don Luis had been grateful for the appointment; the death of his wife from fever in Seville had left him empty, and he had no other close relatives apart from his daughter, Angela, whom he adored. The girl had come late in the marriage, after two infant sons had died, so he treasured her all the more. She had been in Europe when Mansvelt attacked;

he would do his best to see that nothing occurred to her now.

After three years on the viceroy's staff in Mexico City, Don Luis had heard that the position of mayor in the town of Campeche was for sale; by gathering all his assets, he'd managed to secure it. And it was exactly what he required: isolated, profitable, and growing in prosperity. Only the threat of piracy had interfered with the port's progress. Yet that he'd viewed merely as another problem to be solved. As an administrator, Don Luis had been clever and successful. In the seven years since he had purchased his office, he had seen the terror of the pirates die.

Mansvelt's attack had been the last and one of the worst. After that Don Luis decided that whatever gold or silver or jewels the pirates demanded was not worth the value of the town or the destruction they would commit in searching. What they did to the women was inevitable, but what they did to the town could be avoided. So he had begun to trade with them, to pay the ransom and thereby save the sacking.

Don Luis thumped the table, and a servant appeared with hot coffee. "Call Manuel," Don Luis ordered. "I want him back here at once."

"*Sí*, señor." The servant disappeared, and a moment later Manuel entered the stately room.

"I need to speak to senior members of the council," Don Luis said. "In my rooms in half an hour. Capitán d'Avila I particularly want to see. Understood?"

"Of course, Your Worship."

"Where is Angela?"

"She is coming, señor."

"Hurry, hurry." Don Luis thrust sugared bread into his mouth. "Don't you realize we might all be attacked?"

"Yes, señor, I have heard the rumors."

"They might be more than rumors. Think about it. You were here when Mansvelt came. You know just how horrible it can be."

"I do, señor. My wife died when—"

"Then hurry, man, hurry. Send out now for those I want to see."

Manuel, bowing slightly, backed from the room.

Christopher Stone bent over the chart table in his neat, simply furnished cabin. He was exhausted now that the storm had passed, and he was deeply aware of the new dangers all on the *Courage* faced. The ship was in need of repairs and fresh supplies; the men would be frustrated by the thought of the loss of Spanish gold. They required a further target, a sense of future purpose— his years in the navy had taught him that. It was part of his task to show them command.

He glanced up when Cramer the Black entered. "Your watch is slack," he said without ceremony, returning his attention to the maps spread before him. "Lost its bollocks, perchance?"

Cramer's dark skin flushed. "McBride were one of the watch," he said carefully. "We lost him."

Stone's tight-boned face came up again. "I'll have no rot, I'll have no mewling," he said without raising his voice.

Cramer frowned, uncertain of what was next to come.

"Have every man who's not crippled move 'tween decks," Stone continued evenly. "Have them hang their hammocks between the guns. Get them from the fo'c'sle."

"Yes, sir."

"Then scrub the fo'c'sle clean."

"Scrub it?"

"God's blood, Cramer. Get the smell of shit and vomit and fear out of it." Stone's voice was steady. "Clean the *Courage* until I can walk into that fo'c'sle and not taste your panic."

Cramer swallowed. "The storm were bad, Cap'n. We thought we were done for. All of us, not only McBride. It were bad, you know that for yourself."

"Then sweep its memory clean."

"We will, but—"

"Sweet Jesu." Stone walked away from the table; he breathed deeply, knowing that Cramer would pass on the command. "There is nothing like weather to weaken a man," he added in a milder tone.

Cramer did not reply. He watched Stone peer through a porthole at the sunlit sea. The tall Englishman wore a leather jerkin over an unbleached linen shirt, breeches that were tucked into turned-down seaboots. When he turned again to Cramer, his expression was openly concerned.

"We've lost a forward hand, and another's dying," Stone said quietly. "There's timbers in need of repair. Water in the biscuit. The salt beef's rotting. We'll needs put in somewhere, and I want the men in heart."

Cramer nodded; he understood now the Englishman's drive. "There's talk of the Laguna de Términos," he said.

"Aye. It's no place for milk-livers there." Stone's voice was thoughtful as he continued, "It's the home of logwood cutters, mainly English. Slaves that've escaped Jamaica. Blackies, like yourself. They'll give none of us a real welcome."

Cramer cleared his throat. "I know it," he said softly. "I put in there with Bartolomeo the Portuguese once. We were sick with yellow jack. Those already there helped themselves to what we had. They was more like animals than men."

"They lived hard," Stone replied. "They've had to, to survive." His eyes did not leave the Negro's face. "You know what a slave's life's like, Cramer. Better than most. Especially in the hands of the Spanish or the Portuguese."

"It was Bartolomeo that freed me," Cramer said quietly.

"That's as may be." Stone grunted and returned his attention to the map laid out on the chart table, his finger pointing. "Now, look, Cramer, from what I reckon—"

Stone was interrupted by a cry. "Ship, ship ahoy," shouted a lookout. "*La Petite*. The Frenchman's back."

Stone lifted his head. "Well, well," he said, staring at Cramer, his eyes hardening. "I wonder what he wants from us now."

*   *   *

Don Luis de Córdoba, mayor of Campeche, stuffed a warm sweet roll into his mouth while he waited for his daughter to descend and turned over in his mind the reports he'd heard of a ship—or ships, no one seemed certain of the number—sighted off the coast. His first reaction had been to hope the rumors were unfounded; now he was not quite so sure. He had learned to deal with these invading corsarios, as they had learned how to bargain with him.

However, it was possible, Don Luis thought as he chewed ponderously, that an invasion from someone who would be content to accept a reasonable ransom and leave the town untouched might suit him quite nicely now. Restore him, as it were. All was not quite as smooth in Campeche as it had been a few years ago; they'd benefited too well from his management. González, the town treasurer, had designs on the mayoralty, would buy it any way he could. D'Avila, the garrison commander, was becoming more puffed up and arrogant by the day; they could both benefit, in Don Luis's eyes, by being firmly reduced to their offices.

And a raid by pirates, carefully handled by himself, without bloodshed and loss of life? Don Luis nodded thoughtfully. It could suit him very well. Do him untold good. Of course, he would see that Angela was safely out of the way, just in case. And then he would watch the coast carefully or move sooner if he thought it prudent.

Jean-Marc Cazaux wore his hair long enough to curl into the collar of his broadcloth doublet; about his neck was a scarf of Chinese silk. He was five years older than Stone and almost as tall; from his right cheekbone to the corner of his mouth ran a fine scar that lent his expression a smiling aspect. He sat opposite Stone at the chart table, and behind him stood Sartou, his fat, foul-breathed mate, who wore a gold ring in the lobe of his left ear.

The only other occupant of the cabin was van Staal; he watched both Cazaux and Sartou with open dislike.

"Laguna de Términos?" Cazaux was saying with a graceful gesture of dismissal. "It is so inhospitable there."

"It's close. We'll manage," Stone replied carefully. "Anyway, a little opposition will keep my crew alert."

"Perhaps." Cazaux shrugged; his English was only slightly accented. "I know well what this storm has meant," he continued. "Your ship needs refitting, your men are beginning to, shall we say, lose faith."

"You've no damage?" van Staal asked gruffly from where he stood behind Stone.

"A little water." Cazaux waved an indifferent hand. "But Laguna de Términos?" he went on, returning his attention to Stone. "It is as its name implies, the end of all civilization." He smiled at his own remark and, carried by it, added, "That is where half the population is the color of coal. Maroons, we call them." He laughed aloud. "You'll find yourself marooned, my friend, fighting for your life."

"We'll survive," Stone said. "And it's close," he added doggedly. "We need a port."

Cazaux spread his eloquent hands. "Would Campeche not serve as well?" he asked. He watched with further amusement the surprise that swept over Stone's hawklike features, that stilled the round face of van Staal, and smiled. "I know it is a garrison town," he went on easily. "They are proud of their fort. They have a commander fresh from Spain. But that does not mean that certain arrangements cannot be made. And it is not all that far from here."

Stone hesitated. "I do not know the port," he said.

"Ah, but I do. I was there . . . when was it?" Cazaux questioned Sartou. "Four? Yes, four years ago?" Sartou nodded.

"With more success, I trust, than we've had on this miserable venture," Stone said cuttingly.

"My friend, you are growing tiresome." There was a trace of impatience in Cazaux's voice. "M'sieu Sartou," he said, turning to the mate of *La Petite*, "be kind enough to tell these gentlemen what ransom we made four years ago."

Sartou cleared his throat, and Cazaux leaned away from his mate's foul breath. "There was much," Sartou began clumsily, his accent thick. "We left rich."

"Really?" Stone's tone was dry.

Sartou blinked.

"Forgive his English," Cazaux said easily. "That is not where his talent lies." He spoke rapidly to Sartou in French, listened, then translated. "We took more than thirty thousand pieces of eight. Every man felt he had been well rewarded."

"How many did you lose?"

"One." Cazaux smiled. "For a wager one happy night, he drank a pitcher of rum."

Stone's face showed surprise. "You met no resistance?"

Cazaux shook his head. "There is a mayor in Campeche who does not wish to see his town destroyed. We made him a proposition, and he paid us a ransom. It was very simple, very civilized, my friend. There was no damage."

Sartou snorted with suppressed laughter.

"Well"—Cazaux shrugged—"very little damage. Most of the women should have, by now, fully recovered. So you see," he continued, his eyes on Stone, "even in our reduced condition, it is quite possible that we will succeed handsomely. In spite of what we have been through, our men will have something for their troubles." He leaned back and waited for Stone's reply.

Stone knew that, in part, what the Frenchman said was true. His men were disheartened. They had lost all sight of the Spanish fleet, they had been beaten by the storm. The thought of an easy prize would renew their spirit. But he had no faith in this affected foreigner with the scar on his face.

"Very well," he said at last. "We will go with you. But ready your fighting men. We will make this mayor of yours a proposition. But should it be rejected, we will fight for our purchase."

The thing to do, Don Luis calculated as he waited for Angela, was to present the matter to the council forcefully, make them aware that a real danger waited just beyond the horizon. They must see clearly that only through his own skillful bargaining could the town be saved from burning, the women from brutality, and the would-be pillagers turned away. They must be impressed by the fact that his own unshakable presence was critical to their salvation. Without him, they would be lost.

Don Luis nodded in self-confirmation. It shouldn't be difficult to bring about. If only his daughter would appear, so that he might get her well out of the way before anything began. Just in case, he told himself. To spare her any discomfort.

"Manuel," he called suddenly, impatiently. "Get Angela down here at once."

From somewhere above he heard a muffled reply.

Christopher Stone leaned against the railing of the poop deck. The *Courage* was easy in the little wind, the sea was as soft as cloth. From somewhere to the west came the smell of vegetation, a sense of coastline; beside him stood Cramer the Black.

"You've been to Campeche?" Stone was asking. "You know this quarter well?"

"Aye." Cramer's lilting voice was mournful. "I knows it well."

Stone laughed. "You're a gloomy mongrel, Cramer," he said. "Is it not as easy a town as our friend Cazaux describes?"

"I was locked in jail, Cap'n," Cramer explained. "With Bartolomeo the Portuguese. I was caught with him, and they put us in the largest fort."

"Then you'll know something of their defenses?"

"From the inside. Was more'n a month before we were clear of our irons."

"Did you discover anything?"

"Well, it's the only fort that has any strength. There's another to the east and one to the west, but they're used for storage. Barracks for the men. But the big one's well defended. Very proud of it they were when they put us in their stinking dungeons."

"All dungeons stink, Cramer. What else should I know?"

"There was talk of trenches they'd dug along the waterfront, but I never saw nothing of them."

"You speak their language?"

"Enough. We all speak a bit of something, don't we?" Cramer scratched his woolly head. "It'll suit me to call in there again. I've a few old scores to settle."

"They treat you badly?"

Cramer shrugged in the darkness. "I've been treated worse," he replied quietly.

"How'd you get away?"

"Paid. Gold gets you anything along this coast."

"How'd you get the gold, Cramer?"

"I sang for it, Cap'n." The Negro laughed. "I'm sure you know there's always ways."

Stone did not reply.

She was a tall girl, quite beautiful, with skin like milk. Even now, her dark hair uncombed, her face puffed from sleep, she was lovely. As he watched his daughter, seated opposite him at the breakfast table, Don Luis's eyes softened.

"*Dios mío,* Papá." Angela yawned delicately. "What is this? So early?"

"Have some coffee." Don Luis waved at a servant. "You must wake up."

"At this hour, uf!" Angela's fingers played with the coffee cup. "Why did you not let me sleep?"

Don Luis leaned forward. "Ships have been reported along the coast. Last evening and the night before. Strange sails that made no attempt to anchor. They may be pirates."

Angela's eyes opened wide.

"You were well away from Campeche last time we were attacked." Don Luis crossed himself rapidly. "Thank God for that. But I am not taking any chances. You must be ready to go before I leave the house."

"That is impossible."

"Make it possible." Don Luis spoke with sudden firmness. "Your well-being may depend on it."

"But Papá—" Angela seemed distressed by the harshness of her father's words—"even if they *are* corsarios, I have heard you have ways of dealing with them."

"I have, and I trust we can bargain. But I am not taking the slightest risk as far as you are concerned. You are all I have. I would not see them lay a hand on you."

"My God." Angela's features came alive. "What *do* you mean?"

"Prepare yourself." Don Luis patted his daughter's hand. "I will see to the carriage, and then I must leave."

"But Papá, where would I go?"

"To Mérida. To the governor's house."

"Oh, I hate it there. You know how boring they are."

"Get ready." Don Luis urged his daughter from the table. "There may be little time."

He walked the easy deck, listening to the sound of creaking rope, smelling the fresh tang of tar. It was almost dark, and the line between the sea and sky was dove gray and dying. From below came the sound of lifting voices; he heard the lookout singing. There was a new spirit in the *Courage*, it was replacing the weakness the storm had left behind.

Stone paused by the railing and recalled his first command. He'd come to this part of the world in 1655 with the fleet that made up Cromwell's grand design to the West Indies, it was an aspect of the war with Spain. He'd fought at the capture of Jamaica, and that was where he'd met van Staal. The Dutchman had been a Spanish prisoner, to be executed as a buccaneer in Port Royal, until the English drove in and relieved the Spaniards of both: their prisoner and their port.

Later Stone had sailed with Vice-Admiral Goodson, refining his seamanship and his presence among the crew. When Commodore Mings replaced Goodson, both Stone and van Staal had signed with him to continue their sacking of the Spanish Main. England was still at war, Holland was an ally, they had legitimate commissions to loot and plunder; they were the privateers.

Stone's first command had been a Spanish frigate captured on its way to Cartagena. He'd sailed it back to Jamaica; Rolf van Staal had gone with him as his mate.

It all seemed, suddenly, an age ago, Stone thought as he gripped the railing and watched the line between sea and sky fade to almost nothing. There'd been many changes since then, perchance there'd been too many. He sucked in the soft evening air and shrugged. It paid little to think upon it, he told himself. He was not responsible for the Restoration or the withdrawal of the commissions, those letters of marque that gave them the protection of a country, that didn't brand them as they were branded now: freebooters, pirates, Brethren of the Coast.

Stone spat suddenly into the passing sea. There was no point in further contemplation. There was work to be done. He'd be better employed turning his mind to the task that lay ahead. The morrow: that was where his responsibility lay.

CHAPTER 2

THEY CAME IN LONGBOATS THROUGH THE CRABBED ROOTS of mangroves, past flocks of sleeping flamingos pink as rose petals in the soft gray dawn. They slipped from the boats to creep silently over the limestone foreshore, their weapons wrapped to prevent any sound. Most of them were barefooted as they made their way toward the Campeche fort the Spaniards were so proud of. Its shape grew bulky in the filling light.

The invaders were as mixed and as varied a lot as any in the Caribbean. Some had been logwood cutters on the Campeche coast, men whose hands and forearms were stained dark red from the dye the logwood held. There were others, like Stone, who had fled when their letters of marque were withdrawn, when the commissions they carried were canceled by the restoration of an English king and the end of a Spanish war; they were the sailors who knew the winds and the currents and the bays in which to find shelter. There were cow hunters from the northwest of Hispaniola who had learned the art of the buccan, the smoking of meat from the Indians that gave the name to all their kind: buccaneers.

There were Dutch and French and English, black and brown and white, none any longer with a country; they sailed for no one but themselves. All came with the

knowledge that without any prize there would be no
pay. They came now, silently in the filling dawn, for a
booty that lay within reach.

Wearing a black cloak and a leather hat, Don Luis de
Córdoba hurried through the Plaza Principal toward the
Municipal Building. About him everything appeared normal. A boisterous Indian muleteer, beneath a broad-
brimmed straw sombrero, shouted at a Negro slave leading
a reluctant donkey. A friar with a freshly shaven scalp
walked, grave of manner, across the square, weaving
between the piles of laid-out produce. Three merchants,
as somber in their dress as Don Luis or the friar, stood
in a group discussing the rumors. They looked at the
mayor as he passed, their eyes questioning.

Don Luis did not speak to them. He had seen to it that
the carriage was ready, as was his daughter. She should
now be on her way. He went on rapidly, through an
archway, and came to the colonnaded entrance of the
Municipal Building; its pinkstone façade was fresh and
inviting in the early sunlight. Two guards in red doublets
and off-white hose came to slow attention as he approached, their pikes held loosely before them.

Don Luis made a half bow in their direction and
entered the two-story building. He moved rapidly through
a long, richly furnished chamber toward his offices, nodding his ackowledgment of greetings, mumbling responses,
his mind elsewhere.

Christopher Stone lay behind a limestone outcrop
twenty-five yards from the northeasterly wall of the
Spanish fort. Between his position and the Campeche
defenses ran a narrow, steep-sided trench, which had
collapsed where it ran closest to the wall of the fortress.
There, a wooden lean-to was also in decay. Stone calculated that with the remains of the fallen timbers he could
make a hasty stepway that his men could climb.

He turned to glance at where they were hidden. There
were almost fifty of them amongst the broken rock and
stunted vegetation, but not one was to be seen.

He felt the slightest movement beside him and turned farther to see van Staal come silently closer.

"They are ready," whispered van Staal.

"All know the signal?"

"Aye. Three shots close-fired to say that all is well."

Stone squinted at the lifting sun. "They should come soon if what the Frenchman says is true."

"If."

"Do you doubt him?"

"I doubt all men until they prove themselves." Van Staal shifted his weight. "And he has yet to do so."

Stone did not reply. The men were placed, they were prepared. It was Cazaux's task to make the mayor his proposition. If he failed, the pirates would attack. Now was not the time to question loyalties.

Don Luis de Córdoba sat in the raised mayoral chair at the head of the council table. With him were Muñoz, Campeche's chief constable, González, the town treasurer, and Leal, the municipal architect. Behind the mayor, on the wall of the council chamber, hung a huge portrait of Philip IV of Spain. The king had been dead for over a year, but so far no painting of his successor had arrived, and no one saw any reason for removing the likeness of the dead monarch.

"With all due respect," González was saying, "don't you think your reaction might be premature? There is, after all, nothing known of these ships." He was a thin man with a tiny mouth, and to the mayor, his words always sounded pinched.

"I agree," said Muñoz, a heavy shape in his sixties. He blinked as he spoke. "What is more, we have dealt with corsarios before."

Leal also opened his mouth to protest. None of them had welcomed the mayor's early call, all had been lulled by the tranquillity of the past few years. But before the architect had the chance to speak, the great double doors of the council chamber burst open and the short, bearded figure of Capitán d'Avila, commander of the garrison, hurried into the room.

"Listen, all of you," d'Avila said loudly. "A frigate is approaching the town. She is French. Watermen identify her as *La Petite*."

The force of d'Avila's entry, the threat in his words, silenced the council chamber momentarily. Then Don Luis, with a feeling of great relief, let out his breath very slowly. "Cazaux," he said. "He was here four years ago. For ransom."

Immediately a buzz of comment began.

"Do you still think I am being *premature*?" Don Luis fixed his gaze on González, forcing his intensity. "Last time he took twenty thousand pieces of eight, ten Indian women, and some boys. I saw the body of one of them washed up a week later. It was not a pretty sight."

"Yes, of course." González coughed behind his hand; the pompous merchant was being curiously dramatic, and González wondered why. If this fat, untidy little man had not been related to the viceroy, he'd never have been considered for the post of mayor—money or not. The sooner he was replaced the better. González turned to d'Avila. "How far away is the frigate? How much time do we have?"

"An hour. Or less."

"Are there others?"

"None have been sighted."

"Then we must be ready," Don Luis said quietly, nodding with authority.

"That we will," said d'Avila. "I have ordered the fort to arms. I have called out the garrison. By the time the French land we will be more than ready."

"You do not understand." Don Luis's voice rose quickly. "They will have come to bargain."

"Bargain?" D'Avila's dark eyes flashed. "I do not bargain with pirates."

"You do not understand," Don Luis said with forced patience. "You have not seen what such men can do."

"Of course I have seen the work of pirates. They are no worse here than in Europe." D'Avila spoke fiercely. "But they can be stopped. They can be contained."

"By battle?"

"Indeed. I should like to test my garrison."

"I am afraid you'll find it wanting." It was Leal, the municipal architect, who spoke; he was a broad man in his forties with an open, clever face. "It's not been tested in many years. It has forgotten what the sound of gunfire is like."

"Then it is time it was heard again."

"No." Don Luis thumped the table and lifted his voice again. "There will be no fighting. There will be no destruction. We will find out what these Frenchmen want. If needs be, we will give it to them. What's more, if Cazaux is still captain of *La Petite*, we can negotiate, as we did before." He leaned forward, his eyes going from face to face. "I want you to understand that clearly, gentlemen. I will not see Campeche put to the torch again."

D'Avila stared at the mayor with distrust and dislike.

"Return to the fort," Don Luis instructed. His thick-set figure was full of bearing. "See that your men are ready if you wish, but do not even think of firing a shot."

The garrison commander hesitated.

"Now." Don Luis, rising, pushed the great mayoral chair back from the table. "I order it. The rest of you, come with me to the waterfront."

The offshore breeze smelled faintly of dust and woodsmoke. Gulls wheeled and turned, diving among the frigate's jetsam, filling the air with their cries. Cazaux lifted the telescope and examined once more the knot of men on the great breakwater that ran out from the Campeche shore.

"They await us," he said quietly to Sartou.

"They remember well," replied the fat mate. "With them we will have no problems."

"With our new friends?"

Sartou tugged at the gold ring in his left ear. "That Englishman is more clever than he seems," he muttered.

"Then we must be extremely careful, M'sieu Sartou."

Sartou belched, and Cazaux raised a protective hand.

"However, I do not think that he suspects anything," the mate said.

"Nevertheless, you are right about him. If there is any sign at all, he will guess." Cazaux closed the telescope with a click. "Make sure that all who are informed are silent. There are not many, but speak to them yourself."

"I will see to it, *mon capitaine*."

"Good. and see that they do not drink too much tonight. None of those who are involved. Not until what we have to do is over."

Cazaux turned his attention back to the shore, to the white clustered shapes of the waterfront buildings. The spires of the churches, the dark pattern of the squares, were clear in the early sun. Behind the town the hills were pale as wash, the air buckled by the rising heat. Cazaux's eyes went to the solid shape of the fort; it seemed massive against the landscape. He knew that Stone and his men were already in place and hoped they would not be needed.

"He is untameable," he muttered, almost to himself. "There are times when I fear that Englishman will explode."

Sartou glanced at Cazaux, then shrugged. "He is not as you are," he commented politely.

Cazaux nodded, accepting the flattery. In his own veins flowed the blood of aristocrats. It had been his cousin, governor of French St. Kitts, who had persuaded him to come to the Caribbean. On arrival Cazaux had been given a frigate. Sailing had been a passion of his since boyhood; he'd developed his skills in the harsh waters off St. Malo, absorbing every sea. As a captain he'd proved himself superb.

Three times he'd traded vessels, and now he had *La Petite*; she was as fast and as maneuverable as any along the coasts. He sailed her out of Tortuga for a time under a Portuguese commission, relying on any target for a prize, taking what he was able whenever he could. His shrewdness and his charm carried him; his seamanship enabled him always to escape: he was swift in these clear waters, almost impossible to touch.

Yet now he stared a little troubled at the port they were approaching; there was more than he could see hidden in the landscape.

"He is possessed," he continued, speaking to the shore. "He has this . . . what is it? a frenzy to succeed."

Sartou waited a moment before speaking again. "What he is matters little, so long as he plays his part," he suggested.

"Of course, of course." Cazaux laughed abruptly and turned away from Campeche. "So long as he plays his part."

Capitán Fernando d'Avila marched briskly toward the fort, anger forcing his pace. He had nothing but disdain for these soft colonials. In the six months he had been in Campeche, his dislike for them had grown until he found it difficult to speak to them civilly.

He had been sent to review the garrison and had set out believing the task would be easy, that the reports of its competence were sound; but on arrival he'd been appalled by what he'd found. The garrison was not merely slack, it was slovenly. Of the twelve pieces of artillery in the principal fort, most failed to function. Carriages had rotted in the tropical climate or had been eaten to a shell by wood-borers. Many of the guns had rusted into place; some had been spiked by Mansvelt's men and not redrilled, there was no way of firing them. Round shot had long ago ceased being checked by gauges to see if it would fit into the weapons; successive coats of paint now covered the balls, and many of them would no longer enter the gun breeches.

Powder had moldered with damp; slow matches would not light. Often as not the men on duty would leave their posts to drink in the taverns along the waterfront or to visit the women in the Indian village. Few of them stayed the long nights, slapping at mosquitoes, envying those who had left.

Even now, six months after his arrival, although most

of the guns were serviceable, little had changed in the discipline of the garrison. D'Avila noted with disgust, as he approached the fort, that the party he had set to remove weeds from between the bulwark stones was sitting in the shade; a flask of wine was being passed between them. When they saw him, the soldiers scrambled to their feet, expecting his rebuke. But d'Avila hurried past, his mind focusing on the approach of the French frigate. It was closer now, he heard the crack of sails. D'Avila's pace quickened. He knew that his men, however shabby, would outnumber the pirates. He believed that any invader must be turned back with force.

On the breakwater that ran out from the town's seawall, the mayor and the councilors watched *La Petite* approach. As she came through the morning in the blue-brown harbor, the sun full on her and the wind stirring, she was magnificent.

A voice called in French. A sailor with a lead line answered, and *La Petite* came to, her sails shivering as the wind was held. They loosened, and the frigate swung on her anchor rope. A boat was lowered and began to pull toward the Spaniards on the breakwater. In the stern, beside Cazaux, a sailor held a white flag aloft.

"They come in peace," muttered Muñoz, the chief constable. Under sparse gray brows, his old eyes shifted their gaze to Don Luis. "It is to be hoped they leave that way."

"They have come to ransom," Don Luis replied; he coughed. "*I* will have to see what can be done," he added significantly.

"We have—" González broke off, nervous. "I mean, what could we afford?"

"Nothing." Don Luis's reply was sharp. "But I will deal with them; don't you worry about that."

"It is possible," said Leal, the municipal architect, "that they have other needs. Food, perhaps, or water. After all, there has been a storm."

"Perhaps." Don Luis wondered if Angela had left and

was certain that she had. "I will attend to them as I have before."

The longboat came abreast of the breakwater. French hands reached out for Spanish. There was a hollow grinding as the sleek craft come to rest. Cazaux leapt ashore and smiled broadly at the members of the Campeche council.

"It is a pleasure to see you, gentlemen." Cazaux's Spanish was as fluent as his English. "Especially you, Don Lorenzo."

"Luis," the mayor corrected.

"Of course." The genial scar on Cazaux's cheekbone deepened. "I see that your pretty town is as pretty as it was . . . before. Let us all hope it remains that way for many years to come." His mocking eyes went from the turrets of the fort to the careful stonework of the church of Guadalupe. "It would be a great pity to see any harm come to so lovely a place."

"We trust none will."

"Of course." Cazaux spread his hands. "That is why we are meeting, no?"

"What is it you want, Señor Cazaux?" Don Luis lifted his chin and stared levelly at the Frenchman. "Do not play games with me any longer. You know, very well, how I function here."

"Ah, so commercial you have become." Cazaux's smile disappeared; the line of his scar was thin and distinct. "Fifty thousand pieces of eight."

All the council members blinked.

"And a few novelties to amuse my crew."

"You mean women?" Leal enquired.

"And others. We do not want to leave anyone unsatisfied, do we?" Cazaux's voice was hard. "Neither my men nor those on the ships you cannot see."

"What ships?" Don Luis turned hurriedly toward the horizon. "What do you mean?"

"They wait," Cazaux replied confidently. "When we have completed our negotiations I will signal them—to let them know if the results are good or bad."

"How many are there?" Don Luis's eyes were suddenly concerned—the advantage that he'd seemed to possess was being taken from him. "What other ships?"

"Four. All larger than *La Petite*. All with so much hunger."

"Fifty thousand pieces of eight is impossible." González moved his thin lips carefully, as if feeling his way into the exchange. "We do not have so large a sum."

"Are you sure of that, Spaniard?"

"I am certain it could not be found."

"My men would find it," Cazaux said, leaning closer to the lean treasurer. "If I let them loose to search, they would find it easily."

González swallowed; on his taut neck his Adam's apple was stark. "Half that amount—"

"Gentlemen . . ." Don Luis coughed to ease the tension, to regain his fading influence. There was sweat in the band of his leather hat; his cloak seemed suddenly heavy, but he knew he must maintain control. "Perhaps if we were to examine what funds we have . . ."

González shrugged. "Our resources are low," he said uneasily. "The wars with the Indians in the north have been expensive. There have been taxes—"

"*Merde*," said Cazaux bitterly. "How you Spaniards barter." He turned toward the longboat and spoke softly and swiftly to Sartou in French. He listened to the response, then laughed and returned his attention to the councilors. "As you may have heard," he began, "my mate informs me it will take him little time to find the money. He would start with the church and move from there to the larger houses. Then the convent and, perhaps, the hospital. It may require some effort, and there would, of course, be a little damage. But he would find it, señores. Of that he had no doubt."

"No." Don Luis shook his head vigorously. "I'll not permit it."

"Mind you," Cazaux continued smoothly, ignoring the mayor, "it would mean that they might find more than fifty thousand pieces of eight. And some of your citizens may be made to feel . . . uncomfortable." He spread his hands. "What is more, normally my men are satisfied with Indian women, but should they sniff what else there is in this pretty town, how would we stop them? Gentlemen, I ask you, once they had that flavor in their glands, who knows what they might demand?''

''Very well, very well.'' Don Luis knew it was time to agree. ''We will give you what we have.''

''You will give me what I ask.''

''We will try.'' With an effort Don Luis's jaw jutted forward. ''But you understand—''

Cazaux smiled suddenly. ''I am not a greedy man, Don Luis,'' he said. ''Guarantee me forty thousand pieces of eight, or goods to that value, and your town will be safe.''

''I will do my best.''

''Of that, I am certain.''

Don Luis turned toward the town, trying to hide his feeling of sudden satisfaction. The sum was twice that taken by Cazaux four years ago, but in that time Campeche had prospered. Forty thousand could be afforded. It was less than the mayor would have settled for and far less than the pirates would have taken had they been set loose among the houses.

''Are we agreed, gentlemen?'' Cazaux's sharp eyes were on the other councilors. ''Is that a bargain?''

The others exchanged quick, nervous glances and nodded.

Van Staal lifted his round head and peered into the near distance. His eyes took in the anchored *La Petite*, the longboat, the cluster of men on the stone causeway that ran out from the shore. ''They talk,'' he muttered as he crouched again by Stone. ''And yet there is no signal.''

'' 'Tis not yet time.''

''They've had their time.''

''Be patient,'' Stone whispered.

''I'm coming not to trust him.''

''Be patient,'' Stone said again, his own tension rising. He felt the violence in the air that came from the men who hid and waited. ''We will know soon enough.''

* * *

Capitán Fernando d'Avila had watched impatiently as the last of the workable cannons was prepared. There were four in all; they'd been lumbered into the embrasures facing the sea by soldiers who'd sweated and cursed as they'd heaved. The guns were trained on *La Petite*; now, loaded and primed, they were almost ready. Touchmen stood by with lit matches, waiting for the order to fire.

In spite of what the mayor had ordered, d'Avila intended to fire on the French. He had seen the frigate drop anchor and the longboat pull into the breakwater. There was no sign of any other craft. With his four guns trained on *La Petite,* and her captain already ashore, he had an excellent chance of crippling the enemy. Immediately after that was done, he would send a troop down to the waterfront. There, they would take the corsario captain and his men.

Then they would see what bargains were to be made, what his garrison was capable of. With the slightest amount of good fortune, his men would redeem themselves and once again be in control of the defense of the town.

Jean-Marc Cazaux turned to his mate. "M'sieu Sartou," he said loudly, a smile quirking the corners of his lips. "I think it is time to make our signal."

"*Oui, mon capitaine.* Three muskets, close-fired."

"Three muskets close-fired it is."

"But?" Don Luis frowned; a trick was being played. "The frigates beyond the horizon? They will not hear muskets."

"Forgive me, señor. I have told you some little lies."

"There are no other ships?"

"There is a ship, but she is some distance from here." Cazaux help up a warning hand as he watched the expression on the mayor's face. "But there is a party of men who landed before sunrise. They are in position behind your pretty fort. If they do not hear the three shots soon, they will attack. Do you understand?"

with a cherub in her arms. A seaman died with a splinter of oak in his throat.

As soon as Cazaux heard the cannon he jerked a pistol from his belt and fired at the nearest Spaniard. Leal, the architect, fell dead on the stone breakwater. As Don Luis and the others, their faces drawn with fear, scrambled for safety among the low stonework at the head of the causeway, Cazaux leapt back into the longboat.

"To the ship," Cazaux shouted, his face livid with rage. "We will skin these motherless Spaniards. We will kill every whore in the town."

Berniard, the chief gunner of *La Petite*, seeing what had occurred, immediately ordered a return of fire. Hurriedly, guns were wedged and sighted on the fort. Most of their shots fell short to land in the shallow harbor or went over the battlements to the town beyond, but two crashed into the embrasures, filling the air with dust and the shouts of frightened men.

"Load again," Capitán d'Avila ordered as he staggered among the wreckage, a bloody cloth torn from the shirt of a dead gunner held to his face. "Fire again."

D'Avila's lieutenant, Reyes, approached and saluted. "The troop to attack the breakwater?" he questioned. "Shall I send it down now, sir?"

"Immediately, Teniente."

"Yes, sir." The lieutenant fumbled another salute. The morning was rich with excitement. He moved away urgently, calling to his sergeant. "Use your muskets," he cried. "Single out the captain. Do not let him reach his ship alive."

"Now," Stone roared above the confusion. "Up the wall with the broken timbers. Now. Follow me."

For all his size, Stone ran lightly across the broken ground. Van Staal followed closely, and out of the seemingly deserted landscape came the rabble of pirates. Some wore bandanas around their foreheads, others had their hair braided and tarred. They carried pistols, muskets, or pikes. Almost all had a broad-bladed cutlass or

a shortsword stuck in their belts. They were ready and
dangerous. Their greed lent them courage.

As Stone put the first of the fallen timbers into place,
other hands reached for planks. A carriageway began to
form up the wall. When it was ready, Stone was the first
onto it. He swung himself level with the nearest parapet
and looked over it to see what lay below.

The three working cannon were primed, ready to be
fired again. Dust hung heavy about them, speckling the
air. The cries of the wounded and the desperately afraid
filtered piteously up to Stone as he fixed his attention on
the short, bearded figure of d'Avila, the bloodied cloth to
his face, urging his men to action.

Then movement on the waterfront caught Stone's eye,
and he saw the scarlet jackets of the troop led by Reyes
form parallel lines, drop into a firing position, and train
their long-barreled muskets at the escaping longboat.
There was a sound of scattered shooting. A sailor in the
longboat shouted and fell into the sea. It was not Cazaux.
His tall shape remained in the stern, mouth open, hurl-
ing curses at the shore, arms waving, flailing the men
toward *La Petite*.

Then the three cannon boomed and jerked on their
trucks; roundshot was flung into the air. This time two
went home. One smashed a gunport, bursting the cannon it held; the other struck a yardarm, sending deadly
splinters to the men below.

Immediately Stone knew what had to be done. *"Now,"*
he yelled, and went over the wall. "We'll have them
before they load again."

With cries as fearsome as the Spaniards had ever
heard, the pirates threw themselves over the bulwarks
and down onto the gun platforms. They fell on the
garrison force like hail, mercilessly swinging their cutlasses, driving their pikes, bludgeoning as swiftly as fear
and blood and the awful tension of the moment would
allow. Their slaughter was wholesale.

Stone led them, a pistol, drawn from the six he carried
in the sling across his shoulders, level in either hand. He
paused to fire, and a Spanish soldier fell.

Van Staal passed Stone, his great double-bladed axe, free of its holster on his back, glinting in the sunlight. He swung his powerful arms, and a soldier's head flew clear of its body to fall among the broken stonework; the body toppled sideways, hands to the bleeding stump.

D'Avila staggered back, the cloth clamped to his eye, not believing the sudden butchery, the panic, the animal intensity, the blood. As his fingers scrabbled for the dagger in his belt, a tall rawboned man with madness in his eyes reached him, drew back his head, and planted a pistol under his chin.

"Surrender," Stone shouted in Spanish. "Or I'll blow your brains to the sea."

D'Avila tried to speak, but the muzzle in his throat would not permit it.

"Surrender," Stone cried again above the carnage, screaming at them all. "Throw down your arms or every man will die."

There was a moment's uneasy pausing. A Spaniard lowered his musket, and an Englishman ran him through with a pike. A soldier turned toward a gun, and van Staal split him in two like a stake.

"Fight," d'Avila croaked. He twisted his head, attempting to say more, but the grip he was in silenced him. Blood began to trickle down his neck.

"Surrender," Stone shouted for the third time. "Or you *and your families* will all be killed."

"No," d'Avila spluttered.

But it was over. Defeat had invaded them all. Spanish soldiers dropped their arms, covered their wounds, tried to preserve what remained. They were no longer a fighting force, however ragged.

"Cramer," Stone called, seeing the Negro. "Fetch a gunner. Load the best of these. Train it on the waterfront."

Cramer shouted to a tall Breton, Henri the Stain, whose face was covered with a purple birthmark. Henri ran to the cannon, Meredith, another gunner, with him.

"Use grape if they have it," Stone instructed.

"Aye, Cap'n."

Stone watched as the gun was sighted, as fineshot was poured into the muzzle. As soon as it was ready, Stone gave the order to fire. The gun jumped as its deadly cargo was hurled below.

The troop on the waterfront was unprepared when the rain of death fell upon it. Grapeshot tore through the packed soldiers like a scythe, halving their number. Men fell, spun, cried, and tumbled into the reddening sea. Teniente Reyes, untouched by the shot, turned back toward the fort, his sword drawn, his young face defiant. He called his men, but none was prepared to follow.

"Reload," Stone said, his voice even, his eyes determined. "Fire when ready."

"No," d'Avila managed to shout. "They are defenseless."

Henri the Stain held the lighted match aloft, his eyes going from Stone to the Spaniard.

"In the name of God," d'Avila urged. "Do not fire on them again."

"Then order their surrender."

"I—" D'Avila's voice was a whisper. He felt the hatred all around him. The dead, the wounded, the dying, all condemned him by their presence. His order to fire the fort's cannon had precipitated all the bloodshed. "Very well," he croaked. "But do not fire again."

Without a further word, Stone dragged the Spaniard to the parapet overlooking the waterfront, the pistol still under his chin. "Tell them," Stone hissed. "Order them to lay down their arms."

"They, they are broken," d'Avila whispered at the sight.

"Order it."

"I cannot," d'Avila choked. "The pistol—"

Stone removed it, and d'Avila called down to his men. Those who could, listened. They placed their weapons on the stonework and stood with their hands above their heads. Teniente Reyes was the last to do so.

Cazaux waved from the longboat. It turned and headed back toward the shore.

*   *   *

Guadalupe Santoya listened to her mother, Magdelena, and then she shook her head firmly. "It is true," she said. "I have just come from the hacienda, where they all speak of it. He is blind. He has been taken prisoner."

"Then forget him, my daughter." Magdelena turned her face to the cooking fire in her thatched hut in the Barrio de San Román, on the southern outskirts of Campeche, where Indians like herself were forced to live. "You are rid of him now."

"No." Guadalupe closed her eyes; she would never be rid of him. The memory of what had happened in the barn was too close, the kindness that had followed too disarming. "He is my protector still."

Magdelena did not reply. She, herself, was an Indian with a Spanish name; Guadalupe's father had been a Spaniard she had almost forgotten. She looked again at her daughter, at the graceful figure and the simple beauty that never ceased to surprise her, at the pride that came from somewhere so foreign.

"These animals from the sea have disgraced him," Guadalupe continued. "They have blinded him. They have filled him with shame."

"That may be, but what can you do?" Magdelena queried, knowing Guadalupe's answer before it came.

"Avenge him," Guadalupe replied in a voice that would not be questioned. "I have no other choice."

" 'Lupe . . .'' Magdelena began, but did not continue; she knew that her daughter would not listen to her now. There was no point in attempting, yet again, to persuade Guadalupe to forget the man who had first raped and then protected her.

The rape, as Magdelena knew, was almost to be expected; the kindnesses that followed had come as a surprise. It was because d'Avila was fresh from Spain, Magdelena had reasoned, that his ways differed from those of his countrymen here. Guadalupe had responded to d'Avila's generosity with loyalty, and Magdelena knew that that would not be put aside lightly. Now she watched as Guadalupe took a basket that hung on a wall and a knife from beside the cooking fire, and she could contain herself no longer. "Do not go from here with that," Magdelena whispered, her eyes on the knife. "You owe him nothing."

"On the contrary," Guadalupe replied, her voice distant, "apart from you, he is all I have."

Christopher Stone leaned back in the raised mayoral chair at the head of the council table. Beside him was a flask of black Jamaican rum. At the far end was Cazaux, seated on the table itself, his long legs swinging over its side. Between them, Don Luis de Córdoba, González, and the bound figure of Capitán Fernando d'Avila awaited decisions that would affect the lives of them all.

Also present at the table was Jaime Toledo Flores, the youngest of the town councilors. Flores, a straight-backed man with unblinking eyes, had ridden out with horsemen from his hacienda before dawn; he'd known nothing of the early meeting. Consequently, he'd been absent when death had carved its way along the waterfront. Now he stared insolently at the pirates. They had not touched him yet.

The other councilors, like most of the Spanish townspeople, were locked in the white interior of the church of Guadalupe. Those Spanish soldiers still alive were in the dungeons below the fort, chained to the damp and mildewed walls. Already from the streets outside rose the sound of foreign voices, many of them thick with drink.

"Mon Dieu," Cazaux called down the table to Stone. "You are a fighter, Englishman. Never have I seen such a storm." His eyes swept to d'Avila, trussed in his chair. "What did you think, little Spanish captain? *Merde,* eh? In your head and in your breeches." Cazaux laughed a high, excited laugh. "I could smell you from the sea. All of you. All you Spanish dung."

D'Avila said nothing; he was wretchedly ashamed. His blinded eye throbbed painfully; it had been bandaged roughly, and blood seeped down his face. There was dried blood in his beard; it came from where Stone's pistol had torn the skin of his neck. He felt helpless and soiled, and wished himself dead. The only force that sustained him was a sour, growing hatred: one day he hoped to kill the shambling Englishman who had caused this humiliation.

"Eh, little captain?" Cazaux's bantering voice persisted. "Have you lost your tongue as well as your eye?"

"Do not torment him," said Don Luis. His voice was uneven, his face ashen. His eyes moved from one Spaniard to another. Apart from Flores, they all displayed aspects of fear. They'd all seen Leal die: he who had been clever among them had been reduced to a heavy corpse. None knows what to do, Don Luis thought. Yet if we are careful, these men may yet show reason. "It was not his fault," he added carefully.

"He was the whoreson who fired the cannon." Cazaux's expression altered; his scar burned red. "He is the shit-cater who ruined my ship."

"He thought that the musket shots from the breakwater signified— "

"He did not think." Cazaux's voice became razor thin. "I am so glad we have him alive. It would give me no satisfaction to see him dead. Not yet."

"What . . . what will you do now?" asked Don Luis.

"Ah." Cazaux raised a long finger, enjoying his power. "An interesting question, Spaniard. You will understand, of course, that the price has become elevated."

"The price?" Don Luis felt his fear ease. While they spoke of money, hope remained: what price?

"For this town of yours. For those good citizens of yours who are now, like all good citizens, in church. For the damage you have done to my ship and my men you have killed. After all, we had concluded an honorable bargain."

"But . . ." Don Luis swallowed. He glanced at González; the town treasurer would not catch his eye. He turned to Toledo, the youngest of the councilmen, and became more aware of the curious defiance on the man's smooth face—of them all, he alone was unafraid.

"But it was a mistake," he continued, wondering what the price would now be. "An error . . ."

"It was no mistake." D'Avila croaked the words, wincing at the pain caused by the effort. "The only error was timing. If we'd had time to aim, you would now be dead."

"No," Don Luis contradicted quickly. "I ordered the garrison not to fire."

"I intended to ignore that order." D'Avila turned his ravaged face to Stone, who sat impassively at the head of the table. "These men are swine. I would have slaughtered them like swine." The garrison commander's voice was thick with bitterness.

"No," Don Luis repeated. "That is not what I intended." He appealed to Cazaux. "You understand. . . ?"

"I understand only that the damage and the insults will all be paid for," Cazaux replied easily, his humor restored by the Spaniards' distress. "And that the purchase will be ready this day."

"Today?"

"I would have thought you would have welcomed the urgency. The good people of Campeche will not want to remain forever in church. There is little food and drink, and certain, shall we say, *accommodations* will be less than adequate." He laughed and called in French to Sartou, leaning by the door. "*Putain de merde,* can you imagine what it will be like in there by the time the sun has cooked them for a while?"

Sartou's small eyes closed. "*Mon Dieu,*" he breathed. "I would not like to share it." He put two fingers to his nose in an expression of exaggerated delicacy.

"Those poor ladies." Cazaux shook his head mockingly, speaking again in Spanish. "Those high-born gentlemen. They have my sympathy."

"What is it you want?" Jaime Toledo spoke for the first time. He stared defiantly at Cazaux. "We have had enough of this churlishness."

"Have you?" Cazaux seemed amused. "And who are you *again,* my little Spanish friend?" he asked, pretending he did not know.

"I am Jaime Toledo Flores, member of this council. Landowner in Campeche. Born here and—"

"A Creole." Cazaux interrupted with a laugh. "More Spanish than those born in Spain." He gave a derisive wave of the hand. "I am pleased to make your acquaintance."

Toledo's eyes flashed. "Tell us what you want," he said angrily.

Cazaux leaned forward, the smile dying on his face. "I want everything you have in this pretty town. I want gold from the necks of women. Everything of value from the houses and the church. I want silver plate and jewelry and anything else we can find." His voice was chilling. "Do you understand? That is what I want, Creole. That is what I intend to take."

Toledo stared, wetting his lips. His dislike was vivid.

"Is that not so, Englishman?" Cazaux slipped from the table and walked to Stone. "The time has come for us to be paid."

"Bravo." Stone belched and reached for the flask of rum that stood by his elbow. The fight had left him empty. In the heat of it, while he held and took the lives of men, it carried him wrapped and unthinking. But now a hollowness invaded, a numbing, unsatisfied afterwash of death. He was prepared to leave these negotiations to Cazaux, none of them held his interest. He lifted the rum and was grateful for the way it weighed in his hand, the way it burned his belly. "Bravo," he repeated. "We'll be given what we came for."

"You see." Cazaux turned back to Toledo. "Your moment of delivery has arrived."

"Where would you have your payment?" Toledo asked, his hot eyes not leaving the Frenchman's face.

"On the breakwater," replied Cazaux. "We will hold it safe on *La Petite*." His eyes flicked toward Sartou and away. "Only until the *Courage* arrives," he said to Stone. "We will share tomorrow morning."

Stone grunted; prizes meant little to him now. Cazaux continued, and the interweave of language ebbed and flowed. All spoke Spanish, even van Staal in the crude form learned in the Venezuelan mines. Yet when Stone leaned back in the great mayoral chair, it was English that came to his tongue, as it was French that Cazaux spoke in his asides to Sartou. However, the fabric of many voices, the lingua franca learned between decks on endless voyages, shared in bars and brothels in the hundred ports they visited, was understood, or understood enough, by all.

Suddenly Van Staal, who stood against a wall, leaned forward, his weight on the head of his two-bladed axe. "Why do not we share today?" he asked gruffly.

Cazaux smiled and waved a hand toward the noise rising from the streets outside; voices had thickened, there was the sound of breaking glass. "I think it would be better tomorrow," he said smoothly. "When your ship is here and some of the, shall we say, excitement has been exhausted. Do you not agree?"

Van Staal glared, but Stone laughed openly. "Tomorrow, Rolf," he said to his mate, his tongue loosening. "God's blood, there will be time enough to quarrel then."

For a moment no one seemed to understand, then Cazaux smiled uncertainly. "Ah, my English friend. You have such a sense of humor." He slapped Stone on the back and turned toward the defiant Creole. "Are you ready?"

"Very well." Jaime Toledo lifted his voice. For the moment he had no choice but to follow these arrogant invaders. He would keep close to them; perhaps his presence might lessen their damage. "Shall we begin?"

"Are you to lead us, my little Creole?"

"I wish to see it done."

"So do we all," said Cazaux. He turned to Don Luis. "You have been doubly unfortunate," he said, a touch of understanding in his voice. "If it had not been for the storm, we would not have come to your town. If it had not been for your stupid little captain here"—he jerked a thumb at d'Avila—"there would have been no bloodshed. In a way, I almost pity you."

"We pity ourselves," replied Don Luis, hoping that by now Angela would be clear. There would be others who had fled, their valuables with them. They also would be on their way to Mérida, and no pirate would follow them there. Campeche would not be burned. Those in the church of Guadalupe would emerge poorer, but, it seemed, their lives would be spared. The situation was not quite as bad as it might have been. The mayor shuddered inwardly. "We have not been fortunate," he concluded.

It was Berniard, whose long arms were more accustomed to wrapping themselves around the cannon of *La Petite*, who lifted her kicking from the carriage. With a laugh he handed her to Cordier, his yellow-bearded bosun.

"She would have run from us," Berniard said.

"She would have succeeded," Cordier replied, glancing at the loaded carriage, "if she'd not wasted time packing her entire wardrobe."

"Let me go, you pig," Angela shouted, twisting in Cordier's grip. "You hear me, pig? *Cochon*," she added in French for good measure. "Let me go."

"Let you go?" Cordier grinned and shook his head. He turned to the group of pirates who had halted the carriage in the back streets of the town; they were beginning to pull down the hastily packed trunks. The driver lay dead by the side of the road. "Leave this intact," he ordered firmly. "Take the coachload to the waterfront."

A pirate grumbled, and Cordier swung on him. "Later," he said levelly, "you will get your share."

"Let me go," Angela repeated, but less aggressively. These invaders were cleaner than she had expected, and he with the yellow beard was both handsome and forceful. "I am the daughter of Don Luis de Córdoba, mayor of Campeche."

"Are you now?" Cordier smiled broadly. "Then we have a prize on our hands."

"What will you do with me?"

"That is to be seen." Cordier shrugged. "Get into the carriage. You will be safer there."

"Safer?" There was a note of curiosity in Angela's voice. "What do you mean?"

"Exactly what I say. Get in."

"No." It would be more seemly to resist, certainly at first. "Take me to my father immediately."

Cordier nodded at Berniard. The long-armed gunner came forward. Together they bundled the struggling girl unceremoniously into the carriage and closed the door in her face.

Christopher Stone leaned back in the mayor's great chair and smiled; the rum was beginning to release him. He needed more. Sartou and van Staal stood by the double doors leading from the council chamber, ready to depart. With them was Toledo, who had been accepted as their guide. The mixed band of pirates would wade through the town taking all they could. Soon, Stone mused, it would be over; soon they could be gone from here.

Abruptly he called to Cramer the Black. "Take the others to the church," he said, indicting Don Luis, d'Avila, and González. "Lock them away."

"Be my pleasure, Cap'n."

Stone laughed lightly; he came to his feet, and the chair fell behind him with a crash. "Be kind to them," he said. "The way they were to you."

As the tall Negro turned to them, Don Luis and González stood quickly, then left the room, but d'Avila did not move. As Cramer reached for him, d'Avila twisted his head toward Stone, his seeing eye burning.

"I will kill you," he said, and his quiet intensity stayed Cramer's hand. "One day, I will see you die." Then he came to his feet and marched stiffly from the council chamber.

Stone stared a moment, then shrugged and reached for the flask of rum. As his fingers closed about its weight there was a scuffling sound from outside, the crash of a door being thrown roughly open, and Berniard came into the council chamber leading Angela by the hair. Cordier walked beside them.

CHAPTER 4

GUADALUPE SANTOYA PUT THE KNIFE IN THE BASKET, CON-cealing it with a loaf of bread; she added fresh fruit and covered it all with a cloth. "I know who he is," she told her mother, who watched in silence. "I have discovered who was responsible."

"Do not do it, my daughter," Magdelena whispered.

"I have to." Guadalupe took a shawl and put it over her head. "He has a face as thin as the devil's. His hair is the color of straw."

"They will kill you."

"He is tall and ugly," Guadalupe continued as if her mother had not spoken. "It will be a pleasure to see him die."

"They will not let you near him. You will not succeed."

"Tonight, when it is dark, when all are drunk, I will find him." Guadalupe turned and stared at her mother. "I will not fail."

"Please, my daughter, do not leave the barrio."

"I must."

Magdelena closed her eyes; she could no longer look at Guadalupe, at the beauty that had hardened, the expression that was so distant, the pride that burned. She wished there was some way to dissuade her daughter but knew that nothing would prevent this attempt to avenge her protector's shame.

"What have we here?" Cazaux asked Berniard, his eyes bright with interest. "What is this treasure you have found?"

"The mayor's daughter, *mon capitaine*," Berniard replied in French, releasing Angela's hair. "She thought to run from us."

"That I cannot believe."

As Cazaux reached out both hands toward the girl, Don Luis pushed past Cramer to reenter the council chamber. "Angela," he cried.

"Papá!"

"Have they touched you?"

"No, they stopped me and they brought me here. But I am unharmed."

"Of course she is." Cazaux led the girl to a chair; he held it while she sat. "Who would want to harm so lovely a creature as this?"

Berniard laughed.

"My God," Don Luis began, but Cazaux raised a hand. "She will be safe with me," he said quietly. "I will see to it that she is very well looked after."

"If she is touched—"

"If she is touched, there is nothing you can do about it." Cazaux nodded at Cramer, who moved forward and took Don Luis by the arm. "Now, go to the church with the others and do not worry about your daughter."

"No." With a clumsy thrust, Don Luis pushed Cramer aside. "I will not leave her. She is . . . she is all I have." He placed a hand on his daughter's shoulder; she clutched at his fingers, her eyes not leaving the Frenchman's face. "She must remain with me."

Cazaux smiled easily. "I understand your concern," he said politely, "but I cannot allow any exceptions to be made. If I were to do that, I would have the wives and daughters of all the councilors clamoring at my ears and . . ." He paused to smile. "Condemning *you*."

Don Luis opened his mouth and closed it again. There

were too many decisions to be made, there was no time to think. He needed to plan, to balance, to assemble his emotions.

"I give you my word," Cazaux went on smoothly, "my solemn word, that she will not be harmed." He raised his eyebrows. "Have I ever broken my word as far as you have been concerned?"

Don Luis shook his head; he felt some of the pressure go from his daughter's fingers.

"Papá?" Angela said, beginning hesitantly. "Does he speak the truth?"

"Well, yes . . ."

"Then might it not be better for me to remain here?" Angela glanced about her; she would quite like to know more about the great scar that ran down the French pirate's face. "I mean, in the church there will be all those people, and crying babies . . ."

"I assure you, señorita," Cazaux said persuasively, "you will be much more comfortable with me." He glanced up at Don Luis. "And you," he added, "have my word."

"Please, Papá, what do you think? . . ."

Don Luis swallowed; his head pained him now, and his throat was dry. He needed to believe. With a last despairing look he allowed himself to be led away.

Stone, who he'd watched the proceedings with a smirk, sauntered forward, swinging his rum.

Cazaux turned to him. "Would you like her?" he asked in English.

Stone shook his head. "She is not to my taste," he replied, and drank a little more rum.

Angela stared at Cazaux with curious eyes as he sent Cordier from the room for something cool to drink, as he drew up a chair and sat opposite her, smiling all the while with ease.

"You have been frightened, my pretty," he said, leaning toward her. "For that, I apologize. Some of my men are a little too basic, it seems."

Angela lowered her eyes. "They killed my driver,"

she whispered, trying to recall the unfortunate man's name.

"The men responsible will be punished," Cazaux replied smoothly. "I can see the entire experience has shaken you severely."

Angela nodded her head. This was more than she could possibly have expected. The man was refined; his accent was most attractive. She put a hand to her brow. "I do feel a little faint," she said. A movement from Stone caught her eye, and she turned to see him pour rum down his throat. "Who is *he*?" she asked Cazaux breathlessly.

Cazaux's voice became confidential. "He is a famous English cutthroat," he murmured. "Be careful of him and his men. I have seen him— But no"—Cazaux's voice dropped even lower—"I could not even whisper some of the things he has done."

"My God, what are you doing with him?"

Cazaux shrugged. "It is a matter of convenience," he replied. "I owe him some little favors, so I have come here with him, to assist."

"But you are not like him." Angela studied the fine-boned face, the superior clothes, the elegance. "You are not like any of the others."

"That is true," Cazaux agreed.

"Will you, will you help me?" Angela thought of the long, boring journey to Mérida and widened her eyes. "I am still a little afraid."

"Of course, my pretty," Cazaux replied as Cordier returned with a pitcher of orange juice. "I will do everything in my power to protect you from these men."

"I thank you."

"I will take you to the protection of my ship," Cazaux continued smoothly, handing Angela a drink. "You will be secure there. I shall see to it personally."

"Do you think that is best?" Angela's eyes were huge with curiosity. "My poor father would be desperate if he knew."

"Then we will have to see that his mind remains at peace," Cazaux replied easily. "For I can assure you he

would be much more concerned were he to know that
certain others had their way with you.''

Angela's eyes flew to Stone.

Cazaux turned to the Englishman. ''Would you mind
leaving us?'' he said in English. ''This little chicken
seems to be afraid of you.''

Stone smiled thinly. ''Now I wonder why that should
be,'' he said.

''It is your cool English manner, my friend.''

''God's blood.'' Stone laughed. He belched and left
the council chamber.

The late-day sun beat down upon the squares, the
archways, the neat-packed colonial buildings stretching
back toward the foothills that formed the town of Campeche. There were black shadows at the feet of white-
plastered walls; heat curled in dancing waves above the
flat and domed and tiled roofs of the town.

There were no Indians in the Plaza Principal, no bright
serapes were to be seen. The little piles of avocadoes,
mangoes, and mamme had been trodden into the paving
or scooped up by foreign hands. The Indians had fled to
the hills behind the town or to their barrio in the south
where no pirate would follow.

A lean dog sniffed in a corner of the square, then lifted
its leg to urinate.

Pirates lounged in the sun along the seafront. A group
was gathered about a wine barrel whose head had been
smashed in; they were drinking from mugs of pewter or
glass. One or two dipped their hands into the broken
barrel to scoop up the wine, which ran in red rivulets
down their arms and chests. They would begin to sing
soon and quarrel, to stagger again through the town,
taking whatever caught their fancy, seeking anything to
release them from the fears they had known in the
morning's bloodshed. They would take what they could,
and what they must leave they would mark, like the dog
in the corner of the square.

In the church of Guadalupe the rich of the town—the
merchants, the bankers, the landowners and the council-

men, with their wives and children, those who had had neither the time nor the presence of mind to flee—waited with their arms about each other, comforting their children as best they could.

There were more than two hundred and fifty of them in the lofted, pink-walled church, and as the day turned and the weakest of them grew faint from lack of water and fresh air, they began to wonder what the night would bring. From the waterfront the rising voices were becoming harsher, and after a while the dancing from seafront fires gave a menacing illumination to the interior of the church. When the sound of the first woman's scream came to their frightened ears, they turned their gray faces toward each other and began to lose all hope.

Christopher Stone stood outside the church of Guadalupe watching the pirates decay. Of his own, he knew how they could be handled; for the French, he was not so sure. He hoped the looting would occupy them and, later, the transfer of the purchase to *La Petite*. After that, many would be too drunk to cause further damage. Those with women would become the quietest. He had no desire to witness more bloodshed, he had no desire to see the citizens dragged from the church. Mindless seizure angered him, made him almost sullen. He would be glad when it all was done. The *Courage* would be back by dawn. She had waited beyond the horizon, and the windless day had left her idle. Now, Stone felt a night breeze on his cheek and knew he would see his own sails against the skyline in the morning. He spat and drank a little more rum, and an image came to his uneasy mind. He saw again the body of Munro hanging grisly from a gibbet at Port Royal, Jamaica. Munro had swung between the corpses of his men, his rotting flesh bound with chain to make its message doubly clear.

"This is no Spaniard," Stone had said angrily to van Staal. "This man has paid the king's share in his time." He'd eyed the corpse bitterly as it turned, black and sinister, on its rope. "He held a commission like the rest of us."

"That paper in your sea chest's worthless now," van Staal had replied. "Your king has dealings with the king of Spain. 'Tis mine they'll be fighting next. What's more," he'd added, "this Munro plundered an English vessel. He should have had the wit to stay away from here."

" 'Tis politics," Stone had continued stubbornly. "I want none of it. They can make their wars, not mine."

Van Staal had smiled: he'd tapped the freshly resined railing of the *Courage*. "Then we'd better swing her round and run," he'd suggested.

Stone had turned to his mate: an idea had been voiced that he'd held frequently in mind these past unsettled months. "You'd sail with me, Rolf? As a freebooter?" he'd asked.

"Aye, and fight with you, Christopher. So will all the others in the crew."

" 'Twill mean risking their necks."

Van Staal's smile had become a laugh. "They do that every day at sea as it is," he'd answered. "And, at times, more often ashore."

So, not for the first time nor the last was an immediate decision to alter Christopher Stone's life, and the lives of those who sailed with him. They'd run the *Courage* along the Main, trading, carrying contraband, taking what they had to, reliving those boisterous days they'd known after the capture of Jamaica. The world again was theirs.

The *Courage* was lean, newly sheathed in cedarwood, fast and maneuverable. She carried twenty-four guns, and Stone captained her with only sixty-seven men. She became famous among the Brethren of the Coast; there was never any shortage of those who wished to join her.

For four years she'd sailed between New Amsterdam and the Spanish Main, with a crew from any country, speaking a barrage of languages, understanding that what they gained they shared. They'd sold their cargoes for half the price Spanish-taxed goods demanded. They'd carried their private war against those they considered their only true enemies: the Spanish crown and the officers of that state.

And now? Stone stood alone outside the church in

Campeche, the last of their overrun towns. Once more he'd succeeded in what he'd planned; once more success had left him empty. About him tension rose in the air as fear from the morning's fight was given a resting place, as the right they believed they had to take was exercised so brutally.

He filled his mouth with rum and held its burn. For the moment, there was nothing for him here. He hoped the night would pass as undemandingly but knew in his heart it would not.

When the loot began to appear, English, French, and Dutch alike gathered on the stonework at the neck of the breakwater to paw over it, to play with the purchase they had come for. Later the bosuns would distribute it; now it lay like a rich new toy.

There were heaps of silver plate, candelabra with many branches, a chandelier or two, finely fitted boxes of silkwood and mahogany filled with gold-worked jewels and heavy coins. There were pearls from the Pacific and emeralds from Peru, bolts of silk from China and lace from Amsterdam. Tapestries had been torn from walls and swords wrenched from scabbards. Everything had been taken with violence, a force that seemed to display something more than mere greed. It was as if by ripping the treasure from the houses the pirates could further humiliate the town. It was theirs now, they would own it until they left, until they sailed from its shell.

A squat Frenchman with tarred hair reached his thick fingers toward a string of pearls that rested in a carved silkwood box. He hung the pearls about his neck and flashed a coquettish, gap-toothed smile. Beside him, a young companion lifted the corner of a bolt of fine black silk and wrapped the material about himself. The group they were with began to laugh.

"Ho, la la," someone called loudly. "How pretty you look."

"Perhaps we will have a wedding," declared another voice. "Some entertainment for us, no?"

"I would not marry him," said the squat Frenchman

with the tarred hair. "I have had him already. He is a whore."

Men laughed and moved closer.

"That is not what you told me, Jacques, the night of the storm. Then you held me close." The young man giggled. Someone passed him a bottle, and he drank, spilling wine on the silk. "Then you said I was your own true love."

Jacques lifted his head and roared with laughter, the big veins in his neck swelling beneath the pearls. "I knew you were a whore from the beginning," he shouted. "I would not marry you if you were the last *matelot* in the whole of the filthy Caribbean." The gaps between his teeth were black through his laughter. "But I will tell you what I will do, my pretty little whore."

"What is that?"

"Dance with you." Jacques reached for the young man and began a clumsy jig. "What do you think of that, eh?" Jacques pulled him closer. "It is better than a marriage, no?"

Jacques spun his partner until both were wrapped in silk. They laughed. About them rose the sound of singing. A bottle crashed amidst silver plate. The young man fell, Jacques on top of him, and they rolled amongst a clatter of silver knives and spoons scattered over the flagstones. For a moment there was nothing but a tumbling, boisterous chaos in which glassware broke and fabric shredded, and then van Staal and Sartou were among them, pulling them apart.

"Up." Van Staal's round face was furious. "You break this before it shared?" His French was poor, but the meaning clear. "Get from it. All."

"*Fous le camp.*" Jacques staggered to his feet, a massive fist drawn back. "You have no right—"

"I make my right." Van Staal held his axe before him. He glanced at Sartou. "Get your men off," he said savagely. "If you want them alive."

Sartou blinked. He spoke, and his men began to sidle away, releasing the prize, kicking flatware back to the pile.

"Who is he to give us orders?" Jacques's angry eyes were on van Staal. "We were having a little fun, that is all."

"I understand," Sartou replied. He winked suddenly. "Perhaps you made him jealous when you danced with Pierre."

Jacques shrugged, some of his anger died. "He should find his own whore," he said. "If he wants mine, he will have to fight me first."

Sartou smiled. "That will not be necessary, there are plenty in the town." He lowered his voice a little and spoke rapidly, knowing that van Staal would not comprehend. "Get this booty on board," he urged. "Let us be sure it is all stowed away before we lose our heads. Remember, the English ship is not yet here, so be sure we are loaded well." He tapped the side of his nose significantly.

The men shuffled and grinned. They returned to the pile of loot, carried it farther down the breakwater, and began to load the longboats that waited there.

"They will behave," Sartou said to van Staal. "It will be better when all this is out of sight on *La Petite*."

"Will it?"

"What else would you have me do?" Sartou leaned closer, and his breath stung van Staal. "It has been agreed."

"I know. But I not like it." Van Staal watched the longboats put out from the mole and row toward the lean line of the French frigate—she was a black shadow in the dying light, about which the water lapped silver. "It would not have been my choosing," he muttered to himself.

Guadalupe Santoya waited until darkness filled the hut of stone and palm thatch. When she could no longer see across the room, she stood, knotted the shawl more firmly, picked up the covered basket, and turned toward the huddled shape of her mother. It was just visible in the glow from the coals of the untouched fire. She opened her mouth to speak but said nothing. She left the house quickly and went from the safety of the Barrio de San Román. From the town, drifting in the little breeze, came the sound of drunken voices.

Van Staal stood on the breakwater and felt the coldness rise up from the sea. He heard a step beside him and turned to see Stone, rum bottle in hand, come close. The Englishman held out the rum, but van Staal shook his head.

"Take it," Stone urged, his voice thick now. "Drink to our great victory over the Spanish garrison."

"No."

"Lost your taste for it?"

Van Staal shrugged.

"It will keep me through this night," Stone said, and drank more. "God's pox. What great goad there is in greed."

"They have what they fought for," van Staal said simply.

"They do not even want it." Stone spat into the sea. "They will take their shares to Tortuga and sell them for nothing. Give them to whores if it pleases them. Trade them for scabs."

" 'Tis always the same."

"Later it will be worse. Then they'll fight over the women."

"Christopher—" Van Staal's voice showed concern.

"Where is Cazaux?" Stone asked abruptly.

"On board. With the daughter of the mayor."

"Poor little bitch." Stone belched. "Those in the church?" he asked. "Have they been given food or drink?"

"Not that I know of."

"Send them something." Stone's voice was empty. "Have Cramer take them sustenance. In the morning we'll let them go. I have no desire to bury them as well."

"What of the soldiers of the garrison? Those in the dungeons beneath the fort?"

"Give them victuals also. 'Tis not their fault they're

there.'' Stone drank more. ''The commander, the fool responsible. Send him to the hospital. There's no point in his dying, either.''

''I'll see that it all is done.''

Stone stared at the shape of van Staal. ''You have no more liking for this than I,'' he observed.

''I've seen more of it than you.''

''That does not make it any better.''

''No. Merely more predictable.''

''Pray to God this night is over soon.'' The moon was a gold coin riding the sky. ''We should not have come with this Frenchman.''

Van Staal paused a moment, then said, ''I will see that all the prisoners are fed.''

''And I will find more rum,'' Stone answered. ''Later I will meet you by the door of the church. We must quarter there until the worst of this is over.''

''To protect those inside?''

''Perhaps to protect ourselves.'' Stone stared along the waterfront at the groups of men, their voices raised and ragged. ''We must all face the morrow,'' he said quietly.

The great cabin of *La Petite* was immensely richer than its counterpart on the *Courage*. Darkly stained walls carried tapestries in claret and gold. A vast four-poster bed filled one corner. Above it, draperies entwined with silver cord floated to the swell of the sea. All the furniture was elaborately carved. On the floor were rugs from Turkey, and in the air was the heavy scent of woods and pomander and something darker, not quite familiar, which lay on the tongue.

Angela sat in a plushly upholstered oaken chair. Behind her stood Cazaux, fondling her long dark tresses. Through the stern windows and their curtains of bone lace filtered the palest night light. Outside was the soft lapping of the gentle waves and distantly, as if part of a farther world, an occasional shout from the shore.

Angela seemed part of the velvet-covered chair, so deeply did she sit in it. Her face was completely relaxed.

She still wore her traveling clothes of the morning: a circular blue cape with a folded collar, open to show a white mantilla and a high-necked bodice. In the glow from the sea lanterns on the chart table, her milky skin was luminous, almost ghostly.

Now, Cazaux slipped the cape from Angela's shoulders and let it rest on the back of the chair. "Take a little more," he said gently. "It will ease you."

"I am eased," Angela murmured. Before her, on the table, was a silver tray bearing a silver-bound crystal flask, a sugar shaker, and two finely chiseled goblets, each of which contained a little cloudy green liquid. "What is this?" she asked.

"An elixir," Cazaux replied. "I discovered it in France, but it comes from the East, I am told."

Angela sipped a little more and made a face. "It is so bitter."

"I understand the ancients used it as an aid to meditation in their search for a perfect peace."

"In France?" Angela smiled lazily.

"No." Cazaux emptied his own glass. "Those of the true Indies. Ah," he sighed, watching the girl closely. "If we were only in France now. It is February. There would be snow along the branches of the trees. We would sit before a fire and sip mulled wine. How romantic it would be."

Angela's smile grew; she gazed deeply into the flickering flame of a sea lantern. "I so love it in Europe," she whispered.

"If you relaxed, my pretty, you could imagine you were in Europe now."

Angela reached up to touch her hair, and the fingers of Cazaux's hand approached. "You have been very kind to me," she said softly.

Cazaux moved closer. "It is easy to be kind to one so beautiful," he said. "Anyway, I am not as evil as I am rumored to be."

"You are not evil."

"That is true." Cazaux smiled; he moved to lean against the chart table, to look down into the soft loveliness gazing up at him. "Life at sea is not always easy," he began gently. "There are times when one must fight for one's life. One's passions become aroused." His intelligent eyes seemed to pierce, to probe her. "When one is at war it is difficult not to give in to evil."

"But you are not at war now?"

"No, I am not at war now," Cazaux whispered, his lips near her ear. He reached for Angela's hand. "And yet, yet I am aware of a sense of evil with you here."

"Oh." Angela smiled languorously. In the light of the cabin his face was finely sculpted; his eyes, with their great pupils, were extraordinarily bright. She felt as if she were floating in a warm and friendly sea, close to the substance of her dreams. "Do you feel evil with me?" Her voice drifted.

"Yes."

"Would you care to kiss me?"

Cazaux bent and brushed his lips against hers and was aware of her strangely willing response. "You are lovely," he whispered.

"Do you, do you desire me?" Angela breathed, and her own utterance filled her being, it soothed and it softened; a luxurious warmth entered her bones. A knight stood on a hill. A phantom maiden waited to be taken. "Do you feel that way?"

"I, well, yes I do."

"Then—" Angela sank deeper into the chair. The corners of the cabin were filled with aching shadow, the sound of the sea was basic. She was conscious of a curious need to touch herself. "Will you?"

"I would . . ." Cazaux paused significantly. "But—"

"Do not be concerned." Angela pressed his hand. She felt warmth surge through her, was conscious of a new, deeply profound freedom that overrode all else. "It would not be evil."

"I am afraid I cannot."

"What? . . . But why?"

"It is a wound." Cazaux's eyes were stricken. "It has rendered me incapable."

"Oh, my sweet." Angela came forward in the chair;

her hands went to Cazaux's face, her lips were close to his. She shared his melancholy. "What can I do?"

"Nothing."

"But I must."

"You could—" Cazaux drew his face away. "No. It is unthinkable. Out of the question."

"What is it?" Angela's cheeks were flushed, her lips reddened. "Tell me, please tell me."

"I cannot."

"Please, anything. The way I feel for you now . . ."

"Well . . ." Cazaux sighed heavily. "If I were to substitute— But no, that could never be."

"Substitute?" echoed Angela.

"Yes . . ." The cabin rocked silently in the easy tide as Cazaux searched for words. He felt her warmth and knew he had again succeeded. This was his game, and he'd played it often. Yet for a moment he felt himself hesitate, wondering for the briefest instant who had captured whom. Then abruptly he looked away and heard his voice continue.

"Someone to help me give all that I would give you. So that I might cherish you and rejoice in your most complete pleasure." He listened to his own, yearning tone and was glad his eyes were averted.

"I—" Angela's cheeks flushed. She felt deliciously released.

"I knew you could not." Cazaux drew nearer again and touched her gently. "It was evil to even suggest such a thing."

"No." Angela took a slow, deep breath. "It is not evil. But could you?"

"Take you that way?" Cazaux's speech quickened. "Oh, I could, my sweet. I would hold you, kiss you. I would be with you in each and every moment. It would be as if I were there."

"Are you sure?"

"Positive."

"Then?"

"Would you agree?" Cazaux spread his hands in front of him. "Have you, before?"

"Yes," Angela said as she regarded the long, delicate fingers. "Once, with a nobleman from the court of Seville. And—"

"Oh." Cazaux was not eager to hear more.

"Now," Angela breathed, and turned her gaze full upon him. "Who will it be?"

Cazaux tapped the chart table with his empty goblet. The door of the great cabin opened, and a gentle duty boy stood before it. His doublet was loose and his breeches slackened. He stepped into the cabin's interior, a smile on his youthful face.

"I am prepared, *mon capitaine*," he said softly. "I am here to serve you."

CHAPTER 5

CHRISTOPHER STONE LEANED AGAINST THE OAK-PANELED door of the church of Guadalupe, his long, angular body curved by the rum he'd consumed. His face was paler than usual, his eyes dull. One hand was pressed against the doorway, in the other swung a fresh flask of black Jamaican rum.

"God's pox," he said thickly. "The stench inside is rising."

"There's nothing more that can be done," van Staal replied. "They've been given food and water."

Stone grunted. He lifted his head to look across the Plaza Principal, where fires burned and drunken men danced travesties of reels and jigs. They danced with each other, with women who were reluctant, with women who were ingratiating. One man danced with a light-skinned Indian boy who stared about in confusion and fear. Shouts curled across the square. Flames leapt along the waterfront, throwing the shadows of those who crouched about them in grotesque patterns onto white plaster walls. Out from the shallows of the shore, the etched-black silhouette of *La Petite* swung on her mooring. Above, the night was an inverted valley, full of fading stars.

Stone lifted the flask and swallowed another mouthful of rum. "Where's Cramer?" he asked.

"At the fort, checking the guard."

"Who watches the prisoners?"

"Meredith."

Stone belched. He placed the flask on a step beside the door and moved away clumsily to a corner of the church. There, he loosened his breeches and urinated against the stonework. He was returning when Guadalupe Santoya, the shawl covering her head, approached.

"Forgive me, señor," Guadalupe said; her voice had the peculiar singing cadence of Indian-spoken Spanish. 'I have some food here for the capitán."

"What?" Stone turned as she followed him up the steps. "What do you want?"

"Capitán d'Avila, señor. He who was blinded."

"That mongrel. He's gone to hospital." Stone scowled. "Who are you?"

"One of his servants. From the hacienda at San Pedro. He has need—"

"He has need of a rope." Stone peered at the basket she carried, its contents concealed by the cloth. "What's there? What have you hidden?"

"It is only some medicines, señor. And some food."

"Show it to me."

Guadalupe moved a little closer. Then, in one swift action, she threw the cover from the basket, drew the knife, and raised it to thrust, with all her strength, at the Englishman's heart.

"I will show you," she shouted, her face a mask of hatred.

Astounded, Stone tried to leap away as the blade slashed downward. He slipped and felt a line of fire along his ribs. He landed against the wall of the church, Guadalupe on top of him, her hand ready to plunge the knife again.

"Sweet Jesu," Stone gasped, reaching for her wrist.

"Animal!" screamed Guadalupe as van Staal ran from the steps and kicked her sideways. He unholstered his great axe and raised it above his head. "No," shouted Stone. "Leave her be."

Breathing deeply, van Staal held his blow. Christopher Stone scrambled to his feet, a hand to his side to hold back the wetness of his blood. "God's body," he gasped. "What does this madwoman want?"

"You are hit," said van Staal.

"I am cut on the ribs," Stone replied; he stared down at the sprawled figure of Guadalupe. "Get up," he said.

Very slowly Guadalupe began to rise. When she was on her hands and knees Stone said, "Move no farther." He bent and ran a hand over her body, searching for weapons. "You are well made," he said, straightening. "Get to your feet."

Guadalupe stood. The shawl had fallen away to reveal the handsomeness of her graceful face. Her eyes were full of beauty and defiance.

Stone stared. "Why would you kill me?" he asked.

"For what you have done."

"I have done no more than others." Stone was clearly puzzled. "Less than some."

"You are their leader." Guadalupe's voice was flat and cold. "It was you who blinded Capitán d'Avila."

"Sweet Christ," Stone said. 'He was blinded by his own idiocy."

"It would not have happened had you not come."

Stone sighed. Gingerly, he reached for the rum that lay beside the church door and drank deeply. "That may be so," he said to Guadalupe at last. "But would my death return sight to his eye?"

She stared at him bitterly. "It would avenge his shame," she whispered.

"It would do nothing." Stone pointed savagely over the plaza. "It would make no difference to them." In a corner, two men had a woman on her back. Their grunts could be heard amid the sounds of the laughter of others. "Nor would it affect the lives of those in the church." He moved closer to Guadalupe and lifted her chin with his hand. "Are you his woman?" he asked.

"I work at his hacienda."

"Answer me, are you his woman?"

"I have been with him, yes."

"How old are you?"

"Eighteen."

Cursing, Stone walked away from the girl. "Put her in with the others," he said to van Staal, gesturing toward the church. His gaze swept the plaza once more. "Tell her to pray that none of those get her. For then she will know what animals are truly like."

Stone opened his shirt and poured raw rum into the wound on his side; the quick pain of the spirits caused his breath to catch. He drank a little and cursed the girl again.

"Are you hurt?" asked van Staal as he returned.

"It will heal," Stone replied dryly. "Good Christ, that would have been an irony. To die by the hand of a Spaniard's doxy."

"Can you fight still?"

"Fight? Aye." Stone lifted his head. "Will there be need?"

Van Staal, grim and tightlipped, responded with an abrupt nod.

Stone sighed and pushed the linen of his shirt into the wound. The rum burned, and he felt wearied; he slumped down against the church. Van Staal did not reholster his axe but sat with it across his knees beside his captain. They were silent as they watched the frenzy begin to build on the far side of the plaza.

In the great cabin beneath the poop on *La Petite*, Angela lay on the chart table, her legs spread, her eyelids drooping. Beide her, his lean face empty, a hand still in the girl's long dark hair, sat Cazaux. The duty boy had gone; they remained alone with the tapestries and the carvings, the silver tray and the crystal flask containing its tincture of hashish, and the memory of all that had happened.

Angela let her eyes close and felt again, through the avenues of her swirling mind, Cazaux's long fingers undo the buttons of her high-necked bodice. His voice went through her, whispering, breathing words she did not understand. Hands reached for her, lifted her from the upholstered chair. Beneath her was the chart table; she lay on its embroidered cover.

She was aware again of the great and growing excitement; it was as if all that was about to occur would happen to another. Fingers, once more, spread her riding gown, her underskirt was lifted, she knew the delicious freedom of her own exposure, it contained neither fear nor shame.

Hands moved, anew, to take her. There was weight on the table and the heat of another. Her legs were divided, urgently she was entered, and, from somewhere near and far, a voice or voices cried in ecstasy. She did not know where the voices came from. But now, as her mind heard the sound again, suddenly she realized that the voice was hers, and Cazaux's also. She turned her head to find him, and his lips caught her own.

Now as then, the cabin rocked. Shadows deepened, the light from sea lanterns grew overpowering, waves of a deep and infinite pleasure began to roll through every portion of her being. Beside her, Cazaux's head went back, the threads of his neck tightened as the very air in the cabin roared and the green and bitter gratification in her loins rose and gathered, rolled through her like all the movements of the sea. She put a hand to her mouth and tasted salt. She bit into the mound of her own flesh as her voice sprang forth and was released from everything that had ever restrained her. Tears melted her eyes, and her lips were trembling.

She lay for a long time, now as she had done then, waiting for time and the waves of pleasure to re-form.

Cazaux lay beside her now, but she had no memory of his moving. Amidst the roiling of the sea he had come to her, his hands everywhere, filling her with their fire. She wrapped herself about him.

"You are there?" Angela whispered after what seemed to be an endless time. "You are with me?"

"I am here." Cazaux's throat was dry. "You have captured me."

"Are you happy?"

"No, I am caught."

The ship rolled, and the air was velvet. After a time Cazaux moved from the table, then returned to cover Angela with a soft woolen blanket. His fingers did their work with care; they were wrapping something precious. He bent once, suddenly, and pressed the scar on his cheek against her thigh.

Christopher Stone lay slumped against the oak church door, a flask of rum beside him. From time to time he clumsily splashed the wound over his ribs with the spirits. On one side of him sat van Staal, his axe across his knees; on the other was Cramer the Black, his cutlass drawn. All three watched the French on the far side of the plaza and the riot that was about to form.

"Where are our own?" Stone asked after a time.

"They know better than to flaunt themselves," replied van Staal.

Stone grunted. "That what you think, Cramer?"

"Hard to tell, Cap'n," the tall Negro replied, scratching his short, curly hair. "I thinks they're lost without the vessel. They've no home no more. My guess'll be they're lying low."

"That what you'd do?"

"Aye, it would."

Stone stared at the black shape of the man. "How'd you lose your ear?" he asked abruptly.

Cramer paused. "Cut from me in Jamaica," he replied after a moment. "I was held in slavery there."

"What'd they take the ear for?"

"They said I stole."

"Did you?"

"Aye, I did." Cramer smiled briefly. "But it wasn't worth no ear."

Stone laughed hoarsely, sipped his rum, and passed the bottle to the others. They drank and waited, silent as a flame leapt on a distant side of the square. The night air seemed alight, as if at any moment it would spark and the slow tension that had been building all the afternoon would burst like a storm.

*   *   *

"I must send you back," he said softly.

"No." Angela's eyes widened. "Can I not remain with you?"

"You must return." Cazaux gazed into the radiance of her face; her pupils were smaller now. "You will be secure. I will leave a guard. There is nothing to fear."

"When, when will I see you again?"

Cazaux turned away.

"Tomorrow?"

"Of course." Cazaux placed the blue circular cape about her shoulders and rebuttoned her bodice. "Do not concern yourself," he said softly. "I have great need of you."

He took her to the ship's rail and helped her down into a longboat where Cordier, the bosun, was in charge. When she saw him Angela drew back, but Cazaux spoke gently and she continued.

"Take care of her," Cazaux called to Cordier. "See that she is safely delivered."

"It will be so, *mon capitaine*."

"It will be your life if it is otherwise."

"She will come to no harm."

Cazaux leaned on the rail and looked down at the pale face against the darkness of the sea. He lifted a hand, and she put her own to her lips. For a moment they remained, joined though separate; then the oars moved, the longboat turned, and the two vessels parted company.

Jacques, the squat Frenchman with the tarred hair, emptied a brandy bottle and threw it into the flames. The glass broke; a small puff of blue fire jumped amid sparks. Jacques wiped his lips with the back of his hand and turned to a sailor who lay on a woman near the steps of the Municipal Building.

"Hey, *matelot*," Jacques shouted. "Now is not the time for sleeping."

The sailor did not move. Jacques touched the man with his boot, but there was no reaction. With one massive hand, Jacques reached down and lifted the unconscious form away from the woman. A little blood trickled from between the woman's legs. She moaned painfully and rolled onto her side, her hands clutching her stomach.

"They are all used," Jacques shouted. "I want fresh meat." He stared into other faces lit by jumping flames. "Eh . . ." He grinned, showing the gaps in his teeth. "We want the taste of something fresh. Isn't that so, my friends?"

"In Christ's name, yes," a voice replied. "Fresh meat in this whoremother's town."

"In the church they've not been touched."

"The festering English have them. They save them for themselves."

"Come, my friends." Jacques bent and took a brand from the fire; he started across the square. "Let us take our share of the Spaniards."

A ragged collection of eight or ten accompanied him across the Plaza Principal, some so drunk they could barely walk. One stepped on a mango, slipped, and fell laughing; he got to his feet, fell again, and continued on his hands and knees. Others, more sober, reached for weapons.

Cramer and van Staal saw them coming; they turned to Stone, who dozed against the oaken door. "Cap'n," Cramer whispered. "Wake. We've trouble." Stone grunted and rubbed a hand over his face.

"English," Jacques called a few yards from the church. "If you value your whore-bred lives, move away."

"Stay as you are," Stone said quietly to those beside him; he poured rum into his mouth, swirled it round his tongue, and spat it out. "Are you ready, Rolf?" he whispered.

Van Staal nodded, his bald head catching the light.

"Do not yet stand," Stone added. "Let them come closer."

"I'll kill that big French fart-sucker," van Staal grunted.

"Stop him. Do not kill him."

"We three's enough," Cramer observed. "Most of them's drunk."

"So am I," said Stone, "but that doesn't mean I'm useless."

"Well, English?" Jacques held his brand high; its flame lit them all. "Do you move, or do we move you?"

"Tell him if he comes any closer I'll shit on his head," Stone said quietly.

Van Staal got to his feet and spoke in his fractured French. Jacques listened, and his face darkened. He dropped the brand, turned to the man closest to him, and savagely tore a pike from his grasp. *"Vas te faire foutre,"* he yelled, and charged at the church.

As Jacques came up the steps, van Staal used his axe like a staff. With a movement to the left he parried the pike; it slid past to bury itself in the door. With a movement to the right, he brought the axe head up under Jacques's jaw. There was a soft crunching sound, and Jacques fell to his knees, scrambling backward, one hand holding the remains of his jaw. Blood ran down his chin, broken teeth dribbled from his lips. He tried to speak but was unable to; his tongue seemed to be missing.

"What, scum?" Van Staal's voice was loud in the shocked silence. "Who you going to move?"

"It seems he made a mistake." Stone leaned against the church door, a pistol in either hand. "Tell them to scatter."

Van Staal spoke again, and the French began to sidle away. Two of them helped Jacques to his feet. Half carrying, half dragging, they led him toward the waterfront.

"Hurry." Stone fired a shot into the air. "Get out of my poxy sight."

The French staggered, stumbled away, and the sound of their departure faded into the soft lapping of the sea.

"They'll not return," Cramer said. "That's the last of it for tonight."

"Nevertheless, we'll stay." Stone passed the rum to Cramer. "With enough of that you'll sleep in comfort here."

"Enough of that and I'll sleep in comfort anywhere."

Stone laughed. "You're a good man, Cramer. Tell me about that ear of yours again."

"I'll have another wet first, Cap'n." Cramer drank and passed the bottle to van Staal. For a time his soft, dark voice wound through the square, then it faded into silence as he, and the others before the church door, slept.

"How many are still to come aboard?"

"Not many," replied Sartou. "Those with Jacques."

"The longboats?"

"Gone for the last of them."

"Get it done as soon as you can."

"I will, *mon capitaine*."

Cazaux stared across the water to the dark and fitful town. Fires were dying along the waterfront; there was no movement to be seen. Soon all his men would be aboard *La Petite*, and they would be complete. He leaned forward suddenly, peering into darkness as if seeking something beyond his reach. He shook his head.

No, he told himself. I cannot afford to be concerned about her now. But he was, even more deeply than he knew.

CHAPTER 6

CHRISTOPHER STONE AWOKE, SUNLIGHT BEATING DOWN ON his throbbing head with a force that sent stabs of fire through his brain; his eyes seemed full of sand. He moved and was stilled by pain. The wound in his side threatened to tear; his shirt was stuck to the flesh. For a dizzy moment he thought he would vomit. Then, very slowly, as if he were either old or crippled, he pushed himself to his feet.

"God's blood," he muttered thickly. "I am poisoned."

" 'Tis the rum," said Cramer, who sat next to Stone, peering down at him through bloodshot eyes.

"Is there more?"

"Aye," said Cramer, and winced. "If you've the strength for it."

Stone reached for the bottle and took a mouthful. The rum was warm; he gagged on it and spat it out, his eyes running with the effort. He poured what remained of the spirits over the wound on his ribs and loosened the shirt that stuck there.

"Where's van Staal?" he asked.

"Our men's assembling, Cap'n," Cramer replied, his voice solemn. "But the French's gone."

"*What?*" Stone spun round in anger, then clamped his hands to his throbbing head. "God's mercy, no."

69

"Aye. In the night."

"Christ Jesus." Stone covered his eyes against the merciless sun. "Is there any sign of the *Courage*?"

"Yes, Cap'n. On the horizon now."

"Thank God for that. Organize the men." Stone felt his stomach heave. "Dry them out. Clean them up. Throw them into the sea if needs be, but have them ready in the square here in an hour." He coughed and spat out the bile that burned his throat. "Fetch me a clean shirt and bring it to the house of the mayor. I'll go there and purge myself." He turned his ragged eyes toward the horizon. "The poxy mongrel," he muttered, shaking his throbbing head. "He has a wondrous ability to take the chances as they come."

"Aye. 'Tis the secret of his survival." Cramer ran a hand over his black-bristled chin. "What can be done?"

"Nothing. Not yet." Stone's tongue stuck to the roof of his mouth. "For God's sake find me another flask of rum. One that's not been cooked in this festering sun. It is all that will cure me this day."

"Yes, Cap'n." Cramer hesitated. "What'll I tell the men?"

"Tell them to clear their heads if they want to see their share again." Stone's eyes went to Cramer. "We'll get it back. Tell them that also," he added defiantly.

Cramer nodded. "What about them's that are in there?" he asked, jerking his chin in the direction of the church.

"They'll keep." Stone watched the expression on Cramer's face. "I know, it stinks like the jakes, but they'll need to hold awhile."

In the slanted light that came in through the high ovoid windows, Don Luis de Córdoba moved through the Spaniards gathered in the church of Guadalupe, his mind on his daughter. She was nowhere to be seen. She was not amongst the company in the church. He had not expected her to be; yet in spite of what he feared, some distorted hope in a corner of his exhausted mind led him to believe she might suddenly appear—used, perhaps, but somehow whole, her hands held out toward him.

All night he'd remained by the great oak door, barely moving, not sleeping, hoping the nightmares that plagued him would go with the dawn. But the shape of Angela did not come to him.

Once he'd climbed to the pulpit and spoken to the townsfolk, assuring them that all would be well, that their lives would be spared and their losses less than any of them expected. But his words had an empty ring to them, and his heart had been heavy. As he spoke he'd thought of Cazaux and the value of his word.

Later, when the church door had actually opened and Guadalupe had been thrust into their midst, Don Luis had moved forward eagerly, only to see in the dim candlelight before the heavy oak door slammed in his face that the female figure was not that of his daughter.

So, when the first thin light of morning filtered down, he started among them, threading his way through the assembly, peering at each face, turning whenever long dark tresses moved in the corners of his vision, pressing his forlorn hope through tired eyes. But Angela was nowhere to be seen.

Don Luis did, however, come to realize how well the townspeople had survived the night. In spite of the scarcity of food and water, the cramped discomfort, the absence of sanitation, most were now on their feet, reassmbling, trying to begin a new day. Fear was stamped on all their faces, yet they greeted him as he passed, and some of them tried to smile. An old woman had died, he discovered, and a baby had convulsed just before dawn, but they had been fortunate: their women had not been taken.

From the far side of the high-walled church, Don Luis saw Fray Alonso de Campos, bishop of Campeche, coming toward him through the fetid air, counting his congregation.

"Our Lord has watched over us," the bishop said as he came closer. "He has protected us through this night."

"Yes, yes, Your Grace." Don Luis nodded. "Were all you saw alive?"

"Don Fernando is not long for this world," the bishop replied quietly. "But apart from him—" He shrugged.

"Have you seen my daughter?"

The bishop slowly shook his head. "I have not seen her at any time during the night." His hands were clasped before him. "I shall pray for her."

"Thank you." Don Luis's tongue was heavy. "Thank you, Your Grace."

"It is nothing, my son." The bishop cleared his throat. "Do you know how long we will be kept like this?"

"No," Don Luis replied, his eyes looking past the bishop.

"But pray it will not be long. Another day, and many more will perish."

"I will pray it is not so."

Don Luis's portly figure moved on.

A wetness had come to his eyes, his stomach held a hollow knot. Pray for her, he whispered to himself. Pray she is alive. Or has died quickly. Pray for her. Pray that Cazaux has kept his word. Pray he was to be trusted.

He pressed on through the packed bodies, the stench of vomit, feces, and urine that came from all sides; he pressed on unseeing, his tired legs barely supporting his weight.

Stone was shaving with a Spanish blade in the court-yard when Cramer and van Staal came to the house of the mayor. He had washed his wound and bandaged it. He'd taken a purgative he'd found in a chest of medicines; it was bitter and had done him no good. As he pulled the fresh shirt they had brought him over his aching head, he felt as if he were going to die.

"Did you bring me rum?" he whispered.

"Here, Cap'n." Cramer held out a tankard. "Try this, they say it'll cure the devil."

"What is it?"

"Rum and gunpowder. The buccaneer's cure."

"Must I drink it?"

"Well, Cap'n"—Cramer's eyes were laughing—"there's

another way to get it into you. If you takes down your breeches, I'll— ''

"Go to hell." Stone reached for the tankard and drank, emptying it in a swallow. For a moment he stood very still, his eyes watering, his face puckered. Then he turned and vomited against a whitewashed wall. "If that doesn't cure me, I'll cut your other ear from your poxy head," he managed to say. "Now, give me the rum."

Angela woke in her bedroom. The air was clear, her head felt strangely light; she lay long moments examining the familiar walls. They, too, should reflect the change she felt, the dream or the reality or the amalgam of both that filled her like the beginnings of a morning breeze rippling the surface of a deeply stirring sea. Idly she moved her limbs.

And then she heard foreign voices in the courtyard below. They lifted, and someone laughed. They had shattered her peace. Angela lay so still she did not seem to breathe. Then, very slowly, she crawled from the bed to a wide balcony overlooking the courtyard. Stretching her head around the corner of a square pillar, making no noise at all, she peered over the railing—and froze.

Directly below stood a tall Negro with a cutlass in his hand. His left ear was missing. He had seen Angela immediately and was watching her intently. Her hand flew to her mouth; she held her scream.

"Cap'n," the Negro called to someone she could not see. "I think we just got lucky."

"What can we do?" van Staal asked. "We are less than fifty, now the French have gone." His eyes in his round bronzed head were wary.

"And the men we have?"

"Most of them are on their feet, but some are useless." Van Staal hit the wall of the mayor's house with the flat of his hand. "The miserable, pox-ridden, fart-sucking Frenchman. Do you think he ever meant to share?"

"God's heart, who can tell?" Stone studied the Dutchman's open face. "The Frenchman sails as the winds blow." He shrugged. "But he offered us purpose. Something to drive for, after the storm."

"Sweet Christ." Van Staal's baldness glinted in the morning sun. "I, at least, should have had the wit to set our own guard on the purchase."

"To what end?" Stone drank a little rum and shuddered.

"To stop the thieving mongrel."

Stone closed his eyes. "If we'd done that, Rolf, we'd now be burying our dead. Or theirs. If Cazaux was determined, it would have achieved nothing. There's been killing enough as it is."

Van Staal turned away. "If I ever get close to that pox-mucked, whore-mothered scum-eater, I'll stuff his guts down his throat," he muttered.

"Please." Stone put a hand over his mouth. "Spare me this until my stomach is healed." He managed to swallow a little more rum. "Are our men armed?" he asked.

"They are. For whatever good it may do them."

"Are they before the church?"

Van Staal nodded.

"Good," said Stone, his head beginning to clear. "And we have the daughter of the mayor." He breathed deeply. "Listen, and I will tell you what we'll do."

Christopher Stone sat at the head of the council table, with van Staal and Cramer standing behind him. To his left were Angela and the mayor, to his right Capitán d'Avila and Jaime Toledo Flores. D'Avila had been brought from the hospital of San Juan de Dios; his face was pale, and he could not keep his fingers from the bandage that covered his blinded eye. Toledo sat coldly erect. The mayor was haggard. His eyes were fixed on his daughter, who slouched with her shoulders slumped, her countenance vacant.

Stone watched them for a moment or two; they should be enough to furnish him with what he required. "You have come through this well," he began boldly. His head no longer ached, his stomach had ceased to heave;

he was active again, and the industry renewed him. "I understand that one or two of your citizens died during the night, but I, too, have lost men. However, those who survived have been given their freedom. They can begin their lives again." He addressed himself to Don Luis. "We have treated you fairly, under the circumstances. Would you not agree?"

The mayor did not reply; it was as if he had not heard. He was aware that his clothes were sticking to him and that his throat was dry. He felt defeated. What they had done to Angela he did not know, but from the moment he had seen her being led docile into the council chamber she had not uttered a word.

"Do you not agree?" Stone repeated, interrupting the mayor's silence.

Don Luis's head twitched, and he licked his lips. "What do you want from us now?" he asked hoarsely. "Why did you not go with the French?"

"We differed over certain matters," Stone replied evenly. "You may have heard part of it outside the church last night."

Don Luis had nothing to say.

"Nevertheless," Stone continued expansively, "we will go as soon as we are able. In the meantime I need supplies, my ship some refitting." He cleared his throat. "While this is being achieved, the soldiers of your garrison will remain in the fort. They will be cared for, but they will not be released."

He turned to Toledo and d'Avila. "I need beef and I need water," he said. "That is why you are here. I understand you both hold property, and I expect to be supplied from that source."

D'Avila did not speak; his eye throbbed, and he felt the fever of rage in his blood. It took all his effort not to pitch forward on the council table in a faint.

Jaime Toledo stared back at the hawk-faced Englishman in undisguised defiance. "How many head will you take?" he asked as if speaking to a servant.

"Fifty," Stone replied. "It will needs be salted and stored in barrels."

Toledo nodded, his young face contemptuous. "It will take time to prepare," he said.

"How long?"

"A week, perhaps longer. And we require certain considerations in return."

Stone smiled thinly. "What are they?" he asked.

"You will release from the dungeons all those who are wounded or ill. They will go with Capitán d'Avila to the hospital of San Juan de Dios. And you must agree to contain your men while they remain in the town."

Stone seemed amused. "Tell me, Señor Toledo, why should all this be granted?"

"We must work together," Toledo answered, his voice barely civil. "Otherwise nothing will be done."

"Is that so?"

Toledo nodded. "You are not many. You will be unable to achieve anything without our cooperation."

Stone stared at the Creole, at his smooth young face, the determination he found there. "You sound very sure of yourself," he said at last.

"I am. I was born in Campeche. I know what is required to survive here."

"Unlike some others?"

Toledo glanced at Don Luis, noting the man's distress. The mayor's eyes did not leave his silent daughter. "The mayor is tired," Toledo replied evenly. "The others also. I am the only member of the council who has withstood your coming. It is my duty to do what I can for Campeche."

"Very well," Stone agreed. "You shall have your conditions. But I insist on one of my own. We will hold the mayor's daughter as security."

"No." The cry broke from Don Luis. He half rose from his chair, sudden anger stiffening his features. "Do not touch her." His voice was stubborn. "She has suffered enough."

Stone peered closely at the girl; as he did so tears welled in her eyes. She did not move, nothing about her showed any sign of life save the heavy tears forming. She had not spoken in all the time she had been with them. She had dressed in her room and come with them silently, and Stone had thought her condition was due to fear. Now he realized it was more profound. She was not the same wench he had seen yesterday; whatever had occurred during the night had altered something within her.

"Please," urged the mayor. "Show some decency."

Stone nodded and had opened his mouth to speak when van Staal bent to his ear. Stone smiled. "However," he said a moment later, "in lieu of the mayor's daughter we'll hold the captain's woman."

D'Avila turned his fevered face to Stone. "It is a pity she did not kill you," he whispered.

"Was it you who sent her?"

"No. When my turn comes I'll need no assistance." D'Avila's voice was like a knife blade. "But it is a pity that she failed, all the same."

Stone shrugged. There was rancor all about him. He would be glad to be away from this place.

"I did not kill him," Guadalupe said to her mother; she stood in the center of the house in the barrio looking at the coals of the dead fire. She had been released with the others from the church. No one had questioned her going, their thoughts had been too occupied with the French who had vanished. "I tried, but I was not quick enough."

"Thank God for that." There were dark patches beneath Magdelena's eyes; her face was gray from lack of sleep. "If you had succeeded, you also would be dead."

"It would not matter."

"It would to me."

Guadalupe looked at her mother for a long time, and finally some of the enmity left her face. "I must go back to the hacienda," she said. "There is much to be done."

"Stay with me."

"I cannot. I must return." Guadalupe pulled the shawl firmly across her shoulders. "It is the least I can do."

"Be careful, 'Lupe," Magdelena cautioned. "One day your pride will destroy you." She stared at her daughter, wondering how so slender a shape could hold such strength of will. "Be careful," she repeated. "If only for love of me."

Guadalupe turned away.

"How was it the French were able to leave?" Jaime
Toledo asked scornfully. "It was their ship that took our
shot."

Stone grunted. "They were urged by a considerable
greed," he said. "One quite capable of taking the place
of food or water or even equipment."

"They went with everything?"

Stone nodded.

"Why do you not look for more?" Toledo asked, his
voice contemptuous. "That's what your kind usually
does."

Stone shrugged. "I have no taste for it." He smiled
ruefully. "I am a pirate, not a bloodsucker. You have
suffered enough this visit."

Toledo's expression altered. He opened his mouth to
speak again but held the comment. He stood abruptly,
and the others at the table moved on his signal. The
mayor helped his daughter to her feet. Cramer would
have done the same for d'Avila, but the Spaniard thrust
his arm away. The ragged group headed toward the
double doors leading from the council chamber.

"What's more, we'll have our purchase back," Stone
called. "It is only a matter of time before we catch
Cazaux and cut his black heart from his poxy body."

As the words filled the stately room with its great
chairs, handsome table, and portrait of the now dead
king, Angela fainted. Her knees sagged, she sobbed
aloud and sank into her father's arms.

CHAPTER 7

CHRISTOPHER STONE SPENT THE REMAINDER OF THE DAY inspecting the town. He rode through cobbled streets, under arches, past squares of white-and-pinkstone houses. He examined the fort and checked the condition of the Spanish soldiers in the dungeons. He went out to the haciendas owned by Toledo and d'Avila and saw the cattle from which his beef would come. He watched the people of Campeche begin to emerge.

Merchants reopened, Indians in the Plaza Principal repiled their multicolored fruits; all moved warily as the pirates patrolled the streets. They watched carefully as the *Courage* came close to the town and anchored broadside to the waterfront, her cannon primed and aimed at Campeche. They spoke little and laughed less, but they were returning to the surface of their lives.

Jean-Marc Cazaux sat in a sea chair clamped to the deck, his eyes fixed on the horizon. All night he'd remained staring into darkness. When dawn was a thin red line severing night from day, Sartou approached and coughed discreetly, his foul breath filling the air.

Cazaux moved his head to windward. "How is Jacques?" he asked in a voice as flat as water. "The idiot who had his jaw broken outside the church."

"Dying, *mon capitaine*. Marcou is with him but says nothing can be done."

"He is a fool."

"Marcou? He is a good surgeon and an even better cook."

"Jacques. He brought it on himself."

Sartou shrugged. "There is wine and biscuits," he began. "I have warmed the wine—"

Cazaux lifted a hand to silence the mate. Sartou cleared his throat, and once more Cazaux raised the Chinese silk scarf he wore about his neck to cover his nostrils. "What course should we sail?" Sartou began again. "We are headed due north at the moment."

"Make for Florida. We'll go to Tampa Bay."

"Yes, *mon capitaine*." Sartou paused. "Anything else?"

"Leave me. I must think." Cazaux waited until he was alone again before removing the neckerchief.

He had grown hollow-eyed from staring outward, at the line of the sea, and inward, where demons pursued him and an emptiness prevailed. The demons nagged at him until he flung himself from the chair and began to pace the deck. They remained, tied to his footsteps.

It had not begun this way; it was unjust that he should be captured now. He, who had always been free. His plan to trap a limping Spanish galleon, struggling north from Veracruz, had been a splendid idea at the time.

"It will not be the first occasion on which I've taken so handsome a prize," he'd said to Stone as they'd peered at each other through uncertain light in a tavern in Tortuga, and he'd smiled easily to cover the lie.

Stone had said nothing; he'd drunk more rum.

"What is more," Cazaux had continued smoothly, pointing to himself and Stone, "a Frenchman and an Englishman. What Spaniard do you know of who could touch us on these seas?"

"What do you want with me?" the Englishman had asked.

Cazaux had laughed aloud. "You're well reputed here, my friend," he'd answered. "They say you have never been known to resist a given challenge."

"And the challenge in this?"

"Two frigates against a galleon?" Cazaux had leaned forward over the deal table. "Even if the galleon be captained by a Spanish blockhead."

Stone had turned to spit on the sawdust-covered floor.

"And they say you know how to fight, my friend," Cazaux had added quietly. "Don't tell me I've been misinformed."

Stone's eyes had come up, and Cazaux had seen their frenzy; for an instant it had chilled him in his chair. But he smiled again, and he'd persuaded, never quite knowing why Stone agreed, only sure that, whatever the outcome, he'd be able to use this tall, rawboned Englishman in some manner from which he'd profit.

And so it had occurred. The storm had destroyed any chance they might have had with the Spanish fleet, but Stone had proved his value when he'd thundered down on the Campeche fort.

Now, Cazaux paused by the rail on his northbound ship: so why had it come to this? The fact that they had missed the fleet mattered little. He'd enjoyed the norther that had struck them down. To see the damage caused to the *Courage,* knowing how little *La Petite* had suffered, had filled him with glee.

So why was it he was captured now? Torn back toward a girl he knew practically nothing about? Her eyes had filled him, and her passion was something he'd been unable to resist.

Cazaux walked his decks again and shrugged. It was monstrously unfair, this tugging at his heart and loins; he deserved no part of it. What had begun as a further adventure now threatened to anchor him: the demons had him bound.

Toward evening, Stone sat in a corner of the flagstoned courtyard of the mayor's house, a tankard of rum in his hand. He watched light from the setting sun turn white walls the color of flamingos, the shadows in the arches from indigo to black. The town was quiet; a scent of peace was in the air.

He heard Manuel, the majordomo, laying a table for supper in the dining room. The silver had gone with Cazaux, and the plates being placed were pottery, but their clinks sounded gentle, hospitable.

Installed above, in Angela's bedroom, was Guadalupe Santoya. She had come, resisting, from the hacienda of d'Avila, her eyes furious and her mouth sharp. But when she was told the welfare of the commander of the garrison depended on her presence, she drew herself upright and stared at Stone with such loathing that he was forced to turn away.

Now she lay on Angela's bed; Piet the Mulatto, a half-breed buccaneer from Hispaniola, squatted beside her door, a cutlass across his knees.

In a bedroom on the opposite side of the house van Staal slept, his round head pressed into pillows, his mouth open in a mild snore.

Cramer the Black walked the town; his was the evening watch.

Stone sipped a little rum. It was mixed with water and the juice of limes, its flavor refreshed. He was not displeased with the events of the day. When he thought back to his condition of the morning, and the emptying shock when he was told that *La Petite* had sailed, he felt he had reason to be content. He was quietly counting his small advantages when Manuel approached stiffly in his striped jerkin and tight hose.

"Excuse me, señor," Manuel began with rigid formality. "The señor Jaime Toledo Flores wishes to speak with you."

"What does he want?"

"I did not ask, señor."

"Have the goodness to do so." Stone was amused by the ceremony. "I wish to be spared further surprises."

Manuel bowed and went away. A moment later he returned and bowed again. "Señor Toledo says it is a private matter," he said. "But he wishes you to know that it might compensate you for the losses you suffered this morning." The majordomo's face was devoid of expression.

"Is he alone?"

"Yes, señor."

"Bring him in."

Jaime Toledo came into the courtyard with the slightest hesitation in his step. His comportment had altered from that of the morning; his eyes no longer held such hatred, some of the scorn had gone from his voice. "It is good of you to receive me," he began.

"I am surprised you have come," Stone commented. "I would have considered myself the last person you might visit."

"This is not a social matter."

Stone smiled thinly. "I did not expect it to be," he said.

"It is—" Toledo wet his lips. "It is that I have a prospect in mind which might interest you."

"Really?" Stone's voice was impassive. "Why should you care to interest me?"

"I, I also will benefit."

Stone drank a little rum, his eyes not leaving the Creole. He offered Toledo neither a seat nor any refreshment. He waited to see what would be said.

"How much do you know of this country?" Toledo proceeded. "This part of New Spain?"

"Some. Yet little enough."

"The Indians? Those who call themselves the Maya?"

"Nothing." Stone shrugged. "Well, very little."

"They once were many. Now there are few."

"So I have heard," Stone said dryly. "You've killed some. Others have succumbed to the plagues you brought."

"They have been defeated here," Toledo went on, "but not completely. There is a tribe that, to this day, remains independent. Leading its old life, believing in its false gods, and retaining its gold."

Stone leaned back in his chair. "And are you to suggest that we relieve them of it?" he asked lightly.

"I am suggesting that it is time they were made loyal subjects to the Spanish crown. That their wealth was rendered to my king. That they were taught to abandon their idols and to believe in the one true Church."

Stone shrugged. "I have no concern with increasing the wealth of your king," he said. "Nor do I hold much credence for your church. And I cannot say that the idea of defeating a band of savages has much to do with my way of life."

"Forgive me," Toledo said carefully. "But I do not believe you."

Stone smiled. "You would call me a liar?"

"No. I would call you a man who responds to a challenge." Toledo's eyes were level, his gaze calculating. "And I would have you know how great a challenge this is." His voice quickened. "The great Cortez was not able to achieve victory over these Maya. Montejo, the conqueror of Yucatán, could not defeat them. What I am offering you is the opportunity to do what no man has done before. Does that not stimulate your very soul?"

"And, of course, there is the gold?"

"More than you could ever imagine. It would make what Cazaux has taken a mere nothing."

"In spite of what would go to your king."

"Without his share you would still hold enormous wealth."

Stone nodded slowly. "And you would achieve your dream. Is that not so?"

The Creole's eyes flashed. "Six generations ago one of my forefathers came with Cortez. It has always been my ambition to follow him. With you, I have the chance."

"Regardless of your detestation of what I am."

Jaime Toledo looked away. "When you came I hated you," he replied quietly. "This morning, I could have killed you. Since then I have learned what you did to protect us. And when you spoke of what Campeche had already suffered—" He shrugged, and his eyes went back to Stone. "I believe you live by certain principles. Not my own, but they exist."

"And you would use them."

"I would use anything I could to make this journey into the interior. I have had this dream for as long as I can remember. To conquer the Itzá, the last of the Maya." Toledo smiled, and his face was suddenly very young. "I wish to become the last conquistador, Captain Stone. I ask you to help me."

Stone watched the enthusiasm glow in the Creole's eyes; it was curiously infectious. "What of these Itzá?" he asked carefully. "What right do you have to dispossess them of their wealth? To say nothing of their lives."

"They are heathen." Toledo's face stiffened. "They are sodomists. They eat human flesh, and they sacrifice their prisoners to blasphemous idols." He breathed deeply. "By conquering them we would do them a service. We would bring their souls to God. We would offer them redemption."

"Perhaps," Stone said. "But I am not of your papist faith."

"Your God is my God." Toledo's reply was sure. "We approach Him differently, but we know He is the one true God."

Stone drank from his tankard. "You may be right." He wiped his lips. "I will think on what you have said. I will talk to my men."

"They will be eager. Of that I am certain."

"Why?"

"For them it is a challenge also. You see, the city of the Itzá is on an island in a lake among mountains. To conquer it one would need to be both soldier and sailor." Toledo smiled confidently. "I am sure your men could prove themselves most capable as both."

Stone leaned forward; his eyes held a new look, a touch of sudden intensity flickered. "I will think on it," he said again. "But I do admit you begin to interest me most strangely."

For long moments, the Creole and the English pirate examined each other's faces. These two men, who were to be welded, wondered how they might use each other, how far each of them was to be trusted.

Late in the evening, in the house of the late municipal architect, she began to speak. After her collapse in the council chamber, Don Luis had taken her to Leal's home, his own dwelling having been appropriated by Stone. All afternoon she had lain as if sleeping, her breathing shallow, her pale face covered with a veil of sweat.

Leal's servants and his widow, her own grief restrained
behind red-rimmed eyes, ministered to the girl, but it
was not until Angela was alone with her father that she
woke abruptly and smiled softly as she gazed up into the
haggard face of the mayor.

"Papá," she said, her voice dry and dreamy. "He will
come back, won't he? He will come back for me."

"He—?" The word was like a dry biscuit in Don Luis's
throat. "Who?" He refused to accept what he'd heard.

"Jean-Marc. I know it. He will come back."

Don Luis could not speak; he took a cloth to wipe his
daughter's forehead. She avoided him and sat upright on the
bed in which she'd lain. "This is the house of Leal," Angela
said, looking about her. "Why on earth are we here?"

"It—it is only for a while," Don Luis managed. "Soon
we will go home."

"But I must go now." A note of excitement entered
Angela's whispery voice. "I must prepare."

"Prepare?"

"For Jean-Marc. I must be ready when he returns."

Don Luis stared. Angela's skin was creamy; her eyes
were very bright. "What—?" he began, but got no further.

"*Must* we remain here? Really? I've never liked this
house. It always smells of babies. It feels closed in. And
Señora Leal is such a stuffy woman."

"She—she is a widow now."

"Oh. Poor creature. What happened?"

Don Luis did not answer. He tried to compose his
thoughts as he seated himself beside Angela and took
her hand. "What—what did he do?" He forced his un-
willing lips to form the words. "What—?" He saw again
Leal fallen on the breakwater: murdered by the hand
that had led his daughter away. He saw again the
Frenchman's face and heard the empty promises. He
tried to force himself to anger, but as he gazed at Angela
he was confused. "Tell me what he did," he asked.

"Who, Papá?"

"The Fren—" Don Luis swallowed. "Jean-Marc
Cazaux."

Angela smiled. "Nothing," she replied with some truth.
"He was kind, he was gentle. And he will come back for
me. Of that I am absolutely certain."

Don Luis stared; color was returning to Angela's cheeks, her voice was stronger. Her eyes covered the room; she frowned and shook her head. Then her hands went to her hair, lifted it from her slender neck, and she tossed it, teased it, combed it with her fingers. She turned to him, smiling; in a rush all her loveliness returned. And with it came a certainty, a quick, sure enchantment that sparkled in her eyes. Her smile widened, and Don Luis was forced to turn his head away.

Van Staal welcomed the plan. " 'Tis what we need," he said. "It will occupy those who go, and keep those who remain alert."

"I could secure the safety of those who remain by taking the commander's doxy," Stone said thoughtfully. "What is more, we will have the Creole as an additional bond."

"I am for the venture."

"What do you know of these Indians?"

Van Staal smiled grimly. "I was chained to a number of them in the mines of Venezuela," he said. "They are fierce and they are cruel. But they have no weapons such as ours."

"You have no scruples at taking their gold?"

"None. It once belonged to others. We have as much right to it as any."

"What else do you know of them?"

"A little of their language." Van Staal rubbed a hand over his near bald head. "One learns something even in a salt mine," he said reflectively.

Stone grunted. "You do not hesitate to join forces with the Spanish? It was they who put you to the mines in Venezuela."

"It is a choice of evils," Van Staal replied. "We go with them, or we remain with them here." He shrugged. "I would choose the action."

"I too," said Stone simply, and so it was decided.

Toledo found him talking to Meredith, one of the *Courage*'s gunners. The pirates stood on the breakwater on either side of a four-foot culverin, the slender cannon's brass sheen catching the evening light. Stone glanced up at the young Spaniard, then continued his conversation in English.

Finally he turned to Toledo. "Well," he began, "as you see, we will be well armed for our attack on the Itzá gold."

Toledo nodded, dismissing the gun; waiting, for Stone had annoyed him. "I have a request to make," he said crisply.

"What is that?" Stone took Toledo by the elbow to lead him away. Meredith watched them a moment, then returned his attention to the cannon. "Tell me," Stone continued, "does something trouble you?"

"Yes." Toledo shook Stone's hand free; he stopped to stare up at the tall pirate. This man was too independent for his liking. "The prisoners. I want them released. One has died, and another's dying."

Stone frowned. "You're asking that I free them all?" he enquired.

"Yes," Toledo replied forcibly.

Stone shook his head. "Those who are ill may go, I have already agreed to that," he said, "but the others must remain."

Toledo flushed angrily. "Have you any idea what it's like in there?" he asked.

Stone nodded.

"Then—"

"Señor Toledo"—Stone began to walk again, to pace the breakwater slowly, his eyes on the vermilion orb of the setting sun—"I cannot release all your soldiers, that you must understand. While we're away, and God knows how long that will be, your Capitán d'Avila will recover. And if his men were free, he might just be tempted to employ them. He is not, as you know, a very level-headed man."

"He has given his word," Toledo countered, keeping step. "Is that not enough?"

"On his mestiza?" Stone shook his head.

"He is a Spanish officer."

"He is also incredibly stupid."

Toledo halted once again, this time in front of Stone, causing the Englishman to pause and stare down into the face of the Creole. "I think we should be clear about something," Toledo said, his voice rising. "*I* am the leader of this expedition."

Stone felt a sudden pressure behind his eyes; he sucked in breath, controlling his irritation. "No one is in charge of this expedition," he said slowly and evenly. "We go together, and we will work together. I will supply my experience in the manner best known to me. You will use your experience when it is needed." He stared, unblinking. "*That* is what we must understand, Señor Toledo, nothing more."

Toledo's face withdrew; a line appeared about his lips as he stepped back, holding any reply. He needed this overbearing pirate to give substance to his dreams, but he knew, as clearly as did Stone, that a battle, other than any they would fight with the Itzá, lay clearly now before them.

All around, the setting sun bathed the dying afternoon in simple golden light.

Guadalupe Santoya lay on the bed in the room above the courtyard in the house of the mayor, listening to the coming and going of footsteps and the sound of foreign voices. She had eaten nothing since her arrival and felt weak and dispirited. Yet she sat quickly and smoothed her skirt into place when Stone entered the bedroom. She stared at the gaunt, straw-headed pirate with open defiance.

"You are to come with us," Stone said without ceremony. He turned to Piet the Mulatto, who had followed him into the room. "Have her prepare what she needs," he added. "But do not let her near a weapon."

"What is this?" Guadalupe lifted her chin. "What do you speak of?"

"You are to come with us," Stone repeated. "We are to make a journey together."

"I would not go anywhere with you."

"You will." Stone smiled thinly. "Your protector has given his word on your life."

"What do you mean?"

"D'Avila will behave himself if we assure him of your safe return." Stone's voice was even. "He has already committed one stupidity against us, you are to guarantee he will not attempt another." He moved a hand impatiently. "Now, go back to the hacienda for whatever you need. Piet will accompany you."

Very slowly Guadalupe eased herself from the bed, trying to evaluate the importance of what had been said. She realized that if she went with this barbarian, sooner or later she would be given the opportunity to accomplish what she had endeavored as he'd swayed drunkenly before the door of the church. Yet at the same time, she began, vaguely, to wonder whether if she were taken as assurance of the word of d'Avila, that sacrifice, in itself, might significantly ease the burden of her debt. The wisps of thoughts confused her; she required time. It was impossible to conclude anything in this unfamiliar room with this ugly pirate and the other, he who held the curved weapon, he whose skin was the color of her own.

"Come along," Stone urged impatiently. "There is much to be done."

"When, when do we depart?" Guadalupe asked, her voice uncertain. She needed to be told a great deal more.

"Tomorrow. The next day. Whenever we are ready."

"Where do we go?"

"To the interior." Stone frowned. "To the land of, what are they called, the Itzá."

"The Itzá." Guadalupe's reaction was immediate. "They who are the last of us."

"Us?" Stone questioned. "What are you talking about?"

"My, my mother is a Maya," Guadalupe said, her voice low for the first time. There seemed no point in not explaining. "I am a mestiza."

"Your father was a Spaniard?"

"He was a seaman who spent one night with my mother. She has nothing of him apart from me and a name. We are not considered of any value in Campeche."

"So you have a protector?"

"Capitán d'Avila has been kind," Guadalupe replied, a note of challenge coming back to her voice. "He has treated me well. He has taken care of my mother."

"And they are not all so generous in this prosperous little town," Stone said, understanding for the first time part of what she owed. He studied the dusky face, the fine bones of the cheeks, the almost Oriental slant to the eyes and the pride that dwelt therein. "You don't, perchance, speak the language of the Itzá?" he asked.

"I speak the Maya tongue as well as I speak Spanish."

Stone smiled. "By my soul," he said, "you may be of some value on this journey after all." Without a further word he turned and left the room.

"I've been thinking I was coming," the tall Negro said grudgingly. "Seems you'd want me there."

"I need you here," Stone said, seeing the disappointment on the big black face. "Someone's got to watch over the *Courage*."

"What about Gottberg, he's bosun."

"I need his skill where I'm going."

"Van Staal?"

Stone shook his head. "It's you to hold the town," he said. "Watch over the Spanish in the dungeons, be sure our newfound friends don't let them out. There's no one else I trust."

"As you say." Cramer swallowed his discontent. "How long will you be gone?"

"A month." Stone watched him. "Think you'll hold?"

Cramer shrugged. "I hopes so, Cap'n," he replied.

"You will," Stone said evenly, then added, "What cannon should I take, harquebus?"

"Culverins'd do you better. They're light. They fire straight."

Stone nodded. " 'Tis what I thought. Have Henri the Stain prepare a pair. I'll take him along as well. And as many muskets as you can spare."

"Is that all, Cap'n?"

"All the powder and shot the men can carry." Stone clapped a hand on the Negro's shoulder. "Cheer up, Cramer," he said. "You'll have the best of it here."

Cramer wondered about that last remark; it was to return to him frequently in the weeks to come.

Toledo chose Teniente Reyes to command the Spanish who were to make the journey into the interior.

The young officer, who had led the troop down onto the breakwater just a few days earlier, now approached Stone and saluted crisply. "It will give me much pleasure to accompany you, sir," he said enthusiastically. "It is our duty to pacify this land."

"Really?" Stone studied the optimistic face. "Who is your sergeant?"

"Ocaño, sir. He's been in this part of the world for years." Reyes pointed toward a man with an unshaven chin, whose doublet hung half-open on a thin, almost concave, torso. "He may not look it, sir, but he knows how to control his men."

Stone grunted, unimpressed. "What bearers do we have?"

"Fifty. Indian and Negro."

Stone handed Reyes a list. "See that all this is prepared for them," he said. "And if there's room for more, make it up in small shot for the cannon."

"I shall see to it at once, sir. It will be a pleasure."

Stone smiled thinly. "I should have been glad of a release from the dungeons also," he commented.

"It's not that, sir. I feel, well, that this will prove to be a most significant mission." He saluted again and left smartly.

Stone watched him go, wondering how many more there were like him in this strange, isolated town.

CHAPTER 8

THEY LEFT EARLY, WHILE THE SUN REMAINED A LOW BALL in the eastern sky. Pink-edged clouds ran level with the land; the air was soft, cool as the sound of the sea.

Before departing they assembled in the Plaza Principal before the half-lowered eyes of Indians shaping their produce and the servants who had come to buy. They gathered with the clink of harness, the stamp of hooves; the polyglot voices were uneven as they made their way southeast of the town.

Those from the *Courage* were twenty: buccaneer-marksmen, toughened on the shores of Hispaniola, whose skill with the long-barreled muzzle loader was legend; logwood cutters from along the coast. Each man knew how to live from the land through the ways of the Indians; every one was worth ten of any other breed.

The Spanish consisted of twenty also: the fittest of the garrison, taken from the dungeon. Most were unshaven, their uniforms soiled from their days of imprisonment; without d'Avila to preen them, they were even more slovenly. Only the eager Teniente Reyes showed any pride in his appearance.

Their weaponry was diverse. It ranged from the short-barreled muskets and fighting swords of the Spanish to the great axe of van Staal, slung across his back; it varied from the six pistols Stone carried in the holster over his shoulders to the two brass culverins, each in a sling between four bearers.

But, of them all, Jaime Toledo Flores was the most bizarre. He wore a dented, well-polished breastplate, the like of which no one had seen in use for many years.

"It belonged to my ancestor," he told Stone with pride. "He who came with Cortez."

Stone nodded solemnly. "It is not an inconvenience in the heat?" he enquired dryly.

"It is what each foot soldier wore," Toledo explained. "Day or night. Hot or cold. It was both their protection and their emblem."

"May it bring you the same success."

"Of that I am certain." Toledo's chest filled; he turned in his saddle, reviewing the collection of mounted men, the bearers who went on foot. Seeing Guadalupe, he frowned suddenly. "Who gave the mestiza a horse?"

"I did."

"That is not necessary. She is capable of making the journey without it."

"She travels with the same comfort as you or I," Stone replied evenly.

Toledo shrugged, and his breastplate caught the light. "Very well," he agreed. "But she will bring us trouble sooner or later." With that he turned his horse and rode to the head of the column. His back was stiff, his shining token gleamed like a beacon in the emerging sun.

Don Luis de Córdoba, in the house of Leal, heard the sounds of departure. He lifted his head abruptly, listening for more, as if the rattle of harness and the hollow crack of hooves might signal some relief, might lessen the weight that had settled on his shoulders: none of his calculated schemes had achieved anything at all. Now, there was nothing more than the dying echoes of distant men and the shouts of those who controlled them.

Then, from another part of the house, he heard his daughter singing. Her voice was light and tuneful. She sang a folksong from the south of Spain that captured the movement of feet, laughter on the faces of dancers. Angela was assembling the few possessions she had with her. She had insisted that they return to the house near the Municipal Building with its cool courtyard and its glimpses of the sea as soon as the gaunt English pirate was gone; she insisted on returning to her own comfortable room.

Angela's voice rose. Don Luis closed his eyes and poured more cognac into his coffee. He did not know how else to abide the waiting, to consume the empty time. The daughter he loved, the only link he had with that frail creature, his wife, who had died of fever in Seville, had been returned to him damaged, her mind overtaken by some monstrous fantasy whose precise nature both eluded and frightened him. She was in some foreign place, beyond his reach.

And the town he loved, that which had absorbed and profited him, that which he'd seen grow also, that had given him a future to believe in—that, too, was overtaken: robbed and occupied. The mayor's hand shook as the brandy poured; he drank the hot, harsh mixture quickly and added further cognac to the empty cup. There was little to believe in now, nothing to achieve, nothing that his care could accomplish. He paused, the cup halfway to his lips, but the sound of the departing column was no longer to be heard.

From the outset the going was hard. Away from the cooling sea the land became dry and daunting: savanna stretched as far as the eye could reach. The dry, coarse grasses and the thin ground between their roots gave the bearers trouble; no rain had fallen for more than a month, and dust rose chokingly. Their eyes became reddened, and toward evening their pace had turned so slow that those with horses were forced to rein and wait for long and longer periods.

Finally Stone approached Toledo. "We'll camp here," he said, pointing to a clump of stunted, flat-topped trees half a mile to the east. "There's shelter there."

"No." Toledo's eyes were impatient. "We have

made less than twenty kilometers. I had planned on twenty-five.''

Stone stared into the determined face of the Creole, seeing some of the fanaticism that marked the ancestors. ''Do not push these men too hard,'' he said. ''Allow them to become accustomed to the journey. We have need of them for many days to come.''

Toledo shook his head. ''They are natives,'' he said as if speaking of cattle. ''They are capable.''

''They are men. And we need them.''

Toledo watched as Stone trotted his horse to where van Staal waited for the exhausted bearers to approach. Then, his young face hardening, he followed.

What had begun as sport had ended by possessing.

Cazaux sat in the darkness before another dawn, listening to the passing of the sea, trying in vain to deny the force that drew him and the shape of the girl who called him home.

He'd almost convinced himself that women were playthings, toys to be had by proxy, enjoyed as he wanted to enjoy them, then left behind and forgotten. Now he was no longer sure.

He'd lied about his injury. There was none to the body, unless you counted the long scar on his face, caused by the razor of a Tortuga whore he'd laughed at. Although, he had to admit, his use of substitutes had begun shortly after that. He wasn't impotent, he merely preferred watching others and attending to himself. It excited him more to control them all.

Or so he'd believed until the tall girl with skin like milk and eyes that held such wonder had made him alter his ritual, had had him beside her on the table after the duty boy had gone, attending to her as he attended to himself or—it was too full and clouded and overwhelming to bring clearly to mind. Or what?

Their pleasure cloaked a mystery he did not understand; her desire had consumed his own, had sown a need for more. She bored in his brain like a worm. There was only one way to assuage this demand, and he was not prepared to give in to that—yet. He must continue, sail north to the new French colony near Tampa Bay in Florida. There his men could repair the damage caused by Spanish cannon in Campeche; there he could begin a renewal. Yet he was profoundly affected and knew it, was drawn in a manner he could not have imagined possible. It gnawed at him without mercy.

And he could not begin to explain it, not even as he sat, hour by hour, watching the endless sea. He was consumed.

"These Spanish are less prepared than I'd thought," said Stone to van Staal. His eyes were on the soldiers spread, without order, beneath the flat-topped trees. The bearers, Indian and Negro alike, were as abandoned in their weariness. Those from the *Courage* squatted about their cooking fires, crouched in the lee, using the smoke to keep away the insects the others swatted at. "None but our own have experienced this country before."

"Are you concerned?"

"At the moment no."

"How long before we're there?"

"Ten days." Stone shrugged. "The Spanish will have toughened by then, or they'll no longer be with us."

That night, despite the guard set by Teniente Reyes, ten bearers disappeared. They slipped silently between the dozing sentries, leaving their packages, taking nothing but themselves in the stillness of the night. All were Indian, and not a trace of them was found, although Toledo, Reyes, and Ocaño spent an hour the following morning galloping back toward Campeche.

On their return to camp Reyes assembled his men. He strutted before them, shouting in their faces, attempting to bring some form of military bearing to their ranks. But his performance had little effect: no backs straightened, no uniform was rebuttoned. They stared insolently until he ceased.

Before Reyes had quite finished, Stone and his men prepared to leave. "Where are you going?" Toledo called, his face red with anger.

"On," Stone replied calmly. "To this city of the Itzá I have heard so much about."

"We are ten bearers short," Toledo shouted. "Who will carry their loads?"

"Others," Stone replied levelly, his hand on his horse's bridle. "And I do not mean bearers, Señor Toledo, they are weighted enough. I mean my men and yours. You and I."

Toledo turned his head furiously to catch sight of Guadalupe. "You," he called roughly. "Get down."

"Stay where you are," Stone contradicted.

"She can walk. We need the horse."

"We need her more." Stone mounted. "My men are ready," he informed Toledo. "I shall wait a little while yours prepare. Then I will proceed." He smiled briefly. "Do not lose me, Señor Toledo. I do not have a breast-plate which shines so brightly. I might be difficult to find once I've gone."

Toledo stared at the big Englishman who sat so easily in his saddle. Then he spurred away, calling to his men, ordering the sharing of the packages the bearers had left behind. His voice was strong, but in his heart was a growing unease about the man he could not control.

"Why did you not let him have my horse?" Guadalupe asked.

Stone glanced at her; her face was losing some of its bitterness, her eyes were curious.

"Why?" Guadalupe persisted. "He had the right to make me walk."

"Because you are a mestiza?"

"Because I am a woman and a mestiza. Neither is worth much in the eyes of a Creole."

"Then be grateful I am no Creole."

"Is there no more to it than that?" Guadalupe's voice held a note Stone had not heard before. "Would you have done the same for any of the others?"

"Of course. It is my duty to protect all those I need."

"And you need me?"

"Who else would translate?"

"There are others."

"None who will stay." Stone leaned closer. "You will stay because the life of your protector depends on it. Were you to be seen in Campeche, Cramer would have d'Avila's head."

"That does not mean I could not walk rather than ride," Guadalupe replied with some of her earlier defiance.

Stone smiled. "I need you healthy for the task that lies ahead. I want you alert when it comes to talking to these people whose gold we are to steal."

Cramer the Black awoke in the captain's cabin beneath the poop of the *Courage*. He lay in the simple bunk listening to the movement of the ship, the murmur of men at their tasks. The day was warm and humid, the sea air clung to his skin. Later it would rain. It was a day like any other, here on this curve of the coast; it was a day that lacked a spark.

Cramer scratched his chin and thought of shaving. Perhaps he should prepare himself, change his clothing, visit the house of the mayor. Campeche was his port now, he must be seen to be in command. As he must attend to the slaughter of the cattle, the salting of their carcasses, the storage of water and biscuits, beans and peas and lentils, fresh fruit and cheese. The list, like the time he had in hand, seemed endless.

With an effort Cramer climbed from the bunk to stare out the stern windows. Heat danced on the sea, the air in the cabin was clammy, a little mildew grew in the corner of a pane of glass. Cramer wiped it away with a thumb and breathed deeply. He must display himself, maintain himself, or he too would be captured by the mold that grew on everything in this damp, seductive climate. He must not become like those whose cannon had failed to fire, who had been so easy to defeat as they stumbled, confused and bewildered, in the dust of the fort.

Cramer shook his head to clear it. It was too easy to allow one's thoughts to meander. It was his duty to protect what he had been left to protect, or he would become another victim, and so would those who depend on him. He grunted and reached for the captain's razor.

*   *   *

The bearers dropped their packages and sank to the ground, as exhausted as they'd been the night before. Toledo, Teniente Reyes, and Sargento Ocaño approached. From their saddlebags they had extracted a number of fine iron shackles.

Stone watched, his face hard, as they began their task. The bearers did not protest but moved their legs to accommodate the irons. As the shackles were placed and locked, the metal made a small singing, clinking sound that blended in with the noise of the foddering horses and the low conversation of men.

When the work was complete Toledo turned to Stone, conscious of his critical stare. "You object to this?" he asked.

"Yes," Stone replied. "And no."

"They would run away like the others if we did not prevent it."

"Perhaps." Stone's voice was noncommittal.

"They would run to escape," Toledo persisted.

"Or in order not to see the last of their kind in irons like themselves," Stone said evenly. "But a thought like that would not cross your mind, would it, Señor Toledo?"

"Nor theirs," Toledo countered. "They are inferior creatures. They need to be taught."

"And you would teach them because you are superior?"

Toledo nodded. "As we will beat them because we are superior. We will triumph because we have the right to triumph." His voice was sure, his eyes determined. "I have faith."

"My congratulations."

"You too should have faith, Captain Stone. Without it you do not have the right to be a leader of this venture."

"Be grateful that my head is clear," Stone replied levelly. "That your mania has not yet touched me."

"Will it?" Toledo's eyes were searching. "Will you find faith on this journey?"

"I doubt it."

"Or will you find something among these savages we

are about to conquer? Will they give you what you are looking for?"

Stone stared at Toledo.

"For you seek something, Captain Stone, do not deny it. Why else would you be voyaging so far from your ship?"

"For gold."

"No, not you." Toledo stepped closer. "Not with those eyes that are always questing."

For a moment Christopher Stone said nothing, then he smiled very slowly. "Perhaps the Itzá do hold a secret," he said, and his voice was distant. "The secret of their own survival."

"And you would learn it?"

"We shall see." Stone turned away. The camp was settling, the fires had begun to smolder, men of all colors were lying on the ground. For the first time since he had left Campeche, he was aware of a sense of real purpose. "We shall see," he repeated softly. "When we get there, we shall see."

She could not keep him from mind, this Englishman she did not comprehend. He was unlike anyone she had ever met. D'Avila had used her but had been kind; he had taken her but had treated her honorably, had provided her with her livelihood. Any of the others she had met in Campeche had wanted her, heedlessly, for themselves. But this Englishman cared for the comfort of others. He drove them all, but no harder than he drove himself.

She had attacked him because she believed he was responsible for what had occurred to d'Avila: the blindness and the shame. She had been intent on procuring his death because he had destroyed the only security she had ever known. Now she was with him, watching his every move, and he did not appear to notice her.

He was an enigma, this ungainly pirate, he treated her as equally as any of the others, and it seemed unimportant to him that she'd attempted to take his life. His indifference confused her, reduced her certainty; she was no longer convinced that his death would erase d'Avila's humiliation.

*   *   *

Capitán Fernando d'Avila lay in the cool half-light that came through the barred window of his white-walled room in the hospital of San Juan de Dios. His eye was healing. An elderly nun had just visited him to wash his forehead, to tell him that his fever was on the wane. Soon he would be able to leave his bed. She had departed a moment ago with words of reassurance, and he could still hear the bustling of her robes as she walked down the corridor.

There was no doubt in his mind that he would recover, he had known it from the beginning, had known it as clearly as he knew that someday he would have the opportunity to take the life of the barbarian who had pulled his head back by the hair and forced a pistol into his neck.

It mattered little that he, d'Avila, had given his word on the life of the mestiza; when they returned that bond would be canceled anyway. Truly, no matter: she no longer occupied his thoughts.

In the meantime he would begin. As soon as he was able he would start to assess the strength of the force left behind to police the town; he would calculate the vulnerability of the *Courage*. He would visit the men of his garrison still chained in the dungeon below the fort, evaluating their ability to fight, preparing them for vengeance.

The moment would come, and he was determined to use it; his belief in it fired him while he waited. He moved in his bed and watched a shadow crawl up the cool white wall, rising as the sun set. All he required was time and determination, and he possessed enough of both. Very soon he would begin to plan the details of the death of the English pirate. When Stone returned from the interior, he, Capitán Fernando d'Avila, would be ready for him.

CHAPTER 9

FOR SEVERAL DAYS MORE THEY TRAVELED THE DRY AND
dustbound savanna. For several more days they wound
through the short tussock, their pace increasing as the
men and the horses grew used to the work. Each night
the bearers were put in irons, and each night Christopher Stone heard with distaste the gentle chink of the
singing chain and watched uneasily the docile acceptance of the men who were bound.

Then late one night he was awakened by a cry he
could not place. It came from the far side of the encamp-
ment where the pirates had made their shelters. It came
thick and muffled, as if a hand had been placed over the
mouth of the crier. At first Stone was not even sure the
plea was human, but when he heard it again, low and
fearful, ending in a grunt, he was certain.

Immediately he was on his feet, running toward the
sound. It was that of a woman in distress. Someone held
Guadalupe, and she was struggling. As he ran Stone
became aware of footfalls matching his own; he turned
to see van Staal beside him.

"The girl," Stone grunted. "Who has her?"

"God knows."

Stone held a pistol in one hand. "I'll kill the whoreson," he muttered. "We want none of this."

Now there were voices on all sides, calling in English, in Spanish, in all the tongues of the camp. There was laughter, and someone shouted coarse encouragement. Stone and van Staal arrived to find Meredith, the gunner, holding Guadalupe firmly. Before Stone had time to act, the mestiza tore Meredith's fingers from her lips, swung in his grasp, and clawed at his face. Meredith cried aloud as blood ran from four gouges in his cheek. He raised a fist to strike the girl, and Stone kicked his legs from under him.

Meredith fell into the embers of a dying fire; he grunted at the further pain and rolled from the cinders. He was a tough, muscular man who had been a logwood cutter before he joined the *Courage*, and he came up from the ground spitting, a knife in his hand.

"Stay," Stone called. "It is over."

"Not yet," growled Meredith, his eyes flickering between the crouched shape of the girl and the wild-eyed figure of Stone.

"Stay," Stone repeated, this time raising the pistol in his fist. "If you move, you are a dead man."

"Cap'n—" Meredith wiped his lips with a dye-stained hand, his expression altering; he was puzzled now. "You've no right."

"If you move, I'll kill you, right or no."

"The doxy was—"

"You shit-brained idiot," Stone said furiously. "Could you not take her quietly? Didn't you have the snot-nosed sense to get what you wanted without disturbing the camp?" The pistol trembled in his fist, and he wondered at the intensity of his own rage. "Did you want a poxy audience?" he roared.

"I was—" Meredith shook his head, he wiped blood from his torn cheek. "I was awake. She was walking. It was almost as if she was looking for something." He put his knife away and took a step backward, careful of the pistol in Stone's white-knuckled hand. "I'm not one of your buccaneers," he muttered bitterly. "After the arsegut of all he sees. She's a woman. She belongs to no one here."

"She belongs to me," said Stone, not knowing fully why. "Leave her be." His eyes covered all who stood in the darkness. "Let that be understood," he shouted. "The girl belongs to me."

There was a moment of disbelief. Then Meredith nodded and wiped his cheek again. "You should have said so earlier," he grunted.

"I say so now." Stone let the pistol fall to his side; he turned to Guadalupe. "Come with me," he said in Spanish. "I will protect you."

Guadalupe stared at the fierce-eyed pirate. "I have a protector," she replied, her voice uncertain.

"Not here," said Stone. "Unless it be me."

He turned and walked back to where he'd been sleeping. After a moment's hesitation Guadalupe followed. Behind them the men's voices lifted, and someone laughed again.

Meredith watched them go with dislike. Van Staal approached and put a hand on the gunner's arm. "Do not bear him malice," he said quietly. "He did it to keep peace among us all."

"A pox on him." Meredith spat, and the embers hissed. "I had always thought him fair."

"He is."

As Stone returned to his blanket, Jaime Toledo came out of the dark, appearing curiously naked without his breastplate. "I see," he said, his eyes on Guadalupe, "you have started already, Captain Stone."

Stone stared at the Creole and did not reply.

"The secrets of the Indians," Toledo persisted. "You are to begin with hers."

Stone's hand came up, the fingers clenched into a fist. Then he brushed past Toledo, pushing him aside, and went on to his bedding. The sound of his breathing was suddenly loud in his ears.

"Sleep here," he told Guadalupe, indicating a space a little distance from his own. He tossed a blanket at her feet. "Sleep there and stay there. Do not do any more midnight walking."

Guadalupe lay for a long time staring up at the carpet

of stars; they came and went with the passing of the clouds. Beside her, Stone shuffled abruptly in his bedding, his violence barely contained. After a time he relaxed, and later she knew he was asleep. Only then did she move. She reached out carefully and laid a hand on the Englishman's cheek, allowing her fingers to run over the gaunt shape of his bones; gently she touched the line of his lips. Stone grunted in his sleep, he brushed at her fingers as if they were some small creature of the night. Guadalupe removed her hand, and soon she too slept.

"There's a pretty chicklet ashore, *mon capitaine*," Sartou said one evening as he picked his teeth with a splinter of wood. "She would suit you very well."

Cazaux moved his head away to avoid Sartou's breath.

"She would be willing."

"I do not desire her," Cazaux replied.

Sartou waited a moment before continuing. "The men are talking, *mon capitaine*. They say you are ill." He coughed discreetly. "They also wonder when the purchase will be shared."

"When I am ready." Cazaux lifted an impatient hand. "Anyway, they have already been given a portion."

Sartou nodded. "But they are accustomed to more. They say, with some right, that it belongs to all of us." His voice was very controlled.

"They can say what they like."

"They ask that they be permitted—"

"They are premitted to leave if they are not content. They are permitted to confront me if they have questions to ask." Cazaux's voice rose; the scar that ran from lip to cheekbone was a livid line. "Who causes this trouble?" he enquired.

Sartou looked away.

"Answer me."

"Cordier, the bosun, spoke to me, but—"

"Send him here."

Sartou examined something he had dug from a tooth with the wooden splinter. "I do not think that would be wise, *mon capitaine*," he said calmly. "We do not want more trouble than we have. I will speak to the men. I will tell them that this stay is only temporary. When the repairs are complete we will leave, and when we arrive at some other destination the purchase will be full shared." He turned his eyes to Cazaux, seeking approval.

Cazaux nodded. "Do that, M'sieu Sartou," he said, his voice easing. "Tell them what you will to keep them calm." He rubbed a hand over his tired face. "And I thank you. Forgive me, I am not myself."

"You have some illness?"

Cazaux sighed. "The worst known to man," he replied.

Sartou blinked. "I do not understand," he said.

"Neither do I, neither do I, and that's the curse of it." Caxaux stared at the horizon. "What's more, there's nothing that will cure me here."

Sartou explored another tooth with the wooden splinter and, after a time, drifted away. He looked back once; Cazaux did not even seem to notice that he had been left alone.

Christopher Stone rode moodily, moving from the head to the tail of the column, forcing the men onward, treating all with the same detached drive. Food was beginning to run short, and the land offered up less than had been expected. The bearers were being fed iguana flesh and that of the few birds brought down on the dusty plain. Once a herd of deer was seen in the distance, and half a day was lost while the animals were pursued.

The only water found was slightly salt; each day the throats of all grew a little more arid, a little more raw. Some faces browned; others burned and peeled, then burned again and developed sores.

Small fights broke out between the pirates and the Spaniards. One morning a bearer was found dead, and no one knew the cause. All were begining to feel lost in the seemingly endless savanna, the stretched desert of yellowing grasses, stunted trees, and thornbushes. It was as if there were neither beginning nor end to their journey.

When a scuffle broke out between Henri the Stain and Mateos, a Spanish horse handler, Stone rode between them, knocking both aside, not turning back to see how either had fared.

He barely spoke to Guadalupe. He treated Toledo with disdain. The sole person he had any contact with was van Staal, and that was terse, related only to the forward movement of the caravan.

"We needs be out of this," he said one evening. "Or we will succeed only in destroying ourselves."

"They say there are hills to the south."

"They say many things in this poxy country. I know not what to believe."

"It must be so. By all that's natural this plain must end."

"By all that's natural?" Stone spat onto the dry ground. "Do not make jests about this awesome land."

Later, he sat staring into the remains of a fire. The night air was chill, he wore an Indian serape over his shoulders; about him the camp was almost silent. Then, suddenly, to the south, the sky was lit by shimmering reflection, sheet lightning burned a moment and died.

A storm? Stone thought. Perhaps there are hills at the end of this soulless savanna.

He picked up a stick and began to stir the fire. The stick caught, and Stone held it a moment, looking into the dancing movement of the yellow-orange tongue of fire. Then he threw it amongst embers. It was late, the night was still, even the singing of the bearers' chains was hushed. He stretched, yawned, and was about to go to his bedding when a small motion caused him to turn. There, on the far side of the campfire, crouched like a cat, was Guadalupe Santoya, staring at him.

Stone blinked. "Why are you not abed?" he asked. "In a few hours we begin again." For the first time, his words were gentle.

Gaudalupe did not move, nor did she speak. It was almost as if she had not heard.

"Are you not tired?" Stone continued. "Or are you about to take another of your midnight walks?"

"I was waiting for you," Guadalupe replied softly.

"For me?"

"I do not sleep until you lie down."

Stone peered. In the remnant firelight the girl's face was finely molded, it seemed both savage and calm; the hair that framed it, the deep, impenetrable eyes, were noble. "You have no cause to wait for me," he said, frowning.

"You are my protector." The words themselves were simple. "Is that not so?"

"I am yours," Stone replied. "But that does not make you mine."

"I would be."

"No," Stone replied, his voice oddly affected. "I want nothing from you now."

"It is your due."

"Come." Stone held out a hand. "Come and sleep. What is due and what is taken are not always the same."

"Those are strange words to come from a man like you," Guadalupe said.

"They are even stranger for me to utter." Stone led the girl to her bedding. "Sleep," he said. "Now is not the time."

"Why do you say that?"

Stone shrugged. "I no longer value taking for the sake of it," he said quietly.

Guadalupe stared at him steadily for a long time. "You do not even know what you want," she said finally.

Stone smiled his agreement. "Then it is to be hoped that I recognize it when it is found," he replied, and, turning, went to his bed.

Guadalupe stood without moving; she watched Stone lie and cover himself and go to sleep. She wondered what it was that she felt for him and could not give it a name. He had neither taken nor rejected; she remained unplaced. He was unlike any other man she had ever known; he was more than any other man she had ever encountered. She no longer thought of taking his life.

* * *

Cramer the Black sat opposite Don Luis the mayor, watching Manuel place a heavy wooden tray, inlaid with small blue tiles, on the dining table between them. It bore a bottle of French cognac, a ceramic coffeepot, cups and glasses, and an earthenware jar that held several conical cigars. No one spoke as the majordomo poured coffee and brandy into separate vessels; when Manuel offered Cramer a cigar the Negro hesitated.

"They are excellent," Don Luis explained. "From Havana. The best I have ever smoked."

Cramer took one. Manuel lit both cigars, then left the room.

"The supplies?" Don Luis puffed smoke, his voice held no real interest; he was merely passing time. "You are being provided with all you asked for?"

"Yes," Cramer said. "We get what we want."

"Good, good." Don Luis nodded.

The mayor was not quite sure how to treat the Negro who had remained to patrol Campeche; he did not really know what the black man sought. Each evening, just before dark, Cramer would arrive to sit in the courtyard. With a glass of rum in hand he would speak slowly and unevenly, his Spanish clumsy, and listen to the sound of Angela singing in her room above. When Manuel appeared to announce that the evening meal was ready to be served, he would accompany the mayor into the long, comfortable dining room and there sit rigidly and eat stolidly, saying little. Invited or not, his presence became accepted.

At first Don Luis had merely supped with him and then gone upstairs to join his daughter, who had eaten accompanied only by her dreams. But, gradually, in a manner he did not understand, the mayor had come to look forward to the Negro's presence, and his hospitality had grown. He began by offering Cramer brandy after dinner and tonight, for the first time, a cigar. Nevertheless, he remained uncertain over the black man's role, he did not know what the stranger was looking for in this unfortunate house. Yet he must treat him with some respect; after all, the *Courage* remained with her guns trained on the port.

"There have been no problems?" Don Luis made a further assault on the line of conversation they followed day by day. "No one has caused any trouble?"

The Negro shook his head.

"Everything else goes well?"

Cramer nodded. "I visit the . . . the men from the garrison, in the fort. They are well," he said, lying only a little about their miserable conditions.

"Yes, yes." Don Luis did not wish to know more of the prisoners; they were a reminder of his failure. "And d'Avila, he has almost recovered."

"Soon he can go from the hospital."

"Excellent." Don Luis swallowed a mouthful of brandy. "That is very good news." He wondered if d'Avila realized just how much misery he'd caused.

"He say he will be good."

"I know, I know. The mestiza—" Don Luis coughed and turned uncomfortably away from the deep brown eyes. "He is a man of his word."

Cramer nodded again; very slowly he reached for the cognac and sipped from the glass. "Good," he pronounced, and drank a little more.

"French," Don Luis explained. "The very best."

"Most time, I drink rum."

"Yes, of course." The mayor picked up the brandy bottle. "A little more?"

Cramer pushed his glass across the mahogany table and watched the mayor refill it. He lifted it with delicate fingers and raised it to his lips, already pursed to receive it, when there was the sound of running feet across the courtyard, and, a moment later, Angela burst into the dining room.

"Oh," she said, her hands clasped before her, her eyes wide and very bright against the paleness of her skin, "you are here. You have come."

Cramer held the glass very still.

The mayor rose to his feet in astonishment.

"I knew it," Angela continued breathlessly. "I knew

he would send someone." She came farther into the room and stood by a chair, waiting to be attended to. She looked superb. Her long dark hair was arranged in elaborate ringlets laced with pearls; they glittered in her tresses like pebbles in a stream. She wore a low bodice of the palest pink, about her waist was a sash of purple, her skirt was full, bell-shaped and delicately fashioned in silks of lavender and gray. "Oh," she went on, "I am *so* glad to see you. I know you have been here before, but I did not descend until I was sure."

Cramer blinked; he looked at Don Luis, then away. He replaced the glass on the table and pulled on his cigar. It had gone out.

Don Luis, shaking his head in confusion, hurried around the table to where his daughter waited; he stared into the wildness of her magnificent eyes, and then, very slowly, he pulled the chair away from the table, seated her, and remained behind her, his presence that of a guardian.

Angela sat primly, smiling at Cramer, who continued unmoving, the dead cigar in one hand, the other pressed flat against the tabletop.

"My blackamoor," Angela went on as if the others were as animated as she. "My blackamoor, you have come to attend me. Is that not so?"

"Señorita?" Cramer swallowed. He had never been as close to so beautiful a creature, nor been seated with anyone so finely clothed. "I—"

"I knew it." Angela beamed. "And how is he? Where has he been? Tell me, tell me everything about him."

Don Luis stared at the faces below him, his eyes going from the brown to the milk white, from the deep eyes to those that shone like stars. He opened his mouth as if to speak, but nothing issued. Then, very slowly, he returned to his chair.

"Where did he go?" Angela leaned across the table, her face flushed with excitement. "What took him away?"

"I—" Cramer wet his lips, incapable of denying anything to this beautiful creature who was waiting for his answer. "He—he went away," he stammered.

"Of course he went away." Angela laughed, and the gaiety of the sound brought a smile to the Negro's face. "I know that, you silly blackamoor. What I really want to be told is when he will return."

"I do not know."

"But he will, you know that, don't you? He will come back for me."

Cramer nodded his head. He could not do otherwise; the brightness of this beauty, the fullness of her laugh, would permit no rejection of any kind.

Angela's smile grew; Cramer bathed in its radiance.

Don Luis stared as the conversation flowed, as an exchange he could not comprehend began and instantly flourished. Some form of transaction had begun, two disparate forms of loneliness reached out and touched. His eyes round, he grasped his glass and, with a hand that trembled slightly, emptied it. Then, like a man in a dream, he refilled it.

CHAPTER 10

LATE ONE AFTERNOON, SOME EIGHT DAYS AFTER THE DEPAR-
ture from Campeche, when the heat was beginning to
die and the men were weary of their dusty progress, the
first of the lowland hills was glimpsed. It came out of the
shimmering air like a dimly purple cloud, and its substance held new promise: an end to the plain was in
sight; the invading dust seemed stilled.

The vegetation began to alter, becoming gradually
thicker; shrubs and small, straight-trunked trees appeared,
soft grasses grew underfoot. More birds were abroad;
gray doves fluttered and hummingbirds spun, and above
the tree line black dots that were eagles hung on their
wings. A day later the party reached the hills.

Slowly, almost imperceptibly, men straightened beneath their burdens, and the horses stepped more briskly.
When the ground began its gentle upward slope and they
entered the cool of the rain forest, all believed that the
worst of the journey was over. The scent of damp earth
gave them heart.

On the crest of the first low hill, Stone peered through
a break in the bushes to where a line of taller trees grew
in an arc.

"There?" he questioned, pointing. "Does that mean

114

there could be a river?" He addressed the nearest of his men.

"It does, Cap'n," the man, who was Meredith, replied dully. His wounds still smarted. "There's water there."

"We could camp by a stream?"

"Aye." Meredith wiped his lips with a logwood-stained hand; his further words came grudgingly. "And there could be turkey for supper."

Stone turned in his saddle to look into the gunner's face. It was scarred where Guadalupe's nails had torn the cheek; loyalty and resentment were in conflict. "Now, how could that be?" he asked easily.

"They'll be there, by the river." Meredith turned away. "It's their country."

"You've stalked them before?"

Meredith nodded. "A treat they was, along the coast. Pox turkeys, we called them; they've red warts on their heads. They come out in the evening." Meredith glanced at the sky; he had broken a barrier. He scratched his chest. "I don't suppose there's a fowling piece among us?"

Stone observed the changing expressions, the effort to overlook the indignity of the fire and the girl. "I think we have one," he replied. "The Spaniard Reyes has something that looks much like a game gun to me."

"If I was to go ahead a little, they'd be down by the river. Maybe I'd get half a dozen or so, if I had my wits about me."

Stone seemed surprised. "That many?" he asked.

"They're not what you'd call clever, them pox birds. Shoot one and lie quiet, and the others'll go on pecking the dirt. I think I could manage six or so."

Stone smiled. "I'll get the gun," he said.

"Thanks, Cap'n." Meredith swallowed, and his stained hands seemed to need something to do. "And, ah, Cap'n, I'm—"

"Say nothing." Stone felt his throat tighten against the blunt words. "So am I."

He turned and spurred his horse toward the reddoubleted Teniente Reyes. Meredith watched him go, then blew his nose on the back of his hand.

D'Avila's eye was healing, his health improving, his determination growing every day. He had taken to wearing a black leather patch over his blinded eye, and although he slept in the white-walled room in the hospital with its barred window and its bustle of nuns, he walked the streets of Campeche during the hours of daylight measuring the strength and the decay. His short, black-bearded, patched, and resolute figure became a familiar sight on the waterfront.

He had not been permitted to visit his men, chained in the dungeon below the fort, but he had heard of their survival. He hoped that when the time came they would be able to assist, but in truth it mattered little. What had to be done he could do alone. He had strength enough to carry him.

He detested what was happening to the port, hated to see the ruffians from the *Courage,* their muskets held loosely over their arms, their cutlasses clanking beside them, policing this place he had been sent to guard. And, if he'd had nothing but contempt for the slovenliness of the Spanish garrison, what he felt for the pirates was a simple driving fury.

Their stamp was everywhere. The *Courage* lay facing the waterfront, her guns trained on the shore. The Indians in the marketplace were servile when the pirates were among them and the townspeople ingratiating. There was no pride in Campeche anymore; none of the faces he passed in the streets showed any aspect of hope. At times he felt he was watching the spread of a sore in the flesh of a man who was dying. Soon nothing healthy would remain, soon the pustular wound would consume all the living tissue.

It sickened him, it was worse than he could have imagined; it was due, all of it, to the English cutthroat who had brought him this impotent shame. He could still feel the pressure of the pistol beneath his chin, knew still the pain as it tore at his throat. And he welcomed the memory, it was a sensation he had no wish to lose. It drove him, fired him, it assured him daily of what he had to do.

Occasionally at night, as he lay unsleeping in the hospital bed, he prayed. He prayed to the Holy Virgin that Christopher Stone was still alive, that no harm would come to him on this journey into the interior. He wanted the Englishman returned safely so that he could be killed surely; he wanted him untouched so that he, Capitán Fernando d'Avila, could watch him die.

Meredith's turkeys had been stewed with the roots of wild yams. There was fresh water to drink. As the men sat in the smoke of their small fires and rubbed oil in their exposed skin to keep the mosquitoes away, they conversed with an ease they had not known for days. A new mood of confidence had entered the camp.

Stone set his bedding in the roots of a great ceiba that grew beyond a bend of the river. From where he was, a fire at his feet, he could see the black water curve into a deeper darkness that bore the reflections of the flames on its banks like an offering of candles. In the subdued voices of the men was the sound of comfort.

Stone slapped at an insect that had stuck to the oil on his arm; he stood and began a final tour of the campsite. He spoke to van Staal, paused near the Spaniards to exchange a few words with Toledo, congratulated Meredith in front of his friends. As he began back to his campfire, he noticed a feather lying on the ground. It was a tailfeather from one of the turkeys, a long, handsome silver-and-gray piece with a circle of turquoise like an eye at one end. Stone picked it up, absently tapped it against his lips as he returned.

Guadalupe had already settled. She lay in a fold of the rooted tree, her eyes watching; her gaze followed each movement Stone made, but she did not say a word.

About them were the sounds of the wooded night: the soft chirp of insects, the flutter of a large bird settling and resettling itself in a tree, the echoing screech of

something that could have been bird or beast or even
man as it made its presence known.

Stone kicked back his blanket, removed his boots,
shunted off his breeches, and wrapped his shirt about
himself. He lay back in his bedding, glancing at Guadalupe. "You are not yet asleep," he said casually.

"I never sleep before you do."

"Then you are fortunate I do not suffer from insom-
nia," Stone said lightly. "Otherwise you'd have no rest
at all."

"Do you think I am foolish?"

Stone shrugged. "Here," he said, picking up the feather
he'd placed with his clothing and leaning toward her,
"I've brought you a gift."

Guadalupe sucked her breath in carefully; she reached
for the delicate offering and stared at it in the light from
the dying fire. "It is beautiful," she whispered finally.

"Yes, it is pretty."

"It is more." Guadalupe's fingers smoothed the feather,
touching it as if it were made of gold. "You, you brought
it to me?"

"I thought it might amuse you."

"Is that all?"

Stone shifted against his blanket, then looked at the
girl more closely, at the fullness of the lips, now softly
parted, at the questioning eyes, shadows tracing their
graceful contours. The garment she wore, a cotton shift
embroidered in yellows, reds, and blues, had fallen from
a shoulder; her dusky flesh glowed in the flickering light.
Stone, unable to take his eyes from her, felt desire move
him and sensed that she recognized his response.

"Is it," Guadalupe persisted, "only to amuse me?"

"Of what other use is a feather?" Stone replied, his
voice betraying him.

"Perhaps to say that you wanted me."

Stone moved his legs uncomfortably. "I have said—"
he began as Guadalupe came forward to interrupt him.
She leaned on the root that separated them; her eyes, in
the half-light, were sure.

"Do not say," she said. "Just look. Look at me."

"I," Stone said, then looked away. "I am uncertain."

"I am not. It is right."

"Is there right and wrong in this matter?"

"Yes. It is the difference between wanting and taking."

Stone smiled; his cheeks were stiff. "You appear to have given much thought to his," he said.

"I have given much." Guadalupe seemed to flow over the ceiba root. There was the blurred brown passing of her feet as they went beneath Stone's blanket. There was the sudden closeness of her breath. "But now is not the time for words," she whispered.

Stone's hands came up and pulled her close. He kissed her, and for a moment Guadalupe seemed unsure what to do; then her own lips opened and captured his. Her arms were around him now, he felt her heat through his shirt. She rolled, and he with her, tearing at the garments that lay between them. Her legs parted, and for an instant he stayed, looking down into the fire in her eyes. Then he plunged, and his breath was a harsh sound in his throat. She encircled and gripped him; he was deep, and he was fulfilling. They clung for the few moments that it lasted, its power and its demand too great for delay. It carried them, and they were lost, spun into a deep, sweet darkness; it drowned them until the little sounds of the night returned.

Stone stirred and eased his weight. Guadalupe touched the hard-boned face beside hers. It was peaceful now, its lines were softer. She smiled and whispered something.

"What?" Stone's voice sounded far away.

"Cristóbal," Guadalupe repeated. "I have not used your name before."

"Animal was what you called me first," he said.

Guadalupe's fingers went to the scar on his side; it was rough now, almost healed. "Is that where I cut you?" she asked, pain in her voice.

"It has cured. I put rum on it."

"*Dios mío,* I am sorry."

"You were not sorry then."

"I did not know you then."

"And now?" Stone lifted her hair away from her face

and smiled at her beauty. "What I felt with you was more than I have ever felt before," he said.

"Perhaps you have never been wanted as much before."

Stone wrapped his long arms around her and was unable to reply immediately; he held her, nuzzling, scenting the musky aftertones of what they had achieved. "Perhaps," he said finally, and felt her fingers, delicate and trembling, trace the line of the scar along his ribs. "Perhaps it is so."

Guadalupe lay against him, her eyes grew heavy. She heard him begin to sleep, and she nestled closer. Clumsily, he tightened his arm about her and grunted in his sleep. The campsite was quiet and the horses still.

To the south, on the far side of the ridge under which they slept, a group of hunting Maya lay by their weapons and waited for the dawn.

The repairs were complete; the crew of *La Petite* had grown restless once again. They'd roamed the taverns, the brothels, the streets behind the waterfront. The share of the prize they'd been given was spent, their thirst had dulled, too many found that their old shoreside companion, the pox, was back. They needed action once again, something to help them forget what alcohol had done to their bellies and scabs had done to their flesh.

Sartou approached Cazaux. "Little Pierre," he began, spreading his hands in an eloquent gesture. "He is the second, in less than a week."

Cazaux, who spent long hours locked in his cabin, days seated on the poop staring across the low green marshland toward an unseen Spanish seaport in the south, turned his hollow eyes to the mate.

"Mon capitaine." Sartou's voice held pity for all parties. "It is time to go."

Cazaux breathed in deeply.

"Think on it, I beg you. Before it is too late."

Cazaux nodded, and Sartou went away.

"You have become a romantic fool," Cazaux told himself, but the words did not accomplish their task. He tried again. "Your head is touched, and you are more than stupid," he whispered; and then, finally, "What you are about to do will probably cost you your life."

"M'sieu Sartou," Cazaux said next morning. "We leave. Tell the crew to prepare."

"Good news, *mon capitaine*. You have decided our destination?"

Cazaux nodded.

"We return to Tortuga? St. Kitts, perhaps?"

"We go back to Campeche."

"Campeche?" Sartou's eyes were wide, nervously he pulled at the gold ring that hung from the lobe of his left ear. "What cause do we have for that?"

"It is my wish."

Sartou shrugged broadly. "The crew may wish to know what there is for them in Campeche," he said as evenly as he was able.

"Tell them whatever you care to," Cazaux replied, spreading a chart on the table. "Tell them that the English will have gone. Say that the Spanish garrison will not yet have recovered. Suggest there is more to be taken from that pretty little town. Tell them whatever comes to mind, but make sure that we sail with the tide."

Sartou shook his head. "I understand nothing of this, but I will do what you say," he muttered.

"Good." Cazaux sniffed the air. "We have a wind. The crew needs work. Do not be easy with them. See that we make all the speed we can." He bent over the chart and began to whistle.

Sartou backed away, scratching his chin. He did not know what was in his captain's head, but he recognized a look he had not seen for weeks. And that, for the moment, would suffice. When Cazaux was in such a mood, all were likely to benefit.

Christopher Stone strode through the camp rousing his men, calling the Spaniards, ordering the unlocking of the bearers. Each action he performed decisively, almost with challenge, as if seeking a response to the night. None gave it; perhaps they believed it already done.

He saw van Staal coming toward him and turned to face the Dutchman, but van Staal's mood was easy, although his eyes were a little cautious. "We should change our order in this country," he suggested. "We'll need to send scouts before us."

Stone nodded his agreement.

"A pair to east and west would do."

"Send them off," said Stone. "But none of the Spanish. Our men—and ones used to negotiating country." He returned to his bedding to find that Guadalupe had prepared it ready for the horse. "I thank you," he said, and was surprised by the clumsiness of his tongue. "But it is a task I can do for myself."

"Cristóbal." Guadalupe's voice was light. "Let me attend you a little."

"Well, I thank you again."

"You do not mind?" Guadalupe asked. "About anything?"

"No," replied Stone. "I am grateful to have you attend me." As he reached for his bedding he noticed the feather he had given her the night before. Its colors shone, but its spine had been bent with their rolling. "This is yours," he said simply, handing it to the girl. "A little worn, but yours still."

Guadalupe smiled. "I will keep it with me always," she said, smoothing the feather.

"Always is a very long time."

Guadalupe's smile grew.

They followed the river. Winding between trees, it shone like a scimitar in the morning sun. After a time, Toledo reined alongside Stone. "We must cross the ridge," he said brusquely.

Stone nodded.

"We must begin the crossing soon."

"When we hear from the scouts, we'll turn."

"Are they necessary? We are still some days from the land of the Itzá."

"Nevertheless, this is their country, I am told." Stone

peered into the forest, which thickened on either side of the river. "What lies before us will be testing."

"What we have *done* is proof of what we are." Toledo's voice rose suddenly. "To defeat a tribe of heathen Indians will be no test at all."

Stone turned to stare into Toledo's heated eyes.

"You disagree, Captain Stone?" There was almost fanatical determination in the Creole's face. "You do not recognize the accomplishment of crossing the savanna that lies between here and the coast." Toledo leaned forward in the saddle. "No one has ever done that with so many men before," he exclaimed triumphantly. "No one. Ever."

"Nor have they ever beaten these Indians," Stone replied evenly. "You told me so yourself."

"But *we* will," Toledo exulted. "You and I, Captain Stone. We will beat them. We are, both of us, conquistadores." He drew himself even more erect, and his breastplate flashed. He spurred his horse and galloped away.

Stone watched him go, his mind uneasy.

The Maya hunting party walked through a valley of splendid richness. The air was warm, lively with the sound of bees. The skin of the Mayan warriors, in the early morning air, was already beaded with sweat.

Cramer the Black came in the afternoons now, whenever Angela was ready for him. He came while Don Luis sat in a corner of the cool courtyard in a split-cane chair beside a table containing his brandy. He would come quietly, sometimes to find the mayor asleep: the unshaven chin resting on the chest, the doublet hanging loose, the hose crumpled about the ankles.

On these occasions Don Luis would awake to the sound of singing; his daughter's tuneful voice would be lifted in Spanish folksong, and accompanying it would be the soft, deep tones of the Negro, the words fractured but the harmony sound. Then there would be a pause, a quick dying of voices, followed, a while later, by Angela's rich, full-throated laughter—a sound that made Don Luis fumble for his brandy, fill his mouth with the coarse, comforting spirits.

Those were the worst of times: the periods of silence leading to the sound of spilling laughter and its voluptuousness.

When González, the treasurer, called, as he sometimes did in the mornings, Don Luis became critically aware of his sense of failure. There were days when he could not meet the contemptuous stare of the councilor or listen to the words that came from the tiny mouth deploring the fact that the council no longer met; reviling the standards of the port, which, especially now that the Negro had neither the time nor the inclination to discipline or punish, had declined steadily until they met the crude needs of the pirates.

These confrontations were bad, but Don Luis managed them. With a little cognac and an avoidance of the gaze that excoriated, he was able to survive until the thin treasurer had gone. Then he drank until his memory failed, until a temporary peace arrived.

Almost as difficult to sustain were his encounters with d'Avila. Each time the mayor ventured from his dwelling, he seemed to find the one-eyed ex-commander of the garrison prowling the town. But, whereas González's tone was censorious, d'Avila's was openly challenging.

He ranted, his bearded face close to Don Luis's, about the decay in the air, the stench that was everywhere, the appalling condition of his men in the dungeons, and his detestation of the Englishman who had brought this plague to Campeche.

As he listened to the fury that poured from the crippled soldier's lips, time and substance seemed to hold no meaning for the mayor. Try as he might, he could no longer recapture the pride he'd had in the town. Nothing seemed to be clearly positioned anymore. He found it difficult to recall when the corsarios had actually arrived.

Often he would lift his head and listen: was it the snapping of d'Avila's nagging tongue, the harmony of magical voices, or González's tiny mouth snipping out his words of reproof that beat into his brain? He was, quite often, never sure.

Very occasionally, in the early dawn, when he awoke with a mouth as dry as a corn husk, before he reached for the bottle that remained always by his bed, would he wonder about time and its passage, considering, for an almost clear moment, how much longer this nightmare could last. And then he'd drink again, unable to face a single instant more without the bite of cognac in his throat.

He was sinking, and he knew it; he was drowning in his own despair and could imagine no salvation. And with him, always, was the sound of Angela's singing.

CHAPTER 11

STONE TURNED IN HIS SADDLE TO SEE A FIGURE APPEAR. IT
was Cooper, one of the scouts; he rode rapidly out of the
forest, glancing over his shoulder as he came.

When he reached Stone, near the river, he reined; he
was a small, neatly built man, and his movements and
the horse's were one. "There's a path over the ridge
here, Cap'n," he said controlling his voice. "Leads down
to a valley. In the valley there's Indians. More'n a
dozen, with bows. They've a sort of satrap with them.
Carrying their chief in it, they are."

"Have they horses?"

"No, Cap'n, they're afoot."

"Tell the mate. Have him and the Spanish leader meet
me on the ridge above. Tell all the others to wait."
Stone nodded at Cooper. "Well done," he said. "You
sure they didn't see you?"

"Certain of it, Cap'n."

"Then off you go. Have the others come up quietly."

Stone rode carefully up the ridge, away from the river.
The forest closed above him, the air grew damp and
velvet. Underfoot, the leaves thickened, and the sound
of the horse became muffled. When he neared the top he
dismounted, walked forward to the crest silently and,
with care, parted the bushes that grew there.

The sight below made him catch his breath. The ground fell away steeply, and for a moment he had the impression that the valley spread almost from his feet. In it the grass was thick, rich with yellow flowers; they were like jewels in a crown of jade. Threading its way through the simple loveliness was a group of Mayan hunters, and with them, carefully guarded, was an elaborately covered palanquin borne by four men—slaves? Stone could just discern, in the hooded litter, a figure wearing a brilliant array of colors that seemed to float on the breeze.

As Stone watched, the party stopped, and two of the leading warriors went to the palanquin. They approached with a posture of deference, of reverence. It appeared that some discussion took place; then the warriors retraced their steps without turning their backs on the palanquin.

The procession resumed, heading a little more to the west, coming ever closer to the cliff on which Stone crouched. He heard the slightest sound behind him and turned quickly, a finger to his lips, as van Staal, Toledo, and Teniente Reyes crept up toward him. Quickly he pointed to what he'd seen.

"They come for the birds with the long green tails," van Staal whispered. "They call them the quetzal. They use the feathers for their cloaks."

"Call our men," said Toledo excitedly. "We will run them down as they pass." He spoke to Reyes, his voice quiet but its animation clear. "Quick. Go now."

"Wait," said Stone, holding Reyes's arm. "We may speak to them peacefully."

"They are armed," hissed Toledo impatiently.

"Be quiet." Stone's voice was like a razor. "I will go with the girl. She speaks their language. I'll take ten marksmen for protection."

"No," Toledo whispered harshly. This was no sweep of conquistadores, this was no taking of a prize. "You will not go without me. I will accompany you with ten of my own." He turned to Reyes once more. "Bring them now. Our best. Our fittest."

This time Stone did not protest, he nodded. "Go with

him, Rolf," he told van Staal. "See that they return with caution. Do everything with the utmost quiet."

Stone and Toledo remained unspeaking as they watched the Maya approach; they strained to see more of the man in the palanquin. His face was long-nosed, its air aloof; his forehead sloped back steeply to meet the head-dress he wore, stiffly feathered and decorated with colored stones. Here and there a gold bead caught the sunlight. His cloak was superb; closely interwoven with red, gold, and green feathers, it fell from his shoulders like a sunset. Its richness reached up toward Stone and Toledo: they were in the presence of a man of noble birth.

The warriors who accompanied the litter were simply dressed, they wore loincloths only. Their hair was long and braided, wound about their skulls. Each carried a short bow and a quiver of arrows; some held spears and a throwing stick. They marched in stolid grace through the rich green grasses and the yellow flowers, raising swarms of small white butterflies and neat black bees.

Presently, Stone and Toledo heard the muffled sounds of horsemen approaching and turned from the cliff to join them. Quietly, Stone urged the riders to a point some hundred yards ahead of the Maya below. Then, on his signal, they began down toward the valley through a small rocky gorge, gathering speed as they went.

They came out into the sunlight suddenly, their saddlery chinking, the sound of hooves bursting from the gorge. They came out into the valley in a cloud of dust, and the Maya halted at the sight of the strange, multicolored assortment of men. Immediately they moved to form a semicircle about the palanquin and the man who sat within. The bows of the Maya were bent. In each an arrow, with a fire-hardened point, was directed at the group of approaching horsemen. The man in the litter made no movement at all.

"Hold," Stone called, and raised a hand, slowing the pace of the horses. "Stay a moment. We will speak with them."

"Run them down," shouted Toledo, his young face flushed. "Now, while we have the advantage."

"Into their arrows? Don't be a fool." Stone watched the Spaniard pause, then turned to Guadalupe. "Tell them we come in peace," he said.

Guadalupe rode a little ahead, her hands lifted, palms toward the Maya. She spoke rapidly, the words seeming suddenly harsh to Stone after the liquid Spanish he had heard from her tongue. She waited while the warriors chattered among themselves; two of them went to the palanquin, spoke, and a moment later retraced their steps. The bows of the others remained steady, their arrows trained on the chests of the horsemen. Then one of the warriors called, and Guadalupe relaxed; her hands dropped, and she looked back at Stone.

"They will talk with us," she said simply.

"What did you tell them?"

"That we were looking for horses we had lost."

Stone smiled briefly. "That was clever," he said.

"We must approach now. As few as possible."

Stone beckoned van Staal and, after a moment's pause, Toledo. "We will accompany the girl," he said. "Have five men with muskets follow a few yards behind. If there is any sign of attack, I will use my pistols and we'll turn aside, leaving them open to the marksmen." His voice hardened. "Whatever happens, do not kill the man in the litter. We must take him alive." He stared at them all, the beginnings of fire in his eyes. "Is that clearly understood?"

Van Staal nodded; he went to speak to the men.

Toledo said, "I will have Teniente Reyes with me." His voice was stubborn.

"Very well," said Stone. "Let us begin."

Cautiously they moved their horses forward: Stone, van Staal, Guadalupe, Toledo, and Reyes, riding all in a line. Behind them came the marksmen. Ahead the Maya crouched, their bows ready, their eyes fixed on the riders.

When they were ten yards from the bowmen, Stone

said, "Ask them where they're from." His voice was soft, almost casual.

Guadalupe put the question; for a moment there was no reply, then from the far side of the palanquin came a man none of them had noticed before. He was young and slightly built, he walked delicately and wore an ornamented loincloth and a short feathered cloak. On his right arm he carried a spider monkey whose round inquisitive eyes peered up at the strangers. The young man spoke to Guadalupe in a gentle tone.

"What does he want?" demanded Toledo; his back had stiffened, there was outrage in his voice. "He is—"

"He wants to know why we are here," Guadalupe replied. "He does not believe the story of the horses."

"It is none of his business."

"It is. He speaks for his master."

"He is an invert. A sodomist." Toledo swung angrily in the saddle. "Reyes!" he shouted. "Kill him."

"No," Stone cried. "In the name of God—"

"In the name of God, he dies," Teniente Reyes called clearly.

He drew his sword and spurred his horse. As the animal sprang forward, one of the Maya warriors moved also. He leapt as the horse leapt, and they met together, rising from the ground. The Maya drove his shoulder into the horse's chest; he reached beneath it and took hold of the foreleg on the far side. Wrenching, his whole body heaving, the Maya turned the horse in midair. It spun. Teniente Reyes, his sword lifted, his fresh face a mixture of horror and disbelief, was hurled to the ground. He landed on his side, his sword snapping. He struggled to his feet as an arrow caught him in the chest. For a second he hung, half-risen, about to fall, dead before he realized what had happened to the bright and valiant morning. He collapsed among the grasses and the wild-flowers, a soft groan on his lips.

By now the others were in motion. As Reyes's horse was thrown, Stone reached for the reins of Guadalupe's mount; he jerked them savagely, and Guadalupe fell.

"Lie still," he cried, and drew one of the six pistols he carried and shot the nearest warrior.

He swung away as his marksmen fired, their aim uneven in the skirmish. Two more of the Maya fell; others unleashed their arrows. One sang as it bounced from Toledo's breastplate, leaving a long, running dent in the shining metal. A Spanish soldier cried as a spear pierced his throat.

For long minutes the handsome valley burst with the sound of gunfire, the shouts of men. Their muskets spent, the marksmen drew cutlasses and closed in on the Maya, who aimed, fired, and reloaded with amazing speed. Stone charged among them, disturbing their aim, his pistols exploding. Toledo spurred forward and drove his sword at a bowman. Van Staal leapt from his saddle, axe in hand, and used it twice, murderously.

Finally it was over. The twelve Maya warriors lay dead or wounded. Four Spaniards and two pirates had died from the spears or the fire-hardened arrows. The bearers of the palanquin had fled, but the youth at its far side, his monkey still clutching his arm, had not moved since the fighting began. He remained by the litter, comforting the frightened creature, eyeing the bloodshed with the detachment of one watching a play, as if the deaths held no reality. And, still, the royal figure had not emerged from the palanquin.

Stone dismounted; he went to where Guadalupe lay in the grass and helped her to her feet. Together they approached the litter. "Tell him to get out," Stone said. "He is now our prisoner."

Guadalupe hesitated, not quite bold enough to address the splendid personage within the litter; her bloodline forbade her to speak with him at all. She turned finally to the young man who stood beside his master and told him of Stone's order. Soon, from beneath the cover of the Palanquin, the man of noble birth appeared. He was short and young, and his face was deeply pockmarked.

"Who is he?" Stone asked.

"His name is Tutul Katun," Guadalupe explained after a further exchange with the youth. "He is the second son of Canek, king of the Itźa."

"And the other?" Stone inquired. "The one who speaks for him?"

"He is Ah Cuc," Guadalupe replied after another question. "His servant."

"He is worse than that." Toledo's voice cut through the air. "He is an offense. I will have him burned."

"Do not lay a hand on him." Stone's words were controlled, but his eyes were furious. "Any further stupidity and I'll have you in irons."

"You would not dare."

"Try me." Stone could barely contain his rage. "That is all, merely try me."

Toledo opened his mouth but did not speak. Spots of color flushed his cheeks. He turned and marched stiffly away. Be patient, he urged himself, ignore his insults. Use him for the fighting animal he is. Once that function is no longer needed, you can be rid of him as you will. In the meantime, maintain your dignity.

Tutul Katun watched with interest the exchange between the tall gaunt man with the pistols and the younger officer with the breastplate. He did not understand a word, but their attitudes told him a great deal about both.

These must be the men he had heard of but never seen. The sons of the sons of the Spaniards who had come and killed his people, who now held almost all the rest in this land in slavery. Whose greed for gold was such that when one of them, called Tonatiuh by the Maya, came to the Yucatán he could not wait for the gold plugs to be taken from the ears of the nobles but cut them free, the more quickly to hold them in his hungry hands.

These were the men who brought the plagues that had swept through his land killing millions, the pestilences that had taken his grandfather's life, that had pitted his own face. Tutul Katun watched them; they were curious and their language soft.

Of them all, the Pale One seemed the strongest, but he who wore the Silver Chest also had power. Tutul Katun observed their confrontation and wondered how it might be used to take them apart. He had been correct not to fight them hand to hand. He was a king's son, above brawling, and although he was not yet twenty he knew his position in the land.

He turned to the girl who was with them, but not of them, who spoke the language. "Why have they come?" he asked. "What brings them here?"

The girl remained silent.

"Speak," Tutul Katun demanded. "I have addressed you. What are these savages doing on my land?"

"They have come to rob you." Guadalupe stared at the ground and was incapable of lying. This prince was, in a sense, her prince also. "They have come for your gold."

"Really?" Tutul Katun seemed amused. "They have not even attempted to disguise their crime in the name of what they call their true religion?"

"That also. They march under the banner of our Lord."

Tutul Katun peered at her. "Is he your god, too?" he asked.

"Yes," Guadalupe whispered. "I have their gods as I have their names. I am nothing to them, and yet they made me what I am."

Tutul Katun nodded. Much was being explained. "And who is he?" he asked, indicating Stone. "The Pale One who leads them."

"He came from the sea," Guadalupe replied. "To steal from the others. But, in turn, he was stolen from."

"And so now he comes to take my gold?" Tutul Katun's pitted face creased into a tolerant smile. "Do they all live by robbery, these invaders?" he asked. "Must they steal all the time?"

"Yes, that is the way they live."

"Then I do not understand them."

"Nor do I."

There was a moment of pressing silence, which Stone broke. "What does he say?" he asked abruptly, watching the Maya's eyes with their intelligence and their disdain. "What have you told him?"

"The truth," Guadalupe answered simply. "He knows we have come for the gold of his people."

"It does not seem to surprise him."

"It has happened before." A strange confusion troubled Guadalupe. She was affected by Tutul Katun's authority and the way his questions searched her soul. She felt a touch of shame, not only for herself, but for Cristóbal also. "He knows too well how the Spaniards come with the images of their gods in one hand, while the other is held out for gold," she added sadly.

Stone studied her face, puzzled by her downcast tone. "In your heart, are these your people?" he asked in a gentler voice. "Is that it? Do you feel you belong with them?"

"I belong nowhere." Guadalupe shook her head, attempting to clear it. "What else do you wish to know?" she asked in a whisper.

"Nothing." Stone understood her confusion but could not allay it. "Tell him he will be treated with dignity. We respect his position."

Guadalupe held Stone's look, then spoke again to Ah Cuc. The hard, guttural words of the Maya tongue passed between them for several minutes, and then Tutul Katun, catching a particular remark, laughed openly. He repeated what Ah Cuc had said, laughed again, and turned away. Guadalupe watched, seeming not to know how to react; then a smile touched the corners of her own lips.

Stone took her arm. "What did he say?" he asked.

"There is no gold," Guadalupe replied. "He said to tell you there is no gold among his people. They do not worship the yellow metal."

"I have seen it about his neck."

"Trinkets, nothing more. They have less value than the feathers of the quetzal bird."

"Are you sure?"

"I am certain," Guadalupe replied firmly. "Tutul Katun would not lie about so trivial a matter."

Stone stared as the Maya prince walked easily toward his lover; his back was straight, the magnificent headdress was part of his bearing, the cloak of green and red and gold was splendid in the sunlight.

Tutul Katun neither looked at his dead hunters nor

seemed aware of their presence. He went to Ah Cuc and took the spider monkey from the young man's arm; he whispered to it quietly and stroked its nervous head. He could have been anywhere but on this plain of death.

You may not have gold, Stone thought as he watched the prince. But you do possess something. Whatever it is, I shall find it.

When he had time to spare, Cazaux spent it on the foredeck, eyes to the south, counting the days as the slim frigate made her long tacks down toward Campeche. He urged the crew arduously, yet worked with them, doing his share: hauling ropes, bending canvas, taking his turn at the wheel.

When Claude le Grand, a gangling youth with arms and legs like broomsticks, fell from a spar in a hook of the wind, breaking an arm, Cazaux was the first beside him. When the arm festered and black gangrene began in the wound, he was at the side of Marcou, cook and surgeon, while the butcher performed his bloody task.

Cazaux held Claude's head as the fevered boy drank as much black rum as he was able; he waited until the lanky youth's eyelids lowered and his voice thickened, then he gripped him firmly by the shoulders.

"He is yours now," Cazaux told Marcou. "Be as rapid as you can."

Marcou stripped the bandage from the wound; the arm had shattered above the elbow, bone had pierced the skin, and infection was increasing rapidly. Already a pinkish fluid, bright with gas, ran from the puncture. Where Marcou's fingers touched the infection, it crackled as though alive.

"Fetch the tar," Marcou said to a sailor assisting him. "Have it hot. Ready to apply."

The assistant hurried away.

Marcou took up a knife, tested its edge, and lifted Claude's arm. The first cut he made was above the line of the gangrene in the red and swollen flesh. Claude cried out sharply, and Cazaux struggled to hold the boy in place. Blood ran freely now, Marcou pulled the arm over a wooden bucket beside the bunk. Claude screamed again as the surgeon made a second cut on the lower side of the arm. Claude managed to free his other arm; he clawed up at Marcou's face as the surgeon shaped a flap of flesh, which he let hang while he set aside the knife and reached for a bonesaw, and Cazaux, catching Claude's free arm, held the boy in place.

"How does it go with him?" Marcou asked without lifting his head.

"Be quick," was Cazaux's struggling reply.

Marcou sawed rapidly, and the festering arm fell into the bucket below as the assistant ran in with the tar. When the tar was beneath the stump, Marcou lifted the stump, wrapped the flap of flesh about it and bound it tight. Then he nodded at Cazaux, and together they plunged the remains of the arm into the boiling pitch. Claude le Grand heaved, his mouth became a hole of open shock, his roar of agony was heard the length of the ship. Then, his face a ghastly white, he fell back in his bunk in a faint.

Two days later the fever abated, and all aboard were aware that the lad would survive; an eagerness fired every plank of the frigate. She lifted in the water, determined in her stride. None knew why Jean-Marc Cazaux drove them back to Campeche, none dreamed what lay ahead, but all believed in the journey now, all had faith that great gains lay before them.

Not one of them, Cazaux included, could have imagined that the *Courage* still straddled the harbor, her guns arranged on the town.

CHAPTER 12

WITH THE SUN SLANTED TOWARD THE SOUTHERN RIDGES AND
the dead buried among the wildflowers, Christopher
Stone sat on a fallen pine tree, looking down the long
valley. Beside him was van Staal.

The remainder of their party had camped in a pine
grove not far from the morning's short but brutal battle.
Henri the Stain, one of Stone's gunners, had an arrow
wound in the thigh; it was clean and would heal. Two
Spanish marskmen were injured, one of them badly: a
spear had pierced his upper chest and broken to leave
the point within; now he lay beneath a blanket, his
breathing harsh.

Nine of the Maya had been killed outright or had died
of their wounds. The remaining three were bound to a
tree. The four who had carried the litter—Tipu Indian
slaves, Guadalupe had learned—had been recaptured.
They also were chained, with the bearers.

Tutul Katun and Ah Cuc rested beside their palanquin. Their voices, and at times their laughter, rose
above the mutter of the camp. They appeared indifferent
to all that had occurred.

"He will take us there?" Stone asked again. "He has
no hesitation in leading us to the city?"

Van Staal shook his head. "He is confident, Christopher. I know little enough of their language, but I understand him sufficiently. He has no fear of us. He believes his father's city to be untouchable."

Stone grunted. "He has reason to be brave. They have survived the Spaniards for more than a hundred years."

"And will for many more." Van Staal rubbed a hand over his bald brown skull. "Or so they believe."

Stone spat on the ground at his feet. "And what of the gold?" he asked. "When he talks of that, do you think he speaks the truth?"

"Yes," van Staal replied after a moment's thought. "I detect no falseness in him."

Stone nodded; he lifted his head and watched the sky shimmer into twilight: it was red and gray, vermilion as a maple leaf in autumn. Everywhere was a sense of peace. He could not fathom the inconsistency between its beauty and the bodies buried below.

Later, he listened to what Toledo had to say. "It is a lie." Toledo's voice was bitter. "A filthy pagan lie." The Creole breathed on his breastplate and polished it with a sleeve. He fingered the dent the arrow had made. "There is no doubt about the gold. All these Indians have it. There was so much in Mexico, Cortez and his men were unable to carry it away."

"Why should he lie?" Stone asked.

"To deceive us." He stared at Stone with fanatic's eyes, bright in the dancing firelight. "Give him to me for an hour. We'll see what he says with a red-hot sword before his face."

"We would all answer to that," Stone commented dryly.

"The truth would come out." Toledo put his arms through the straps of the breastplate, shrugged it on, and buckled it into place. "We would learn not only of the gold, but of the secrets of the Itźa defenses. Give him to me."

"No."

"Why not, Captain Stone?" Toledo's eyes were suddenly close. "Have you no stomach for the truth?"

Stone stared at the Creole.

"They *must* have gold." Toledo's voice was almost a whisper. "It is essential that they do."

"I thought your purpose was nobler." Stone gestured toward Toledo's armor. "I thought you dreamed of glory."

"It is not myself I speak of," Toledo replied. "Think of your men, Captain Stone. Those here and those who wait in Campeche. If there is nothing for them in this pagan city, they will have no prize at all." His eyes were full of cunning. "How would you control them then?"

"My men have sailed for nothing before," Stone replied, but something in his voice betrayed him. For days he had subdued all thought of the *Courage* and the men who waited on the coast. Cramer was with them, and he trusted the Negro. Yet Toledo was right—their wait would be long, and they would be bitter if he returned with nothing at all. After the treachery of Cazaux it would be more than some of them would take. "What is more," he added, forcing his argument, "if my men become impatient, they will find ways of amusing themselves."

"Do not be too sure." Toledo's tone was confident. "Campeche has a way of absorbing everything. That is the secret of its survival. If you have nothing for your men, you may find you have no men at all."

"I shall concern myself with that when I return," Stone said tightly. "Gold or no."

Toledo smiled, and his face seemed to dance in the light of the fire. "If I am not to touch the prince," he said, "give me the sodomist. A heated sword up his rectum will loosen his tongue."

"You will touch neither of them," Stone said quickly. "Understand me, your life depends on it."

Toledo shrugged, too pleased with Stone's reaction to be touched by the threat. "You are becoming soft, Captain Stone. These people are savages. They play with monkeys because *they* are monkeys, they deserve to be treated as such." His voice was taunting. "Do not be fooled by their trappings."

"I am fooled by nothing," Stone replied angrily. "For us they have value, as guides and hostages. I will not have them touched."

Toledo spread his hands, then moved away. For a moment his breastplate caught the firelight and flashed a cold ray into Stone's eyes; then it was gone.

Tutul Katun wore only a loincloth now, a band of woven cotton elaborately embroidered with feathers; on his feet were sandals of untanned deer hide, with beads of jade on the ends of the tying thongs. His great headdress, and the splendid feathered cloak, had been put aside until his homecoming. A prisoner now, he would not wear them again until he crossed the lake on his way toward his freedom.

Without his trappings, the Maya prince seemed smaller, the slope of his flattened forehead more pronounced. The aristocratic shape of his head had been created just after his birth: boards had been bound to his infant skull and left until the slope had formed; at the right moment they were removed, and the forehead maintained its backward slant.

He was seated on a leather cushion, feeding the monkey pieces of fruit; beside him Ah Cuc squatted on the ground. The campsite encircled them, preventing any escape, although the thought would have occurred to neither of them. They were content to return to Tayasal with the invaders, to witness their destruction.

"They are crude, these men," Ah Cuc observed. "They have no dignity."

Tutul Katun smiled, his pocked face creasing in the glow of the dying fire.

"The Pale One and Silver Chest are not in accord." Ah Cuc continued. "There is no harmony between them."

Tutul Katun scratched the monkey's neck. "Their dislike will aid us greatly," he said.

"My lord"—Ah Cuc bowed toward the prince—"your cleverness never ceases to delight me."

"Thank you," Tutul Katun replied, "but when the time comes we must be cautious. It is important that we preserve the lives of the leaders. Itzamná welcomes the hearts of warriors, no matter how crude they may be."

Ah Cuc laughed quietly. He went to the palanquin and returned with rugs of softened skins, spread some on the ground, and covered Tutul Katun with others. Then, placing the monkey between them, he crept into the bedding and took his master's hand. For a while they lay, the firelight playing on their serene features; presently they slept.

"Why do you not touch me?" she asked. "Are you angry because I told the prince the reason for our coming?"

"No." Stone shook his head in the darkness. "It makes no difference that they know."

"They would not have believed another lie." Guadalupe moved a little closer. "They did not believe the first."

"Do not concern yourself."

"But you are worried. You are unhappy."

Stone moved his legs and said nothing.

"Please, Cristóbal, what worries you?"

"It has nothing to do with you," Stone replied; he sighed. "It is, I do not know what it is. Perhaps the killing this morning—" He shrugged. "It was unnecessary."

Guadalupe was silent. The slaughter had horrified her; as she'd lain in the grass it had sickened her to know that he was part of it. Perhaps that was why she had told so much, so readily. Part of her shame came from what he'd done. But she had forgiven him, as she must. She had no choice; he was more important to her now than his actions.

"It was stupid," Stone went on. "We could have taken them alive."

"Yes, that is sad."

"It is grievous." Stone grunted. "What's more, I have no rum to ease it."

"I, I will ease you."

Stone's tone became softer. "Just lie with me," he said.

"You do not want me?"

"At the moment I want nothing, except sleep."

Guadalupe put her arms about him and lay very still.

Stone remained on his back, staring up at the needle-pointed stars framed by the pines. Beside him he was aware of the breathing of the girl, but he did not touch her.

The singing stopped; Don Luis raised his head. Today, he told himself, I will challenge it. This terrible silence. She is my daughter. This is my home. No matter what strength he possesses, I have my right, as father and as mayor.

He stood and paused. There was sudden pain in his head, a trembling that went through his whole frame. There was a desperate need for brandy. Do it now, he urged, or it will never be done.

Don Luis reached for the glass that stood on the table beside his split-cane chair, then took his hand away. Do it first, he told himself. With what you have. For what you believe in.

He breathed deeply, determinedly, crossed the courtyard, and began up the stairs; his step was heavy, he seemed to weigh too much. At the top of the stairs he paused, his heart beating uneasily. Then, resolutely, he walked down the arched corridor to Angela's bedroom and reached for the handle of the paneled heavy-nailed door.

As his fingers closed on the doorknob, he heard his daughter's voice. "Now," she said in her rich full tone, "it is time, my blackamoor. Time for you to substitute."

Don Luis's hand remained where it was, held by the words that made no sense yet said more than he could contain.

"Come now." Angela's voice was breathy. "Substitute, my blackamoor."

Don Luis turned and walked silently away, incapable

of acting otherwise. He descended the stairs, recrossed the courtyard, and drank the brandy. He reached for more, his fingers white where they gripped the bottle. If only he were not so alone.

Then he stayed his movement, closed his eyes, and shook. "No," he whispered, "you have lost her, but there is Campeche. The town remains. The post you purchased is still yours." In his mind's eye he saw the pattern of the curved portals, the cobblestones, the towers of the fort, the pink façade of the church of Guadalupe, all the neat squared colonial buildings that clustered on the shore. It was his, it would survive, it held the past and the future in its stonework.

Don Luis opened his eyes; he replaced the brandy bottle, touched his unshaven chin with an uncertain hand. Begin again, he told himself. Before it is too late. here, in Campeche, there is enough to cling to.

The forest became an unending passageway of vine-covered trunks and gnarled roots. On all sides it appeared impenetrable, only the narrow paths the Maya followed had any course at all; without the Maya the men from Campeche would have been lost a thousand times.

Sargento Ocaño was now in charge of the Spanish contingent, and the authority gave him new bearing. He sat more upright in his saddle, he kept his men in line. The soldier with the spear wound died the second day away from the green valley; he was buried in a shallow grave scraped out among the roots of the great trees growing beside the narrow jungle path. Ocaño saw to it that the man's musket, powder, shot, and boots were added to a bearer's load; the rest of him was left to the ants that swarmed through the leaf mold.

Stone and Toledo barely spoke. The gloom of the forest seemed to penetrate them both; the uncertainty of a rich reward was beginning to erode their vitality. Toledo's breastplate developed spots of rust that he forgot to rub away; an angry red sore began at the corner of his mouth. Stone's face lost its healthy tan; his eyes seemed to sink deep into his head.

Among the invaders, Guadalupe was most at ease. At night she lay beside Stone, and when he slept she touched him. She provided for him, saying little. Once again, she was a mestiza; she expected nothing to change.

Of them all, only she had contact with the Maya.

"You, the Pretty One," Ah Cuc asked her gently, "why are you with these people? You know you do not belong."

Guadalupe looked into Ah Cuc's curious eyes. "I speak the language," she murmured. "I am here to translate."

"Is that all?"

Guadalupe paused; there was something about speaking the language that reached down into a well of truth. It was as if she were with her mother, to whom she never lied.

"Tell me," Ah Cuc persisted, "is that all?"

"I am a hostage also," Guadalupe replied.

Ah Cuc laughed. "These people"—he made a careless gesture of the hand—"have they no scruples at all?"

Guadalupe did not reply; it was easier to remain silent.

"Pretty One"—Ah Cuc's eyes were still laughing—"what do you guarantee amongst these dreamers?"

"You call them that?"

"What else? They exhibit no reality." His voice became even gentler than usual. "But answer me, why are you really here?"

"I have told you, I am a hostage."

"Has that not changed? From what I see—"

"Yes, you are right." Guadalupe's words were so quiet they could barely be heard. "Now, I would not leave if I could."

Ah Cuc was delighted. "So, you have become hostage to yourself, Pretty One. Bound as the prince and I are bound."

"Yes."

Ah Cuc smiled; he learned more each day of these

graceless invaders. Soon, all their secrets would be his. They had no right to be here, and the sooner they were disposed of, the better.

"There is talk of returning, Christopher. Some believe there is nothing to be gained."

"How many have lost heart?"

"Enough. Half a dozen or so. They want to go back to Campeche and take what's there."

"Tell them—no, ask them to be patient. All can see how rich our prisoner is. Ask them to wait until we reach this city before a decision is made."

"That, I have requested. But they are not impressed by the feathers of his cloak, nor the few gold beads about his neck. It is real wealth they have come for. It is bars of gold they want."

"Then they shall have it."

"How?"

"They shall have it, I say." Stone's eyes were suddenly fierce. "When we conquer this city on the lake, they shall have all the gold they can carry."

"Are you sure?"

"Yes," Stone replied, defiant, determined, reckless. "There will be more gold than they have seen in their lives before."

Van Staal stared at his captain, for a moment or two poised as if to speak. Then without a further word, he turned and walked away.

Stone watched the loyal figure depart. There was nothing he could do for anyone. He felt incompetent and isolated. And about him the green jungle menaced, mocked with its vines and creepers, its impenetrable gloom. It taunted with its damp decay, and he knew of no way out of it, forward or back. It surrounded him, bled him. There was no way in which it would respond to any command he made; he could not negotiate its seas.

CHAPTER 13

THE CITY OF TAYASAL CAME OUT OF THE SUNSET LIKE THE skeleton of some long-dead creature, bleach-boned, immense, majestic. White limestone buildings stood upon an island shore; the island was a black-green leaf in a lake of splendid silver, shattered by shards of gold cast upon it by the westerly sun. It glittered defiantly into the eyes of all who rode over the tree line to stare down at it in wonder.

Those who belonged, smiled. They knew their strength; the gods had never withdrawn their favor from this place. Those who saw it for the first time were silenced: alluring and impregnable, Tayasal gave them new hope and filled them with despair.

The knitted buildings formed a solid fortress; on all sides the island was distant from the shore. As they watched, the dying sun caught the peak of a temple, held it an instant in a white-and-golden beacon, issuing a challenge none could take.

After what seemed to be an interminable time, Christopher Stone turned in his saddle. "God's heart," he whispered to van Staal, and the words were almost a prayer. "I had not dreamed of such a place."

"Nor I."

"It is a true city."

"It is a stronghold."

Stone smiled then, for the first time in days. "Let us descend, and see it nearer," he said excitedly. "Let us assess what it is we have to conquer."

Van Staal nodded, doubt in his eyes.

Stone galloped alone, down from the trees to the lake, urging his mount, increasing his pace on the leveling ground. He galloped to where the shoreline spread, to where rushes grew and the little waves the water made lapped in the fiery light. He galloped with increasing heart, amazed at the lift the city had given him; his rawboned face was active, his eyes were alive again. The gloom of the forest was behind him, the new prize lay ahead.

He swung around a clump of cabbage palms and stood in his stirrups to gain a better view, then fell across the saddle as his horse reared, slipped in the grass, and shied in fright at the sight and smell of a naked Indian woman hanging by her heels from a scrubby tree. She was dead, as was the dog that dangled beside her. Both had been freshly killed.

Stone's stomach rose at the butchery before him. Gagging, his throat hot with bile, he tried to steady his horse, tried not to look at the corpses hanging at his height, but he could not take his eyes away. Both had been eviscerated; blood ran from them in sticky black streams, flies and yellow-banded hornets hissed in the reeking air.

Stone turned as Toledo ranged beside him. The Creole's face was white as cotton, his body stiff with shock. He raised a hand and crossed himself. "Pagan," he whispered. "It is an offense."

Stone spat copiously. "What does this signify?" he asked.

Toledo did not reply; his eyes were fixed on the corpses, his lips moving in silent prayer. Stone turned as Guadalupe approached. "Get back," he shouted. "Tell them to send me the prince."

"What is it?" Guadalupe saw nothing but the men and the horses. "What is wrong?"

"Get him." Stone waved an arm. "Tell van Staal to hold the others. I want no one here but the Maya."

Guadalupe swung away. Stone saw her speak to van Staal, before he returned his attention to Toledo. "What meaning has this slaughter?" he asked, and spat again.

"It is a challenge," Toledo replied, color returning to his face. "I have heard of such offenses."

"They knew we would come?"

"They are animals." Toledo's voice was rancid. "They live in these forests like animals. They have been watching us all the time."

"Then they will know we hold their prince."

"Let me torture him." Toledo's eyes were burning; the sore at the corner of his mouth glistened. "Let me find from him their defenses. How many warriors they have. What they will give for his life."

"We need him alive."

"I would not kill him."

"He would die before he told you anything."

"I would make him talk."

"Do not touch him." Stone's hand went to the butt of one of the pistols he carried. "I am though with warning. The prince is the only hope we have of negotiating with these people." He paused to control his breathing. "If what you say is true," he added, "and his warriors watch us, they would fall upon us instantly, the moment we harmed their lord."

Toledo licked his lips, he turned away to find Tutul Katun watching him with curious eyes, a small smile on his intelligent, pitted face. "You will be punished for this," Toledo shouted at him. "The Lord will see you suffer."

Tutul Katun remained unmoved; he seemed quite satisfied with the barbarian's reaction to the woman and the dog.

"You will burn in hell for what you have done."

Tutul Katun turned his gaze from the voluble Silver Chest toward the Pale One.

"I will see your soul damned and your body dismembered." Toledo raged on, and lifted a hand to strike the Maya. But Stone was beside him, gripping his wrist.

"Go," Stone said with more calm than Toledo would have expected. "I will speak with him."

"He is an abomination."

Stone nodded. "I too loathe what I have seen, yet we need the man alive." His voice was now controlled; he released the Creole's arm. "And he is clever," he added quietly. "Do not display too much, for he will pass such intelligence on."

Jaime Toledo breathed deeply, holding back his outrage. "Very well," he whispered. "But I will remain to hear what he has to say."

"As you wish." Stone looked for Guadalupe. She stared at the tree of death, one hand clamped to her mouth. "Come here," he called almost roughly. "Ask him what he means by this butchery."

When Guadalupe spoke directly to Tutul Katun her voice was subdued. "This is our warning," she translated to Stone a moment later.

"What are we being warned of?"

"To go, or become like these dead."

"Who put them there?" Stone asked.

"We, who are everywhere," Tutul Katun replied through Guadalupe. His voice was firm, in command, as if it were he who sat in the saddle. "When the time comes, you will find us all around you."

"Why did they use a woman and a dog?"

Tutul Katun's eyes hardened. "That is what the Spaniards take," he said. "Our women and our food. And, of course, the yellow metal when it is to be found."

"Who was the woman?"

"A slave, quite worthless. Fit for your people and their needs." Tutul Katun listened while Guadalupe translated, his eyes going from Stone to Toledo in haughtiness and scorn. "Make your decision," he added. "Time is passing."

Almost on signal, as if the players had been listening, a hollow drumming and a ring of trumpets came across the still waters of Lake Petén Itzá. As they turned toward the sound, those on the shoreline witnessed the last of the sun's rays pick out the bones of the splendid city. Tayasal glowed; its temple stood magnificent.

"Well?" Tutul Katun queried. "Have you the sense to depart?"

Stone leaned from his saddle to stare down at the short, finely clad figure of the Maya. "Tell him," he said through Guadalupe, speaking to the prince directly, "that he has challenged me obscenely. For that reason alone I would not go. Tell him," he added quietly, "that I accept his challenge. I am a pirate, and his city shall be my prize."

Stone continued to stare while Guadalupe repeated his message. He saw the Maya's eyes flicker; he waited for the prince's response and Guadalupe's translation of the short, hard words.

"He says that you are brave and you are foolish," Guadalupe said. "That you will regret not going when the chance was yours."

"So be it."

"Is that all?"

"Yes," said Stone. "That is all." He spurred his horse, and it moved ahead, forcing the Mayan prince to step aside. Stone did not even glance at him but rode on his way, his final words drifting back to those who remained in the malodorous air. "His city shall be my prize."

Guadalupe waited; she told the Maya nothing more.

From across the water, the sound of drums and the ring of trumpets continued throughout the night. Those in the camp slept fitfully, not knowing what the dawn would bring or what lay in the days ahead. Only Christopher Stone and Rolf van Staal moved in the darkness. They walked the shoreline endlessly, eyes on the island, darker in the darkling sea. Planning.

"What boats do they have?" the Englishman asked, his boots squelching the wetness. "Have you questioned any about them?"

"Canoes, Christopher, no more."

Stone paused. "They carry that satrap he travels in by canoe?" he queried, a new note in his voice.

"They must, placed across two or more."

Stone stared into the darkness, willing his eyes to see.

"They possess no other craft," van Staal continued. "None that I have heard of."

"Then we shall surprise them." Stone laughed suddenly as the idea came to mind; a short hard sound went skipping over the lake. "We shall build a vessel, the like of which will astound them."

Van Staal looked up at Stone, caught by the infection of his words.

"We shall build a battleship," Stone shouted, his eyes on the darkness. "With the satrap on its fore. Culverins in the place of the prince. By God, Rolf, we'll go to war."

Van Staal laughed then, also. A chuckle: the sound of pleasure as an image formed. "With muskets bound like organ pipes, all along the stern."

"Built high on the sides to keep their arrows out. Sweet Jesus, it is possible."

"Aye, it is. We've men to fight and men to row. And timber all around us."

"Tomorrow." Stone hurled his words over the water, into the sound of the trumpets and drums. "Tomorrow we cut and tomorrow we build. By the sweet living Jesus, then you'll see a ship." He laughed again. The savanna with its dust, the forest with its melancholy, were problems of the past. The new, the immediate, the exciting, lay ahead in darkness. Stone had never felt so alive. "A castle on the sea," he cried. "It waits for you. It bids you on, it challenges."

He turned from the water and walked back to the camp, van Staal beside him. The bodies of the woman and the dog were buried now, put from sight; no matter how grisly their memory, there was a new spring to his step.

Before dawn Stone was up again, talking to Simmons. They calculated, the short fat carpenter sweating heavily, that enough timber could be cut in three days to form the basis of a galley, a wide, flat-bottomed craft large enough to carry the thirty or more fighting men they would have to attack the city.

Gottberg, the bosun, began plaiting ropes from the vines that grew in profusion. Henri the Stain, whose arrow wound was healing, planned a gun carriage on which to mount the culverins in the ornamental palan-quin of Tutul Katun. Van Staal designed an assembly of muskets, each bound to the next and the whole to a plank whose collective discharge would scythe through the enemy like grapeshot, like a thresher through young corn.

Toward midafternoon on that first dynamic day, Mer-edith, ex–logwood cutter, his face still scarred by Gua-dalupe's nails, his back still feeling the fire into which Stone's blow had sent him sprawling, climbed from the pit where he'd been cutting timber. He'd been working below, Piet the Mulatto above; they sawed planks from logs laid across the pit, heaving the ripsaw up and down.

" 'Tis poxy work," Meredith grunted, wiping dust from his mouth. "I'd thought it all behind me when I joined with Cap'n Stone."

Piet spat on his blistered hands. "I'll take a turn in the pit," he offered.

Meredith grunted. "You have faith in him still?" he asked casually. "The cap'n?"

"Oh, aye. I've been with him four years now. He'll not fail."

"He did in Campeche."

"We all did." Piet tapped the saw for emphasis, and it rang. " 'Twas the women and the rum. I don't blame him, alone." He peered into Meredith's eyes. They were red-rimmed from sawdust, but their gaze was level. "What's with you, anyway?" he wanted to know. "Is it because his cat got you before you laid her down?"

Meredith shook his head. "That's settled," he replied.

"What, then?" Piet's tone hardened. "Do you doubt *me*?"

" 'Twas you who'd have left when they said they had

no gold." Meredith scratched his chest. "I'd want to think you was with us now."

Piet spat on his hands again and smiled. "You're a foxy dog," he said.

"I want us to be strong, that's all. We've no room for them that's got no heart."

"We've all heart now there's work to do."

"Aye." Meredith stared at the half-cut log with dislike. "More'n enough of that."

Piet laughed lightly. "Just promise me something when we fight," he asked.

"What's that?"

"Stand beside me. I'd feel better knowing you were there."

Meredith nodded; he took the saw. "Get into the pit," he said easily. "If we don't cut these, we'll be going nowhere."

The saw tore, and wood dust fell into Piet's eyes; he closed them and pulled until his muscles were fire. Above him, Meredith drove as hard. About, others cut and carried, wedged the planks into the shape they'd form; they gummed the joints with sapodilla resin, rubbed sawdust over the caulk. The vessel would be heavy, but it would float. Everywhere was the sound of industry; there was energy in the air. It was a time of great assent.

Tutul Katun and Ah Cuc observed with care the galley's growth. As they noted the spirit of the men, saw the competence of their hands, they thought anew of the outcome.

"He is an excellent commander, the Pale One," Tutul Katun murmured one afternoon as he teased the monkey with a blade of grass. "He gets the best from them all."

"His heart will be valued by Itzamná," Ah Cuc agreed. "We will be given many good seasons for its bloods."

"Yes, he is powerful." Tutul Kutan's voice became more thoughtful. "My brother will need to be most careful when he faces him."

Ah Cuc's eyes flickered with new curiosity. "You do

not think, my lord, that he might overcome Lord Paxbolón?"

Tutul Katun turned his face away, hiding his expression. "It is not impossible," he replied quietly. "The Pale One, and he who carries the axe, Round Skull, are great fighters. Of course"—he shrugged—"in the end they will die, but my brother could also lose his life."

"That would mean great changes, my lord."

"Great changes, Ah Cuc." Tutul Katun threw a piece of fruit, and the monkey ran after it, its copper chain jangling. "It would mean that I would become Canek. When our father dies, I would bear the name of all our kings."

Ah Cuc's voice became even smoother. "And would that please you, my lord?" he asked.

"Yes." Tutul Katun's face remained averted, his voice told Ah Cuc nothing. "It would save me from the priesthood. I really have no taste for that profession." His tone became harsher. "They are no longer the inspiration they used to be."

Ah Coc coughed discreetly. "Of course, it is to be hoped that nothing befalls Lord Paxbolón," he said carefully. "I would not wish anyone to think that I was disloyal."

Tutul Katun smiled. "It is safe to speak with me," he said, looking back to his lover.

"Should we"—Ah Cuc frowned—"should we not warn the Fighting Lord?"

Tutul Katun slowly shook his head. "That would be almost impossible," he replied. "It would shame him too much to be advised by a younger brother." He turned to the vessel the invaders were constructing: it was big, it was clumsy, it also possessed great strength. He wondered, not for the first time, how it might affect his destiny. When it was put to sea he would know; then the revelation might prove to be more far-reaching than any he could ever have imagined when the barbarians rode down into the green valley with their firearms and their murder. "No," he added, "my brother would only be angered if I were to offer him counsel."

Ah Cuc smiled. "You are so extremely wise, my lord," he said, his eyes also on the vessel growing on the shore. "But tell me," he continued, "what are they doing to the palanquin? It will never be the same again."

"It matters little what they do to it," Tutul Katun said easily. "What is important is how it is carried to Tayasal. With how many and how fast."

"Then you believe they may succeed, my lord?"

"No," Tutul Katun replied surely. "They will not succeed, but they may alter our lives considerably."

Each day the Maya from the island put out in their canoes. They paddled toward the campsite, toward the shape of the growing galley. They came, beating their drums, blowing their trumpets, well within musket range, seemingly without fear. In the canoes the warriors were painted red. They shouted across the water to the men working on the shore in what became a ritual of mockery and defiance. Each morning they drew a little closer.

"Have they no fear?" Stone asked Guadalupe. "Do they not understand how far our guns will carry?"

"They hope we will use them," she answered. "They have challenged us, now we must reply. They will do nothing until we respond, that is the custom."

"So, if we were to shoot one?"

"They would land on this shore in their hundreds."

"And if we wait?"

"So will they."

Stone turned to van Staal. "See that each of us knows that clearly," he said crisply. "Including the Spaniards. They will wait until we are ready. And when we are ready we will go."

As van Staal hurried away, Stone asked, "What is it they call to us? Can you hear?"

Guadalupe nodded; when she spoke her voice was subdued. "They say they will give our hearts to their gods, and our flesh to their women," she whispered. "They have the cooking pots ready, and the chilies for flavor."

"Sweet Jesu, they would eat us?"

"After we have been properly sacrificed."

"God's pox," Stone said in English, his face a mixture of expressions, his eyes calculating. "That means they would take us alive." He looked at the downturned head of the girl. "Would they then try *not* to kill us in combat?" he asked.

"If they had to, they would, but they will capture us if they can. Especially, especially the leaders." Guadalupe's eyes came up quickly. "We are in great danger here," she said. "More than I believe you realize."

"We are strong," Stone replied. "Stronger than we seem."

"But they, they are so many. They are everywhere."

Stone reached out and touched her cheek. "*We* and *they*?" he questioned. "Does it trouble you still?"

"Yes, but less so."

"You do not feel as close to them as you did?"

Guadalupe shook her head.

"Nor do I have as much respect for them as I first believed," said Stone, and held her a moment. "What is more, I have less to learn from them than once I thought."

Later, when the sun had gone and the canoes returned, when the sounds of the trumpets and the drums were almost masked with distance, and the twilight, with its reds and flaming orange, was so heavy it weighed the sky, Guadalupe said, "Give me your shirt. I will wash it in the lake." She smiled briefly. "And your socks," she added. "They begin to smell."

Stone looked up, his eyes curious. "You would be a wife to me?" he asked, but removed his shirt.

"No," Guadalupe replied easily. "I am what I am."

"Stay," Stone said gently. "There is more between us than that."

"Of course." Guadalupe's tone was lightly mocking. "I am to translate also."

As Stone removed his socks he watched the girl's half-shadowed face, but it told him nothing. Guadalupe took the garments to the rush-lined shore; she bent and dipped the clothing, darkening against the deepness of the evening. When she returned she spread the washing on a bush, then examined the inside of her arm in the firelight. There was a thin line of blood running down to her wrist.

Immediately Stone came to his feet. "What is it?" he asked.

"A leech. There are many in the water. I tore it away, and that was stupid. Now it will bleed for a while."

Stone lifted her arm; he placed his lips over the wound and sucked it, and Guadalupe felt herself tremble as the bristles about his mouth rasped her skin. Instinctively she reached out to where his light blond hair curled about his ears. There was a melting within she feared she might not be able to control. He had lain with her since the night by the river, but it had seemed to her that their lovemaking had become less and less important to him. As the forest had closed in about them and the tension between him and Toledo increased, he had at times appeared to use her simply for physical release, had entered her with urgency, almost a frenzy, caring little about her response. Often, when she watched him building his ship, she had wondered if he thought of her at all. Now he was attending her again; his warmth held a honeyed sweetness sharp as pain.

Stone raised his head. "The wound will heal," he told her. "It will bleed, but it will not fester."

Guadalupe nodded.

"Come." Stone placed the serape he wore about her shoulders, leaving his own bare. He seated her on a log. "Rest a little, here, by the fire," he said.

"I am, I am all right."

"I'll put more wood—" He began to move away.

"No." Guadalupe held his hand. "Don't go from me." She stared up at his body, licked by little flames. "Do not leave me now."

Stone sank to his knees beside her; he kissed her with such gentleness that, for an instant, she did not know if the touch were real or not. Her throat tightened; it was as if she had never been with a man before.

"Dear God, I have resisted naming this so long."

Stone lifted her to his bedding. "Love?" he whispered. "Can it be?"

"Cristóbal."

"I have had many women, in many places, but none, my love, like you. I fear . . . this."

"Is, love, what you feel for me?" The words barely passed the tightness of Guadalupe's throat. "Love?"

"What else, it frightens me so."

"Why?" The words were easier now. "Why should you fear loving me?"

"Because it asks so much."

"I ask for nothing."

"Not you, *it*. The binding. My God, what am I to do with you?"

"Love me."

"That I do." Stone's hands removed her clothing; he reached to undo his breeches but found her fingers there before his own.

"Let me," she whispered. "I have never seen a man before."

"That cannot be."

"Not like this, when I have wanted him. It has always been in the dark, not seeing anything."

"Look at me, then."

In the soft yellow light from the fire, Guadalupe examined with her fingers and her eyes. "You are beautiful," she said. "Put yourself inside me."

"I love you," Stone said as he felt her tighten about him. "God help me, but I do."

Her breath in his ear whispered, "Cristóbal, Cristóbal. Stay there forever."

The firelight died, the moon was a fingernail behind a film of cloud. About them an occasional voice was lifted, a log was added to a fire, scattering fans of sparks. The lake rippled about the galley growing on the shore. Across the water, in their island stronghold, the Maya waited for their challenge to be accepted.

PART TWO

THE
KINGDOM
OF
FEAR

CHAPTER 1

HE CAME AT NIGHT, SILENTLY, HIS LEAN SHIP CARVING THE velvet seas, his men ready by the longboats. Four boats put out to land noiselessly on the breakwater; four more, oars muffled, encountered the shape of Stone's *Courage* as it nestled on the midnight tide.

The first that Cramer the Black knew of the arrival of the French was a pistol to his head as he slept in the captain's cabin.

"Where are the others?" Cazaux asked in the light of the lantern Sartou held. "Stone? The Dutchman?" He could not believe his luck. "Half your crew is missing."

Cramer licked his uncomfortably dry lips; his eyes were restlessly cautious. There were three other Frenchmen in the low-beamed cabin; he could hear the voices of others rounding up his crew.

"Where?" Cazaux asked clearly in English, tapping Cramer's head with the pistol muzzle. "Where have they gone?"

"Inland," Cramer grunted. "They went with the Spaniards for gold."

Cazaux smiled. "And left you, the Negro, in charge." He shook his head in mocking wonder. "*Mon Dieu*, I could never have imagined anything like this. You did not even set a watch."

Cramer did not reply; he eased himself upright in the bunk, condemning his own incompetence.

"What happened, black man? Do they not obey your orders?"

"They were drunk," Cramer confessed grudgingly, and wiped sweat from his face. He had ignored what was happening to himself and the men, he had been enchanted in a manner that shrouded all reality, he had been caught in the lunacy of another's fabrication. He stared into the eager Frenchman's eyes, hating their triumph, knowing that the truth could no longer be avoided. "This waiting has been bad for us," he muttered.

"It has not been good for me, either," Cazaux replied.

"What brings you back amongst us?"

"Ah"—Cazaux's tone grew gloomy—"that is a long story, but you would not understand it, black man." He prodded again with the pistol. "Tell me, are the Spaniards from the garrison still imprisoned in the fort?"

"Some are." Cramer watched the Frenchman carefully, wondering what he knew. "Some's died, and some we freed."

"And he with the wounded eye? What of him?"

"D'Avila. In hospital still. We leave him there for mercy's sake. He's agreed to keep the promise he made on the life of his doxy."

"His *promise*?" Cazaux's laugh was cynical. "With *you*? Have you all become ill with the same disease? This lack of watch, these promises. You all have the tropical fever, no? The fever of the damned."

Cramer shrugged; he straightened his back a little. "We've'd nothing to do but wait," he said, hoping all would be accepted as it seemed.

"With plenty of women and too much rum." Cazaux nodded solemnly. "I know of that, my friend. I have seen it happen. But tell me, has no one here disturbed you? No other ships have come to this busy little port in the weeks we've been gone?"

"Some," Cramer replied. "Merchantmen for hides and dyes. Cotton. They've come, and they've traded."

"With no questions asked, eh?"

"Surprising how little some wants to know when there's business to be done." Cramer cupped the palm of his hand, indicating money. "If you knows what I mean."

Cazaux nodded, his expression altering. "What then, of this gold you speak of?" He leaned forward. "Where did you say your captain had gone?"

"Inland. To the Indians."

"Ah, to the Indians for gold. That interests me greatly. Almost as much as . . ." He paused, thinking. "What have you heard of the daughter of the mayor?" he asked. "The girl, Angela?"

Cramer's eyes flickered. "They says she's ill," he replied carefully, but knew considerably to the contrary. "They says she's mad."

"Never," Cazaux replied with confidence. "Once she knows I'm here she'll be full of life again. But first, the gold. Tell me more about it."

Cramer scratched his head thoughtfully, aware of the pistol's presence. There was no point in concealing anything of the expedition from the Frenchman; and the more he talked, the better he felt. So he explained how it had come about and watched Jean-Marc Cazaux's eyes shine with interest and calculation.

"Most fascinating," Cazaux said when Cramer stopped. "So there's more gold to be brought to this pretty little town?"

"That's what they've said." Cramer shrugged. "But we've heard nothing now in almost a month." He added a mournful note to his voice, presenting his plea. "We've been left behind," he added. "That's why we've become so loose."

Cazaux smiled. "How many men have deserted you?" he asked.

"Enough. There's them that's gone with the merchantmen. There's them that's living with mulattos. We've half of what we came with, if that's what you wants to know."

"That is exactly what I want to know." Cazaux's scar deepened with mirth. "But now, my friend, what I have to think about is what to do with you."

"Do?"

"You cannot remain free, and it would seem, shall we say, inconsiderate to fill the dungeons with both English and Spanish, considering the conditions of our arrival here."

Cramer's eyes narrowed.

"After all, we came as associates."

"Aye, and you left as a thief."

Cazaux spread his long hands. "The fortunes of war, my friend," he replied easily.

"What's become of our purchase?"

"I have it still." Cazaux peered at Cramer mischievously. "Perhaps I have returned to present your share."

"And perhaps my foreskin's white."

Cazaux laughed openly; he turned to Sartou and translated the remark. Sartou chuckled, his little eyes creased.

Cramer watched them, his anger rising. "Why've you come at all?" he asked, his voice hardening. "There's nothing for you here."

"Ah, there you're wrong." Cazaux's tone was admonishing. "There is something of the heart."

"The heart?"

"Well, one of the delicate organs, shall we say."

Cramer's lip curled. "From what they say, you can't get that up," he said with new incisiveness.

Cazaux stepped forward and slapped the black man's cheek; the sound was shotlike in the cabin. Before Cramer had time to react, Cazaux spoke rapidly to the two Frenchmen who stood behind Sartou. They came forward quickly, each taking Cramer by an arm. The six-foot Negro rose in the bunk, shaking them free like dogs. He caught one by the neck and hurled him against the cabin wall; he took the other by the shirt and threw him straight at Sartou.

Cazaux lifted his pistol, but Cramer held out a hand. "I'll go where you want me, Frenchman," he said in a voice that burned. "But keep your mongrels away. I don't know how many you've got, but there'll be two less if you sets them up again."

Cazaux paused, then gave a mock salute. "You still

have your spirit," he said. "Not everything has deserted you. You *are* far too dangerous to be left uncaged." He tapped his nose with a long forefinger. "I was about to take the girl and go, but now you have given me reason to wait. I will exchange you for the Spaniards who remain in the dungeon. That way it will be possible to use you more than once. First, to keep these Spanish pigs content, and second, to trade with Captain Stone when he returns here with the gold." He smiled. "Is that not clever?" he asked.

Cramer stared at Cazaux. "You're a scummy crew," he said contemptuously. "You'd take the coins from your dead mother's eyes."

"Scummy? That is a word I do not understand," Cazaux replied pleasantly. "But if it has anything to do with coming aboard and taking you by surprise, then I can only agree. As for the coins you refer to, they were spent many years ago, my big black friend. Now go. Follow my men. We will lock you in your forecastle tonight. Tomorrow we begin our exchange."

Paxbolón reached for another piece of roast dog and listened to what his father, Canek, king of the Itzá, had to say about the invaders and the vessel they were building on the far side of the lake.

"Perhaps it could be burned," the old man suggested; he patted his stomach thoughtfully. "With fire taken by canoes?"

Paxbolón shook his head. He was taller than Tutul Katun, and his face was untouched by smallpox; his forehead sloped back in the same noble way, but his eyes were narrower. "The wood is green," he replied, chewing. "Fire would not harm it."

"Could it not be holed?" Canek sat cross-legged on a cushion of deerhide covered with a jaguar skin. He had become heavy in the past years, and it was no longer comfortable for him to remain unmoving for any length of time. "What do you think, my son?"

"When it comes close to the shore." Paxbolón picked his teeth. "Then we can sink it."

"But by then they will be here with their arms of fire and their swords."

"Good. Here is where I want them."

"You do not fear their firearms? The new ones we have been told of, that shine like the yellow metal?"

Paxbolón shook his head again; he poked among the bones of the roasted hairless dog, his favorite dish, looking for a further piece of the delicate meat. He was eager for the fighting to begin, to test the invaders, to see what they brought with them this time.

He recalled with amusement what he'd been told of the horse that had been left behind when Cortez came and went. The Itzá of the time, who had never seen such an animal, thought it a god. How naive they must have been.

They had taken the lamed horse and placed it in a temple, feeding it chickens and flowers, and, of course, the creature had died. Then they built a stone image of it, called it Tzimin Chac, and worshiped it until the Spaniards returned and destroyed it, telling them they were fools. They had come in peace then, the invaders, bringing with them the image of a woman with a child at her breast, asking that it be worshiped as the one true god, more powerful than Itzamná or his father, Hunab Kú.

Paxbolón smiled as he found another piece of dogflesh. What would they worship now that they came in war? he wondered. They would need something more powerful than a woman and a child. Tayasal had enough of each already.

Canek shifted his bulk uncomfortably, watching his son. "What preparations have you made?" he asked. He was a simple man who appreciated a clever answer to a direct question. The clothing he wore was uncomplicated; his loincloth was decorated, as his rank demanded, but not excessively so. About his neck was a heavy collar of jaguar claws separated by small cylinders of gold; there were gold plugs in his earlobes, his hair was plaited high and interwoven with quetzal feathers. In spite of his rank, he dressed no more elaborately than many of the nobles of his court; he felt no need to display himself. How ready are the warriors?" he wanted to know.

"They are ready, Father," Paxbolón answered patiently. "And we have prepared many new arrows. Swords, too, those with blades of obsidian that cut sharper than the metal of the enemy."

"And what of Bacal?" Canek asked quietly.

At the mention of the head priest, Paxbolón's eyes narrowed. He had no liking for Bacal and feared his power; he cleared his throat and sipped a little cornwater. "Bacal has offered Itzamná the hearts of two young boys," he said. "It was done this morning." Paxbolón pushed the food away. "It seems that all the signs are fortunate."

"Do they indicate a day?"

"Any time before the moon is fat. Now it is thin, but the sooner they come, the better we will receive them. They are few and we are many. I welcome their arrival."

"Is there anything that can be done to hasten it?"

Paxbolón nodded, his expression brightening. "We will extend the challenge," he said, and smiled cruelly. "One of them, strung by the heels, might bring them closer."

"An excellent thought. I suggest you arrange it quite soon."

"I will do it myself, Father. It will give me much pleasure to go to the place of the invaders and offer one of them to He who looks over us all."

"Take care," Canek warned, moving his buttocks uncomfortably. "Your brother is already in their hands."

"My brother is a fool," Paxbolón replied impatiently. "If they did not hold him, our task would be much easier."

"It is unfortunate, I admit."

"What does he think he's doing? Hunting with so few men? Taking his pets, the monkey and Ah Cuc? It will please me when the day arrives for him to join the priesthood."

Canek stretched. Paxbolón's intensity was tiring; he

much preferred the company of his younger son but could not alter their birthrights. He wondered what it would be like when he was gone, what would happen to his people. Perhaps Tayasal would go the way of Tenochtitlán, the city of the Aztecs, and the Canek of the time would be like Moctezuma, a prisoner in his own palace, a plaything for the conquerors. Canek hoped not. It would be much better if Tayasal, like Tikal and the other great abandoned cities of the Maya, returned to the jungle from which it had sprung, became covered with the vines, creepers, and saplings that grew with such rapidity. That would seem more natural. Canek sighed, looked into the noble face of his eldest son, and wondered if he, Paxbolón, represented the last of his line.

"When do you think the new challenge might be issued?" Canek asked. "And whom would you choose?"

"I will do it soon, Father. And there are many who would suit the purpose. There is Silver Chest, and others of the Red Vests. Also, there is the woman who speaks the language. Her loss would mean much to them."

"Then we would not be able to converse."

"When we offer their hearts to Itzamná it will not be necessary to converse."

"So be it." Canek held back a yawn. Soon he would go to his mat and sleep. "Leave me now, my son," he said wearily.

"Yes, Father." Paxbolón stood. He was tall for a Maya, and his shoulders were broad. He looked as if he had every right to be what he was: the foremost warrior of the Itzá, the best ball player in the whole of Tayasal. "I shall inform you when the new challenge has been laid."

Canek nodded, watched his son bow and walk backward from the room. He sighed; he would be glad when it all was over, and he could sit in peace once more, thinking of the glory of his people.

*   *   *

The mayor had drunk a little less in the past few days, consciously attempting to maintain control. The need for brandy remained, but he did not indulge it as frequently.

One morning he went to the Municipal Building, seated himself at the council table, and penned a letter to the governor of Yucatán, assuring him that in spite of what rumors he might have heard to the contrary, Campeche prospered. Merchantmen continued to use the port, trading local produce for wines, oils, and hardware. It was true, Don Luis wrote, that foreigners were in the town, but some of them were actively helping to subdue the Itzá; their aid had been invaluable. There was no need for concern, Don Luis promised Mérida, soon all would be richer with Itzá gold.

After completing the letter the mayor had hurried home, feeling that he had made a beginning, had arrested a decline. In time he would attend to more.

Two days later he found himself awakened by Manuel before it was light. The servant had dressed hurriedly, his jerkin hung half-buttoned and part of his undershirt showed through.

"What is it?" Don Luis's mouth was dry, and an ache pressed from behind his eyes. "What do you want?"

"Your Worship"—Manuel's voice was uneven; a lantern shook in his hand—"there is something I must tell you."

"You have nothing to tell me." Don Luis covered his eyes. "Get out of here. Take that light away."

"The Frenchman"—Manuel could not stop himself— "has come back."

"*What?*" Don Luis sat bolt upright.

"Yes, señor. That is why I woke you, señor." Manuel's nervousness increased. "*La Petite* returned during the night. Now the French are aboard the English frigate. Many are in the town. They are everywhere."

"They have taken the *Courage*?"

"Yes, señor."

"The blackamoor also?"

"He too."

"My God." Don Luis put his hands over his face, not

knowing what to think. One was as bad as the other. Or worse. "What time is it?" he muttered.

"The hour before dawn, señor."

"Listen," the mayor said, trying to assemble the fragments that darted through his brain. "The Frenchman? Has he come ashore?"

Manuel shook his head.

"Good." Don Luis pressed his fingers to his temples. "When he does, I will speak to him. First, you understand, before another has the chance."

"Yes, señor."

Don Luis swung his bare feet from the bed. "Now, make me some coffee," he said. "Bring me brandy. And make the coffee hot, do you hear? Hot enough to burn."

Manuel hurried away.

The mayor dressed clumsily, his hands fumbling with his garments as his mind fumbled with the changes that had occurred. He examined his gray, bristly chin in a mirror and decided to shave. He looked at his trembling hands and thought better of it, then realized he must. As he tucked his shirt into his breeches, he called Manuel again and asked for hot water and a newly sharpened razor. Then he sat very still while the majordomo cut the growth away. He wiped his own face with a steaming cloth and watched Manuel pour coffee.

"Put a measure in," he instructed, indicating the brandy. "Then take the bottle away."

"*Sí*, señor."

Don Luis cupped both hands about the steaming coffee mug and was surprised by their sudden steadiness. He held the fragrant mixture beneath his nostrils and breathed deeply.

"Is that all, señor?" asked Manuel.

"Is my daughter awake?" the mayor asked abruptly.

Manuel nodded.

"What is she doing?"

"The same, señor." Manuel's eyes came up and went away. "She is preparing."

"Holy Mother of God." Don Luis sipped the burning

liquid as Manuel arranged his black broadcloth doublet and straightened his hose.

"I will go to her."

"*Sí*, señor."

"See that there is more coffee waiting for me at the Municipal Building. And something to eat."

"You will take breakfast, señor?"

"Get away from here, Manuel. Do as I ask."

When he was alone, Don Luis examined himself in the mirror: his face had become puffy, red veins stood out on his cheeks, little sacs surrounded his eyes. It was the brandy, he knew, but without it he would not have survived. He took a wide black cravat and knotted it about his throat; for reasons he could not comprehend, the arrival of Cazaux had braced him. Perhaps it was that something, this day, would be settled. He straightened his shoulders and went up to his daughter's room.

Angela was seated at her dressing table, interweaving pearls with the ringlets of her hair. In the light of the many candles arranged between mirrors on her polished mahogany *tocador,* she appeared incandescently lovely. She was singing when her father came into the room and bent to kiss her cheek. She turned, rapidly, to glance at him, and her expression altered: color flooded her cheeks.

"He has come," she said. "Is that not so, Papá?"

"Angela—"

"You have dressed, you have come to me for the first time in so many days." Angela's voice rang with certainty. She had never doubted herself or Cazaux; she knew where the future lay. "And you have shaved. None of this would be done for anyone else."

"I have a meeting with the council."

"Of course." Angela turned back to the glass. "Tell him I am prepared."

"Angela, be calm." Don Luis closed his eyes; the moment pressed, but he withstood it. If he failed now, he knew, he would never be given another chance. "Be patient," he went on doggedly. "The Frenchman may have returned for other reasons."

"Nonsense, Papá, don't be so silly." Angela had never

been so sure: she knew that the world was what you made it. "Now, leave me. I have much to do."

"I intend to speak to him first."

Angela hesitated only a moment. "Very well," she agreed. "I will wait until you are ready. But call me as soon as you possibly can."

Don Luis left the room, then half turned as he heard his daughter's singing begin again. But his step was relatively steady as he left the house. Outside, on this new day, he saw the first spines of sunrise cut into the sky. At least the waiting was over. Time had meaning again.

CHAPTER 2

THE FINAL TIMBERS WERE HAMMERED INTO PLACE. THE PALanquin, with the culverins mounted, was positioned on the rough foredeck. Each of the bearers was shown how to work an oar.

Tutul Katun would be placed in full view of those at Tayasal, and behind him the three remaining hunters and Ah Cuc would stand in line; all would form a shield for the new conquistadores.

In the center of the galley, surrounded by Stone's men, would be the Spanish soldiers protected by the gunnels. Behind them, facing out, were the muskets van Staal had mounted on a plank. Already the battleship was taking its shape.

In his mind's eye Christopher Stone could see it clearly, riding through the water. In his blood he felt the excitement beginning its heady surge. "What shot do we have?" he asked Henri the Stain, the birthmarked gunner, holding back the enthusiasm that crept into his voice.

"We've round and grape," Henri replied. "The heavy's for the stonework. The grape's for them." He pointed to the Maya, who shouted from their canoes.

Stone nodded; he handed the gunner a telescope. "Look," he said. "There's a narrow break in the fortress. It's where the canoes land on the island. On each

173

side of it stands a building. Either one down would give us room to beach."

"Aye." Henri studied the waterfront. On the left of the landing place was a solid-looking house of stone and plaster, on the right a round-walled building with a roof of thatch. "The one with the rush roof, Cap'n," he said. "That's the one I'd take."

"Mark it well," Stone replied. "And save the grape 'til I order it."

The gunner nodded slowly.

"See that the musketeers bottle their powder," Stone later told van Staal. He could leave no detail alone. "They'll go through water on their way ashore."

"Aye, I will." Van Staal rubbed a hand over his head. "The Creole spoke to me this morning," he said in a different tone. "He wants the bearers chained to the oars. Without it, he won't board his men."

"He thinks they'll run?"

"Aye, he does."

Stone grunted. "I suspected as much," he murmured. "If—"

"There's no more ifs, Rolf," Stone interrupted loudly; they were all committed now. "We're bound and we're going and we'll do what must be done." He shook his head and smiled thinly. "I'd chain the Spaniards themselves," he added, "given half a chance."

The dream was past, misplaced by the longboats that had drawn silently alongside, broken by the pistol pressed against his forehead. Now, Cramer the Black sat on the stone floor of a Spanish prison, chained to a damp wall, his ankles fettered by heavy irons that bit to the bone. The air in the confines was used, already soiled; the Spaniards had only recently been taken away.

All dungeons stink, the captain had said. This stank more than most. He knew it too well, this was the second time he'd been here.

As for the dream? Cramer could not have resisted it if he'd tried. In all his restless life, he'd never touched such finery, nor had such beauty within reach of his own black hand. He scratched the stub of his missing ear and wondered how much he'd have to pay. Everything had its price along this Spaniard's coast; everything took its weight.

And yet, who could value it? If the magic had not tempted, if the girl, what she wanted and what she gave, had not absorbed him so witheringly on all those afternoons inside the singing room, where would he be at this moment? Dead, most likely, killed defending the *Courage*, cut down by the boarding French.

Cramer shook his curly head. There was no answer to any of it, the thoughts were pointless to pursue. But even here, part of the dream clung still, like silk to his skin. It gave him something to cleave to in this dank and rotting place; it endured in spite of the gloom.

He peered at the men around him, in the green and fetid air. They were twenty-three, chained by the wrists, shackled by the ankles, all that remained of the crew of the *Courage*, all that was left of the sixty or more who had come to the port of Campeche. He wondered how many would leave.

Paxbolón squatted above the campsite, staring down at the invaders clustered about their fires. He had twice tried to get near the girl who spoke the language but had failed. She slept too close to the Pale One to be touched; she lay in his arms, and there was no approaching her.

But there were others. Paxbolón studied the arrangement of the camp. A group of pirates sat about a blanket, playing cards with leaves of the signature tree that had been dried and inscribed and were now like leather. Others hung in their hammocks over the smoke from their fires. His brother lay with Ah Cuc, their chained monkey between them. Silver Chest spoke to a Red Vest. His little hissing words rose up to Paxbolón like water on hot stones, they contained the heat of steam. Behind them all, just visible, was the vessel they were building; it was almost complete. He could see the dull glint of the large firearms made of yellow metal inside his brother's litter; he could just make out the high walls

of the craft under which they would hide when they
came. It would not be easy to sink the vessel, but he
would find a way.

Paxbolón shifted a little. For two nights he had been
waiting—tonight he would strike. The invaders must be
provoked, they had lived long enough on the shores of
Lake Petén Itzá, on the land of his people. Tonight they
would be told that their time was over. He waited a little
longer; then, his mind made up, he disappeared silently
into darkness.

"I intend to stay here," Cazaux said softly and slowly,
with great emphasis, his voice echoing around the almost empty council chamber, over the oiled surface of
the portrait of the still dead king. "I wish to make
Campeche my home."

Don Luis, the only other occupant of the ornate room,
dropped his coffee cup loudly onto the table. He stared
at Cazaux in astonishment. The Frenchman was assured
and elegant, his broadcloth was clean, the neckerchief
new, his hair appeared freshly combed.

"I must confess, this is not what I had intended,"
Cazaux went on expansively. "But certain circumstances
have altered my point of view. This is a pretty town, and
prosperous, but poor in terms of defense. It needs someone with experience of the coast. Someone like myself."

"Here?" Don Luis managed to speak, sounding as if
he had understood nothing. "In Campeche?"

Cazaux nodded; he bowed toward the mayor. "I will
also marry your daughter. That is, if you will give me
permission."

"Marry Angela?" Don Luis felt like an oaf. Following
the Frenchman was like trying to scrape sunlight off
water. "You would wed her?"

"With your blessing, of course."

"But—" There was too much to grasp and none of it
expected. "If you were to stay, I mean, what of the
others, the rest of your crew? What would happen to
them?"

"Very simple," Cazaux explained patiently. "We now

have two ships, the English frigate and our own. Those who wish to go can take the *Courage* and leave. Others may care to remain and, like me, find their future here."

Don Luis shook his head in disbelief: the light was too bright, too penetrating. He picked up the fallen coffee cup, pushed aside the sugared bun Manuel had provided, and reached for the bottle of brandy. Very carefully, as if the act were all that occupied his mind, he filled the cup and drank it dry.

"Listen to me, *mon père*," Cazaux said unhurriedly, watching the mayor's performance. "I understand how, shall we say, *unexpected* this may seem to you, but believe me, it is all for the best."

"The best?" Don Luis closed his eyes. "How can you say that?"

"Easily. I love your daughter. And I am a fighting man; you have need of me here." Cazaux presented each clause slowly, as if speaking to a child. "What is more," he added, "we are allied in war."

"*What?*"

"We, you and I, are at war with the English. And the Dutch. I was given the news by a merchantman I passed on my return." Cazaux raised his eyebrows questioningly. "Don't tell me you had not heard?"

Don Luis dumbly shook his head, wondering, like a man listening to a confession, what else he would be told this day.

"Nevertheless it is true," Cazaux went on. "The French and the Spanish fight the English and the Dutch."

"You, you are sure of this?" Don Luis asked stupidly.

"I swear it in the name of my king. On the head of my wife-to-be."

"We, we have not yet been informed."

"That does not surprise me," Cazaux said. "But I assure you, *mon père,* that the news will be commonplace among the warlords of the sea. English pirates, Dutch freebooters, any with the vaguest hint of a claim will know of it already. Even now, they may be planning their attacks." He watched the effect his words were having on the mayor and nodded with satisfaction. "Understand me, Your Worship," he added cleverly, "we all need to see Campeche strong."

Don Luis stared at Cazaux. He was incapable of knowing where the truth began or ended; he could touch nothing that was solid. Don Luis swallowed, held like a victim in the eye of a predator.

"So, you see, *mon père*"—Cazaux's gesture was gracious—"we are bound together now."

"But . . ." Don Luis shook his head doggedly. "The governor in Mérida, the viceroy in Mexico, they, they will want to know."

"A simple matter, for someone as political as you." Cazaux smiled engagingly. "Tell them you made me a proposition, one of those you are famous for." His smile grew, the scar on his cheek deepened. "As long as there is peace here, as long as Campeche is profitable, no one will give a curse how you govern it. You might even be congratulated for having taken one more corsario from the sea."

Don Luis put his elbows on the table and held his head in his hands. It throbbed with uncertainty, with the weight of the arguments he could not avoid or deny.

"*Bien.*" Cazaux clapped his hands; the sound bounced off all the walls at once. "What do you have to say?"

"Angela?" Don Luis whispered, the word hollow. "What of Angela?"

Cazaux seemed vaguely surprised. "I will marry her," he replied carefully. "She will be my wife. We will live together, happily. Believe me."

"*You?*" Don Luis's uncertain gaze came up. "How in God's name can I believe *you*?"

"Please." Cazaux smiled with genuine warmth. "I understand that you find this difficult to accept, but what I say comes from the heart. She is all of life to me."

Don Luis stared. Was it possible? Could it be so? He did not know. In all honesty, he could not begin to know. And that uncertainty frightened him most of all.

* * *

It was raining when Sargento Ocaño found the dead sentry hanging by his heels from the branch of a tree. The drifting veil of rain made the sight of the man, strung up on the outskirts of the camp, seem unreal.

Ocaño took a step closer, peering, then put a hand to his mouth and stumbled away. The sentry's stomach had been opened, his entrails spilled downward, covering his face; in spite of the fine drizzle, flies were thick on the body, and leeches covered the arms that reached down into the grasses.

It was several minutes before Ocaño could bring himself to identify the man, then he discovered him to be the sentry whose position had been that closest to the heart of the camp. The arrogance of the threat could not have been more pronounced.

"God's pox," Stone breathed when he was shown the corpse. "They are a bloody people." He sent for Tutul Katun at once.

Tutul Katun viewed the dead sentry for a long time, fine rain misting the coil of his plaited hair. "It is the work of my brother, Lord Paxbolón," he told Guadalupe, moving away from the flies. "He grows impatient."

Guadalupe translated, her eyes on the ground; not once had she looked at the body.

"Is he impatient to die?" Stone wanted to know.

"Death has no terror for him. He is a warrior." Tutul Katun waited for Guadalupe to relate the remark to Stone, then added, "Death is what he lives for."

"Then, by God, he shall have it." Stone stared at the prince with furious eyes. "For I shall use this challenge to spur my men. All will look at it. All will hate him. And then we will sail. Do you understand me?" He waited while Guadalupe's voice reuttered his angry words. "We will sail today and give him all the death he could possibly wish for." Stone glared up at the lowering sky. "This is as good a day as any for your brother to die," he said, and turned and walked away.

As Tutul Katun watched the Pale One stride off in the rain, as he had listened to what the tall invader had to say, there was fresh interest in his eyes. He was pleased that his brother had come in the night and left the new challenge. No one would forgive Paxbolón now, no one would show him any mercy, should he fall into the invader's hands. Paxbolón had a great chance of dying whatever happened when the two sides met; there was much today that could possibly occur, there was much that could be decided.

Once again the campsite buzzed with activity. The drifting rain slowly faded, and by the time the galley was eased into the water, a pale sun had begun to filter down on the men who labored. They loaded the powder and the shot, placed the bearers on their benches, and shouldered the oars into position. Then Toledo went among them, chaining the bearers to their seats. This done, he bound Tutul Katun to one side of the palanquin and Ah Cuc to the other. Toledo's hatred, fired by the death of the morning's sentry, burned with a force that shook his hands; his eyes scorched with their gaze.

Stone was everywhere: speaking to Gottberg, the bosun, as he checked the ropes, and to van Staal about the positions of the men, encouraging Henri the Stain and Meredith as they primed the guns. He was a storm of activity.

The pirates, now, were eager to begin. The slaughtering of the sentry, the readiness of the galley, had filled them with a new resolve. Soon they would set out against the savages who had taunted them endlessly, soon they would be filled with the charge that was the headiest of all: that of winning, gaining, taking what they earned.

"The Spaniards, too, were carried by the moment. Catching some of Toledo's fanaticism, they saw themselves in a more brilliant light. They were no longer the listless garrison sweating in Campeche's heat, but a new force bearing the pride of their country.

Altogether, thirty-four fighting men would board the galley with its muskets and its cannon, its gunnels and its prince in the prow offering protection.

Only a single Spaniard would remain on the shore: Grajales, the soldier who had been wounded when the prince was taken in the long green valley almost a month ago. His wound had healed, but one arm was useless. He would stay with the four Tipu slaves who had borne the palanquin, and together they would guard the horses. All the rest were zealous to go.

"What of me?" D'Avila's fingers scrambled with irritation over his black leather eye patch like crabs across a rock. "I am the commander of the garrison here."

"I told him that." The mayor cleared his throat. "There will be no conflict. You will remain as you are. His position would be merely civil, he says."

"Civil." D'Avila spat the word.

Don Luis shrugged. They stood on the breakwater, facing the *Courage* and *La Petite* as the ships hung on the falling tide. Both vessels now carried the flag of France, both were sleek in the afternoon sun.

"This war?" D'Avila continued in the same rancorous tone. "Do you believe what he says about that?"

Don Luis sighed. "That is possible," he began carefully. "For some time now there has been talk—"

"Do not patronize me." D'Avila stared savagely at the mayor. "Less than a year ago I was there. In Spain. Witnessing events take shape. Louis of France and his Spanish queen have legitimate claims against these pirating nations. I know, I was there. Part of it."

"Then you will understand—"

"Of course I understand. I understand an alliance is *possible*. But whether this pirate speaks the truth or not is a different matter altogether."

"If he came ashore—"

"He would still be a pirate. They are all pirates." D'Avila pointed an outraged finger at the twin frigates; he swung his arm to a group of the French sunning themselves on the waterfront. "First it was the English. Now Cazaux's men are among us. There is no difference between them. They look the same. They smell the same. Their hearts carry the same greed."

Don Luis could not respond. He stared at d'Avila, at the fury that burned in the single eye. He prayed that the man was wrong, but he possessed no argument with which to convince him.

"It is the gold he stays for," d'Avila went on. "That's what he really wants. He waits for the barbarian Stone to return." As he mentioned Stone's name the little Spaniard felt hatred seize him. He paused, breathing rapidly, holding this personal fury. He must betray none of it to anyone. When the invader who had caused his shame returned, he, d'Avila, would kill him and be redeemed in the eyes of all. But until that precious moment came he would keep his plan to himself. "Cazaux will take all the gold," he continued steadily. "Our share. The king's share. Every last ounce. He will take the gold—and your daughter with it."

Don Luis closed his eyes and restrained his tongue. "They are to be married," was all he permitted himself to say.

"And you believe that lie?" said d'Avila evilly.

"Yes," the mayor replied. "I do."

D'Avila laughed harshly.

Don Luis controlled himself once more. For a day he had considered Jean-Marc Cazaux's words. Carefully, ponderously, he had weighed them, balanced them as best he was able. He had spoken to his daughter and watched the light in her eyes; he had listened to the excitement in her voice. Finally he had decided that he must give the Frenchman an opportunity to prove himself; he had no other choice. What was more, this was not the first time a corsario had come in from the sea. The English were famous for it; it had occurred with the French; it was possible here in Campeche also. He prayed to the blessed Virgin he was not making a mistake, and he believed his prayers might still be answered. The French in the town *were* restrained. Cazaux had kept them supplied with liquor and women, and there had been no rioting. Also, the French captain had handed responsibility for the English prisoners over to the garrison. Don Luis had almost begun to believe his way was becoming smoother when the short, furious figure of d'Avila caught his arm, dragged him down to the waterfront, and pointed to the strength that floated off the shore.

Now, Don Luis was uncertain again. He stared out to sea. The frigates were splendid in the slanting sun, gulls wove patterns in the air, the shallow seas lapped gently. Yet the vessels contained a frightful power, and the thought of it being unleashed on Campeche filled him with dread. It sickened him to imagine what the combined cannon could do.

"We should get help from Mérida," d'Avila muttered. "We should ask the governor to send us troops."

Don Luis said nothing; he clung to his frail determination. There must be more he could do, some way of ensuring that Campeche and his position remained intact. But, as always, he needed time to calculate. Time. Time. Time. Its unremitting force dragged him on.

No, he told himself, struggling against time's pull, I will prevail. One day soon this town will be mine again. But he wondered where his strength would come from.

"I let the monkey go," Ah Cuc said. "I thought all the fighting would scare the poor creature to death."

"That was kind. We will find another."

"I wish I were as free. These ropes are making my fingers swell."

CHAPTER 3

MAGNIFICENT ON THE SHORE, PAXBOLÓN WATCHED AS THE
invaders' craft was released from its moorings. All day
he'd kept his unwavering eyes on the invaders' activi-
ties. Even as his slaves had dressed him, he'd maintained his vigilance. Those from the north had responded
to his challenge. Their attack was about to begin. Now
he saw the clumsy vessel splash unsteadily across the lake.
It went in one direction, then in another, as it lumbered
toward Tayasal like a huge ungainly bird seeking refuge.

Immediately, Paxbolón assembled his commanders.
He called back those canoes already on the water, or-
ganized the fleet in ranks, and ordered it out to attack
the galley. It went, like a swarm of flies.

Paxbolón wore his jaguar fighting mask. His fighting
cape, from the same animal, swung across his shoulders.
In his right hand he carried a stabbing spear. His head
was high, his eyes were level. He was the Fighting
Lord, and this was his hour. He urged those who prepared the special weapon to hurry it into the water, his
mind untouched by doubt.

On board the galley, there were many with equal
confidence. Gottberg, the bosun, beating out a rhythm
for the bearers at the oars, felt calm as the vessel slowly
gained way. Although they were unaccustomed to the
task, those chained to the oars pulled steadily.

Toledo intently watched the city he had come to conquer. His breastplate was freshly polished, the sore at the corner of his mouth forgotten. He had no eyes for the insignificant canoes. Only the sight of Tayasal drawing closer, delivering itself to him by God's grace, held any importance now. It was his dream made real.

Stone waited. He counted the canoes and found their number formidable; yet when he looked at his men he saw they were poised and ready. The Spaniards, as well as his own men, were eager to fight. Even when the first arrows fell, their determination was unaffected: all saw that the high gunnels protected them, and they felt secure, insulated by a belief in their own invincibility. As they made their way over the afternoon water, all were ready to seize their prize.

The Maya in the canoes were as resolute. Although Tutul Katun, his headdress glinting in the pale sunlight, his quetzal-feathered cloak splendid and shielding, was prominent on the bow, and the vulnerability of his position made the Maya bowmen wary, they knew their gods were with them. And even though firing from the canoes would have been difficult enough had he not been placed before them, and most of their arrows missed or thudded into planking or skittered away into the water, they were many and the invaders few.

The Maya could see, behind the palanquin to which Tutul Katun and Ah Cuc were bound, three more of their own, and recognized them as hunters who had gone with the prince. The two guns of the yellow metal were in the palanquin; there were invaders behind them, as there were rows of invaders, and their firearms huddled down throughout the vessel. But none of them came forward with their weapons; none appeared eager to assume any fighting position the Maya knew. Soon those in the canoes began to believe the battle would be swiftly over.

They raised their voices and beat their drums. The cries of their carved wooden trumpets grew shrill. The warriors were painted red, their hair plaited high for battle; in their ears and noses they wore plugs of bone

and pieces of jade. As they paddled toward the limping
craft, they knew their gods would not fail them now.

So when the canoes closed in for the first time and
those on board the galley saw the warriors as true savages bent on death and destruction, the wall of noise
that came from the Maya was suddenly truly frightening.
Faces took shape, eyes rolled, the arrows continued to
hail, and a note of alarm sprang up aboard the galley. All
those who carried muskets lifted their guns and began to
sight them. Their fingers curled about triggers, their
ears were ready for the signal to fire.

Watching them, his eyes excited but his mind clear,
Stone said, "Do not fire yet." In English and in Spanish
he repeated the order. His voice was relaxed and his
command precise. "Wait for me."

More arrows fell; this time a man cried out. A pirate
pulled a barb from his arm; he bound the wound with a
bandana he took from about his neck and waited as the
restlessness increased. There were mutterings now, a
low hum of rising alarm that rumbled below the cries
from the Maya.

The Maya grew more confident. They had fired frequently, without return; they sent more arrows over,
and this time a Red Vest clutched his chest and fell
among his fellows. A great roar went up among the
warriors. Their trumpets shrilled.

Real fear now rippled through the Spanish. The hands
that held their muskets were white and strained, sweat
ran down their faces, one of them began to vomit. And,
from where she crouched behind the palanquin, Guadalupe Santoya heard the shouting, smelled the panic, and
shuddered.

Jaime Toledo felt the tension mount in him like the
winding of a steel spring. He had never fought like this
before, had never faced so many men whose sole desire
was to kill him, and the sight of the twisted features, the
arrows, the bruising sounds that came from all about,
gave him a sensation of crippling restlessness. He did
not know what to do with his hands; he tugged at the
straps of his breastplate, and his breath grew short.

Finally he could wait no longer; he seized Stone's arm. "*When* will you fire! They are almost on us."

"I will fire when I am ready," Stone replied, his eyes on the Maya and their approaching canoes.

Toledo glanced about him: all aboard had turned wide, questioning eyes to Christopher Stone, telling him their time was short.

Then, the canoes almost upon them, Stone gave the signal. "Fire!" he shouted, his voice lifting massively. "Shoot well. Pick your target. Be sure." The guns began before he'd ended.

The volley of shots was ragged, the effect among the Maya one of carnage. Many died. Were wounded. Fell struggling into the water. Their cries of astonishment and pain were piteous. The lake about them turned to red as bellies and chests, heads and limbs, were shattered by the blast. They clawed at each other, they clawed at their own canoes and others', overturning many.

"Reload. Fire again," Stone roared. "As rapidly as you can."

Again the shots went out. Again the Maya died. The redness in the water grew deeper, richer. The musketmen were sure now, the enemy was shattered. They had all the time and courage they needed to concentrate their deadly work. Now there was neither the blare of trumpets nor the boom of drums in their ears, only the cries of the Maya attempting to flee. The very sound improved their aim.

From the island, Paxbolón watched with concern. He stood with his legs apart, his spear clutched as if in use. He bellowed to his commanders: The canoes must return, re-form, ready themselves for another attack. The special weapon must be taken out to where it would be effective. They were yet many, the invaders few; if he held his men together now, the victory would be his. But it must be done immediately, before the desire to flee the dreadful guns tore his troops apart.

Paxbolón knew that if the monstrous vessel, with its firearms and its walls, its core of seasoned men, landed,

it would menace all of Tayasal. Once beached, it would
be twice as difficult to capture: the invaders would have
a fort in which to hide. This knowledge gave him strength.
He seemed to grow as he stood, rocklike, on the shore.
He became a splendid anchor, unmoving, immovable;
his great voice boomed encouragement, urging his captains, restoring his men. Gradually the Maya began to
recover.

"They are beaten," Toledo said triumphantly, watching the disorder. "The Lord has given us a great victory."

"Wait until we are there to take it," Stone replied, his
eye on the jaguar-cloaked figure of Paxbolón. "Wait
until they surrender."

The Mayan canoes attacked again.

Now they spread more widely on the lake, presenting
a less concentrated target, coming to the galley in scattered knots. Twice, a number were close enough for
warriors to attempt to board; each time the cutlasses of
the invaders drove them back.

Jaime Toledo found himself amongst the cutlass bearers, sweeping with great strokes at those who would
dare to touch him. He killed two easily, then a third was
upon him. Toledo drew back his blade and buried it in
the heathen chest. Blood surged from the warrior's mouth,
staining Toledo's breastplate. Then the Maya, the cutlass still protruding from his ribs, slipped back into the
red-running water. Toledo staggered onto the deck,
astounded by how fast his heart was pounding, how
rapidly his lungs dragged at the fetid air.

Then a third attack was mounted, and while those on
the galley were absorbed fighting it off, a cluster of small
boats divided to reveal a pair of larger canoes connected
by a device supporting an underwater platform. On it a
fresh-cut tree trunk, to which massive flints had been
secured, protruded toward the invading craft: a ramrod
fiercely armored. Before any aboard was aware of what
was happening, the heavy flint-tipped trunk, driven by
the paddlemen aboard the large canoes, began to pound
against the galley's woodwork, sending tremors through
them all. There were cries, men reeled, the whole ship

shuddered. The bearers dropped their oars, frantically attempting to escape their chains.

"Sweet Christ," shouted van Staal. He turned toward his captain, but Stone appeared to be indifferent to the thundering. He stood between Henry the Stain and Meredith, each by a culverin, each with a slow match in the hand. "Fire," Stone said, his voice steady. "Fire when ready."

The culverins exploded; the thatched, round-walled house on the island shore was hit. Part of its stonework collapsed, and some of the roof came down. The Maya in the canoes recoiled from the flame, then came in again with their deadly intensity.

"Fire again. Use heavy shot." Stone's voice was even; he could have been at practice. "Then reload with grape."

Henri the Stain and Meredith reloaded and fired again quickly, and more of the building crumbled. Only then did Stone lift his head as if suddenly aware of the pounding. "What is it?" he called. "Are we aground?"

" 'Tis a ram they have," van Staal replied.

"Shoot them away." Stone turned to Gottberg. "Heave," he cried. "Pull, bosun, get the stroke again."

"Aye," Gottberg replied, but his task was hopeless.

The bearers were terrified. Captive on the rough planking, chained to their discarded oars, they struggled against each other, frantic to be free, as once again the Maya closed, climbing onto the flapping oars, hauling themselves up the gunnels, in their efforts to board the galley.

Van Staal assembled marksmen, but the steady battering of the ram made aim almost impossible. The Maya swarmed about their special weapon, removing the dead from the driving canoes, providing fresh power to send it anew into the fresh-caulked, unseasoned timbers of the hastily constructed galley. Their shouting was redoubled now they saw the great ship stagger, as they heard the cries of panic from within.

"Fire!" Stone was among the musketeers. "Row," he yelled at Gottberg's elbow. He knew well the danger that faced them. They were too far from the shore to abandon the galley, the Maya in the water were too thick to pass. They must get closer if they were to have any chance at all. "Move her in," he shouted. "Make way."

Gottberg's eyes grew round, impotent.

"God's blood." Stone leapt down the planking to the center of the galley, where Toledo stood still gasping for breath. "Your men to the oars," he cried.

"What?"

"Get your men to the oars."

"My men are soldiers."

"Dead, if not used. Unchain the bearers."

"No."

Stone argued no more. He reached for the keys that hung from Toledo's belt and ripped them free. He pushed Toledo aside and unlocked those at the oars. He went among them like a cyclone, roaring, his long arms pulling out the wounded, the dead, those too paralyzed with fear to move. He grabbed Spanish soldiers by their red doublets and hurled them into place.

When he looked up, van Staal was beside him doing the same. "Row," the Dutchman shouted. "Take an oar. Closer to the island, or all will drown in this bloodying lake. Row, you whoresons, row!"

Slowly the galley limped closer to the shore. Sluggishly, crippled, attacked from all sides, pounded steadily, she lurched toward the shallows like some great dying monster plagued by ants and leeches.

Now Paxbolón breathed more easily. The special weapon had worked. The craft was drowning. When it came closer the invaders would have to abandon it, and then his men would be ready. Steadily, his voice sure, he ordered the formation of two rows of archers and, behind them, the heaviest of his warriors, who swung the two-handed sword with the obsidian blade, whose blow could cut the head from a horse in a single stroke.

On board the galley, once the bearers were freed they leapt from the doomed vessel, splashing their way through the water, not toward Tayasal but away, back to the shore they had come from. The Maya in the canoes ignored them; many gathered around the stern of the invading ship in an attempt to board her from the rear.

Stone turned to see them begin to claw their way aboard. "God's Blood," he shouted, and caught the nearest in the chest with a bullet. "The muskets!"

Piet the Mulatto and three others raced to the armory bound to the plank. They fired a rattling of close explosions with devastating effect. Some of the Maya were less than two feet from the guns that erupted in their faces. They fell. They screamed. They slipped in their blood. They were blown back into the water by a gale of fire. In a moment the stern was cleared. Those who lay dead or dying were heaved over the side.

Scarcely looking at the slaughter, Stone ordered, "The culverins. Now. The grape." He took a fresh pistol from his belt and fired toward the shore.

Henri the Stain said to Meredith, "We'll cut the shitpots into shreds." He watched the dyed hands of the ex–logwood cutter put the match to the touchhole. "We'll make it now," he added, and lit the cannon before him. "They'll not stand this."

A fearful destruction lashed out at the Maya lined at the landing point. It obliterated. It tore through the two rows of archers like a scythe; it shattered the bowmen like figures of straw. All were strewn as leaves in a bloody wind, red streaks along the waterfront. Fear swept the rest of them away.

"Fire again," Stone roared as the galley lurched and the oars grounded. "Then to the shore. Find cover in the houses. Go while they run. This vessel's done. She will carry us no farther." The cannon blasted again. "Go," he shouted yet again, "before they begin to recover."

Throughout the carnage, the shouting, and the screaming, the stench of gunpowder and of opened men, Guadalupe remained crouched behind the palanquin, her eyes open but unseeing, her face gray with disbelief. She was numbed by the unremitting slaughter; she felt it would never end.

A movement broke her terrified stillness: a hand reached for a fallen cutlass that landed beside her. The hand was Jaime Toledo's. Weapon raised, he turned to

Tutul Katun, bound to the palaquin in front of her. "You pagan sodomist," he shouted, his eyes bleak with fury. "You, at least, will die."

As Toledo raised the cutlass, van Staal knocked it from his grasp. Then Stone was among them. He thundered past Toledo, went to the Maya prince, and drew a knife from his belt.

"We are sinking," the Englishman said. "Take what chance you can." He cut the Maya free.

Tutul Katun stared at the pirate; the words were foreign, but their intent was clear. Then the prince's glance went to Ah Cuc. Stone freed him also. Of the three hunters who had been ranged behind the palanquin, two were dead; the other Stone released.

Then he reached for the unmoving figure of Guadalupe. Lifting her to her feet, he leapt with her into the water and, half carrying her, took the girl ashore. Raggedly, the remainder of the invaders followed, their muskets held above them as they waded away.

As he eased the blood back into his cramped fingers, Tutul Katun watched the disorderly retreat from the galley with calculating eyes. The invaders had proved themselves to be deadly. Even ashore they would be difficult to overcome. Their arms were impressive, their courage significant, and their resourcefulness impressive. He wondered how long it would be before the last of them died and, again, who might be taken with them. Then he turned his pitted face to the sun and was surprised to see how low it was, how little of the day remained. Fighting would now cease, that was the rule of his people: nothing new would occur until tomorrow.

"My lord . . ." Ah Cuc's voice was beside him. "You are untouched?"

"I am well, Ah Cuc," the prince replied.

"I am so glad, my lord. For a time I thought there would be no ending to it."

"The ending is not yet close," Tutul Katun said. "It would be foolish to even give it thought."

With that, his headdress bold in the late afternoon sunlight, his cloak resplendent, he walked to the bloodied stern and waited for his people to arrive and take him away. Soon, Ah Cuc joined him.

Ah Cuc's careful tongue was quiet a moment, then he asked, "What will happen now, my lord?"

"Of that I am not sure," Tutul Katun replied. "But I look forward to the new day with great interest."

"Perhaps someone should speak with these invaders, now that they are among us," Ah Cuc suggested quietly.

"Perhaps someone should."

They looked at each other and smiled briefly, then turned to watch the final scramble for safety as the enemy went ashore. They watched until the invaders went to the stone-and-mortar house opposite the one that had been destroyed by cannonfire. They watched until the last of them had disappeared, and only then did they acknowledge the canoes that waited to take them ashore.

Surrounded by tapestries of claret and gold, seated at the chart table with its elaborate legs and splendid covering, Angela de Córdoba Martinez and Jean-Marc Cazaux dined off silver plate pirated from the citizens of Campeche and sipped the cloudy greenish liquid that gave shape to dreams.

"They said I was mad, but I knew you'd come back," Angela said, her voice resonant with satisfaction and amusement. "My poor father, how he despaired." Her laughter filled the cabin. "And now, to think he would permit me to marry a corsario. I am amazed."

"A corsario of noble blood," Cazaux said with a flourish. "His manner improved when I told him that."

"Nevertheless, a cruel and ruthless pirate."

"True." Cazaux touched her satiny-smooth shoulder and felt desire. "Though I become less cruel and ruthless every day." He gazed at her beauty as if seeing it for the first time. "I could not exist without you."

"They say you are here for the gold," Angela said, her tone teasing, her eyes level. "Not for me at all."

"Who speaks such lies?"

Angela shrugged. "There are rumors," she said, her voice sly.

"Who utters them?"

"I do not know." Angela laughed again. "But I do not believe them for a moment." She lifted a forkful of meat to her mouth and chewed on it heartily. "May I," she began, then lowered her eyes modestly. "May I ask a favor?"

"Of course." Cazaux leaned closer. "Anything."

"The, the blackamoor, is he well?"

"The ruffian I captured on the *Courage*?" Cazaux spread a long-fingered hand. "As well as any in the dungeons. Why do you ask?"

"He was"—Angela's voice dropped chastely—"he was good to me while, while I waited."

"Good to you?" Cazaux's tone had altered.

Angela nodded her bowed head. "I, I pretended you had sent him," she continued quietly. "It was a game that gave me hope." She lifted her gaze suddenly and saw Cazaux glow. "So, you see, I would wish to help him now, if I were able."

Cazaux cleared his throat. "He was, he was good to you, you say?"

"He is a true gentleman," Angela replied, then reached for another forkful of meat. Survival was largely a selfish matter, but she would do what she could. "He deserves to be repaid in kind," she added.

"In kind?"

"Some food, a blanket, whatever he might need." Angela sipped a little green liquid, shuddered, and reached for a glass of wine. "Something to repay him for the gallantry he showed me."

"Well . . ." Cazaux shrugged. "I will do what I can. After all, it is to my advantage to keep him alive. But as you know, in good faith, I have handed the prisoners over to the garrison. However—"

"Oh, I thank you, I thank you." Angela wiped her lips; she took Cazaux's hand and placed her cheek against it. The fire in her body burned like fever. "Anything to make his stay more comfortable."

Cazaux nodded. With his free hand he picked up a piece of wild fowl and returned it to the plate untasted.

Not for the first time, he wondered who had pirated whom. Yet when he looked into the gorgeous eyes, the thought dissolved. She could have known nothing when she was dragged into the council chamber. What could she possibly have planned before he brought her here? The notion was absurd. He pressed his fingers into her flesh, accepting the fact of possession.

"*Merde*," Cazaux breathed, "you will yet render me merciful."

"My love." Angela's lips came closer as there was a knock on the cabin door. The gentle-faced duty boy entered carrying a tray. "*Mon capitaine*," he said as he began to clear the table, "would you wish me to stay?" He spoke in French, and his voice was low.

"I do not wish more than I have," Cazaux replied in the same language. He ran his long fingers through Angela's hair and watched as her gaze went from one to the other, her eyes very bright; she could taste excitement on her tongue. "Go to Sartou," he added. "He always has need for more."

"M'sieu Sartou is rough, and his breath is bad."

"Tell him to be gentle. And give him fresh rum."

"Oui, *mon capitaine*." The duty boy sounded disappointed. "Will that be all, m'sieu?"

"Yes," Cazaux replied. "That will be all." He sighed. "I think my crew will mutiny," he said when the boy had gone. "They will have no desire to sail with such charity."

"Are they not afraid of you?" Angela asked mischievously. "Do you not fill them with terror?"

"I did." Cazaux's lips explored; his voice was becoming light. "Once, I did."

"Will you?" The intoxication was rich in Angela's throat. "Will you fill me with terror? Now?"

"I will." Cazaux stood, lifted the girl, and carried her across the cabin to where the huge four-poster bed lay waiting. "I promise you, I will."

As they went beneath the draperies, entwined with silver cord, Angela's bell-like laughter filled the cabin, its full notes were interwoven with the richness of pleasure. For the moment, her ambitions were complete.

*   *   *

In the dungeons of the fort, tied by wrist and ankle, the twenty-three members of the crew of the *Courage* huddled uncomfortably about the mildewed walls. Rats scuffled in dank corners, the air was foul and cloying, the little light that came through an archer's window was heavy with mold.

Two of the men were now ill. Marchand, a young rigger, slumped in a pool of bloodied feces; his face was drawn with pain, his head hung to his chest, his breathing heavy. He had the flux, and all who watched him knew he'd die unless taken from the dungeon. Another of them, Lambe, a redheaded gunner, had it also, but he was tougher and as yet not drained.

" 'Tis biscuit they need, and beef," murmured Alec Carson, cook and surgeon from the *Courage*. "Not this scummy gruel they've given us. We sent them better than we get."

"I want ale," said Lambe. "That'll bind me."

"It's us to blame," said Percy Flanders, his Cornish accent soft and whispery. "If we'd watched, they'd never have taken us."

"Aye," agreed Cramer, dark in a patch of darkness. "You speaks the truth."

"What's to be done?" asked d'Lesseps. "We'll all be like poor Marchand, soon enough. Wish I'd never left the shores of Guernsey."

"There's nothing to be done," replied another voice. "We've nothing to pay with, so there's nowt to be done."

"Well now, I wonder." Cramer moved his legs, and the sound of irons echoed softly. "Perhaps there's a way."

"How?" Marchand's head lifted slightly. "We've no . . ." he began, but was unable to continue.

"We've promises," said Cramer softly, and there was promise in his voice. "They's greedy swine, the lot of them. But Alvaréz, the fat one who watches over us, he's the hungriest." He scratched the stub of his missing ear. "Now, if I was to promise him a handful of gold, he'd listen."

"Gold?" Lambe grunted. "We've no gold."

"Not yet," said Cramer. "Not till the captain's back."

"The captain?" queried a voice from the darkness. "He's dead for all we know."

"He'll be back," said Cramer quickly. "He'll be back with gold for all."

"What if this Alvaréz did believe us?" asked Percy Flanders, catching something of Cramer's mood, "What then?"

"He'll give us what we asks for."

"Food," someone said. "Good beef."

"Ale," said Lambe.

Other voices joined, there was a lifting of spirit, the stirring of chain, the rattle of irons. "Clean the shit off the floor," said Alec Carson. "Put down some straw." The darkness seemed less dense.

"Will he, will he clean me?" Marchand asked weakly. "And get me a blanket?"

" 'Course he will, my lad," said Cramer soothingly; he knew what dreams were made of. "He'll bring anything we wants."

"Thank you." Marchand's head went back to his chest. "It's so cold down here at night."

"Aye," called the voice from the corner. "He'll fetch you a blanket, just you see."

Cramer listened. It was a trick he had learned from the captain, it was a process he had lived through on all those afternoons. It gave Cramer faith to hear it working through himself. Somehow it was not important to think how many lives, if any, it might save; all that mattered now was to feel the men respond.

"Listen," Cramer said, "this is what we'll do."

His deep voice droned, the men about him listened; he fashioned a shape they could cling to, he spun a dream for them all to hold. The light from the archer's window became less green, cold retreated from the stones.

CHAPTER 4

THE HOUSE IN WHICH THOSE FROM THE GALLEY SHELTERED, opposite the one destroyed by cannon fire, was solidly built on the water's edge. Its occupants had fled when the culverins hurled their round shot at the shore—they had, obviously, been wealthy.

The walls of the room where the survivors assembled were paneled with wood carved in low relief, showing scenes of hunting parties, of warriors gripping prisoners by the hair. In one panel a priest cut the heart from a man held by four others over a block of stone. Cotton tapestries, rich works in bright colors, decorated with features and beads of jade, hung between the wall panels. Cushions were scattered, mats lay where they'd been left. In other rooms were stocks of food and drink.

Of the thirty-four fighting men who had boarded the galley, twenty-seven had survived; four of them were wounded, but surprisingly few had been killed outright by Mayan arrows. Stone moved among them, assessing their strength. Now that they were contained within four walls, they seemed more cheerful, almost relaxed. Their clothing was drying, the shouts of the Maya and the thud of their arrows was behind them. There was the comforting smell of cooking in the house; there was the sound of cutlasses being sharpened against stone.

198

Stone crossed to where van Staal was dressing a wound
in the thigh of one of the pirates. An arrow had ripped
shallowly through the flesh and the Dutchman was rubbing fat from the stomach of a dead Maya into the slash.

"How many of ours are hurt?" Stone asked.

"Only Goode here." Van Staal looked up. "But the
three Spaniards are badly sore."

Stone grunted. "What weapons do we have?" he
inquired.

"Our own. Each Spaniard has his musket. And there's
a barrel of powder Henri the Stain brought with him."

"Thank God for that."

"They'll leave us alone, this night," van Staal went
on. "They'll make their noise, and they'll pray to their
gods. But they won't attack before it's light."

"I hope you are right, but we'll take no chances.
Have guards set at each corner of the building. Change
the watches each two hours. We shall keep alert in spite
of what you say."

Van Staal nodded. "They will return in the morning,"
he said before Stone left, drawing on what he'd learned
of the Maya while chained to them in the Venezuelan
mines. "But whether to fight or talk, we will have
to see."

"Why would they talk?" asked Stone.

"They live by what their gods tell them. They have
faith in the signs. If the signs are for talk, they will
talk."

"And if not?"

"They will fight."

Stone nodded thoughtfully and left to find Toledo in a
corner of the paneled room, bent over a soldier obviously dying. The man's stomach had been opened, he
lay on his back holding his intestines in place. He was
young, and tears streamed down his cheeks. Stone stared
a moment, then turned away.

He went into the kitchen where Guadalupe crouched
by a large earthenware pot embedded in a charcoal fire.
Stone reached down and placed a hand gently on her
neck; she looked up and, in spite of the hollowness of

her eyes and the fear that strained her face, smiled
briefly. They did not speak, there was no need.

Outside, the night was still; the trumpets had died,
and the drums were quiet. There was no moon. Mist lay
over the lakewater, muffling the island and its city.

Canek, the king, eased his buttocks on his cushion
and listened to what Tutul Katun had to say of the
invaders. They were curious, these men who came from
the north. There was no gold for them, that had been
made clear; nor did they seem to be concerned with
taking his people as slaves. Perhaps this attack was
something their gods had instructed them to do. Whatever the reason, Canek prayed they could be dealt with
quickly. Their presence here was uncomfortable, and
the damage they had inflicted was already great.

"They are difficult to kill," Tutul Katun was saying.
"Not many died in spite of the arrows."

"It is because they hid behind you and the walls of
their craft," Paxbolón said with contempt. "They do not
come out and fight as warriors."

"That is true, my brother," Tutul Katun acknowledged. "It is one of the reasons why they are so
dangerous."

"They will not escape us now," Paxbolón said loudly.
"We have them trapped in the house of Tutz."

"Of course," Tutul Katun agreed. "But they are determined fighters. And their leaders are most resourceful."

Paxbolón and Tutul Katun sat at a level below their
father in a long narrow room whose walls were covered
with further panels displaying the pomp and majesty of
Maya nobles. In the flickering light of oil lamps, the
wall-figures came alive.

"You say these leaders fight among themselves?"
Canek asked abruptly.

"They do not fight, nor do they agree," Tutul Katun
replied. "They have their differences. But, of them all,
the Pale One is the strongest. Without him they could do
little."

"There is little they can do now," Paxbolón said

impatiently. "The great firearms of yellow metal, that killed so many, are drowned with their vessel. They cannot escape from where they are."

"Nevertheless, we should be patient." Tutul Katun's voice was humble. "Not that I would presume to suggest strategy to you, my brother. But you might think of talking to them first."

"What is to be said? None will leave Tayasal alive."

"Of course, but we do not wish to kill them all in battle, is that not so?"

"You know that is so. Itzamná demands the hearts of the leaders."

"So, if you were to speak with them, you would be able to assess their strength accurately." Tutul Katun paused and almost smiled. "Also, a way might occur to you in which they could be taken alive."

Canek grunted and patted the mound of his stomach. His younger son was so very clever, it was a pity they had been born in their order. "We will wait to see what the morning sacrifices suggest," the old king said. "But what you say, my younger son, is worthwhile thinking upon." Canek placed a hand over his mouth to cover a yawn. "Tomorrow early we will meet again. In the meantime I will sleep."

Canek watched his sons exit backward. He hoped that the morrow would see the end of these invaders, and he could continue his life without such demanding intrusions.

Stone stared up into almost darkness. In the center of the great hall a solitary oil lamp burned, about it the survivors slept. They were one less now, the Spaniard with the torn stomach had died an hour earlier. He lay where he had lain in life, but in the morning something would be done about the body. Stone felt a small movement beside him and turned his head; he had thought the girl asleep.

"Cristóbal?"

"What?"

"I, I must kill you before they make you a prisoner," she whispered in a voice that was filled with pain.

Stone held his breath.

Guadalupe went on, "If they take you alive, your death will be terrible."

"And you would kill me swiftly." In spite of an attempt to lighten his words, Stone could not keep the stiffness from his voice. "Is that what you would do?"

"It would be better."

"And what of you?"

"I would kill myself."

"Dear God." Stone reached out and held her close. He felt himself tremble. "Would that I could offer as much."

"Will you promise what I ask?"

"No."

"Why not?"

"Because it will not come to that." His long arms tightened around her. "Nor will we speak of it further."

"But—"

"Shhh, be silent while I love you. That, also, is a form of death."

They moved closer; their breathing quickened. About them the others slept. Above, the city of Tayasal, in the white-stone temple, Itzamná, the hideous god, sat poised in his bloodstained courtyard. Out on the lake water, the galley drifted.

The morning began with the sacrifice of quail. As the sun came up in a golden ball, the breasts of the birds— blue black as the night, whose white spots were the stars of the night, were opened, and the fluttering hearts were presented to the sun.

Bacal, high priest of the Itzá, watched as his acolytes killed the shining birds. As the blood spread the sun rose steadily. Bacal was pleased. This will be a better day, he promised Kinich Ahau, the sun god. Soon the disbelievers will die.

The sun rose higher, its light burned into the face of the great temple. On the topmost platform, where Bacal and his attendants stood, all were forced to hide their eyes from the new day's rising power. It burnished the four images of Muluc, patron of the day, as they towered behind the priests; it filled the morning with its promising glow.

Bacal pulled his black cloak about his tall thin body and turned from the sun. He was dark-skinned, and his hair was dark; it hung below his waist in matted braids, and it stank of blood. To show his belief in the power of his gods, Bacal repeatedly slashed his ears and his lips with a finely honed obsidian blade. He allowed his blood to flow freely for all to see. It was never washed away; it reeked of its own decay. Bacal had offered his blood most recently as the invaders came over the lake. He would offer more today and every day until they were scourged from these shores.

They offended greatly, these pale creatures from the north, and now they were in the house of Tutz, second only to himself in the priestly hierarchy. Their presence in so holy a place was a total abomination. Angrily, Bacal stared down at the house by the water. Their deaths would come soon, of that he felt confident: the quail had bled well, the sky had been white, virginal, ready for the fire of Kinich Ahau. The sun had risen steadily. All the signs were excellent. Very soon Itzamná would have his rightful offering. Very soon the city would be clean again.

Christopher Stone woke to the sound of van Staal's voice. The great hall was almost empty, the body of the dead soldier had been taken away. Guadalupe was gone.

"God's blood," Stone said, climbing from his bedding. "What has—?"

"We let you sleep," van Staal said easily. "There was no cause to disturb you"

"The men?" Stone looked about the paneled room.

"In better heart. They have eaten and are rested."

Stone laced up his breeches and began to draw on his boots. He felt amazingly refreshed. He glanced up at van Staal; the Dutchman also appeared recovered.

"What of those outside?" Stone asked.

"I have seen their priests on the temple. But none has

approached us yet." Van Staal rubbed a hand over his
head. "I am having powder chests prepared," he went
on. "With the barrel that Henri the Stain brought ashore.
Some to be wrapped in cloth, for throwing if they
come close-packed."

Stone nodded. He stood as Jaime Toledo approached.
The Creole seemed older, there were deep lines beneath
his eyes. His mouth was drawn, and the sore at its
corner was crusted with dried blood. The fervor that had
burned in his youthful eyes was now replaced with uncertainty. He stared at Stone, trying to assess the
Englishman's state of mind.

"These bombs," Toledo began, then paused to lick
his lips. "These devices they are making? I've not seen
their like before."

"Powder chests," van Staal explained. "Buccaneer's
tools. Powder mixed with bullets, stones, whatever you've
to hand."

"In pots of earthenware."

"Anything will do," van Staal continued. "With a
fuse to fire them. Although some will fire alone."

"Will they?" Again Toledo hesitated. Then he straightened his back: his belief must not desert him now. "Will
they be enough? We are so few."

"Enough to bargain with," Stone said. "The Maya
know our guns, they have felt our cutlasses. If we surprise them now with something new, they will talk to
us."

"Talk to us." Toledo stared, trying hard to maintain
faith. "What will they talk to us about?"

Stone smiled at the Creole, recognizing his need. "If
we frighten them enough, they will bargain," he said,
his voice confident. "After all, they are only Indians?"

"Of course, but—?"

"Inferior people who respect strength . . . is that
not so?"

Toledo's eyes flickered. "You are mocking me," he
said. He felt a touch of his former arrogance and was
grateful.

"Only because it is necessary."

Toledo lifted his chin. "The Lord God is on our side. The Virgin Mary will protect us," he stated clearly.

"Especially if we take some pains to protect ourselves," Stone added. "Now, talk to your men. Tell them we have new weapons. Get them in good heart." He smiled briefly. "We are all needed."

Toledo nodded. He walked away with some determination in his step. Briefly, his breastplate caught a ray of early light.

Alvaréz, the fat Spanish jailer, could not imagine why good fortune should have smiled on him so warmly. True, he had been to mass recently, and he confessed regularly, but he could not think of any particular reason why the Blessed Virgin should favor him so, especially at the moment.

First of all, the prisoners from the *Courage* had offered to reward him with gold if he were to provide them reasonable food, a blanket each, and a little straw for the floor. It was a transaction he had accepted honorably. After all, it was only recently that he had been imprisoned himself, and he knew how unpleasant the dungeons could be. Especially at night, especially if the dead were not removed, with the rats gnawing at them and the water dribbling down the mildewed walls. Alvaréz shuddered. It did not bear recalling.

And then, just when he had begun to consider how their request might be accommodated, food and blankets had arrived from the French. It could not have been better placed. It was bewildering. He could not imagine how it had come about. But he was extremely grateful. All that he needed to search for now was the straw for the floor, and that was a simple matter.

Alvaréz whistled as he went to look for it. Life in Campeche was showing great new promise. He hoped it would continue for a long time to come.

"They are here," van Staal said, entering the kitchen. "They have come to talk."

"What?" Stone looked up from the bowl of food on

the table before him. It was a dish of beans and meat
Guadalupe had prepared. "Who comes?"

"Two captains and two priests," van Staal explained.
"Their hands are empty and held out."

Stone glanced at Guadalupe, who was tending the
cooking pot. She nodded briefly, when he asked for confirmation. "Where are they?" the Englishman questioned
van Staal.

"By the main entrance." Van Staal paused, tapping a
finger to his lips thoughtfully. "I will bring them into the
hall, when you are ready," he said. "Sit above them.
And do not speak to them unless it is necessary.
Let the girl speak, say what you have to say to her."

Again Stone questioned Guadalupe, speaking to her in
Spanish. "That is wise," she replied. "These are not the
leaders who come. It is right that you show you know
it."

"So be it," Stone said. "When I have done with my
breakfast, I will be ready for them."

"That is as it should be," Guadalupe confirmed quietly. "They would do the same."

Stone picked up a piece of meat with his fingers.
"Toledo will be with us," he added thoughtfully. "We
cannot keep him away. So, speak to him, Rolf, easily.
Ask him to control himself. At least until we see what
these people want."

Van Staal nodded and left the kitchen.

When the four Maya came into the long hall with its
carvings of beauty and death, they found the Pale One
seated on a large cushion at the far end of the room.
Beside him, also seated, were Round Skull and Silver
Chest; the girl who spoke the language squatted on the
floor before them.

The Maya captains approached and bowed. They were
handsome men whose terra-cotta skin was clean of
warpaint. Their heads were bare, each wore a short
feathered cloak and a loincloth. The priests shuffled
behind them, their black cloaks held tightly about their
bodies. Their faces reflected their anger at the offense
being committed by the presence of the invaders in the
house of Tutz.

The taller of the two captains spoke, and Guadalupe translated. "They send you greetings from Canek, king of the Itzá. He is impressed with your courage and the power of your weapons."

She spoke without turning, and Stone grunted.

"I shall return the greeting," Guadalupe said. "After that they will tell us why they have come."

Stone remained unmoving on his cushion. From where he sat he could smell the priests: they stank of blood, they reeked of decay. Their presence gave him the desire to spit.

Guadalupe readdressed the captains. They bowed to acknowledge the return of formality, then they spoke at length.

"They say they have come to discuss how further bloodshed might be avoided, but I do not believe them," Guadalupe informed the others. "They say they come in peace, but I think it is to spy."

"What would they discuss?" asked van Staal.

"They say they have a proposal to make us," Guadalupe reported a moment later. "A suggestion which would mean that not everyone should die."

"They seem very confident," van Staal observed.

"Yes," Guadalupe replied quietly, "they are."

"What are their filthy priests doing here?" Toledo hissed the words, his face pale with outrage. He had remained silent, withstanding the blood-caked creatures for as long as he could. Now his furious words boiled for release. "Why have these obscenities come here?"

"Patience," van Staal urged. "Do not display such venom."

"I cannot do otherwise," Toledo replied. "They are disgusting."

Van Staal leaned forward to Guadalupe. "Ask them why the priests are here," he said calmly. "After all, this is a council of war."

Almost immediately Guadalupe had a reply. "This house is holy," she told the others. "It belongs to the second highest of their order. They have come to cleanse it."

"Cleanse it?" Toledo's voice was poison. "Who in God's name do they think they're talking to?"

"Be patient," said van Staal carefully. He leaned again to Guadalupe. "What would they do to cleanse it?" he asked.

Guadalupe spoke to the Maya once more, then said, "They demand a sacrifice." Her face had gone the color of chalk, she stared steadily at the floor, trying to control her shock.

Van Staal swallowed; his mouth had dried. He glanced at Stone, but the hawklike features of the Englishman told him nothing. On the far side of Stone, Toledo's restlessness seemed about to break, but, manfully, he contained himself. "What, what do they require in the way of a sacrifice?" van Staal asked. He was surprised by the loudness of his words in his ears.

Guadalupe questioned the Maya; then she whispered, "They want nine of our people. Including Silver Chest. That is what they call Señor Toledo. If we give them the nine, they will let us go." Her voice trailed away, became insignificant in the elaborate Mayan hall.

"What?" Van Staal cleared his throat. He knew enough of the language to have followed most of the conversation, but he wanted to be sure. "What will happen to the nine?" he asked.

"Their hearts will be offered to the gods." Guadalupe lifted her eyes to a wall panel on which a priest was cutting the heart from a man. She stared at it fixedly; for her, at that moment, there was nothing else in the room. "They will go to Itzamná," she whispered. "He is the god they make such sacrifices to."

At that Toledo's outrage almost broke. He growled and would have come to his feet, but Stone's hand went out and held him, and the Spaniard remained: furious, white-faced with impatience, struggling within, he nonetheless remained.

"And they say that if this is done, the rest of us will be allowed to leave?" van Staal continued.

Guadalupe nodded.

"Do you believe them?"

Guadalupe lowered her eyes. "No," she whispered.

For long moments no one moved. The Maya captains waited; the priests stood behind them darkly, their faces flat with hate. Van Staal remained silent, listening to the beating of his heart. Toledo continued, Stone's hand on his arm, his eyes not leaving the detested figures of the priests. Only Stone appeared untouched. He remained, staring at the group before him, his face still, his expression disclosing nothing.

Then the taller of the Maya captains spoke, and Guadalupe translated. "They want an answer," she said, forcing the words. "They become impatient."

When van Staal opened his mouth to deny the hideous demand, making no attempt to hide his feelings, Stone turned to him, caught his arm, and whispered in his ear. Immediately van Staal's face froze in disbelief.

"Are you sure?" the Dutchman finally asked, his tone bewildered. "Do you—?"

Stone nodded, cutting him short.

Van Staal shook his head in confusion; he licked his lips. At last he spoke, staring bleakly at the Maya. "Tell them it will be done," he said roughly to Guadalupe, biting out the words he wanted no part of. "Tell them their demand will be granted."

"No." Guadalupe stiffened, then turned to Stone, her desperate eyes appealing. "No."

Stone ignored her.

"That is what he said," van Staal gritted. "Tell them."

"I, I do not believe it."

"Tell them." Van Staal's voice rose in anger, in impotence, in release. "Tell them we agree."

As Guadalupe hesitatingly, uncertainly, feeling for words, began her translation, Jaime Toledo came to his feet and moved forward as if to attack the Maya. His face was gray. His eyes were fierce with loathing and betrayal. "*I* will not permit this outrage," he shouted. "I will die fighting if I have to. But I will not be led obscenely to their filthy gods." His outburst caused the Maya to step backward. He swung to Stone. "You mongrel son of a whore!" he screamed.

"Silence," Stone said, his voice was cold as ice. "Keep him quiet," he told van Staal. "Hold him."

"No," Toledo raved as, reluctantly, the Dutchman took him by the arm. "They will have none of us to sacrifice. None, do you hear? None!"

The Maya captains watched the short struggle with curiosity and some confusion. They glanced at each other, and then the taller of them came forward again and spoke to Guadalupe.

"They want to know if he is being given to them now," she said a moment later, her voice as bitter as van Staal's.

"No." Stone spoke again.

"They say—"

"They will wait. Tell them they can have what they ask for in the morning," Stone continued coldly. "All nine of them. But they'll not get a soul today."

Guadalupe spoke again to the Maya. They listened. They questioned. They waited for replies. But Stone had nothing more to say. Van Staal was silent. Jaime Toledo stared at them all with detestation. Finally the two captains bowed formally, retreated a few paces, then turned and marched from the hall. Behind them the priests shuffled, their glances covering, with distaste, the house that remained defiled.

When they had gone none of the others moved. Their eyes remained on the open door through which the Maya had departed, all hoping for another entry, the arrival of someone or something to shatter the appalling unreality surrounding them.

Except Stone. He remained, his eyes hooded, his face closed, for some minutes, then stood abruptly and strode from the room, leaving nothing behind, not even the movement of the air through which he'd passed.

CHAPTER 5

It was late in the day when González entered the mayoral chamber, an hour at which he might ordinarily have been willing to sit in the comfortable little oak-paneled room with its leather-bound books of law and its bundles of municipal papers. Through a mullioned window was a view of the darkening hills behind the nestled town: they looked like softly folded cloth in the dying light.

It was a time at which González might have taken a glass of sherry and a sweet biscuit and talked politely with the mayor. No friendship existed between them, but certain formalities were maintained. But this evening he had no such courtesy in mind.

The town treasurer barely returned the mayor's greeting. He merely nodded and noted with some pleasure that Don Luis's eyes were faintly red, that his face was distinctly gray. Then he leaned forward over the mayor's desk, addressing him without preliminaries.

"You understand that these circumstances cannot be permitted to continue?" the treasurer began in a voice that was cold and distant.

"What circumstances?" Don Luis gazed at the thin and waspish face before him and eased his weight back into his tiled chair, away from his mahogany desk. "What circumstances do you refer to?"

"The condition of the council, of course." González's little mouth clipped out the words. "The state of affairs here in Campeche is appalling."

"How can you say that?" Don Luis inquired.

He'd succeeded lately, or so he'd believed, in drawing the reins of office tighter. He'd made a point of being present at the Municipal Building most of each day. He'd issued a declaration, which had been nailed prominently throughout the town, explaining what it was the French flags on the frigates represented to them all. War had been declared by Spain, Campeche was enveloped by that ordinance, and certain restrictions would need to be applied. But he'd assured every free citizen that when the expedition led by Councilor Jaime Toledo returned with the Itzá gold, the pirates from the *Courage* would be arrested, the curfews would be lifted, and life would continue as normal.

He'd pointed out that Jean-Marc Cazaux, captain of *La Petite,* had been commissioned to act as municipal architect and would give his special attention to defense. Together with Capitán d'Avila, the restored commander of the garrison, they would work to ensure that Campeche remained secure.

So far, Don Luis had been satisfied by the reaction of his declaration. Until this arrival of González, no voice had been raised in dissent. Everyone, it seemed, recognized the need for certain restrictions. No one had drawn attention to the brutal irony of appointing the French captain to the office of the man he'd slain. Perhaps it was accepted that one, quite clearly, led to the other.

The mayor studied González' sharp little features, wondering what the treasurer had in mind. This visit had a purpose, that much was clear, it was designed to accomplish more than the adding of a further sneer; it sought something deeper, that would emerge in a moment.

"Quite soon we will be left in peace." Don Luis spread his hands widely. "I have already written to the governor—"

"Don't be so stupid." González's face came forward

savagely. "Do you really believe you will be rid of them that easily? Do you think—?"

"Why not?" Don Luis lifted the level of his voice to match the treasurer's. "Why should we have problems? Capitán Cazaux—"

"Capitán Cazaux?" González could contain himself no longer. He bent over the mayor, his tiny lips snipping like scissors. "My God, what do you think you are doing? Have you gone mad?"

Don Luis stared up; in spite of his determination, he blinked.

"The council has not had a meeting in over a month," González went on rapidly. "Its power has been usurped. *You* have no *authority* any longer. Not over anything. In the name of all that is holy, have you lost your reason completely?"

Don Luis wet his lips; he was forced to look away. They had no right to bully him like this. Neither of them, González nor d'Avila. They failed to understand the burden he bore, the responsibility he carried, the long hours he lay awake trying to solve the problems that surrounded them all. What is more, he *had* succeeded well enough. The port was active again. The Spanish garrison had been freed. Trade came and went. Mérida's mind had been put to rest. Angela was happy.

"Not even over your daughter," González continued ruthlessly, as if he'd captured the thought. "Is there nothing sane or decent about you anymore?"

"Silence." Don Luis abruptly slapped the desk before him. In that instant he would have done anything to stop the thin venom pouring from the cutting mouth. "I will not have you mention her."

"Don't you understand what is happening to her? With your precious Capitán Cazaux?" González's scissor lips were cruel. "She has become his whore."

"Silence!" This time the word was a roar.

"You heard me."

"Silence." Don Luis stood. He spread his arms, the further to widen what was, in truth, a plea. "They will marry."

"That," said González acidly, "I will believe when I see it happen." He stared at the mayor with contempt.

"They will marry," Don Luis repeated, but some of the certainty had gone from his voice. "Toledo will return with the gold. Campeche will prosper." He mouthed the litany, forcing the prayer. "You will see. Believe me, you will see."

"I will see none of it."

"You will, I promise."

"You are no longer capable of promising anything." González pulled his doublet sharply, and it snapped across his shoulders. "I intend to have you removed from office," he said, stating at last what he had come for. "I intend to take over the council, send to Mérida for troops, and, once and for all, return to Campeche its honor and its pride."

"You cannot."

"I can, and I will."

"No." Stubbornly Don Luis shook his head, fighting back as best he was able, knowing that he must try to maintain what little he possessed. "This is a purchased office," he continued, watching the treasurer's face. "Bought and paid for in full by me."

González smiled; he knew his ground. "That does not mean it cannot be sold from under you," he said confidently.

"That is a lie," Don Luis maintained, realizing that the treasurer spoke the truth. The Spanish crown was in such need of funds that almost any office could be purchased nowadays. If González were to offer a sufficiently attractive sum, which he, Don Luis, couldn't match, the proposition might easily be accepted. "This post is mine until I care to renounce it," Don Luis went on, painfully now. He could no longer hold the treasurer's eye. It was days now since he'd had a drink, but at this moment the need for cognac caused his throat to tighten. "You know that as well as I do," he concluded dryly.

González merely laughed. "If the council were to withdraw its support—" he began, and that was enough.

"But, but," Don Luis protested, "under the terms of the declaration I have distributed, the council will not meet. We are at war—"

"On the contrary," González interrupted savagely, "if it wishes to do so, the council can certainly meet." He smiled then: a thin, unlovely line of stinging pleasure. "I shall see to it, *Your Worship*," he added sarcastically. "I shall see to it that it meets immediately."

With that the confident treasurer turned and left.

Alone, Don Luis remained, attempting to still the trembling of his hands. It was true. Part of it. Enough of it. There could easily be a sufficient number of council members prepared to condemn him. Don Luis closed his eyes and pressed his hands into them as something like a sob rose in his throat. He held himself, wondering what there was he could do now to arrest the damage within and without. Then he lifted his head and breathed deeply: he must find a way to bargain.

"Why do you not believe him, my son?" Canek asked Tutul Katun carefully. "The Pale One is the strongest. If he says the nine will be offered, why should it not be so?"

"He *is* the strongest," Tutul Katun agreed. He sat on the floor of the long narrow room whose walls were covered with elaborate panels between Bacal and Paxbolón, facing up to his father. "But he is also the cleverest. It is possible he requires time to plan."

"What could he plan?" asked Paxbolón impatiently. "What plan is possible? They cannot escape. We can take them whenever we wish."

"Of course, my brother. But the house of Tutz is solidly built. The battle could be fierce. Many of our people would die, and we might not take their leaders alive."

"Their presence in the house of Tutz is an offense." Bacal spoke savagely, his voice a vibrant whisper. "They must be removed from there. Their blood must be used to cleanse it."

"That is true," Tutul Katun agreed quietly, and bowed

slightly in deference to the priest. "But without their hearts to offer, those who watch over us might not welcome their deaths."

"Itzamná demands the hearts of the leaders." Bacal intoned the only tract that applied. "What he demands he must be given."

"Again you speak the truth," Tutul Katun replied. "That is why we must be careful." He turned to Paxbolón and, in a voice hushed with respect, continued. "I am sure you know how these invaders will be taken, my brother," he said. "But it does not seem fair to leave you alone with this great responsibility. We must offer our suggestions, no matter how foolish they seem."

Paxbolón's eyes narrowed a little. "I will do what I know to be right," he said carefully.

"Of course, we seek only to help."

Canek watched and listened. His younger son was as clever as anyone he had ever encountered. He wondered if Paxbolón would pay much attention to his brother but did not think it likely. After all, Paxbolón was the Fighting Lord responsible for warfare. His destruction of the invaders' vessel had been formidable. This was not his moment to accept anyone else's advice.

"Itzamná grows impatient," Bacal growled, breaking the small silence. He drew his cloak more tightly about his stringy body and felt blood ooze from the fresh cuts on his ears. Tonight he would open his penis and offer its blood to his god. He feared the impatience of Itzamná, feared what the god's rage might do to the crops of the coming season or the sons who were about to be born. "We must offer these heathen hearts as soon as we can," he hissed.

"It will be done," Canek said, and eased his buttocks on his deerhide cushion. "It will be done as soon as it can be done."

Tutul Katun cleared his throat politely. "Might it not be wise to send these invaders something?" he suggested. "Something to give the impression that we accept their word. Even if we do not really believe what they say."

"What sort of thing would you send?" Paxbolón asked, watching his brother carefully.

"Some food, a few gifts." The younger prince's pitted face was conciliatory. "Perhaps some women."

"Nothing." Paxbolón shook his head forcefully. "They do not fight honorably. They deserve nothing."

"It might be wise," Canek said thoughtfully. "It may make them less cautious in the morning."

"You would give them our women?" Paxbolón's voice was controlled, but anger bubbled beneath the surface. "The food we eat?"

"Pick out ugly women," Canek replied; with both hands he lifted the weight of his paunch. "Send them inferior food. They will not know the difference."

"It will be seen as a sign of weakness," Paxbolón persisted. "They will think we fear them."

"Do it," Canek instructed. It was time to end the discussion; his word was final. He waved a hand, indicating that they were all to go. The talk was becoming tedious. Later he would have one of the painted boys sent to amuse him. In the meantime, he wished to lie down, loosen his loincloth, and sip a little balche. He wondered what they would do when he was no longer available to direct them and regretted once again that Tutul Katun would not succeed him. "See that the gifts are sent before evening," Canek added. "And prepare yourselves for the morning. Tomorrow will be a critical day."

Don Luis watched Manuel's hands place a bottle of cognac on the walnut dining table between a dish that had held sweet green peppers stuffed with shrimp and another that contained the remains of a caramel-coated flan. Earlier they'd been served pozóle—a spicy corn soup containing pork and raw sliced onion. The meal had been delicious, the most complete Don Luis had enjoyed in weeks. Now he beamed as cognac and coffee were placed before him, then he waved Manuel away.

"Leave us in peace," he said. "I'll pour this. If there's anything further, I'll call."

Manuel nodded briefly, turned, and left, his red-and-gray-striped jerkin a small flag of color in the candles' shadows.

When they were alone, Don Luis turned his attention to his solitary guest: a man who had eaten little of the food set before him, who had barely responded to the mayor's dinner conversation, who'd not touched his glass of Spanish red Riojan wine.

"Capitán d'Avila," the mayor began—through some sense of courtesy he'd withheld this matter until the meal was over—"there is a favor I would like to ask of you."

D'Avila nodded. All through dinner he'd fought back the words that had pressed for release, had restrained the urge to remonstrate as he'd done when he'd pulled the mayor by the arm down to the breakwater and shouted in his face, warning of the danger of the frigates that hung offshore. They called him mad; he'd heard the comment with his own ears, but they were wrong. They did not know what madness was. Nevertheless, he must be careful or he would never achieve the vindication he planned. So now he nodded and refused the brandy the mayor offered him; he picked up his coffee cup instead.

Don Luis cleared his throat. The silence of the garrison commander disconcerted him slightly. "This favor," he continued, sipping a little of his own cognac, "has to do with the council meeting. The one that has been called for the day after tomorrow."

Once more d'Avila merely nodded. He'd been right to wait, to control himself. He realized with a great deal of pleasure that someone was attempting to use him again, and the knowledge gave him strength.

"This, ah, meeting has been called especially by González," Don Luis went on, determined that his discomfort would not show. But he discovered that his hand, as if by its own accord, was reaching for the cognac bottle and pouring more into his glass. "I'm sure you're aware of the treasurer's reasons for calling it," he remarked.

"He would have your office," d'Avila replied abruptly, the words spilling out in spite of his effort to control them. "And you would have my vote. Is that not so?"

"Ah, well . . ." The mayor breathed deeply. Somehow or other his position had been reduced. "You put it bluntly, but yes, I would like to think that you'd support me."

"Why?" D'Avila leaned forward and went on quickly. "Do not bother to answer, I will tell you why. You need me. González has Muñoz in his pocket, the old fool owes him money. Hurtado will probably vote with you, if you promise him enough. Toledo is absent, and Leal is dead." The commander's beard twitched into a smile. "Your Frenchman is constitutionally unable to vote. So you need to be sure that *I* will support you. Is that not so, Your Worship?"

Don Luis did not immediately reply; he raised his glass, then emptied it. Once more the one-eyed face came closer, and d'Avila continued.

"González has already spoken to me," he went on rapidly. "But I am interested in none of his promises. He is not as desperate as you. *You* will bargain."

Don Luis felt sweat begin to moisten the palms of his hands. "Are you bargaining with *me*?" he asked as lightly as he could, and watched himself refill his glass.

D'Avila ignored the question. He had no respect for these petty manipulators, for their fee-paying purchased offices. In the past few weeks his dislike had reached a peak. They cared nothing for what had happened to him, as they'd made no attempt to understand what he'd tried to do when he'd unleashed the cannon on the pirates. In truth they cared little about Campeche itself, in spite of their protestations. They were concerned only with themselves, their profits, their miserable bargains. Well, at the moment that suited him completely; he'd show them that he too could play their mercenary games.

Don Luis coughed to cover the uncomfortable silence. "What is it that you want from me?" he asked carefully.

"The man who took my eye," d'Avila replied hotly, irrationally, his words cracking now like small sharp stones. "The man who caused my shame. It's his life I want. For *that* you can have my vote."

Don Luis wet his lips and drew away. The sudden outflow of vituperation shocked him. It was out of place in this stately room.

"Do you agree?" d'Avila demanded. He stared at the mayor, his one eye burning. "Tell me, *do you agree?*"

Don Luis paused; he had expected nothing like this. The delicious meal, the quiet of the paneled walls, the courtesies, now belonged in another setting. He had planned a simple bargain, nothing more.

"Answer me?" D'Avila's voice shook suddenly. "Do you agree?"

Very slowly Don Luis nodded, painfully uncertain why acknowledgment required such effort. "Yes," he whispered, "I agree."

"Good." D'Avila stood. "In that case you shall have my vote." He stood abruptly, made a mocking bow, and was gone.

Alone again, twice deserted, Don Luis listened to the beating of his heart. He could not understand the depths of his distress. The English pirate meant nothing to him, nothing at all. Yet *they* had made a bargain, and Stone had gone away believing it to be sound. Now it was broken, bartered to another. And he, Don Luis de Córdoba, who had always prided himself on keeping his word, had broken it so readily. It seemed an appalling price to pay to save his position in Campeche.

When he opened his eyes again, all Don Luis could see was his glass of cognac. Quite slowly he extended an uneasy hand, lifted the glass, and drained it. Then, quickly, he filled it again, shuddering as he did so.

Christopher Stone remained apart for almost all of the day. He did not return to the great hall with its carvings of the past and present. He did not reenter the house. Only occasionally was his figure glimpsed pacing a terrace overlooking the lake, his brow furrowed, his footsteps restless.

Once van Staal approached, his honest eyes clouded. "Cap'n," he began, but Stone cut him short.

"I trust all is prepared for the morrow?" he inquired abruptly.

"The powder chests are complete. The weapons also." Van Staal spoke quietly, his voice contained none of its earlier shock. In spite of what Stone had told the visiting Maya, his faith continued. He knew that without Stone they were nothing. "And the men are ready to do battle."

"Are they?" Stone's question was sharp.

Van Staal nodded. "They think you have betrayed them," he added sadly. "But they'll not give in without a fight."

"Good." Stone smiled thinly. "And you, what do you think?"

Van Staal paused; he lifted his head and stared across the lake. "You would not betray us, Christopher," he said after a moment. "But I know not what you plan."

"You will, you will." Stone turned his gaze to the bones of the galley lapped by the little waves. "I want the men to rage," he added, speaking to himself. "I want to feel their anger."

Van Staal glanced at the long figure of the Englishman leaning on the terrace wall but made no immediate comment. But a moment or two later he spoke again. "The girl," he said carefully. "She wishes to speak with you."

"I wish to speak with her also," Stone replied. "But later. Then I will send for her."

Van Staal nodded; presently he left. The afternoon turned. When pale light from the setting sun began to alter the colors of the countryside, when birdcalls came clearly across the flat, dulling water, van Staal returned, a curious expression on his round face. He told Stone about the Mayan gifts.

Stone stared at the Dutchman. "They have sent us food?' he said. "And women?"

"A scurvy lot. But women nevertheless." Van Staal shrugged. "Fowls, fruits, and vegetables as well."

Stone smiled appreciatively. "They are clever," he said, "they are clever. Give the women to the men. See they carry neither knives nor poison, then share them among ours and the Spaniards.''

"They are an ugly collection, Cap'n.''

"All cats are gray when the night grows dark.'' Stone stretched. It was clear to van Staal that his captain's mind had sharpened in the long hours he'd been isolated on the terrace. "Now, send the girl to me. I wish to see her alone.''

When Guadalupe came up into the pink and dulling light, she stood hesitantly, staring at Stone. His back had been to her, his gaze on the lake, but immediately he heard her step he turned and held out his hands.

Guadalupe remained where she stood, studying his pale, rawboned face. She too could see that it was calmer, that the restless eyes were stiller.

"Do *you* not trust me, either?'' Stone asked easily. "I had thought that of them all, you might understand.''

Guadalupe was confused by his gentleness. She had not wanted to believe in his acquiescence, but she had seen him, heard him accept the arrangement. And all day long the angry voices had buzzed about her, condemning him and his action, testing her loyalty. Yet now he was so much at ease, and this alteration puzzled her deeply.

"Do you not understand what it was I did?'' Stone persisted.

"I do not know what is in your mind,'' Guadalupe replied hesitantly. "You have told me nothing, and they say—''

Stone smiled. "I know what they say. But how do they act?''

"They are busy. They prepare to fight. In the morning they will do anything but give the Maya what they ask.'' Guadalupe swallowed; his motives were becoming clearer. "They say they will die before—''

Stone nodded. "And the Creole?'' he inquired.

"He, also, is determined to fight.''

"So be it,'' Stone said. He went to her and took her in his arms. "And still you do not trust me?''

Guadalupe rested her head on his chest. It all seemed

suddenly, stupidly clear. She could now not imagine how she could have seen it any other way. "You said nothing to me," she accused, allowing her voice to rise as relief flowed over her in comforting waves.

"Did you need to be told?"

Guadalupe nodded. She clung to him, and they remained unspeaking for what seemed to them both to be a long quiet time on the palely lit terrace overlooking the still water. Then, from somewhere, came a muffled shout followed by the sound of hooded laughter.

Stone lifted his head. "Listen," he said softly. "Listen and tell me what it is they say. I need your ears."

"Is that all you need of me?"

"For the moment, yes." Stone moved slightly away. "All day I have heard voices. There are men hidden on the roofs about us. I must know what they speak of."

Guadalupe closed her eyes in an attempt to deny the reality that had returned, then she said, "They will attack. That is what they have intended all along."

"Yet they will do nothing until the morning?" Stone asked, seeking confirmation of what van Staal had said. "Is that not so?"

Guadalupe nodded. "They fight beneath the blessing of their god of light, Kinich Ahau. He is what they call the Lord of the Eye of the Sun. The priests sacrifice birds to him each morning. They will not come for us in the dark."

Stone nodded, his mind extremely clear. "So, they have sent us gifts to put our minds at ease. Now they are close, preparing something, and I would know what it is they plot."

There was another shout, distant but distinct. Guadalupe went from Stone to the edge of the terrace, straining to hear. There were many murmurings now, voices she had not been aware of earlier. She leaned outward, her eyes searching, but there was nothing to be seen. Then the shout was repeated clearly, its echo dying over the lake. When she heard it for the second time, the color went from her cheeks.

"What do they say?" asked Stone.

Guadalupe's expression was sad and distant. "It is as it was before we sailed," she said. "They talk of eating our flesh."

"Nothing more?" The threat was irrelevant to Stone. "They don't say how that will be accomplished?"

Guadalupe shook her head.

"When it is dark they will become more boastful," Stone said with quiet confidence. "Then we will return. Perhaps you will hear more. Something of what they intend." He watched her carefully, seeing some of his own defiance replace the fear in her eyes. "They are arrogant," he added. "They are loud. It will not occur to them that we are listening." He shrugged. "Perhaps they believe we are easier than we seem."

Guadalupe returned his gaze. She accepted his strength. Her voice held new determination when she said, "I will do more than that. When it is dark I will go among them."

Stone stared at her: it was his turn to be shaken. "Are you mad?" he whispered.

Guadalupe smiled slightly. "It will not be difficult," she said with increasing boldness. "In the darkness I will be safe. They will take no notice of another old woman."

"Old woman? What in God's name do you mean?"

"There is clothing in the house." Guadalupe kept her voice low, but she could not hide its growing excitement. "I will disguise myself. No one will give me a second glance."

"No." Stone shook his head firmly. "I will not permit it."

"Listen to me, Cristóbal. If they are planning to attack, everyone will know of it. It will be like a fiesta. You are right. All will be talking about it. I will easily hear what they say."

"No," said Stone, but his mind was on fire. "It is not possible."

"It is most possible. There are women's garments here. I have seen them." She smiled again. "These priests are different. They have women, and boys. With what I have seen I will easily pass for an ancient in the dark.''

"No," said Stone, but his words now carried less conviction. ''I will not let you go.''

"You cannot stop me. There are many rooms in this priest's house. Many doors that lead out of it. If I am determined to go, you could not stop me.''

"And . . .'' Stone's heart rose in his throat; for a moment it almost overpowered him. "And are you determined to go.''

"Yes."

"Why?"

"To, to do something to repay you for what you have given me,'' Guadalupe answered simply.

At that Stone's tongue was silent.

Guadalupe saw him tremble. "You do not know what it is like to be a mestiza and a woman,'' she continued softly. "I was nothing, and you have made me proud of what I am. So, please, I ask you—let me do this for you now.''

Stone closed his eyes. "Be careful,'' was all he could manage to say.

"Of course.'' Guadalupe turned and went quickly from the terrace.

Stone did not watch her go. He stood very still, gazing over the lake water, his eyes deeply pained. For the first time in his life he felt humble and inept.

It was the sight of the casks filled with salted beef that affected him most of all. Their presence stung, their rich odor filled him with bitterness. They kept in mind the pirate he had promised to destroy. D'Avila could not avoid them. He spent much time at the hacienda now. Each afternoon he visited the barn where the casks waited, walking through the cool storeroom in which they stood, his mind inflamed with memory.

He had tried to avoid this poignant place, had made some attempt to drill the fragmented garrison, but had failed. It had no desire to conform; he had not the drive to flail. It was defeated. He was not sufficiently interested in it any longer.

As for the salt beef itself? If he were honest with himself, it would more than likely not be needed now, not for the *Courage* now that Cazaux was back, now that he, d'Avila, had made his bargain with the mayor. It crossed his mind to sell it to the next trading vessel to put into the port of Campeche, but something would not permit him to carry out the act. It was like a lure, here in the barn. It was like bait to bring the cutthroat back. D'Avila sniffed the salty, animal air, forcing himself to believe that one day soon the pirate Stone would return, that one day soon he would be killed in the way d'Avila dreamed.

The presence of the casks was one of the reasons he had decided to support Don Luis and not González in the latter's bid for power. Also, González was too impatient, he would have had fresh troops sent from Mérida. He would have brought new arms, new forces, to Campeche. And that would not have suited d'Avila at all. Not now. It might have been something he, himself, had once suggested, but, no longer. Now he wanted Stone for his use only. No other had the right to interfere. When the English pirate returned, he wanted him alone, to deal with alone, in the way the pig deserved to be dealt with: his throat cut from ear to ear.

That is why he had cast his vote for Don Luis in spite of his contempt for the mayor. Because the mayor had *promised* that the English barbarian would be his. When Stone returned, he, d'Avila, would be given the gangling pirate to judge and sentence, to execute as he deserved to be executed: to be blinded and then put to death. It was a bargain that would not be broken.

Yet promise in itself was not enough. D'Avila could not keep away from the casked meat waiting to be loaded onto the *Courage*. He could not avoid the cool barn where he had taken the mestiza who had been taken from him. Amidst the casks, he saw the girl and smelled her. He wondered where she might be now and how she had fared in the pirates' hands. And it was this uncertainty that threatened to destroy him.

If only he knew more, could learn something of the

pirate's whereabouts. He needed to be sure when the heathen would return. D'Avila paused in the barn's deep twilight. What of those in the dungeons? he asked himself. The blackamoor? He who had been left in charge? D'Avila turned to stare out a door into slanted sunlight, at shadows crawling over the grass. He would question the prisoners. There were ways to be sure they told the truth. D'Avila nodded with satisfaction. Anything would be better than accepting this impotent silence; anything would be better than waiting unknowing.

Unknowing—that was the condition kindling the fire in his brain. He'd never known enough about this place. They'd lied to him before he left his beloved Spain. They'd told him the garrison was competent, and he'd discovered, to his cost, *that* to be an ugly joke. They'd said the mayor was a fine administrator, but he'd come to learn that Don Luis was nothing but a scheming trader, more of a merchant than he'd been in Spain. They'd informed him that the Indians were largely conquered, yet Toledo had gone inland to wage a further war, taking with him the English cutthroat merely because it suited him to do so.

D'Avila realized, with increasing rancor, that he knew far too little about this decaying place where no one spoke the truth.

Except, he had to admit, the girl, the mestiza, the one he'd taken in the barn and given his word upon—not that the promise held any meaning now. None of the promises made in this colony held any validity at all. But the girl had been unusually honest.

Even after he'd taken her she'd made no attempt to hide her defiance but had stared at him so bravely, a respect for her had grown. He knew now it had been, in part, this defiance that had led him to force himself upon her in the straw-fragrant barn—that and her undeniable beauty.

It was this respect for her that had led him to become her protector. He was the only Spaniard of his rank who visited the Indian barrio, taking chickens and smoked hams, lengths of cloth, to the girl's mother—who never made any effort to hide the suspicion in her eyes. That, too, was a form of honesty.

In many ways d'Avila preferred the Indians to anyone else in the colony, for at least they knew, with reason, what they were. As the pirate Stone knew what he was—as d'Avila accepted him to be: the only worthy challenger in this moldering place. He'd accepted that, however much he loathed the man himself.

D'Avila walked from the barn out into the sunlight, away from the casks and their resolute tang, out to face again his determination to destroy the uncouth corsario who'd come in from the sea to take his eye and his woman and all the respect he possessed.

D'Avila knew now he must begin to force an ending, to bring some peace to his aching mind. He stood in the sunlight, his eye tightened against the brightness after the dim interior of the barn. *The prisoners?* The thought returned, and he nodded his acceptance. He would discover what they knew.

CHAPTER 6

HEAVY CLOUD HUNG OVER THE LAKE, NO MOONLIGHT reached the city. Guadalupe slipped out a side door silently, into a narrow street that ran up toward the plaza. It was empty. No one saw her leave.

She wore a long skirt of dark, coarse-woven cloth and over it a simple shift. About her body she'd tied a brown cotton wrap that made her bulkier; covering her head and shoulders was a dark blue shawl. She walked slowly, feeling her steps carefully, like an old woman uncertain of her strength. She carried a basket and, with her free hand, supported herself on the walls of buildings. Ahead of her, where the great plaza at the base of the temple spread, light glowed, and the sound of many voices could be heard.

Guadalupe turned a corner, passed a man and a woman who spoke rapidly, their words hurried and excited. They barely glanced at her, and their disinterest gave her courage. It would not be difficult, she believed, to move among these people as though she were part of their world.

Christopher Stone came down from the terrace to the elaborate hall, from the surrounding, clinging darkness to the yellow lamplit air. He walked steadily to the cushion, from which he had addressed the Mayan captains, and turned to the assembled survivors. They stared back at him defiantly. When he spoke, one foot on the cushion, his voice was penetrating.

"Listen to me," he began without preamble, "The girl has gone into the city to learn what she can. When she returns be prepared to let her in. Be ready, it may need to be done quickly."

He said what he had to say in both English and Spanish to make sure that everyone understood. For a few moments no one responded, then Toledo broke the silence. "So you would use any of us," he said bitingly. "No matter who they are."

Stone did not reply; his mouth clamped shut in irritation.

"You would do anything to save yourself, is that not so?" The Creole's eyes were hard. "I must congratulate you, Captain Stone, you have learned something from these Indians already. You have learned how to become a traitor."

Stone breathed deeply, holding back his anger. "We all need to know what they plan," he said, keeping his voice steady. He looked into the other faces; none contained any sympathy. "She, alone, understands what they say."

"What would you wish to know?" Toledo's voice was relentless. "How many *more* they will ask for in the morning? How many you will have to give to save your precious life?"

Stone's eyes flickered. The muscles at the corners of his jaw bunched, he kicked the heavy cushion away from him, but he said nothing. He glared at Toledo and remained silent. And his silence was like a spur to the Spaniard.

"So, you have sent out your woman?" Toledo came closer, pushing his face to Stone's. "Perhaps you have sent a message with her, eh?"

Still Stone waited, but Toledo could not stop himself.

"Your Indian whore has gone out among her own kind." The sharp words penetrated, they cut like fragments of glass. "For all we know she has gone forever. To wait for you. To—"

Stone hit him then. He swung toward Toledo and crashed the back of his hand into the Creole's face. "Quiet," he spat in English, his whole body trembling with rage. "Shut your fart-sucking mouth."

"You—" began Toledo, his hand going to his dagger.

But van Staal was instantly between them, holding them apart, his voice orderly, his eyes going to the others in the room, to any who had begun to move. "Steady," the Dutchman said evenly. "Hold, the enemy is without."

There were murmurings, the muttering of voices, a curse or two, but none came closer. In a moment all were still. Stone turned away, his face a mixture of white and crimson, patched with shock and outrage. Toledo stepped backward, one hand to his cheek where Stone had struck him, the other on the handle of his dagger.

"Easy," van Staal continued. "We are all unnerved. Each of us is tense." He looked toward Stone. "Tell them," he said, his voice in command, "tell them what is planned for the morrow."

Stone's lips moved before any words were uttered. He paused and filled his lungs with air. "Tomorrow we fight," he said in Spanish and English, and stared at them all challengingly. "Live or die, tomorrow we fight."

"Fight?" questioned Gottberg; sweat covered his face. "Fight, you say?"

"Aye, fight." Stone's expression eased a little. "We will battle. It will be short, and it will be bloody. But if we strike quickly, I believe we can force them to our terms."

"Fight?" called a Spaniard. It was Ocaño, the sergeant. "With what?"

"With what we have," Stone continued. "They will come with their chiefs. We will be ready with the nine. When they are close, we attack them. With our powder chests we will break them. If they are enough damaged, they will bargain."

There was silence. Then again the mutterings rose, this time with greater confidence. Stone walked away, down the long hall with its tapestries of wealth and its carvings of death, past them all, back up to the lonely terrace. He burned within, he smoldered. He feared his rage might erupt again, so he went, leaving and taking with him a searing desire to punish.

Guadalupe sat in a corner of the great plaza with excited voices all about her. The whole city was inflamed by a success not yet gained. The Maya stood in small groups chattering animatedly, calling to those who passed, exchanging greetings with strangers.

Earlier, seeming to need a rest, she'd paused by a group of warriors, who boasted how they would capture the invaders the following day. They'd discussed openly how they would assemble, their method of attack.

Seeing Guadalupe, one of them turned to her. "Well, old woman," he'd said cheerfully. "Will you be at the temple tomorrow?"

Fear clutched Guadalupe's heart, but she'd nodded and wiped her lips.

"If you are fortunate, you will be thrown some flesh," commented another of the group. "You look as if you could do with some meat on your bones."

Guadalupe managed to chuckle. She wrapped the shawl even more closely about her and began to shuffle away.

"Don't forget now," the first warrior called. "Tomorrow, old woman, you will eat well."

Guadalupe waved a trembling hand at the group as slowly, sickened by the confidence of all around her, she'd shuffled to a corner of the plaza to hear more. She knew almost all she needed to know, but the glee of the Maya was like a magnet; she could not force herself to leave the language.

Then, pulling the shawl farther down her forehead, she reached for her basket and heard a familiar voice in her ear. "Well, if it isn't the Pretty One," it said. "What are you doing out here, might I ask?"

Gasping, Guadalupe turned, unable to control her reaction. She stared up into the smiling face of Ah Cuc. He held a pine torch in one hand. He was alone.

"It *is* you." Ah Cue's torch came nearer. "For a moment I was just a little doubtful. But something in the way you moved gave you away." His smile grew. "Are you spying on us?" he asked.

"I, came for food." Guadalupe's mouth was dry; her tongue barely formed the words. "We needed—"

"Now, now, Pretty One." Ah Cuc waved an accusing finger. "The house of Tutz is crammed with food. Everyone knows he's a cross-eyed pig. Tell the truth, you've come to hear what's being said, haven't you?"

Slowly, Guadalupe nodded: there was no point in denying what was obvious.

"Well, that's spying, isn't—" Ah Cuc began as Guadalupe made an attempt to run. But even as she lifted her skirt, Ah Cuc's fingers were about her wrist. "Now, don't be silly," he continued, his voice easy, his smile unchanged. "I am very quick. We have to be. So don't be awkward. If you run, others will catch you, and that could be very nasty."

Guadalupe stared, uncertain what to do.

"You *are* a problem," Ah Cuc went on. "I can't let you go, you'd tell all our secrets to the Pale One. And if these people find out who you are, it would be so very messy." He shook his head thoughtfully. "I shall have to take you to a little house I have. You won't be noticed, and you'll be safe." He looked at her sharply. "But you must promise me something."

"What?"

"You must give me your word you won't try to escape."

"Would, would you trust me?"

"Oh, yes. Whatever you are, Pretty One, you are honest. If you made a promise, you wouldn't think of breaking it."

"And if I won't?"

"Oh, dear." Ah Cuc put a hand on her arm. "That would be a shame. These people would kill you immediately. That mightn't be so bad. But they'd cut off your head and put it on a stick to show to the Pale One. Imagine how he'd feel. You'd look so dreadful. The sight might drive him mad."

Guadalupe glanced at the crowd. It was thicker, the excitement more intense. "You are very clever," she whispered.

"We must be clever as well as quick." Ah Cuc bent to her invitingly. "Now, will you come with me?"

"I have no alternative."

"That's a good girl. Just give me the basket and come along. You'll love my house. It has a wonderful view of the lake."

Slowly they made their way through the throng: Ah Cuc walking cheerfully, Guadalupe shuffling beside, her head bent, her steps slow and ancient. Once she paused, to look down the street in which the house of Tutz stood, but Ah Cuc made a disapproving noise with his tongue, and they moved on, away from the glow in the square, into darkness and isolation.

Low, heavy cloud hugged the mountains about Lake Petén Itzá. No god rose in the east, no shadow was cast, as Bacal stood on the topmost part of the temple and asked for a blessing.

The morning quail were sacrificed to an unseen sun, and the beautiful birds died badly. One of them escaped, to flap, dying on the broad roof of Itamná's courtroom, leaving a trail of scattered feathers.

This, as Bacal knew, was a sign of great anger. The plans for today would not be fulfilled. All the cleverness of Lord Tutul Katun, all the eagerness of Lord Paxbolón, would be denied by the fury of the gods. Kinich Ahau had hidden his face. He would not speak, nor would he give his blessing.

The invaders should have been disposed of yesterday when the signs were favorable. More effort should have been made to capture them on the lake. Bacal was certain of that now. Last night the blood had come badly from his penis, and the pain had been severe. All the indications were evil. Now, it would take acts of great generosity from all the gods to capture the disbelievers alive and offer their hearts in the court of the temple.

Bacal shook his long matted hair, to disperse its stink of death. He turned, his cloak hugging his tall body, to stare down at the plaza at the foot of the temple. Already it was full. That, at least, was a promising aspect. The people had faith, there was a sense of festivity in the air, Maya women were already bartering for chickens and dogs, squashes, red and green peppers, tomatoes, and multicolored beans. Perhaps the spirit of the people might renew a little the humor of the gods.

Bacal lifted his eyes to the house of Tutz where the invaders waited. Soon the captain and the priests would return to demand the nine. Whether they came willingly or not did not matter. The warriors were ready; sword in hand they would take the nine along with the rest. Bacal hoped that few of the disbelievers would be killed. The more hearts offered to Itzamná, the more readily he would smile on Tayasal again. But the signs of the morning were far from reassuring.

Silently, his skin crawling with tension, Christopher Stone watched the nine assemble. Eight Spaniards had been selected to accompany Jaime Toledo. With them was van Staal; it would be he who would hand them over.

Stone had not slept. His eyes were red and rimmed with red; his shoulders sagged, and he turned at every sound. All night he'd walked the stone-walled house, pausing by doors, listening for any whisper of the girl's return. As darkness deepened and the excitement in the great plaza stilled, Stone had gone to the end of the narrow street seeking some sign, some movement, that would tell him she was not already dead. He had waited, crouched at a corner, his eyes scraping the darkness, but there had been no trace of her.

As the clouds lightened he had paced the terraces, peering, urging her to return, but she had not appeared; there was nothing to hope for any longer. She was dead.

He'd climbed to the highest point of the house and watched the morning priests crawl like black flies up the temple steps, and the slow, burning hatred, which had been building ever since Guadalupe had gone, threatened to break him open. Sweat stood out on his forehead; a vein thundered in his neck. These people, who feasted on blood and death, had nothing to teach him now. When the time came he would take as many as he could with him in revenge for the death of the girl.

When the Maya captains approached the house, they found the Pale One, Round Skull, Silver Chest, and eight others waiting for them by the door that faced the street.

The Maya had dressed especially for the occasion; they wore long cloaks decorated with the reds and greens of quetzal feathers, and their loincloths were richly woven. Their sandals were elaborately knotted, and on their wrists and ankles clattered circles of jade.

They were pleased to see that the disbelievers were also well presented. Silver Chest's handsome breastplate had been freshly polished. The Pale One wore a mantle of close-woven cotton that he must have found in the house of Tutz. Round Skull was covered in a similar fashion. The others were clean.

The Maya captains came close. They bowed, they touched the ground with their hands, and then they kissed it. It was their sign of peace. When they'd completed this ceremony they looked for the girl who spoke the language and were surprised to find she was not present. They turned to the priests accompanying them, seeking guidance, but the black-clad acolytes said nothing; they stared hostilely at the invaders, their blood-streaked faces unmoving.

Then Round Skull spoke—badly, to be sure, but clearly he knew something of the language. "You are here," he said. "We are ready."

"Excellent," replied the taller of the two captains. He bowed in the direction of the nine. "Are these for Itzamná?"

"Yes."

"Then"—the captain smiled—"we will take them."

"Wait." Van Staal struggled for words. "My lord, he wants to know what, what you do for us. To go?"

The Maya captains hesitated. They exchanged glances, then the taller spoke again. "You will be told that later," he said, his voice faintly contemptuous. "First we must listen to what the gods have to say when these hearts are offered." He made a step toward Toledo, his hand out as if to take him.

"First"—van Staal's voice was even harder—"we will know what you do."

"You will be given canoes," the shorter captain said offhandedly. "With them, you may leave."

"Where are canoes?"

"By the lake."

"Show me."

The short captain laughed and shook his head. "I wish the girl was here," he said to his companion. "This is like talking to a child."

"Perhaps the Pale One got rid of her and took one of the women we sent," the taller captain said. At that even the priests smiled. "These heathen have no taste."

Stone watched and waited, his body burning. Behind the Maya, in the narrow street, he'd caught the beginnings of movement: a face, half-concealed, the end of an obsidian-bladed sword. And once, for the merest instant, a glimpse of Paxbolón, who wore his jaguar headdress. Every inch of the Fighting Lord's skin had been painted black; he was ready for war.

The taller captain laughed again. "Tell the Pale One to ask his new woman to play the game of the frog," he said to van Staal. "Then he will find out what a good woman is like."

"What do they say?" Stone asked, his voice a growl.

"They insult us."

"So I thought." Stone's voice scalded; he could wait no longer. "When I shoot these pox-mucked foreskins, cut down the priests." He watched van Staal nod, then shouted, *"Now."*

As the word roared from the Pale One's lips, the captains stepped backward. They saw him throw the cotton mantle from his shoulders. In each hand he carried a pistol. He raised them both and fired. That was the last thing they ever saw.

The first bullet caught the taller captain in the throat; he stumbled away, a bubbling sound on his lips. The second bullet hit the shorter officer in the middle of the forehead, and his skull seemed to exploded. He died at Stone's feet without a sound.

As Stone fired, van Staal swung the axe he'd held beneath his covering. The great blade flashed upward in the dull air to strike the first priest in the side. It sliced away the top third of his body as the lower part of the trunk partly turned and began to run. It fell into the dust, its feet still moving.

The second black-clad priest swung to follow the corpse as the raised blade descended to catch him in the center of the skull. It cut him almost in two. The four Maya died with such speed that the warriors farther up the street, waiting for the signal to attack, could do nothing until it was over. By then Stone and van Staal were back in the house of Tutz.

As they went in through the door, Henri the Stain and four others emerged carrying cloth-bound earthenware pots filled with gunpowder and flint, the fuses already lit. They raced toward the Maya who were now filling the narrow street, long swords raised in their hands. Then, a mere ten feet from the warriors, the bombers paused, threw the powder chests, and raced back to the house.

The explosives fell among the Maya, some of whom stopped and picked up the strange smoldering devices as they detonated in their faces.

The destruction was brutal and immediate. Those not killed were blinded. Those whose bodies were not pierced by the flying flints were stunned by the force of the blasts. They spun, staggering, their weapons dropped, their ears shattered, their minds crippled with shock and fright.

For long minutes the Maya reeled in bloody disorder, then Henri and his men appeared again and another round of powder chests fell fuming among the devastation. This time the Maya fled, the sound of their pain echoing up through the alleyway.

Alvaréz the jailer was worried; for some days now his mind had been uneasy. His concern had nothing to do with the food he was supplying the prisoners. That came daily from the French, some of it so good that Alvaréz could not resist filling a bowl, or two, for himself. Nor did he have any problem with the prisoners themselves. They were obviously grateful, their health was improving. True, the young one who had been so ill when Alvaréz had begun to care for them had died. But he'd seen to it that the body was taken away the following morning so that the damage done by rats was minimal. What's more, the death had left the others with an extra blanket, which they'd given to another of their number who was also ill. And that made Alvaréz feel better about the one he'd taken when the blankets had first been delivered.

No, what really disturbed the fat jailer were the actions of his garrison commander, Capitán d'Avila, who had taken to questioning him about the condition of the prisoners, their appearance, and what hope they held of the return of those who had journeyed into the interior.

At first d'Avila's interest had comforted Alvaréz. It suggested that the English prisoners were speaking the truth when they made their promises of gold for food. Mind you, it was not that Alvaréz actually disbelieved the black man who made the offer. It was an honorable agreement, and he had carried out his part of it, but to know that his commander was also interested seemed to reinforce his own reliable faith.

That was, of course, in the beginning. But in the past day or so, d'Avila had become increasingly insistent. His questions were now more critical, his eye flashed, and when he spoke of the men from the *Courage,* his tongue lashed mercilessly. Alvaréz knew—in fact, he'd already had a nightmare about it—that it was only a matter of time before the garrison commander insisted on interrogating the prisoners himself.

And that, Alvaréz would not welcome at all. Their condition, the blankets, the absence of their dead, would indicate far too clearly that someone was pampering them. And, of course, the one-eyed, pompous little ferret would jump to the immediate conclusion that it was he, Alvaréz, who was responsible, and not only that, but that he was doing it only for gain. No consideration would be given to charity, concern for fellow men, an abhorrence of an experience in the very same dungeons themselves. No, he, Alvaréz, would be accused of profit. He could be prosecuted, might be tortured, and could end up a prisoner himself.

It was all intolerable. It was unfair, discourteous, and intolerable.

Alvaréz wondered what he could do to prevent the garrison commander from actually confronting the prisoners, but so far he had not been able to think of anything. It was worrying him, it was with him all day long. It had even begun to affect his appetite, and that was the most intolerable aspect of all. That was a shocking sign.

CHAPTER 7

THEY WAITED IN THE GREAT HALL, ALL OF THEM READY, attempting to withhold from mind the passage of their time. They waited as they'd waited for an hour, prepared for whatever was to come. They had reached an ending, a point of no returning, and somehow its finality gave them strength. Nothing apart remained; their future was with them.

"Soon, they will come back," said van Staal to break the silence. "They will re-form, and the real attack will begin." He looked at Henri the Stain, who nodded. His men stood, explosives wrapped, slowmatches burning. With them were the Spanish musketeers, Toledo in their center. About them waited Stone and the remainder of the pirates, pistols and cutlasses in their hands. "We will meet them in the street," van Staal added, clearly in both languages. "When we hear them we will go out to face them."

The Dutchman's eyes went to Stone, who waited like a man already dead: his face was white, beneath his brows were hollows, his lips a narrow slit. Only his breathing held any life at all.

"It is the chiefs who matter," van Staal added. "Once they are down the rest will scatter."

So they waited in the great hall, not thinking or trying

241

not to think, waiting for the rows of savages to begin, what all knew, would be a final battle.

Then, suddenly, loudly, with wooden trumpets blaring and skin drums beating, the Maya came marching down the street, their two-handed obsidian-bladed swords aloft. They came shouting, a solid mass of painted bodies, their faces animated with the presence of death. Among them, taller than most, his jaguar headdress lifting him above them all, strode Paxbolón. His moment had arrived. From here there was no retreat.

At the approaching sound the door of the house of Tutz crashed open; Henri the Stain and his men came out. They threw their powder chests, but now the Maya ignored them. The devices exploded among the packed red-painted figures, and a further redness grew. The round shapes held no fear now: they were merely weapons that killed, not the voices of strange, unknown gods. And death, above all, was the warrior's duty.

The musketeers fired without aim, blindly, into the approaching ranks. More Maya fell as those behind, stumbling over their bodies, slipping in the blood, pressed on. Pirates with cutlasses thrust forward, hacking, stabbing, slashing the hands that held the swords. But nothing halted the down-swirling tide of those who knew that to die in battle was to remain a warrior forever.

They locked and struggled. A Spaniard fell, his head torn from his shoulders by the sweep of a two-handed sword. Another sank as a Maya grappled with him. The soldier thrust. The Maya's eyes jumped. A further warrior raised his blade and broke the Spaniard's skull.

Henri the Stain ran once more into the street, slipped on the bloodied roadway, and fell, a powder chest beneath him. The explosion killed him instantly.

Christopher Stone, his pistols spent, picked up a fallen shortsword. Red eyes starting from the rawness of his face, he carved his way forward through the seething red-painted shouting bodies. Like a madman, thrashing in punishment and pain, he clawed his way toward the elusive, blackened, magnificent figure of Paxbolón, who seemed to be everywhere at once, yet nowhere at any given moment. An obsidian sword came up at Stone; he slashed it away with his own and ploughed ahead. His breathing was ragged in his ears, his pale face was splashed with the blood that flew at him like rain. From somewhere he heard the sound of van Staal calling and the swish of his murderous axe. From somewhere else, it seemed, came the pitch of his own voice screaming.

Then Paxbolón gave a signal, and a single clear trumpet note cut through all other sound. Immediately all his warriors began to fall away. They turned and fled from the slaughter, leaving behind their dead and dying. They went so swiftly and with such order that those they had been fighting were deprived of opposition.

Stone swung his sword, but the target had vanished. Van Staal's axe came up, but the man it would have killed was gone. Suddenly there was none but those who had come from the north and corpses all about them. The noise had died, the shouting and the crash of weapons was no longer heard. Only the groans of the dying and a harsh and ragged breathing filled the air.

In the confused, unnatural stillness that followed the retreat, Jaime Toledo cried, "After them. The Lord is with us. We have won." His breastplate was bloodied; his eyes were alive with victory. "Come," he shouted. "In the name of the Lord Jesus Christ."

"No," Stone gasped. "Wait."

"Wait? What for?" Toledo's young face contained all his old fervor. "They are running in disorder. After them. We will cut their leaders down. The day is ours. The Lord Jesus Christ has saved us."

Toledo began to move up the bloody street. Others began to follow. The heat, the fury, a sense of absurd victory, were too great to resist.

"Wait," Stone shouted. "They plan to trap us." However much he wished to punish, a sense of caution held him back. "We must be sure."

"I am sure," answered Toledo. "I am sure that it is better to die in this cause than to live in shame. We cannot wait like cowards for these heathen to return. Now that we have them running, let us pursue them. In the name of the Lord. In the name of the one true God. In the name of the Virgin Mary."

The Creole's words lashed them all. They rang through Stone's head like thunder, stirring him, urging him on. He felt the same desire to destroy, to die with as much blood on his hands as possible. His eye caught van Staal's, and he saw the response. They were all prepared to give chase now, whatever the consequences. The sound of the fleeing Maya could still be heard, inviting them to follow.

"Come then," Stone shouted. "Away."

With Toledo in the lead they ran, pressing unthinkingly ahead. They ran into a broad avenue that led to the temple. They poured along it, an uncontained rabble, and were halfway to the temple when the first stones fell.

The Maya, hidden on rooftops on either side of the avenue, raised themselves on a signal from Paxbolón and hurled boulders down onto the invaders.

There were screams, cries of confusion, as the enemy that had vanished reappeared from above. A Spaniard sank to the roadway, his neck broken. Simmons, the carpenter, lifted his face as a rock crashed into it, shattering bone, splintering teeth. He was dead before he reached the ground.

Then the Maya swarmed out of side alleys to fall upon the invaders; they came thickly, and many were unarmed. They advanced without regard for safety or death, determined to catch, to pinion, to carry intact the live hearts for Itzamná. But their task was formidable. Those invaders who remained alive fought like animals: cornered, lost, and desperate, they were deadly in defense.

A Maya grabbed Piet the Mulatto by the arms, another took him about the waist. Piet twisted; his wiry body sprang like steel, and his cutlass slashed into the faces of his captors.

"Mucky dogs," Piet shouted. "Mucky dogs."

A wounded Maya with a sword swung clumsily but effectively, catching Piet across the chest. Dark skin opened, blood ran down the lashing body. Piet fell against

a building and stared at the quick life spilling. He lifted
his eyes to see Meredith cut down the Maya with the
sword. The cutlass in the logwood cutter's hands whirled
like a whip.

Piet held his chest and smiled. "You're a foxy dog,"
he said, blood on his lips. "You're a foxy dog—" His
eyes stilled; he was quiet at last.

Meredith stormed. He found himself near Stone, as
insane as he. Van Staal was with them also. Their weapons threshed all who approached. But slowly, step by
step, the three were forced to retreat until their backs
were against a wall of the avenue. There they faced the
ring of warriors—until the blankets fell. They came down
on the three from the *Courage,* muffling them, cutting
out light and sound and all further effort to survive.

Immediately the Maya rushed in, tumbling the invaders onto the roadway, carrying them away like fish in a
net. They were the only pirates taken alive.

Jaime Toledo was also made prisoner, he too bound in
a blanket. All the others who had fought with him died.
Sargento Ocaño lay surrounded by a ring of dead and
dying Maya. He had fallen over those he'd killed to join
them all in death. But one other Spaniard remained
alive: when the Maya came to search the house of Tutz
they found a short frog-faced soldier named Azcaráte
hidden beneath a pile of blankets in the room where the
women, who had been sent the day before, waited. He
and Jaime Toledo were the only Red Vests to survive.

Shouting, bellowing, trumpets blaring, the Maya warriors announced their triumph to all of Tayasal as they
bore the prisoners away. They carried the trussed men
to the great plaza at the foot of the temple, and there, in
sight of all, bundled the invaders into a cage for the
citizens to gloat over. Later, Azcaráte was thrown in to
join them.

As the crowd thickened to jeer, the heavy sky lowered, and rain began to fall. Thick humid air clung to the
shivering skin of all five as loud, brutal voices hammered in their ears. Death was written on all their faces.
The wet, crowded square, the assembled mob with its

hatred and its glee, were as bleakly terrifying as anything any of them had ever experienced.

From where she lay, on the narrow bed in the locked room in the little house by the lake, Guadalupe Santoya heard the triumphant sounds. She pressed her face into the bedding to hide from this dreadful signal of victory and defeat. She hoped that Cristóbal was already dead. She knew, if he survived, what awaited him, and the thought of it was too atrocious to consider.

The old king sat on his raised cushion covered with deerhide in the main court of his palace. At his feet were his sons and Bacal. He studied the expressions on their faces before he asked his questions. He was puzzled: too much, yet not enough, had been said.

"Why is it that you do not want him offered with the others?" he asked Tutul Katun, his second son, carefully.

Tutul Katun paused before he replied, as if balancing the importance of his words. "It is that I am in the Pale One's debt," he answered finally. "He would not permit Silver Chest to kill me when the vessel sank. Then he freed me so that I might not drown."

Canek sighed and eased his weight. "That is his concern, my son," he pointed out. "It calls for no reply. Not from you, nor any prince."

"You are right, my father. But I learned from the girl who speaks the language that he preserved me in many ways. He would not allow my hands to be cut off and sent to you as a challenge."

"Where is the girl?" Canek asked abruptly. "She was not found in the house of Tutz?" He turned his questioning face to Paxbolón.

"There is no sign of her anywhere," Paxbolón replied.

"Perhaps she was sent away during the night," Tutul Katun suggested quietly. "She was precious to the Pale One."

"Too many have escaped," Bacal growled. "Too many have denied Itzamná their hearts. We will regret this day."

"We have their leaders," Paxbolón said defiantly, denying any criticism the priest's words might imply. "The value of a leader is many times greater than any warrior."

"That is so," hissed Bacal. "But they must be offered soon." He turned his slitted eyes to Tutul Katun. "Soon, my lord," he whispered, "soon. All of them, soon."

"You shall have the others whenever you wish," Tutul Katun replied with quiet authority. "But I ask that the Pale One be given a chance."

"A chance?" Canek raised his eyes with new interest. "What chance would you suggest, my son?"

"The Pale One is a warrior." Tutul Katun bowed to his father respectfully. "He deserves a warrior's chance."

"My son"—Canek breathed deeply and with both hands lifted the weight of his paunch—"you have the right to honor a debt, although it is not necessary. But what you ask . . ." He left the sentence unfinished.

"Itzamná also *asks*," Bacal growled savagely. "This morning Kinich Ahau hid his face from us. The birds with the breasts of night died badly. Now the heavens hang low, and rain falls, although the season of the rain is over. These are warnings, great king, they need to be heeded."

"You speak the truth," Canek replied sagely. "It is right that you should make us aware of the displeasures of our gods. But we have other great hearts to offer them. Those of Silver Chest and Round Skull. They have hearts that Itzamná would welcome." He turned his eyes to Paxbolón. "What is your opinion of your brother's request?" he asked gently. "Do you think that the Pale One should be given a chance."

Paxbolón hesitated for a moment, then smiled. "I think my brother should have his wish," he said generously. He knew that the day's victory was his alone, no other could take its glory from him. "Perhaps he will tell us how this could be achieved."

Tutul Katun bowed. "There are many ways," he replied softly. "We have customs, they are clearly written."

"Quite so." Paxbolón's smile remained, but his eyes

had grown cautious. "The Pale One might be tied to a stone, given a sword, and challenged by the best of our captains."

"That is possible." Tutul Katun stared into his brother's proud face. "Or he might be offered a run to the water between lines of spears."

Paxbolón shrugged. "That would seem unworthy of his greatness as a warrior," he said, his mind suddenly more alert.

"Then?" Tutul Katun's voice dropped significantly. "What else is left, my brother?"

"The greatest chance of all," Paxbolón said significantly. He repeated the ancient creed. "The chance to prove his courage and his skill."

Tutul Katun lowered his head in respect. There was nothing further to be said. His brother had accepted; the process was in motion. A smile touched his lips.

"I will play him at the ball game," Paxbolón went on defiantly. "He and I will meet, and all will be decided. We will play with the ball of quic, and the gods will be our judges."

"So be it," said Tutul Katun. He had obtained what he wanted. "The gods will decide."

Canek pulled at a gold plug in his earlobe, his eyes going from one son to the other, aware that there was more being laid before him than the life of the Pale One. He cleared his throat. "Is this fair, my son?" he asked Paxbolón. "After all, you are the greatest ball player in all of Tayasal. Surely this stranger will have no chance against you "

"It is a game of courage as well as skill," Paxbolón replied. "He has his share of both."

"And you are content to face him?"

"I am more than content, my father." Paxbolón bowed with deep respect. "I am honored."

Canek nodded. "Well, Bacal?" he asked the black-clad priest. "Do you concur with this?"

Bacal hissed and withdrew deeper into the folds of his cloak. His clotted hair hung before his bloodied face.

"Whatever you decide," he said to Canek. "Whatever you proclaim."

"Then," Canek said evenly, "the game will be played."

"In that case," Bacal growled, "it would be well if the hearts of the others were offered this night." His thin, whispery voice grated the air. "To persuade the heavens to open."

"So it shall be."

"And after the ball game," Bacal continued, "Itzamná can expect the heart of a further great warrior, is that not so?"

"It is," said Paxbolón. "For he who loses will die."

"Good, my lord." Bacal lowered his eyes. "Itzamná will welcome the heart of the loser, whether it be that of the Pale One or your own."

Paxbolón laughed softly. "It will not be mine," he replied with ease.

"Of course not, my lord." Bacal shuffled in his cloak. "I was merely asking that the old rules be adhered to."

"They will," said Paxbolón, and his eyes were sure.

After that no one spoke. The three below the king sat unmoving, staring at the flagstoned floor before them, each held in the web of their thinking. Canek looked down at the silent heads and wondered what thoughts passed through each and every one of them. Perhaps time would let him know.

The temple rode the sky, it hung over every part of the city. It rose in nine stages, each narrower than the last, to a square, white-plastered chamber on the roof of which were four enormous carvings of the same god: Muluc, patron of the day—long-nosed, broad-faced, he stared toward the east. From the main door of the chamber a wide, steep stairway of eighty-one steps led down to the plaza where the cage containing the prisoners stood.

The cage was square, wooden, its posts were bound with deerhide. On the roof four warriors sat. Below them, Stone and van Staal, Meredith, Toledo, and Azcaráte shivered like horses in the rain. They had been stripped

of their weapons: the pistols, the axe, and the breastplate had been taken as trophies. Their hands were
bound before them, and their feet were bare. Black and
white paint had been daubed on their faces, marking
them as losers of the battle in the streets.

Outside the cage the Maya pressed. Earlier they had
reached through the bars to touch the prisoners. Now a
ring of warriors kept them away, but their presence was
relentless, and their cries caused the five to huddle back
to back in the center of the cage, facing their tormentors
on all sides.

Of them all, Azcaráte, the Spaniard found hidden in
the bedding, was most afraid. None showed any real
courage now, but he clung with his bound hands to
Toledo's arm and whimpered.

"What, what will they do?" he stammered as a loud
and gleeful shout went up. "What will happen to us?"

"They will kill us," said Toledo. Only he seemed
resigned to death. If his Lord God had decided, then this
is what he had come for. "They will sacrifice us to their
idol."

"Dios mío." Azcaráte's jaw chattered. "Can, can nothing save us?"

"The Lord will save your soul." Toledo breathed
deeply; as he spoke he regathered himself. His head
lifted, and he stared out at the Maya with some of his
former defiance. "If you die bravely, the Lord Jesus will
take your soul to His bosom."

"I, I do not want to die."

"Be proud to die." Toledo's chest went out. His own
counsel gave him strength. "Do not let these heathen
see that you fear to enter the Kingdom of Heaven."

"I—" Azcaráte closed his eyes; he felt his stomach
heaving. "I, oh, holy Mary, Mother of God, please
don't let them kill me."

"Be brave." Toledo's voice was encouraging. "It is
all that remains for you to be."

"Oh, Jesus." Azcaráte began to cry.

"I will die here," Toledo continued, speaking to himself, speaking to them all. "This pagan temple will be

my shrine. When the history of this disgusting race is written, my name will be large. I will be known as the Martyr of Tayasal.''

Azcaráte's sobbing continued. Stone lifted his head to stare at the Creole, admiring for the first time the young man's determination, the depth of the belief that rallied him now. Stone could not speak, his own resources were exhausted, but he felt a strange warmth for the Creole's doomed bravery and would have shared it if he could.

"The Lord Jesus Christ directed me here," Toledo went on steadily. "If it is His wish that I die here, so be it." He turned to stare defiantly at the temple.

As if in response, the clouds behind the temple parted, and a last ray of solitary sunlight came from the lowering sky. It laced the four faces of the gods with rings of fire; it burnished the building with shades of bronze and autumn. For one glorious moment it seemed that the whole majestic structure would burst into flame. Then the glory died. The clouds moved to cover the sinking sun, gray filtered light returned, the temple remained intractable in its leaden power.

Toledo let his breath out slowly. The moment had filled him with infinite wonder. He had stared into the future, and it belonged to him forever.

For hours she lay unmoving. From outside came the sounds of ceremony. There was death within and death without. They would meet, and she would perish. So deep was her despair she did not hear Ah Cuc came into the room.

He peered at her closely in the light of the oil lamp he carried. Finally he said, "Come along, Pretty One. It is time to take you away." His words were gentle.

Guadalupe did not move.

"I have a canoe not far from here," Ah Cuc continued. "You'll be able to paddle across the lake. It's quite dark now, and everyone else is really quite occupied."

"Where are they?" Guadalupe's words were like leaves in a wind. "Tell me where they are."

"Who, my dear?"

"Cristóbal, the others?" Guadalupe sat upright and wrapped her arms about herself. "What has happened to them all?"

"They are dead," Ah Cuc replied softly. "The Pale One is dead, he was killed in the fighting." He looked away, knowing that it was kinder to let her believe it had occurred already. "Certain of the others were captured, however. They'll be sacrificed later. It's better if you go before that happens."

"Who are they?"

"Silver Chest and some of the Red Vests. Round Skull is with them also, I believe."

Guadalupe shut her eyes. "No one else survived?" she asked in a dry whisper.

Ah Cuc shook his head. "The Pale One died very bravely," he said. "If it's any comfort to you. He would not let himself be taken alive. Bacal, the head priest, was furious, of course." He sighed and held out a hand to the girl. "Come," he said encouragingly. "I'll take you to the canoe."

"There is no point." Guadalupe made no attempt to move. "If Cristóbal is dead, I have no reason to live."

"Now, that's being very silly. You have lots of things to remember him by."

Guadalupe was silent. The softly flickering light from the oil lamp deepened the darkness under her eyes; her mouth was a crumpled line.

"You . . . well, you might be going to have his baby," Ah Cuc said comfortingly. "Have you thought of that?"

"I am not." Guadalupe's voice eased, and tears formed. "I do not even have that."

"But you do have much to tell," Ah Cuc went on, wondering if it might not be better to inform her of the truth; but then nothing would persuade her to go. "Someone has to go back and report what happened to the expedition," he urged. "I know there's one of the Red Vests on the other side looking after the horses. Even if you only went that far, he could continue the rest of the way. But someone's *got* to do it. You owe the Pale One that.''

Guadalupe put her face in her hands, and tears ran freely. She knew that Ah Cuc spoke the truth, but its finality was bitter: of all who had sailed she, alone, remained. She could not prevent the sobs that filled the room.

Au Cuc watched her patiently. She would go, he realized, once she regained control. But she must go quickly. He himself was in danger as long as she remained in his house.

CHAPTER 8

THE IRON CAME CLOSER, RED AND GLOWING RED, PEELING black cinders like bark from a tree. Its heat was fierce, its nearness extreme. Alec Carson, cook and surgeon from the *Courage*, forced his head away from its menace, thrust backward into the stonework of the narrow cell with a desperation that tore his flesh.

"Well?" said d'Avila—his hand held the glowing iron. "Tell me of your capitán."

"No." Carson's voice was thick with fear. He spoke so little Spanish he understood almost nothing the threatening commander of the garrison said. "My God, take it away."

"When does he come back, Inglés?" The iron shook with d'Avila's intensity. "With the gold? When?"

"Leave me be." The heat of the iron dried the sweat on Carson's skin. "For Christ's sweet sake, I know nothing."

He'd been dragged up here from the dungeons below, pulled by d'Avila, pushed by Alvaréz, the fat jailer, who stood behind his commander now wringing his hands.

As Carson had been shunted away, Cramer the Black had called to him. "He wants the cap'n," Cramer had said. He'd been arguing with d'Avila for almost an hour and knew clearly what the Spaniard was after. "He wants him back to kill him."

"What's that got to do with me?" Carson had struggled, but he'd been chained too long—he was weak with imprisonment. "What's—"

"He thinks we knows," Cramer had replied. "He thinks we'll tell."

"He's mad."

"Aye, but that's no comfort."

"What does he want with me?" Carson had called as they'd unfettered him and bundled him out of the door. "Ask him, by God. He knows I speak little of his tongue."

Cramer had called again to d'Avila, tapping his own chest, attempting to rise. But d'Avila had ignored him; he'd forced Carson up the slime-green steps to this narrow cell and had chained him in a corner. Only then had Carson seen the brazier with its irons firing and felt real fear begin to flow.

"No," he shouted now, his voice pitching, the edge of terror biting. "Get from me. I know nothing. Leave me be."

"Your capitán?" D'Avila inched the iron closer. "Tell me what he told you? Come back? Return? When do you expect him?"

"Nothing." Carson's voice cracked. He could see nothing but the iron near his eye, its heat was everywhere. His bowels loosened, and urine wet his thigh. "Nothing, I tell you. Oh, for God's pity, I know nothing."

"The blackamoor," d'Avila went on, watching the skin on Carson's face change color, seeing the eyelashes curl in the heat, "the blackamoor knows, and he will tell. When he sees you, he will tell. For he realizes that he'll be next."

"Nothing," Carson babbled. "Sweet Jesus, please. A month, he said, but that's gone now. No, take it away."

"When the blackamoor sees your eye he'll speak."

"Señor?" Alvaréz came closer. "I beg you, señor, do not. I mean—" His hands laundered themselves endlessly. "You cannot—"

"He lies," whispered d'Avila, his voice thin, his hand

unsteady. "They all lie. But they will speak. When they see what I have done they'll speak."

"No, señor."

"Watch."

"In god's name,"

"*Watch.*"

The iron went closer; the chains about Carson's wrists shrieked for release. Alvaréz stared, dumbfounded, paralyzed. The veins in Carson's neck swelled. He smelled his own skin burning as his eye began to boil.

"Watch," spat d'Avila. The skin turned red; the eyeball whitened. "What they did to me I will do to them all."

Alec Carson, cook and surgeon, uttered a single shattering scream and collapsed to hang in his shackles. His legs folded, he swung in his chains.

"You see." D'Avila turned to the jailer. "Soon they will all speak the truth."

Alvaréz backed away, appalled, dislocated. He must stop this, must speak to someone, anyone, even Cazaux. He must end this crude lunacy before d'Avila blinded all the prisoners.

The square theatrical throne room was lit by oil lamps and pine torches. Its walls were lined with scented woods carved to show the scenes that were becoming so familiar: dragon-headed serpents with feathers at their throats; nobles with servants; and symbols of death. A figure stretched over an altar block, a priest with a hooked knife in his hand. A victim bound to a stake, bowmen aiming at a circle drawn over his heart. All the carvings were in profile: the arched Mayan noses were arrogant. The heavy-lidded Mayan eyes, sightless and all-seeing, stared down on these, the *last* of their kind.

Stone, van Staal, Meredith, Toledo, and Azcaráte had been stripped of their clothing. Each wore a simple blue loincloth. Their feet were bare. As they'd entered the throne room, they'd been seized by the hair and forced to kneel before the king.

Canek sat on a dais. He wore neither a headdress nor

a cloak; his hair was simply prepared and contained no feathers. To his right, Paxbolón sat in his jaguar mask and his cloak of the same skin. To the king's left, Tutul Katun was dressed as he had been when captured: his stiffly feathered headpiece rose high on his pitted brow, his cloak was a jewel in the shimmering torchlight. Between them, Canek appeared like a plump old owl surrounded by creatures of greater magnificence.

Beside Paxbolón was an elderly, battle-scarred captain, chief of the fighting men. Next to Tutul Katun was the black-wrapped figure of Bacal. His stench was foul, his thick, unpartable hair hung in a screen before his face.

Canck moved the weight of his paunch and cleared his throat. "I am told one of you speaks the language," he began, taking account of all the prisoners.

"Yes." Van Staal's voice was harsh. "If you speak slow."

The faintest smile crossed Canek's lips. "I assure you, I am in no hurry," he replied.

The old king studied the five kneeling before him. Round Skull, who spoke the language like a child, was the most impressive. He was a true warrior; his hard face was defiant, his muscles were firm. There was an open wound on his arm, which he ignored. Silver Chest, also, was formidable; he had eyes that burned with loathing. He was a fanatic, the gods would welcome him. The Pale One was disappointing. True, his long rangy body was scarred in many places, he was clearly a man who had fought often, but he showed none of the pride they spoke of, none of the leadership. The Pale One's head hung to his chest; he appeared abject and greatly defeated. Canek felt somewhat deceived.

He spoke again. "You are here to be told of your sentences," he said slowly and clearly. "Do you know what that means?"

Van Staal nodded. "You kill us—" he began, but disgust rose in his throat, and he added in English, "Your filthy pox-mucked warlocks will slaughter us like sheep."

Canek nodded, he had understood enough. He scratched

the dewlap beneath his chin. "There is, however, an additional matter which concerns the Pale One alone," he said quietly.

Van Staal stared blankly, lost by a turn he had not expected, wondering what was to come.

"The Pale One is to be given a chance," Canek continued. "My son, Lord Paxbolón, has challenged him in the ball game. If he wins, he will go free."

"What?" Van Staal strove to gain more meaning from the words. "I, no—"

Canek repeated what he had said, phrasing the message simply, and saw comprehension begin on Round Skull's face. "Do you understand now?" the king said finally.

Van Staal nodded. "I, ah, tell him," he said uncomfortably, trying to determine the enormity of what he had just been told.

"Please do," said Canek patiently.

Van Staal explained what Canek had said. Stone listened, unmoving: his head hung, his breathing was fast and shallow.

"Do you hear me, Cap'n?" Van Staal leaned closer. "They say, they say you've a chance."

Slowly Stone lifted his pale, skeletal face and stared at van Staal.

"Christopher, do you hear what I say?"

Stone nodded.

"This chance he offers," van Staal persisted, troubled by Stone's silence. "What shall I tell him?"

Stone shook his head savagely, trying to rouse himself from an exhaustion that penetrated to the bone. A chance? The word was meaningless. Yet again he shook his head to clear it—he should hear more. Others were involved.

"Christopher, do you listen?" Van Staal's voice had risen. "Are you with me?"

"Aye," Stone grunted. "What about the rest of you?"

"They've, they've said nothing of the rest."

"Why not?"

"I do not know."

"Then ask."

Van Staal turned to the king. "My, the Pale One, he say, he want to know—" He felt the eyes of all upon him. "He say why we no all have chance for our lives."

Canek pulled at an earlobe. "You had one," he said simply. "And you lost it. But your captain is to be given an extra chance because he gave Lord Tutul Katun a chance on the vessel you came on. He alone did that, so he alone will be given the chance to win back his life." Canek spoke slowly and simply and saw that he was understood. "He will be given his chance in the ball game."

As van Staal told Stone what had been said, he became aware of the restlessness growing in the room: a low growl came from Bacal; shadows moved about the walls.

"This game?" Stone asked when van Staal had finished. "How important is it?" His head was clearing, and some of the numbing fatigue was beginning to lift; his sense of loss was forming its own cocoon. "What do you know of it?"

"I have only heard of it," van Staal replied. "To them it is most important. It is played with a ball of, quic, that is the only word I know for it. The game is hard, and it is skillful. And they take it more seriously than anything, apart from war."

"So there is some prestige involved "

"There is." Van Staal paused, trying to recall what he knew. "The winner is treated as if he were a king. And, and the loser dies."

Stone grunted. This talk of a game among the scented panels and their majesty, between the stench of fear and death, lifted him strangely. It came like a veil, softening the difference between what they were and what they would become. It was a small but necessary relief.

"So, that is the chance you are being given," van Staal continued, unsure how much Stone had listened, how much he cared. "What do I tell them now?"

Stone raised his head to stare at the king. "Tell them I accept," he said, his voice becoming firmer. "But I have a request to make."

"Request?" Van Staal frowned. "What is it?"

"You will see."

The Dutchman began again, halting as he sought words, stumbling as his tongue struggled with the short, harsh sounds. When the court understood what he was trying to say, there were sudden mutterings. Heads turned in anger. Paxbolón straightened his back to stare down at the prisoners. Tutul Katun lifted a hand to cover his lips.

"The Pale One seems to be confused," Canek said finally. "He has no right to requests. A chance to save his life is being given to him, that is all. He can accept it, or he can choose to die with the rest of you."

"Then he choose to die."

Canek leaned forward; there was new interest in the room. "Are you sure of what you say?" he asked carefully.

Van Staal nodded. He had no need to consult Stone.

"Well . . ." Canek paused, curious about the attitude of the Pale One. "Is it that he is afraid to face Lord Paxbolón on the ball court?"

"I say, different," van Staal replied. "I say, lord afraid if he no hear request."

Paxbolón's face flushed darker, and the muscles at his jaw bunched tight. He stared at the Pale One and caught sight of a curious intensity in the invader's red-rimmed eyes.

"Are you suggesting that Lord Paxbolón is a coward?" Canek asked. It was a long time since he'd had so fascinating a conversation. He was beginning to see why the Pale One was regarded so highly. "Are you sure what you are saying?" he asked Round Skull clearly.

Van Staal nodded. "I am sure," he replied.

Canek cleared his throat. "In that case, what does the Pale One request?" he asked.

Van Staal closed his fists. Sweat ran from beneath his arms, the growing tension was like a band of iron across his forehead. Any moment, he believed, the prince in the jaguar skin would leap down and kill them all. Van Staal turned to Stone.

"He wants to know," he said, "what you request of them."

"Very little," Stone replied evenly. His blood was back; he would use it to the utmost. "I will play this game only if all our lives are decided by the same result."

Van Staal rubbed a hand over his face; it came away wet with sweat. "You realize that you may lose all by this?" he muttered.

Stone shook his head. "I think not," he said. "The prince who challenges me is determined to defeat me. Hand to hand, however it may be. I had heard of it before we came. I see it now in his face. He will do anything to achieve it, be it in battle or in this game of theirs."

"But, but the rest of us have already been condemned." Again van Staal hesitated. "You may be sent to join us."

"In that case, so be it. But tell them 'tis the only way I'll play."

Once again van Staal nerved himself to speak. The threats in the room were active now. Bacal hissed like a snake. The battle-scarred captain beside Paxbolón gripped the stabbing spear he held across his knees. Paxbolón's anger stiffened his spine, the desire to rid himself of the Pale One burned white about his mouth.

"My, the Pale One say," van Staal began, licking his lips, "he say if the game played, the prize be all lives."

Canek frowned. "What does that mean exactly?" he asked.

"All lives." Van Staal indicated the five prisoners. "All live if Pale One win."

"No." The word was hissed by Bacal; it stung the air. "Itzamná demands the others now. No—"

"*Yes.*" It was Paxbolón who spoke. He stood, his jaguar tunic alive in the lamplight. No matter what the Pale One asked, the conditions would be met. Paxbolón lifted his proud sloping forehead and stared down in fury. No one would better him now. "Yes," he said again. "I accept."

The lights flickered, a small gust of air went through

the throne room. The figures in the paneled walls looked down in their silence. Canek nodded. There were deeper games being played than any he'd imagined; there were claims that did not involve the Pale One or any of the prisoners.

"Then let it be so," said the old king. "If that is what Lord Paxbolón agrees, then it is decided."

"No." Toledo staggered to his feet, his bound hands before him, his face white with determination. "My life will not be decided by the outcome of some pagan game." He had understood enough of the exchanges between Stone and van Staal; he had seen the acceptance in the eyes of Paxbolón. "The Lord Jesus Christ has led me here. If He so wishes, I will die for Him. My blood will be spilled for Him. Not for—" The Creole's words were cut short by a captain who took him by the hair and threw him to the floor.

As Toledo was silenced Bacal's growl rose, snarling through all the corners of the room, carrying the same fanatical message. "Itzamná demands a sacrifice now," hissed the black-cloaked priest. "The lizard god, the Dragon Master, will wait no longer."

"Be quiet," the old king snapped. "I wish to know what Silver Chest has said." He turned his heavy-folded face to van Staal. "Translate," he ordered.

Stumbling, almost tongue-tied now, van Staal carried out the demand.

"Then it is decided." Canek's voice was final. "Silver Chest and the other Red Vest will be offered to Itzamná this night. The lives of the others will be decided by what passes on the ball court. Let no more be said."

There were whispers, there was movement. All in the ornate room were caught by sudden fire. Stone stared up at the tall, arrogant, jaguar-clad figure with whom he was to play this deadly game and welcomed his defiance.

Paxbolón gazed back in disdain. Yet there was something about the gaunt, fierce-eyed invader he approved. Their meeting on the ball court would be as challenging as any he had experienced. He held no fear of losing. He was the greatest player in Tayasal; it was unlikely that the Pale One would gain a single point. But it would be fascinating to watch the fierceness in the invader's eyes ignite as he was taunted on the stone-layered court, as the hard ball winded him, as the crowd jeered.

Tutul Katun did not move; his eyes remained downcast before him. He would await the game as patiently as he was able. Three days would need to pass for the ritual cleansing. But surely the moment would come. It would come as certainly as Silver Chest, and the Red Vest who sobbed, would be offered this night to Itzamná.

Mist floated and spun; the shoreline was a black scoop within enfolding darkness. Darkness wreathed in every corner of the lake, obliterating all sense of direction, shrouding any memory she might have had of being there before. Guadalupe Santoya pushed at the dark water with a broken paddle as she searched for the campsite. For hours she'd fumbled her way through rushes, looking for somewhere to land.

Behind her, just visible through the floating, misting blackness, was a glow from the city. She'd tried to keep it at her back, using it as a beacon, but nowhere had she found the site she was seeking.

Once she'd nosed the little boat into where she thought it might have been. She'd stepped into cold water to find no footing; her leg had sunk into mud that rose, bottomless, about her calf. Quickly she'd pulled back and held herself steady.

Later she'd come to the shoreline again, and the paddle had caught in the branches of a sunken tree. In sudden panic she'd pulled at the blade, snapping half of it away.

Now she was weary, worn by grief and effort, by emptiness and a fear that seemed to fester all about her. She had never been so alone. The sounds of the forest came and went. Somewhere a monkey howled, and Guadalupe lifted her head, straining at the piercing noise, looking once more toward the city.

From what she could make out, the glow in the great plaza had increased. By forcing her eyes she was able to discern a snail's trail of fire ascending the temple steps.

She heard the muted, clotted sound of distant voices, of faraway trumpets.

Then, with a suddenness that shocked, the darkness around her seemed to be opened by a cold flat shriek of human agony that shot across the lake water, cutting through her like a knife. Guadalupe put her hands over her ears. She heard the sound of her own voice praying.

CHAPTER 9

THE TEMPLE THAT TOWERED OVER TAYASAL WAS ABLAZE with light. Warriors with pine torches lined its perimeter. Priests with oil lamps illuminated each of its descending stages. Light poured from and about the nine-tiered edifice like a finely filtered spray; soft light, yellow light, reached out to cover the city.

At the top of the temple, amassed before the door of the square, flat-walled chamber, the five prisoners waited. Toledo and Azcaráte had been painted blue, the color of sacrifice. Together with Stone, van Staal, and Meredith, they had been marched up the eighty-one steps to the court of Itzamná—Toledo going boldly, his eyes bright, his head high; Azcaráte stumbling, weeping, prodded on by the spears of the temple guards. The three from the *Courage* went sullenly. They were there to witness the ceremony.

Below the shining temple, filling all corners of the plaza, were gathered the citizens of Tayasal. They waited for what would be thrown to them. Stone stared down at them, his eyes flat with detestation. There was nothing noble about their conduct, they had no secrets to share. Beside him, Stone heard Meredith begin to growl.

"This why we left Campeche, Cap'n?" Meredith's voice was hard as stone. "This is what we came for?"

265

"None of this is what we came for," Stone replied hoarsely. "None of it."

"So they died for nowt, the others?" Meredith's gnarled body twitched. "Piet and Henri, Simmons—?"

Stone had nothing to say.

Meredith's voice was unyielding. "We followed you, Cap'n. We came because you said there'd be a prize."

"I believed it also."

"But you were wrong."

Stone turned and stared into the gunner's face; it carried still the marks of Guadalupe's nails. On his back the burns also remained. Stone saw no fear in Meredith, only outrage and something else: an odium for those who were ready for a prize they had not earned.

"You were wrong, Cap'n," Meredith said again, his voice grinding the words to power. "Admit it, you were wrong."

"Yes—" The word caught in Stone's thought. "I was wrong."

"And we'll die for it?" Meredith turned his angry eyes to Stone. "The way the others died?"

"The others died fighting," Stone replied, his own bitterness rising. "Our deaths will not be as bold."

Meredith blinked; his glance flickered toward Toledo and Azcaráte. "We'll go like them?" he asked, and licked his lips. "Is that what you're saying?"

"We'll go like them," Stone answered. "Whatever chance they've given us, 'twill not amount to much."

Meredith breathed deeply; the growl went from his voice. "I'm sorry about the girl," he said a moment later. "There's no chance she got away?" It was all he had to offer.

Stone shook his head, accepting. They stood, shoulder to shoulder, grateful for each other's presence as Bacal climbed the temple steps. He passed them, his body reeking, and went into the flat-walled chamber. Behind him came other priests with torches: black-clad, barefoot, bloodied angels of death.

Roughly, the prisoners were ushered into the court of Itzamná and were further stilled by what they saw.

Blood clung, thick as tar, about the walls. It hung in encrusted folds; it lay in graveled streams across the floor, scouring the unshod feet of the prisoners.

The idol Itzamná was carved from blackened stone. He had the face of an ancient: sunken cheeks and toothless jaws. His eyes were inlaid with jade and turquois; they glittered in the torchlight. About his wizened face, involving it, was a lizard head. The eyes of the lizard lay above those of Itzamná. They too were filled with precious stones; the two pairs watched in concert each movement the prisoners made. The lizard god, the Dragon Master, sat cross-legged on a coiled snake; at his feet was Toledo's breastplate. It had been polished and shone like a defeated sun.

In jade dishes, which rested on the knees of Itzamná, were the hearts of five Indians who had been sacrificed the day before. They were stiff with blood and crawled with flies who, disturbed by torchlight, came out from the walls and their bloody matting.

The stomachs of the prisoners jerked; their mouths filled with saliva. Meredith spat on the filthy floor, and a torchbearer hit him from behind. He fell to his knees, his face a few inches from the encrusted blood; with an effort he held his vomit. Slowly, he climbed back to his feet.

"I'll kill you," he snarled at the torchbearer, all the grinding hatred returning to his voice. "I'll—"

"Wait," Stone urged, his stomach crawling. "Wait, or they'll kill you now."

Meredith snorted but held his rage as Bacal, standing before Itzamná, began to swing an earthenware incense burner made in the shape of the god. A heavy scent of copal, the resin that burned in the censer, filled the rotten air; black fumes drifted.

"Itzamná," Bacal intoned. "You have waited long, and you have waited patiently. Now we ask that you accept our offering."

The priests about the scabbed walls muttered, Azcaráte sobbed steadily, Toledo was quiet, and the pirates from the *Courage* could not keep their features still: they twitched at the offense being performed around them.

Then Bacal turned and stared at Azcaráte. He said nothing; his gaze was enough. An attendant came forward to cut the ropes that bound Azcaráte's hands, and the Spaniard's eyes went everywhere, seeking anything that might assure him that the inevitable would not occur: his sense of disbelief astounded him.

"Mother of God, no," he whispered, his frog eyes bulging from his terrified face. "No, in the name of the Virgin, no."

A temple warrior prodded Azcaráte with a spear, and the blue-painted figure stumbled forward. "Tell him he must dance," Bacal said to van Staal.

Van Staal stared at the priest in silent disgust.

"Tell him to dance," Bacal hissed. "He must dance to please the god."

"What?" Azcaráte asked pathetically. "What did he say?"

"He—" Van Staal cleared his throat. "He wants you to dance."

"Dance?" Azcaráte looked about him. "Will that help me, will it—"

"I do not know," van Staal cut into the pitiable words. "It's what they want."

Almost immediately a drum in the corner of the fetid room began to beat. Over it crouched a black-clad priest tapping its snakeskin cover. As its rhythm grew, Azcaráte began a shuffling step. Shambling from one bare foot to the other, he danced before the hideous god, his eyes never leaving Bacal's, searching for some sign that this would be enough. He hopped clumsily from one side of the chamber to the other, while the priests watched solemnly and the pirates were further sickened. Toledo ignored the shame.

Bacal raised a hand, and all saw what it contained: a knife whose blade was chipped from pale green chalcedony, whose wooden handle was carved to form a pair of intertwined serpents. From the mouth of one of the snakes the green blade grew; the head of the other was the nub of the handle. The bodies of the reptiles were overlaid with gold. High in Bacal's hand, in the softly polishing lamplight, the knife was as beautiful as it was sinister.

Azcaráte saw it, and his dancing ceased. His mouth opened, and his knees collapsed. He fell to the blood-stained floor, and the warm smell of feces joined the stench in the air.

"Present him," Bacal whispered. "Itzamná is ready."

From the shadowy walls four old men in loincloths came forward. Each took a limb of the whimpering Spaniard and dragged him toward a low block of smooth stone shaped like the back of a turtle. They arranged the unresisting Azcaráte so that the arch of the stone went into the small of his back. They held his hands and feet firmly on the floor.

Bacal came close, the sacrificial knife held high, and Azcaráte screamed. His cry sent shivers through all who watched. Even Toledo twitched in his trance. Azcaráte screamed again, and a fifth aged attendant came out of the shadows to put a rope across the Spaniard's neck, choking him short.

Bacal stood above the victim, his eyes on his god. "Itzamná, father of us all, we ask that you accept our offering." His harsh voice was hushed, the words barely seemed to leave his tongue.

"We ask that you accept." The chorus came from other priests about the gruesome walls. "We ask that you are generous."

As the responses died, Bacal struck. The pale green chalcedony blade slashed down to rip open the left side of Azcaráte's chest. The Spaniard gave a strangled cry, and his body jerked convulsively. As the garroted scream filled the ugly chamber, Bacal reached beneath the dying man's ribs and tore the still beating heart from his chest. With two short, practiced blows, the priest cut the arteries from the organ; blood spurted high about the room. It spilled on Bacal's cloak, joining the decay already there. It splattered over his face and hair, adding to the rotting mixture.

Bacal lifted the heart, and as it gave a final palpitation, he touched the cheeks of Itzamná with it, then placed it in a green jade dish that stood waiting on the stone god's knees. In the jumping torchlight the god's four eyes were fire.

Immediately other priests came forward with bowls in their hands, which they dipped into the open wound on Azcaráte's chest. They splashed the blood they collected about the walls of the sacrificial court. Incense burners were swung, the smell of copal again filled the ghastly air. Two old men in loincloths placed long trumpets to their lips and blew high, keening notes that went out all over the city.

At the sound of the trumpets, the crowd about the temple steps thickened, their faces expectant. The attendants, who had held Azcaráte over the slaughter stone, picked up the body and carried it to the top of the great stairway. They swung it once, then flung it down to the waiting crowd. Bouncing, the wound in the chest spilling blood, the arms and legs loosely flailing, the remains of the Spaniard spun like a ragged doll in their descent.

At the base of the temple, priests of a lower order took the corpse and laid it out on a flagstone. With knives and obsidian saws they began to cut the blue-stained limbs from the body. The hands and feet were taken first; they would be reserved for Bacal. The arms and legs were cut into small pieces and distributed among those who pressed eagerly for the meat, their hands thrusting, their expressions eager.

From the top of the temple stairway, the remaining prisoners were forced to watch the butchery. Of the four, only Toledo was unaffected. His face had become blank and pale, and sweat glistened on his waxen forehead like damp upon a stone. His eyes seemed sightless; they gazed beyond the present, beyond the murder and the gluttony.

The others were appalled in a new, a more enraging manner. The death of Azcaráte in the stinking room possessed an aspect of ritual, however repellent. But the scene below was without order. The greed on the faces was sickening. The hands that stretched for the still warm flesh were hooked in their hunger. The noise that rose from the avid throats was an unordained demand.

Stone closed his eyes and turned away. Van Staal stared, his round face ashen, his lips down-curled in horror. But Meredith began to growl anew.

"Filth," he cried suddenly. "Pox-mucked, shit-filled filth." He swung his tight body toward Bacal, his bound hands rising. "You whore of the devil," he shouted, and went toward the black-clad priest.

A temple warrior came between them to tackle the invader. Meredith made a savage chopping movement with his shackled hands, and the man fell to the floor, his neck broken. Bacal backed away. One of the attendants who had held Azcaráte leapt forward, trying to grasp the ex-woodcutter's arms. For a second they struggled; then Meredith, his eyes burning with hate, took the aged attendant by the throat and throttled him.

Others fell upon the pirate, pulling at his arms, taking him by the hair, pressing with spears. But nothing broke Meredith's grip: his wiry fingers tore into the attendant's throat, his arms were like steel. Finally a temple warrior, carrying a short wooden club, smashed the pirate's skull. There was a soft thudding sound, and Meredith's eyes clouded. For seconds the enraged body seemed to hang in the position it had held in life, then it collapsed.

No one moved. Beside him, Stone heard van Staal's breathing. "No," he whispered to himself, to Stone. "There is nothing you can do."

Then Bacal came forward and hissed an order. The corpses of the attendant and the warrior were laid aside, that of Meredith thrown to the crowd below. As the sounds of greed rose once again, Jaime Toledo Flores turned and walked into the chamber of Itzamná. His head was high, his eyes glazed, his step that of a sleepwalker.

The Creole proceeded steadily through the vile air, through the mists of copal that wreathed the malevolent god, to the turtle-backed sacrificial stone. And there he stood, his hands held out for their bindings to be cut, his lips moving softly in an unheard prayer.

Bacal stared, then spat another order: an attendant with a knife removed Toledo's cords. Four others approached, uncertain now their authority had been usurped, unnecessary now that the victim had assumed the conduct of the ritual.

Bacal beckoned van Staal. "Tell him to dance," he croaked.

Van Staal's jaw tightened. "He no dance," he muttered.

"He must." Anger darkened further Bacal's swarthy face. "Itzamná demands it."

"Itzamná can drink his father's piss for all Toledo cares," van Staal said in English. "Take what you have, you shit-faced mongrel."

"Steady, Rolf." Stone's voice was controlled. "Let the Creole die as he wishes to die. But we've nothing to gain by going with him."

"He won't dance for this pox-sired warlock."

"Make it known, easily."

"What is being said?" Bacal's eyes were sharp as flint. "What words do you use to defile this holy place?"

Van Staal breathed deeply. "The, Silver Chest, no dance," he said slowly, biting on each word. "He, big warrior. Too big for dance. God know that." The Dutchman's voice was bleak with hatred.

Bacal hesitated. He turned to Toledo and saw the blankness in the eyes, the emptiness in the face. Round Skull spoke the truth, Silver Chest would not dance. He was in a state of supreme holiness, and his heart was ready. The moment was divine.

"Prepare him," Bacal told the attendants, and lifted the knife with its greenstone blade. "Itzamná waits."

The attendants moved forward. As they reached for Toledo's hands the Creole turned to Stone. "Say a Mass for me, Inglés," he said clearly. "If you ever leave this satanic place, see that a Mass is said for my soul." His eyes were steady as he spread his hands.

Toledo was laid over the arched stone. The green blade lifted. "Itzamná, son of Hunab Kú, we offer you this. It comes from a great warrior. A man who is close to other gods. Take his heart and become them." The knife came down.

Blood spurted, wetting the face and hair of Bacal. Blood was used to dampen the face of the old-man god with the reptile body. The heart of Toledo touched the shriveled lips, then it went to a jade dish. The body was cast down the giant stairway to the greed that stirred below. Blood dripped down the walls of the dreadful chamber; it began to dry on the crusted floor. Darkness filled the throne room of the wizened god, and the flies returned to the matting on which they feasted.

To the hollow sound of bleating trumpets, Stone and van Staal were led down the bloodstained steps. Priests swinging incense burners walked beside them. Bacal remained above.

The marketplace was quieter now. No hands reached out, no faces pressed. The citizens of Tayasal looked at the tall invader with curiosity now. All knew of the ball game, and they wondered how he would perform in three days' time when the rubber ball was thrown into the stone court and the play of life and death began.

Stone and van Staal were taken to a small, windowless cell behind Canek's palace. It was lit with pine torches, and two simple frame beds with cotton blankets were at one end of the room. On a table were dishes containing stewed meats, fruit, flat Mayan bread; there was also a jug of cornwater. The prisoners' bindings were removed, and they were left alone with the images of blood and greed that burned into their brains, with the sounds of pain and pagan ritual that filled their ears.

He'd been broken once and mended, had halted the downward slide; now he was lost again, searching for an ending to his blind and chilling loneliness in the bottom of a bottle. It was absurd, Don Luis told himself, it was ridiculous, it should really make him laugh.

Don Luis coughed and a bubble burst from his nose.

He was alone, so much alone he pitied himself. His wife had died, his daughter had deserted him, and now the town he loved was indifferent to his presence. He had even been forced into a dishonest bargain with d'Avila, a madman who sought nothing but revenge.

It was unfair, Don Luis told himself, as he fumbled for more brandy; it was not right that Jean-Marc Cazaux, a pirate from the sea, should represent the only law, the only order, that functioned in Campeche. It was unjust, monstrously unremittingly unjust that not a soul seemed to care what he, don Luis de Cordóba, mayor of the port, thought or did. They were ungrateful, all of them. How was he expected to withstand so much alone?

Don Luis drank, and wanted more, his need had no ending.

CHAPTER 10

IN THE MAIN CABIN OF *La Petite*, SEATED AT THE ORNATE chart table, one of Angela's hands in his own, Jean-Marc Cazaux looked into the girl's dark-pupiled eyes and sighed.

"We are to be married in the church of Guadalupe," he said. "The bishop will conduct the ceremony. Your father has spoken to him, and he says it will be a privilege."

"Papá is being so sweet about everything," Angela said, her voice rich with content. "He seems quite a lot better, now that everything is settled."

"It pleases him to see you happy," Cazaux replied, a vision of Don Luis's gloomy face in mind. "I feel it gives him strength."

Angela smiled. It had been less complicated than even she might have imagined. Men were such children. All that talk about old wounds and inability made her laugh. Jean-Marc performed as well as anyone she'd ever known . . . well, almost so, and certainly as frequently. He had needed encouragement, that was all, and a sense of unfulfillment. Both had been quite simply achieved. It was amazing how some people responded to ingenuousness, the idea that one could not do without them.

And as far as her father was concerned, it had just

275

been a matter of time, although if she were to be honest about it, he *was* drinking more than he should. Mind you, she reasoned, he'd always drank more than most, especially after his arrival here. Perhaps it was the effect of the tropics. But recently she'd noticed his consumption of brandy had become quite extreme. She realized that it had a lot to do with his idleness, his waiting for something dramatic to occur. The arrival of Jean-Marc somehow hadn't been enough. When the party that had gone to the interior returned, he'd be better. In the meantime, she should set her mind to finding something for him to focus on. That shouldn't be too difficult. Angela smiled radiantly and watched Cazaux ignite. Men were dear creatures, really.

Her cheek went close to the Frenchman's. "When will we be married?" she asked softly.

"Soon," Cazaux replied. "But first we should have a celebration."

"A celebration?"

"Of course. We have much to rejoice in." Cazaux stroked her sensuous flesh. "What should it be?" he asked. "Think of something appropriate."

"Me?" Angela's eyelashes fluttered. "My love, what would please you most of all?"

"Something exciting," Cazaux whispered. "Something which, shall we say, encompasses all our passion and, at the same time, acknowledges that I remain here in peace."

"All of that?"

"Yes, all of that."

It began as a smile, and it grew until Angela's laughter filled the cabin. The veins in her noble neck filled, and the tapestries about the wall trembled with its volume. "I have it," she cried, clapping her hands. "I know exactly what it is you are looking for."

"And what is that?" Cazaux leaned forward eagerly.

"A cockfight." Angela laughed again. "They are famous for them here. They celebrate the best occasions. They are full of color and action and passion. Unfortunately, one of the birds must die, but that is only to be expected." She lifted her tremendous eyes to Cazaux. "What do you say to that?" she asked.

Cazaux sat back and smiled enigmatically. "That is a very clever thought," he said finally.

"Thank you." Angela bowed her beautiful head. "I am so glad it pleases you."

"It pleases me greatly." Cazaux moved closer again. With his long fingers he began to undo the buttons of her high-necked bodice. "It pleases me that you are so clever."

"Am I?" Angela's head came up like a cat's; her eyes were closed, her voice throaty. "That feels marvelous," she said as his hand descended. "More," she purred.

Cazaux continued. "You are quite sure of everything, are you not?" he asked, his fingers not ceasing to explore.

"Perhaps," Angela whispered. She could feel her body burning like an oven. "Perhaps I am."

"You are not, shall we say, quite as silly as you sometimes pretend to be?"

"Oh"—Angela's eyes widened for a moment—"don't tell me I displease you."

"No, of course not," Cazaux replied hurriedly.

"Are you sure?"

"Yes," Cazaux said, his fingers moving lower. "I am sure, God be my witness, I am sure." Again he wondered who had spun the web, and again it did not matter. "I adore you, as you are."

"I am glad." Once more the splendid eyes were closed; once more the voice was purring. "All the way down, please."

Cazaux's fingers touched the flesh that threatened to catch fire. He moved closer to possess it when there was a knock on the cabin door. The Frenchman turned, his expression both angry and perplexed. After a moment the knocking was resumed.

"Come in," Cazaux said impatiently. "What is it?"

The duty boy's face appeared about the door. Angela's eyes grew round with interest. Cazaux blinked.

"Forgive me, *mon capitaine*—"

"I have already told you I have no need of you," Cazaux said rapidly in French. "Do you not understand?"

"*Oui, mon capitaine*, I understand, but"—the boy's voice rose nervously—"there is someone who has come out to speak with you."

"Come out? Out to *La Petite*?" Cazaux frowned. "What does he want?"

"I do not know, m'sieu. He will not say, m'sieu. He wishes to speak with you alone. He persuaded M'sieu Cordier to row him here. He—"

"He must be very persuasive if he managed that," Cazaux replied, a particle of his good humor returning. "Who is he?"

"One Alvaréz, a jailer from the fort." The duty boy rubbed his hands together uncertainly. "He says it is urgent, otherwise I would not have, would not have interrupted you."

"And he will not tell you what he wants?"

"No, m'sieu, only that it is urgent."

Cazaux sighed. He almost moved from his chair, but then he turned back to Angela and saw again the fire in her eyes and lost all interest in an unknown Spanish jailer.

"Tell him to come back in the morning," Cazaux called over his shoulder. "I will listen to him then."

"*Oui, mon capitaine*." The duty boy sounded quietly dismayed. "I will tell him that. In the morning, you say?"

"Yes," Cazaux replied dryly. "In the morning."

"Of course, *mon capitaine*." The duty boy closed the cabin door. "Of course," he repeated as he went away.

Cazaux looked into the depths of Angela's eyes and saw twin images of himself. Very slowly he leaned forward, feeling the fire reach out to him, and kissed each eyelid, closing the door on his reflections.

Guadalupe Santoya woke to the gentle rocking of the canoe. It was not yet light. The sun was a russet cast in the hills behind her, the island an emerging bulk across the water. She shivered; her body was stiff from its cramped position, her face and hands swollen from the mosquitoes that had lifted from the rushes like a plague.

She heard a splash and turned quickly to see the widening rings where a fish had jumped. The action alerted her, and she reached for the broken paddle. She felt empty and incompetent, yet she had no choice but to continue seeking the campsite. She had no choice but to go on, to find Grajales, the Spaniard who had been left there, and tell him what she knew.

She plunged the paddle into the water, and the canoe nosed ahead. Almost immediately she saw the tiny stream by which they had camped. Its presence came up mockingly, smacking her into response. She pushed the canoe to the lakeside.

Ashore, the campsite was deserted. There was no sign of Grajales or the horses. Confused, Guadalupe began up a hill, following the trail that had been used when they first came to the site, stumbling a little over the long skirt of coarse-woven cloth she'd taken from the house of Tutz. She labored upward to a small clearing in the forest, and there she turned to look back across the water to the city. It was radiant in the emerging sun; it was almost impossible to believe it had produced such terror and such loss.

Guadalupe closed her eyes, stilling the pain of memory. Then she heard a long, low whistle, and the suspended moment broke. Fear returned with force, came back with such speed she could not move. Every muscle was rigid, each part of her body seemed separate and frozen. The whistle came again, and she spun, her eyes round with panic. She was about to run headlong from the lake when she heard a voice call her name.

"Guadalupe." The cry was repeated. "Help me. I cannot get down alone."

She looked upward. Above her, in the broad limbs of a sapodilla, was Grajales. He was a small man with round friendly eyes, and his right arm was useless. The arrow wound, inflicted when Tutul Katun had been captured, had healed, but the nerves had not recovered, and the limb swung without purpose; already its muscles were beginning to wither.

Grajales crouched on a branch some ten feet from the ground. "I climbed up here last night," he explained. "When I heard the noise from the city. Now I am caught."

"Wait." Relief washed through Guadalupe with the intensity of cramp. "I will help you."

By standing on one of the high gnarled roots, she was able to get within two feet of the Spaniard. "Give me your hand," she called up to him.

Grajales shook his head. "I am afraid of falling onto those roots," he said. "They are like iron."

"Then can you climb onto my back?"

Grajales raised his eyebrows. "I will try," he said doubtfully. Slowly, his thighs stiff with disuse, he turned cautiously on the branch and extended a foot. Guadalupe took hold of it and placed it on her shoulder. Grajales swung the other leg and felt the girl grasp it. "Now," she said. "Let go."

"I, I don't think I can. I am not very brave."

"Do it. You will be safe."

Reluctantly, Grajales forced the fingers of his good hand to open and allowed his feet to take his weight. With a rush he fell onto the girl, and they both spilled onto grass and matted leaves beside the tree. Gasping, a moment later they climbed to their feet.

"I am sorry," Grajales began. "My arm—"

"Be grateful for your arm," Guadalupe interrupted bluntly. "Without it you would be dead."

Grajales's round eyes opened wider. "You, you are the only one alive?" he asked cautiously.

Guadalupe nodded.

"All the others—?"

"They are dead," said Guadalupe bleakly. "Later I will tell you more." She looked away. "Where are the horses?" she asked.

Grajales stared, noting for the first time the hollows in her face, the lines of grief about her eyes. "The horses are over there," he said, pointing behind him. "Come, I will show you." In time she would tell him what had happened; in the meantime he would do what he could to keep her mind from the pain that shrouded her face.

"You hid them?" Guadalupe said, her voice dry. "That was wise."

Grajales nodded. As they walked to where he had left the horses, he told her what had happened after the galley had put out onto the lake.

As soon as the vessel was clear, the four Tipu Indian slaves who had carried Tutul Katun's palanquin had fled. Each took a horse and released the rest. Grajales had attempted to prevent them, to no avail. They had made no effort to harm him but were merely concerned with escaping and not being followed.

After they'd gone, he'd managed to recapture three horses. These he'd hidden, and he was on his way back to the campsite when he'd seen the galley founder and the bearers begin to come ashore. Quietly he'd returned to the horses, in their hollow in the hills, and had waited until the bearers had gone.

Alone again, he'd watched the city all the following day until the great crowd had gathered in the plaza. He'd seen the activity on the temple steps and heard Azcaráte scream. That was when he'd climbed the sapodilla tree, not realizing he'd be unable to descend.

"As I say, I am not very brave." Grajales smiled ruefully. "When I heard you coming, I was very afraid."

"You have more courage than you admit," Guadalupe assured him. "You could have gone when the galley sank. You must have known that no one would return."

"You are here," Grajales said simply.

"I was lucky." Guadalupe's voice altered. "The companion of the prince helped me escape." She shuddered, suddenly, violently. "I want to get away from here as soon as I can," she whispered.

Grajales took Guadalupe's arm. "Come," he said. "We will go immediately." He looked into the girl's eyes. "You are sure there is no reason to wait any longer?"

"I am sure," Guadalupe replied, and began to move away.

Canek's high-walled palace seemed to float on three great levels. One above the other they spread like beautifully carved ornate tables, decorated as though for a feast. Stately trees grew by ponds with fish and lilies; tame birds strolled past sculptures. The palace held a splendor that went beyond a single race. It was timeless.

Canek, king of the Itzá, stared into the dark water of a pond, watching multicolored fish rise and dive away again to hide beneath the heavy plates of lily leaves. The freshening warmth of the early sun was on his back, the air was cool and its flavor delicate. These mornings were Canek's favorite part of the day. He grunted with pleasure as he listened to what his younger son was saying.

"Bacal informs me that the signs are favorable," Tutul Katun said gently. "This is a good day for the cleansing to begin."

"The cleansing is a part I do not welcome," Canek muttered. "The abstinence. The dreadfully plain food."

Tutul Katun smiled. "The food I can understand, Father. But I would not have thought the abstinence worried you greatly."

"I enjoy the visits of the painted boys," Canek said with a smile. "In that manner I am not unlike you, my son." He paused, then added, "But one day you will have children, is that not so?"

"Of course, Father. I take pleasure in all manner of good things."

"That is wise." The king was pleased. "You will need children."

Tutul Katun made no attempt to reply.

"You understand?" Canek turned to look into his son's pitted face. In the early light it appeared soft, almost childlike. It appeared as it had appeared so often in the past, looking up from its playthings, turning from its study: simple and sensitive and knowing. "You understand that when this is over there will be much to be done?"

Tutul Katun bowed his head in acknowledgment. "From the beginning I have known that all of this would mean much," he replied softly.

"You have great insight." Canek cleared his throat. "You must have inherited it from your mother. I have never seen things quite as clearly."

"You are being modest," Tutul Katun said gently. "All I have learned has come from you."

The old king grunted; he moved his back in the sun for a moment, savoring its warmth, then said, "Now I will go and break my fast with something uninteresting. Later, we may speak more of this."

"Yes, my father," Tutul Katun replied carefully. "Later, we may."

The old king waddled across the terrace to one of the wide stone-framed doors and disappeared between twin columns shaped like feathered serpents. Tutul Katun watched him go, a smile on his lips, then he went to the far end of the patio and looked down at the invaders' galley, half-sunken in the lake. Birds rested on its stern, canoes nudged past curiously. It would be left until rot and the water claimed it. It was a symbol of the forces that had come and the changes that were about to occur.

Tutul Katun heard a sound behind him and turned to see Ah Cuc stepping gracefully over the stonework. They exchanged greetings and embraced briefly, knowing that even this slight contact was against the rules that applied until the ball game was over and the feasting began.

"Tell me, Ah Cuc," Tutul Katun asked a few minutes later as they watched a group of peacocks peck between flagstones, "what do they say about the game?"

Ah Cuc smiled. "Few can speak of anything else," he replied. "Although no one doubts that Lord Paxbolón will win," he added hurriedly.

Tutul Katun nodded. "That is how it should be," he murmured.

"Well, of course. The Pale One knows nothing of the game at all. He has very little chance."

"Very little," Tutul Katun agreed. "Although he will be shown the court and have the rules explained."

Ah Cuc nodded dubiously as they began to walk between broad-leafed plants and colored shrubs, admiring their foliage. "Will he also be told about the Pretty One?" he asked.

Tutul Katun shook his head. "No," he said firmly. "He will be told nothing."

"Perhaps it is better," Ah Cuc agreed. "After all, it would make no difference to him now."

"None." Tutul Katun walked beneath a tree from which a pair of scarlet macaws stared down curiously at the men below. "It would not help him at all."

"And, it might, well, weaken him to know that she was safe. Is that not so, my lord?"

"Precisely." A smile touched Tutul Katun's lips. "For the sake of the spectators, nothing should take the edge from the Pale One's anger."

Ah Cuc bowed low. "I understand completely, my lord," he said with mischief in his voice. "And I must congratulate you on your thoughtfulness."

"Thank you, Ah Cuc," Tutul Katun replied easily. He paused to smell a flower. "Now, tell me what else I might have missed."

"My lord, you never miss anything."

"Not so. I knew nothing of the Pretty One until you told me about her yesterday. So think, there may be other little matters I should be told about."

Ah Cuc was briefly silent; then his voice lifted, and he began again. They strolled the length of the elegant terrace and back, Ah Cuc chattering, Tutul Katun listening. From their perch the scarlet macaws watched, their wrinkled eyes inclined, their huge beaks unmoving, as the couple paraded below.

During the night the food was taken away, but neither of them had heard a sound as they slept. Now, in the early dawn, Stone thought about the game as if nothing else existed. It was the way it had to be. She was gone. That was final. Her death gave him grit to whet his anger

on, and as such he would use it. All else in this alien
place stank of blood and fear. He would rid himself of
the stench by concentrating on the game. Three days
waited until it would be played. He'd keep his sanity
until the moment arrived, working toward the time. It
was the only statement he could make.

He leaned on an elbow and saw that van Staal was
also awake. "Rolf," he called softly. "Tell me what you
know of it."

"The game?" It filled van Staal's mind also. "Is that
what you ask?"

"Aye," said Stone. "It is."

Van Staal sat up and looked at Stone. Some of the
color had returned to the Englishman's face; the mouth
was determined. Van Staal felt his own heart move in
gratitude, in relief. "What games have you played?" he
asked.

"I've kicked a pig's bladder over the common," Stone
replied. "I've thrown wooden balls at fairs."

"But you've not used your hip or your elbow. Or had
a ball hit you over the heart with force enough to kill."
Van Staal's voice gained pace. "They'd talk of it at
night," he added. "In the mines, while others spoke of
wars, the Maya would talk of the game. 'Tis like a war
for them."

Stone grunted. "I expect it to be brutal," he said.
"But, God's blood, we must have some sort of chance."

"Aye, we have," van Staal replied, grasping at what
little they possessed. "A simple chance."

"Then let's make a plan to win." Stone swung his feet
to the floor. "Show me what you know."

Van Staal left the bed and went to the center of the
room. There, with a piece of broken stone he found in a
corner of the cell, he began to draw an outline of a ball
court on the floor.

CHAPTER 11

GUADALUPE AND GRAJALES RODE STEADILY NORTH, BACK toward Campeche. As they rode together, the spare horse following on a lead, Guadalupe told the Spaniard what had happened in Tayasal. As they headed over the hills and down toward the green valley in which they'd first contacted the Maya, she spoke flatly, unemotionally, telling him what he had to know.

Grajales said nothing, allowing the girl to ease herself of some of her pain without interruption. He said nothing for a day, but that evening, as they sat beside a tiny fire, eating fruit and yam roots Guadalupe had baked in the coals, he asked her what she thought the future held.

Guadalupe's eyes came up quickly, as if the question had no place; then she looked away. After a while she said, "I will return to my mother." Her voice was flat as still water.

"You would not consider returning to what you were?" Grajales asked gently.

"What do you mean? Go back to d'Avila?" Guadalupe's eyes shone resentfully. "Pretend that nothing has happened?"

Grajales nodded. "It would be possible," he said.

"Not for me," Guadalupe replied. "I will go to the

barrio and live with my mother. We, we will remain together.''

"That would seem to be a waste," Grajales observed without design. "You are young, and you are pretty. There is much the future holds for you.''

Guadalupe looked at him: his eyes were friendly, in his soiled red doublet he appeared a little like a jester. "What do you suggest?" she asked pointedly.

"Nothing." Grajales raised his good hand as if to dispel any misconception. "This is the present," he added with a smile. "I was talking of the future.''

"I, I do not think of the future," Guadalupe said, but her tone was softening. He was what she needed, this gentle man with the friendly eyes, allowing her to be what she was. "Anyway," she added, showing a new resolve, "the future will not begin until we reach Campeche. And that is some time away.''

"It is," Grajales agreed, "but the time will pass.''

Guadalupe sighed. "In the meantime, thank you," she said quietly. "Thank you for being kind to me now.''

Grajales smiled and did not reply. He reached for a fresh piece of yam, peeled away the coal-black skin, and ate the delicate, scented flesh. She was curious, this girl who had come to translate and had achieved so much more; her future was impossible to define. He watched her and listened to the night and was suddenly grateful for his crippled arm.

Throughout the city of Tayasal was an air of quiet festivity. None could recall an event of such importance. Some of the very old remembered the sacrifice of the lone Castilian priest and his eighty Tipu Indians, half a century ago, but even that seemed insignificant when compared with what was about to happen. Never had a disbeliever taken part in the ball game.

According to custom, the Pale One and Round Skull were treated well while they waited. They were not expected to fast as the rest of Tayasal fasted. It was required that they be healthy when the game began so that the Pale One would play with all his strength, so that their bodies were well filled when the flesh was distributed at the foot of the temple staircase.

As for Lord Paxbolón, he had been seen at practice in the ball court. His game was as skilled as any could remember. The lean diet of breads and cornwater would not affect him. He was able to survive without food or water for a week, he could go without sleep for three days and nights. He was the greatest ball player Tayasal had ever known.

"If I tells him he's dead," Cramer the Black said, breaking the long silence, "he'll leave us alone. Eh, lads? If I tells him that, he'll leave us be."

They were the first words uttered aloud in days. No one had spoken while Carson died. The cook and surgeon from the *Courage* had lain on the dungeon floor for, how long? None knew. Time held no meaning anymore. As he'd suffered, fighting the fever burning brain and body, struggling with the plague that pulsed in the fierce redness of what had been his eye, not a word had been said.

They'd simply waited for the man to die, waited for the whimpering cries of pain and pity to cease, waited for a return of some of the rhythm they'd come to rely on. The dream no longer existed for any of them, but the food and the blankets, fresh straw from time to time, kept them, secured them, and they wanted no reminder that these petty comforts could be taken away.

But they'd awaited in horror and in silence. They'd waited before for men to die. Marchand had died; one other had died. But their deaths had been different: accidents of the dungeon, not violence forced in from outside. All, now, could suffer as Carson had suffered. Cramer might be next, but none of them would escape—until Stone returned or someone stopped d'Avila.

But they did not speak of it. None said a word until Carson's fevered breathing ceased, and his body was taken away, relieving them all of his presence. They were nineteen now, all that remained of the crew.

Then Cramer spoke. "If I tells him they're all dead,"
he said, "he'll leave us here to rot."

Someone rustled. Something moved. Chains were
heard.

"It's the cap'n he wants," Cramer continued, raising
his unused voice. "We, none of us, mean nothing to
him, on our own."

"He's mad," someone muttered. "He's crazed."

" 'Tis 'cos he thinks we'll tell him," Cramer went on,
forcing as much as he dared. "If I tells him we've had a
message. That one of us got back, but the rest is dead.
Then he'll leave us be."

A sigh went around the room. Heads lifted; hands
moved. The tattered dream shuffled in its remnants.
There were the beginnings of something to replace the
fear that crawled over all the faces.

Then Lambe, the red-haired gunner who'd not died of
the flux, said, "If you convinces the madman, Cramer
my friend, you'll convince the jailer also. Where will we
be then, I ask? What'll we do for warmth?" There was a
grain of humor in his voice.

Cramer chuckled; he managed a deep, rich sound that
filled the dank-walled room. "It's an eye for a blanket,"
he said with all the ease he could muster. "That's the
choice we have. An eye for a blanket." He raised the
level of his laugh.

Someone giggled, and that was enough. They were
lifted for a moment. Fear stuck to them like sweat. It
hung in the green-stained air. None could rid himself of
the memory of Carson's dying, but for a moment they
were lifted: there was the sound of the rustling of hope.
It was little enough, but once again they had a frail belief
to cling to.

The door of the cell was opened, and a battle-scarred
captain came striding in. With him were two muscular
warriors carrying carved wooden clubs. When they saw
them, Stone and van Staal moved away.

"Do not be afraid," the captain said slowly. "My

name is Ceel. I am to be the judge of the game." He bowed to them both and waited until van Staal had translated what he'd said. "I am to show you the court," he added.

The prisoners were taken out into bright sunlight. Ceel led them, marching stiffly around the palace, beneath the layered tiers and their walkways, past limestone slabs bearing figures of princes and priests. When Stone and van Staal arrived at the court, they discovered it to be a sunken surface, an imbedded I in a truncated pyramid.

The playing area was in the shape of the letter I, running north and south. The body of the I was a flagstoned roadway that Stone estimated to be thirty feet long by half that distance wide. Sloping walls ran along its length; there were straight walls at either end, extending past the width of the court. About all the walls was an arrangement of benches. In the center of the north wall stood a throne.

Ceel began his explanation by pointing to a narrow gutter carved along the length of the I-shaped roadway. "That is the key line," he said. "One team plays on one side, the other opposite." He waited until he was sure that Round Skull understood and had told the Pale One what had been said.

"Ask him how the points are won," Stone said when van Staal had finished.

A moment later Ceel explained. The hard round ball would be thrown into the court between the teams. Each player had to knock it with hip, knee, or elbow into the other's side. If the ball went out of court, a point was won. A point was lost if the ball was touched with the hand or head of any player. Points were forfeited if the ball was stopped in play, if a player fell on it, if a player was knocked out or killed.

"God's blood, the game *is* a battle," Stone said when he had heard it all. "Who keeps count of all these points?"

When spoken to, Ceel indicated three short, deeply carved posts at each end of the key line. "When it is decided how many points will be played for," he said, "counters are set on the center post. Each time a team wins, a marker is moved to the post in that team's territory. When one team has all the counters, the game is over."

Van Staal listened carefully. Twice he asked Ceel to repeat something; when he was sure of everything he told Stone of the arrangement.

"Does that mean that if five markers are played for, only five points need be won?" Stone asked.

Ceel smiled when given the question. "That would be too simple, and the game too short," he said. "If you win a point, a marker goes from the center to your post. If you lose a point, the marker goes back to the center again. The game continues until one team has all the markers."

"God's heart," Stone muttered. "It could go on forever."

"It is a test of strength as well as skill," Ceel said when the remark was related to him. "That is why it begins at dawn."

Stone grunted. He examined the court thoroughly. He ran his hands over the sloping walls they were to play against: they were plastered and smooth, and their foundation seemed firm. He spent some time staring at the carved marker posts that were sculpted in the form of parrots. Each bird faced in toward the center of the court, like an always present audience, eternally judging the game.

When he rejoined Ceel and Van Staal, the Dutchman turned to him and said, "It seems we both may play. If you recall, he spoke of teams."

Stone smiled thinly. "I would welcome that," he replied. "But I thought the prince in the jaguar skin had challenged me alone."

"So did I. But there was something in the manner he spoke that made me question him," van Staal explained. "It appears the number is to be decided on the morning of the game." Van Staal paused. "He seems to think you'll be given the choice," he added.

"Then prepare yourself," Stone said. "But I have a

question." He pointed to a pair of rings, one set on
either side of the key line high on each sloping wall.
They were made of green-spotted stone, and the holes in
the center were some twelve inches in diameter. "What
are they?" he asked.

Van Staal questioned Ceel. The battle-scarred captain
listened, then smiled secretly before replying. "They are
the winning rings," he replied. "When the gods are
being extremely generous, and the signs are favorable,
the ball will sometimes go through a ring. When that
occurs, it is the end of the game. No matter how many
points have been won by either side, the team that puts
the ball through the ring wins everything."

As Stone listened to van Staal's slow translation, he
went closer to one of the rings. From where he stood,
the hole seemed a long way away.

"He says it's almost impossible," van Staal called.
"The prince you'll play has done it twice, but according
to him, it almost never happens."

Stone turned from the ring. "In that case, what advice
does he give about winning?" he asked.

There began a long, slow conversation between van
Staal and Ceel, during which the captain's face became
stiff and unrevealing. His replies grew shorter and more
brusque.

Finally Stone said, "He'll tell us nothing, am I right?

Van Staal nodded. "He'll do nothing to aid us," he
replied, his voice angry. "He has been ordered to show
us the court, and that is all. Like the rest of them, he
wants to see us beaten to our knees, then hauled up
their temple and sacrificed to their bloodsucking gods."
He spat on the flagstoned surface and lifted his eyes in
defiance.

Ceel spoke rapidly to his men, then slowly to van
Staal. "You will be taken back to your cell. The night
before the game you will return here for the ceremonies."

"What ceremonies?"

"You will see."

"Tell me—"

Ceel cut him short; abruptly he strode away. As van

Staal told him what Ceel had said, Stone walked thought-fully through the sunlight. For reasons he did not under-stand, the sight of the court had heartened him. Perhaps it was because some of the mystery had gone; perhaps it was because now he had something more to work with. Van Staal walked evenly beside him, doubt in his honest eyes.

From the darkness of Itzamná's court, Bacal stared down at the prisoners returning to their cell. The blood in the grisly room had dried, the hearts in the green jade dishes were black and rotting. No new offerings would be made until the game was over. Cornbread and cornwater had been placed at Itzamná's feet, simple reminders of what was to come.

Soon, Bacal was sure, the sunken-cheeked, toothless deity would be placated fully. When the Pale One and Round Skull were opened and their blood rushed forth, it would be a ceremony unlike any other. They would come fresh from the ball court, they would be great warriors twice defeated.

It would be an offering so special that Bacal trembled at the thought of it. He wrapped his long cloak about himself and watched, through his veil of matted hair, the passage of the victims below. He could taste the fresh blood flowing.

"You will be rewarded, O lizard god, O Dragon Mas-ter," he whispered, and his eyes glittered. "You will be rewarded mightily."

Paxbolón came from one of the lesser ball courts behind the palace, wiping sweat from his body with a cotton cloth. He smiled at Varón, the player he'd been practicing with, and stripped away the leather armor he'd worn.

"You play well," Paxbolón said. "I shall need to watch you, this year at the challenges."

Varón, a solid, muscular man with lines of tattooing on his cheeks, smiled in return. "You are very gracious, Lord Paxbolón, but there's none to equal you."

"Not so, the way you use your elbows." Paxbolón

made a savage movement with his arm. "Very skilled. And today I thought you had the ring."

Varón poured water from a gourd over his head. "It is a shot I've never made, my lord," he said. "Unlike yourself."

Paxbolón laughed. He straightened his back imperiously. "I shall need to think of some interesting plays so that this game is not over swiftly," he said. "If the city is to semifast for three days, if our warriors are to deny themselves their women, and no laughter is to be heard, they'll need to be well rewarded."

"To see you play will be reward enough, my lord."

"You flatter me." Paxbolón was pleased. "But I'm sure there's something I can think of to bring the Pale One to his knees." The humour went suddenly from his handsome face. "I shall have him crawling before we are through. He will regret the day he ever heard of Tayasal."

"I feel he must regret that already." Varón spoke softly, feeling the effect of Paxbolón's sudden anger. "I am sure he—"

"You speak of his coming death?" Paxbolón stared at Varón, his eyes narrow. "That will be nothing. It will merely end his misery. I shall have him pleading for death before I'm done."

Paxbolón flung to the ground the cloth he'd been wiping himself with and walked briskly away. Varón watched the tall prince disappear, then splashed more water over his tattooed face. He almost felt pity for the Pale One.

Canek, the king, lay on a pile of woolen rugs and watched the painted boy prepare the oils. "You understand that this is purely medicinal, my child," he said as the boy approached. "We are allowed no real contact until the game is over."

"I understand, my lord," the boy said softly. "That has been made clear to me."

"Oh?" Canek's eyes widened a little. "By whom?"

"The priest, Tutz," the boy replied. "He has spoken to us all."

"Tutz?" Canek smiled. "Is he in his house again?"

The boy nodded. "He returned yesterday. There was a ceremony with much copal. Offerings were placed in all the corners. He was afraid the invaders had defiled the dwelling, but it seems that all is well again."

"As it should be." Canek lay on his back and felt the boy's skilled fingers rub the muscles of his thighs, easing their weariness, comforting the old flesh. "What other gossip have you heard, my child?" he asked.

"Me, my lord?"

"Come, come, you have much more contact with the world than I."

The boy glanced briefly at Canek, his bright eyes calculating beneath their shaded lids. "Well, there is great excitement all over the city," he began, his fingers moving aside the loosely folded loincloth, beginning to rub the warm oil onto the old king's stomach. "They say that wondrous things are to happen. They say it is a time of change for all."

"Do they now?" Canek sighed with pleasure as he felt the boy's hands caress the heavy muscles of his chest. They were soft hands, they were skillful, they gave him all his enjoyment now. "Who would say such things?"

"Certain people."

"What do they say, exactly?"

"Well . . ." The boy's hands went for more oil. The king rolled onto his stomach. He felt the warmth of the oil on his shoulders, fingers kneading the thick hard muscles at the base of his neck. The comfort was exquisite. "I'm only repeating what I have heard," the boy continued. "But they say Lord Paxbolón will wish for greater powers once the game is over."

"He has power enough as it is," Canek murmured. "One day he will be king."

"Some say that one day will not be soon enough."

Canek turned over and looked up at the painted boy's face, at the outlined eyes, the delicate coloring that had been worked into the cheeks. "Who have you been talking to, my child?" he asked without anger. "This is more than simple gossip."

"Please, my lord." The boy's hands spread oil over the old king's chest and began to work down toward the groin, gradually, subtly, as if they were not aware of their movement. "I am only repeating what I have heard."

"Where did you hear it?"

"From others like myself."

"And where had they heard it?"

"I do not know." The hands, warmly caressing, followed the line of the belly, the tips of the fingers stroked the folds of heavy flesh at the junction of the belly and thigh. "I assure you, my lord, if I knew, I would tell you."

"Does Ah Cuc have anything to do with this?"

The boy's fingers stilled momentarily, then their delicate movement continued. "I have heard nothing of Lord Ah Cuc's involvement."

"He is not a lord, my child."

"We, we think of him as such." The boy's hands began to smooth the flesh of Canek's thighs. As if by accident, his fingers touched the flaccid penis, and Canek's eyes began to close. "But I am sure he has nothing to do with what I have heard," the boy continued. "His name has not even been whispered."

"How often have you heard talk of these matters?" Canek asked lazily, his voice barely lifting.

"Not often, my lord. And nothing has been said directly." The boy allowed his fingers to explore further. One rubbed gently the sensitive area at the base of the organ. "Please forgive me, I would not have spoken of this had I thought it might disturb you."

"It does not disturb me, and it is your duty to tell me all you hear."

"Yes, my lord."

"Also, you are not permitted to arouse me until the game has been played."

"I am sorry," the boy said mildly, and made his fingers move more firmly about the penis, which had begun to grow lazily against the old king's oiled thigh. "I had not noticed."

"There is nothing you do not notice, my child. That is one of the reasons why I am so fond of you." Canek laid a hand on the boy's arousing fingers, held them a moment, then lifted them away. "I must wait until the day beyond tomorrow. You will come to me, and we will taste pleasure together, but only then."

"As you wish, my lord."

"It is not my wish," Canek replied comfortably. "But the gods have been good to me throughout my long life. I would desire that they continue to be for some time to come. So, we will not offend them now. We will wait until the time of fasting is over and they no longer object."

"Yes, my lord." the boy wiped his hands and began to take away the oil. "I will come to you then."

"On the other hand"—Canek rolled over onto his stomach—"you may rub my back, and the muscles of my neck, a little longer. I am sure no god could possibly be offended by that."

The boy smiled and returned to his king.

Stone walked the length of the ball court van Staal had roughly sketched on the floor, his mind on the actual playing area, estimating angles, the slope of the walls. From strips of cotton blanket he fashioned a ball, knowing it was nothing like the instrument they would use, but it gave him something to work with.

He attempted to hit it with hip or knee or elbow, clumsily aligning his body to gain thrust and direction. The Dutchman sweated with him in the windowless cell, recalling, imagining, what he knew of the game.

It did not occur to them that whatever they did, the outcome would be the same. They did not consider the foolishness of chasing a ball of rags over a barely legible sketch on a stone floor. There was nothing else to sustain them. They used the hours that remained like weapons of defense. It was all they had to give shape to a future.

And so they passed their precious time until the day of the game.

CHAPTER 12

FIGURES MOVED IN THE CHILL AND MISTY LIGHT, FIGURES drifted even before the copper-tinted clouds announced the rising of the sun. From all over the city of Tayasal they came to see the Pale One driven to his death. By the time dawn's first fingers were in the sky, all the seats that were not reserved for lords or priests were taken.

On the summit of the great temple, Bacal himself performed the sacrifice of the quail. The birds of night died well, the sun began boldly, all the signs were propitious.

Stone and van Staal were ready when Ceel and the guards entered their cell. They followed them out into the thin clear air and filled their lungs with freshness.

" 'Tis a good day," Stone said. "Live or die."

"Aye," van Staal replied. "It is."

They knew, now, more of what lay before them. The night before they'd been marched through the torchlit city, past silent groups of Maya, whose eyes, glittering like the incurve of seashells, never left the prisoners. They'd been taken to the ball court, where priests and the princes waited. They'd seen the leather armor to be worn when the game was played. Stone had made a move to examine it, but a guard with a spear pushed him away.

Bacal had begun to pray. As his strident tones grated the air, a priest came forward with a brown earthenware plate on which the figure of a ball player had been engraved. A second priest entered the torchlit area carrying the round, dark-colored ball. It was some six inches in diameter and sat solidly when placed upon the plate. Its surface was pitted, it was unlike any substance Stone had ever seen before.

Bacal passed among them, spitting the harsh words of his prayer. He sprinkled a little copal over the ball in its dish and bowed to Paxbolón; he repeated the action with the resin and nodded disdainfully at Christopher Stone. Then he turned his attention to the clothing to be worn and blessed it also. After that the dish containing the ball was set in the center of the key line and the clothing arranged about it.

Priests shuffled throughout the court, following the steps of an ancient order. Their black-wrapped shapes moved in and out of torchlight as they laid fruit and flat bread, corn husks and cacao beans, along the key line and about the marker posts. Their lips issuing coils of prayer, the wreaths of burning copal clinging to their dark, malodorous garments, they were like primitive birds of prey that had not yet learned to fly.

As he watched them Stone's courage momentarily wavered. Without the shield of the company of his men, he felt brutally alone. He turned his gaze to the leather armor, trying to discern its use, but it was foreign in the semidarkness. He glanced at van Staal, to see resentment on the hard round face: the Dutchman, quite clearly, would have killed the priests as they stood. Stone breathed deeply and summoned his strength. Tomorrow, he thought. Tomorrow it begins.

Then, the purification ceremony complete, the prisoners were returned to their cell.

Now, in the early dawn, they were once more taken to the playing field. Stone was separated from van Staal and led down into the center of the court. He felt the eyes of all upon him. Van Staal was taken to stand beside the king, a guard with him.

Bacal appeared before the king, the dish with the ball offered for inspection. The king nodded, and Bacal, his razor voice slicing the gentleness of the morning, announced that the game and the players were ready to begin.

Then Canek spoke. "Who will play?" he asked, according to the code.

"I," said Paxbolón, and went to the center of the court.

"Who else?" Canek turned to van Staal.

Van Staal spoke, and Stone moved to stand beside Paxbolón.

"Will the teams be one, or will they be joined by others?" Canek asked.

Paxbolón smiled fleetingly. "I am content alone," he replied. "But perhaps the Pale One should be given the opportunity to decide."

Canek bowed and glanced at van Staal. "Did you understand?" he inquired.

Val Staal nodded. "He will accept," he said, and began to move away.

"Wait," the king added. "The Pale One must speak for himself."

Impatiently, van Staal called down to Stone. Stone listened, then half bowed to the king. "I will take a partner," he said in English, and nodded.

"Then I will accompany him," a voice replied in Maya. The speaker was Tutul Katun. He stood and stared down into the court. "If the Pale One will have me, I will play with him."

There was a hush of astonishment, then voices were raised in babbling excitement. Paxbolón looked up at his brother's pitted face for a long time, realizing that from the beginning he had been maneuvered toward this moment. His eyes narrowed, his mouth became thin—he had never considered Tutul Katun a competitor before.

Canek, the only one present who did not seem surprised, raised his voice. "Does the Pale One accept?" he asked.

Quickly, van Staal told Stone what had happened. The Englishman listened intently, noting the new electricity in the air about him, the harshness of Paxbolón's expression. But before he had formed his reply van Staal continued.

"Take him," said the Dutchman. "I believe he is for us."

Stone nodded slowly, half bowed again, and his choice was understood. Tutul Katun descended to the playing area to stand beside him, his face pale but expressionless.

"Then I choose Varón," said Paxbolón, his words tight. He waited until the player with the tattooed cheeks came down to join him, then added, "Now the teams are fixed."

"That is as it should be," said Canek from the throne. "Put on the dress and let the game begin."

Whispering filled the court as the players prepared to don the leather armor. All had heard the rumors: it was said that when Paxbolón was king, all the Maya in all the land would once again be free. Others called this a lie: all would be sold in slavery, they muttered. Some said that Tutul Katun would never become a priest: that one day he'd be king. Soon, all would know. As they watched the leather fitted, excitement spluttered from their mouths.

Stone was helped to dress by Tutul Katun. The prince arranged a broad belt across the Englishman's stomach and tied it at the back; from it, like a fan, rose a stiffened chest shield. A short skirt covered the simple loincloth Stone wore. He was given a pair of ankle guards and curved protectors for his knees; there were loose leather gloves to cover the hands.

As the beautifully worked, richly decorated armor was strapped to his body, Stone realized how vulnerable he was on the court. Even with the leather in place, he felt exposed. As his bare feet moved on the cold hard pavement, he was tremendously aware of the severity of the walls that surrounded him.

By the time he'd accustomed himself to the unusual clothing, the others were prepared. He was placed on one side of the gouged key line, Paxbolón and Varón opposite him; beside him stood Tutul Katun. Ceel, the judge, then asked how many points would be played for.

Paxbolón looked at his brother. "You decide," he said disdainfully.

Tutul Katun held up a hand and opened the fingers twice, indicating ten. Ceel went to the marker bearers and placed ten flat discs, each carved to show a ball player in action, on the central, parrot-headed posts.

As this was being down, Paxbolón continued a conversation with his brother. "You would have been wiser to choose the priesthood," he said, his voice controlled but his anger apparent. "At least your life would have been spared."

"My life is unimportant," Tutul Katun replied evenly. "It is the future of our people that concerns me."

"Bah." Paxbolón's look was contemptuous. "The future of our people will be what I make it."

"Perhaps," Tutul Katun said softly. "And perhaps not."

They stared at each other a further moment, each attempting to gauge the other. Then Ceel placed himself below Canek, and a charged hush fell upon the court. Bacal sat beside the old king now, his matted hair a frame about his hawkish face. All eyes were on the four who stood in the center of the field.

"We are ready, my lord," Ceel said to Canek. "The players await the start."

Canek nodded; he bent for the ball that lay at his feet and, almost idly, tossed it into the arena. The game had begun.

The ball landed close to the center and bounced high. Varón leapt and with an elbow knocked it to Paxbolón. The tall prince stopped it with a knee, tapped it into the air. As it came down, he dropped into a graceful crouch, caught the ball with a movement of his hip, and shot it into the opposing court. The ball hit the sloping surface.

Tutul Katun raced but arrived late. The ball went high and landed outside the playing area. The crowd roared.

"A point is scored," Ceel said, and moved markers from the central posts to those on the side of Paxbolón. "Bring back the ball. We begin again."

Stone stood rooted, stunned by the speed of the action, the life in the ball, the skill with which Paxbolón and Varón handled it. He'd remained unmoving, bewildered by a swiftness that bore no resemblance to the game he'd attempted with a bundle of rags on the floor of a windowless cell. He turned and stared at Tutul Katan, and for the first time there was doubt on his rawboned face.

From without the playing area, bounded by four dragon-headed columns, the ball returned. This time Ceel took it, held it high for all to see, then threw it to land on the key line between the combatants.

Now Stone moved. He leapt, Varón with him. He lifted an elbow and struck at the round hard material, trying to knock it toward Tutul Katun. He saw the ball flick in the prince's direction as he felt a tremendous blow beneath his ribs. He fell to the pavement breathless, looked up to see Varón glance at him before moving away.

Stone staggered to his feet, gasping, as Paxbolón and Tutul Katun jumped together. The ball became caught between them and rolled loose. It bounced lightly along the guttered key line to rest against one of the parrot-headed markers.

"The ball is dead," Ceel said, picking it up. "It will be entered again."

The players gathered in the center of the court. Tutul Katun turned toward Stone and held up a warning hand. With an elbow he imitated Varón's action, emphasizing to the Pale One that there was much more to this game than striking the ball. Stone nodded, but when he swung to those who opposed him there was the beginning of fury in his eyes. Paxbolón noted it with glee.

The ball was thrown in once more. This time Tutul Katun made a move. He feinted to the left, then, as

Paxbolón began to follow, ducked back, caught the ball with a knee, and pitched it cleanly toward the sloping wall behind his brother. Paxbolón spun, but the ball bounced from the inclined surface high over his head to where Tutul Katun was waiting to receive it. Almost casually, he knocked it out of play on the far side of the court.

Once more Ceel called the point; once more the markers were moved on their posts.

Now the sun was rising higher. There was sweat on the players, it ran down their bodies in darkening lines. Stone noticed that an elbow was bleeding, but he felt neither pain nor stiffness, nothing but an increasing determination to fight this match with whatever he was able.

The ball came in again. Stone leapt once more, both elbows out. He was learning that his height gave him an advantage. None was as tall as he, not even Paxbolón. The ball caught on his chest and dropped to a knee; he tried to kick it, but the effort was clumsy. The ball fell to the ground and bounced slowly along his side of the key line.

"That is a fault," Ceel cried, coming forward. "The ball did not cross the key line." He ordered an assistant to return the marker Tutul Katun had won.

"What?" Stone called angrily up to the solid figure of van Staal standing near the throne. "Why have we lost?"

Van Staal told him.

"Do they invent their rules as they go?" Stone demanded hotly. "God's blood. Ask him what more I should be told."

Van Staal spoke to Ceel. The battle-scarred captain's face stiffened with anger. "The rules were explained when the Pale One was shown the court."

"No say about key line."

"He was told the ball could be struck by hip, knee, or elbow only," Ceel said with controlled patience. "He was told that points were lost when the ball went out of the playing area or if it was touched by the hand or the head."

"No say about key line," van Staal repeated stubbornly.

"If it is played and does not cross the key line, that is also a fault," Ceel said slowly, as if speaking to a child. "It is also a fault if a player knocks the ball out on his side of the court." He paused, then added condescendingly, "Is there anything else the Pale One wishes to know?"

"If it affect his life, yes," van Staal shot back with surprising fluency. "You understand *that*?"

Ceel bowed. "I do," he replied, bristling.

"Then think more what to tell."

Ceel opened his mouth to reply, but Canek leaned forward. The old king could not recall when he'd felt such excitement, known such demanding tension. All the whisperings of the past few days were clear now. The cleverness of his younger son, and the ambitions of his elder, were vividly displayed. It took all his years of experience to appear calm as his heart churned with strange emotions.

"If a mistake was made," Canek said evenly, "then admit it, Ceel."

"My lord—"

"Were all the rules clearly explained?"

"I," Ceel began uncomfortably, "I think so, but—"

"Return the marker, and be sure that all is known." Canek's voice was suddenly hard. "We want no misjudgments here."

Canek watched as Ceel bowed stiffly. Beside him he heard Bacal's sharp intake of breath. He saw Paxbolón's eyes flash and was aware of an expression of satisfaction on the face of Tutul Katun.

"Give me the ball," Canek ordered. "Each side has now one point. I will throw a further entrance."

The ball came down; the players jumped. Stone caught a movement of Paxbolón's elbow and heard Tutul Katun gasp for breath. The ball came off Varón's knee and went high. Stone raced for it, Varón beside him; together they went up. Stone felt Varón's hand on his shoulder, holding him down. Then, his advantage gained, the tattooed player knocked the ball into the opposing court and out of play. Furious, Stone brought his knee up savagely and felt it thud into the Maya's groin. Varón grunted with agony and fell to the roadway. Stone returned to the center of the playing field, gasping for air.

The markers were moved; the crowd roared with fascination. This was more than they had expected. They had come to see the invader taunted on the court, to be beaten quickly and disposed of, to be shamed before them. They had come to witness his punishment, but none had imagined that his shambling form contained such agility, none had considered his determination.

Nor had they dreamed that Tutul Katun would stand beside him, that the rivalry between the princes would be so openly displayed. The men in the front benches turned to each other, recognizing that they were at a game that would be recorded in history. The women, from their positions behind the men, looked slyly at the long legs of the invader and whispered among themselves.

The ball was reentered by Ceel; once more the players rose, elbows flashing, knees battering. Tutul Katun caught it, pitched it with a hip. As it bounced off the wall and Tutul Katun ran to receive it, Paxbolón put out a foot. Tutul Katun fell heavily. Instinctively Stone turned to assist, and Varón scored an easy point.

Now, Paxbolón and Varón were playing as brutal a game as they knew. They butted with their heads, they drove with elbow, knee, and fist. The old rules had been agreed to; none covered anything but the position of the ball and its contact with the player. All else was part of the contest.

Once more the ball came back. Once more the players crashed in their efforts to direct it. Paxbolón and Stone went into the air together; together they fell, and the ball rolled clear. Varón caught it neatly with an elbow, bounced it high to claim a further point.

Relentlessly the play continued. The markers showed that Paxbolón had scored four points, his brother two. Four markers remained on each of the center posts, but all who watched knew the game was not yet decided.

The ball came close to Stone. He flashed an elbow and sent it over Varón's head. Stone raced around him.

Out of the corner of an eye he saw Paxbolón approach. Stone darted to the left, bending beneath the Maya's arms, cracking him with an elbow in the gut as he passed. He straightened as the ball bounced before him, and with a knee he knocked it to Tutul Katun. Tutul Katun kicked savagely at Varón, then slammed the ball over the far side of his brother's court. He now had three to Paxbolón's four. The crowd was on its feet, shouting in praise and excitement.

Van Staal found himself yelling with them. His throat was open; his hands were raised as if to join. There was a fever in the air that infected one and all. The struggle on the court became their own, the skills a talent they wished to share. Beside him, van Staal saw the old king lean forward on his throne, his heavy face swollen with pride.

The shouting lessened as the ball was thrown again and the game endured remorselessly. The sun rose steadily, soon it was savage on the playing roadway. The solid leather the players wore grew heavy and shapeless with sweat. The pavement of the court became damp; in places it was slippery.

Paxbolón scored, and scored again. He caught the ball with elbow and chest, he shot with hip and knee. He was tireless, unwearyingly graceful, recharged by every point he won. It was as if he'd planned each moment of the play. It seemed to Stone he wished the game to go on forever.

Stone was beginning to fall regularly now; each time he recovered he caught the tall prince's eye, and there was joy in it. Paxbolón had the air of a bearbaiter; each time Stone missed the ball, he shouted loudly, applauding the mistake.

Stone's movements became increasingly clumsy. His elbows bled, his knees were bruised, his feet were cut, his ribs and groin were fire. Sweat stung his eyes, his hair clung to his forehead; at times he could barely breathe. Yet he continued, carried by the knowledge that the alternative was death.

Once, as he attempted to regain his feet after an

especially heavy fall, Varón knocked him sprawling with
a casual movement of his hip, striking the Pale One as
though he were the ball itself. Varón looked up for
approval, and the crowd shouted down at him in pleasure.

Stone snarled as he staggered to his feet. For a moment it appeared he would hit the tattooed player, but
his half-lifted hand returned to his side. He had no
energy to waste. He turned and stared at Tutul Katun
and saw, for the first time, a desperation that matched
his own. The final result now appeared decided; it was
only a matter of painful time. When he looked at those
who opposed him, they were black shapes in burning
sunlight, forms that spelled and shouted for his death.

Guadalupe never knew where the fear came from. It
was suddenly with her like a cloak of ice, clouding her
vision, shrinking her flesh, transmitting itself to the horses.

Her own mount threw her. Grajales's reared, its eyes
rolling. The third horse bolted toward the line of purple
hills, and Guadalupe's animal followed.

Fighting to regain control, Grajales gave pursuit. He
rode neatly, his useless arm adding to his skill. He clung
with knees and thighs; the horse's movements were his
own. He rode rapidly, gaining slowly on Guadalupe's
mount. He drew alongside, speaking gently. With his
good arm he reached for the bridle, then rode with the
horse until it came to a halt. He looked for the third
animal, but it was gone.

Guadalupe remained where she had fallen, her heart
beating like a drum. Sweat drenched her; she found it
difficult to see. She touched her skin. It had turned the
color of mud.

When Grajales returned she was crouched beside a
thornbush, shivering as though with fever. He slipped
from the saddle, fastened both the horses, and went to
her. When he spoke he did not think she heard.

He held her a moment, comforting as he could, brush-
ing dust and dead grasses from her clothing. She stared
at him as though he were a stranger, her chin trembling,
her eyes as blank as pebbles on a beach.

It took her a long time to recover, an aching, threatening time during which it seemed, at any instant, she'd slip back into panic. Yet finally she was able to stand and hold herself upright, leaning against the horse. Once more she turned her eyes to Grajales, once more he saw their hollow fear.

Ultimately, she remounted her horse to stare down at the thornbush beside which she'd crouched, at the ground where she'd fallen with such paralyzing suddenness. She shuddered and dragged her eyes away. She did not know where the fear had come from or what had been its cause.

She began to ride away.

CHAPTER 13

FOR NEARLY AN HOUR MORE THEY STRUGGLED ON THE SUN-drenched, pitiless court. Points were won and lost, and won again. The contest had drained them all by now, but it was Stone who suffered most. He moved like a crippled creature of the wild: pausing when he could, fighting when he had to.

Then, when Paxbolón had five markers on his side and his brother three, the tall prince raised an open hand as a sign of request—and asked for water.

The crowd was silent with disbelief. The Fighting Lord had never been known to call for water; he left that weakness to the opposition. Even Ceel was confused. He hesitated, looked into the faces of the other players. Tutul Katun and Varón were as puzzled as the crowd. The Pale One clearly did not understand. Ceel lifted his inquiring eyes to the king and saw the old man nod.

"What happening?" Stone licked his cracked lips, calling up to van Staal. "Is it over?"

"You're to be given water," Van Staal replied, "but—"

"Thank God for that mercy. I am burning."

"Christopher—"

But as van Staal warned, Stone turned to the water bearer and reached thirstily for the gourd. He drank deeply, water splashing down his chest. He held out the gourd for more and felt the water fill his belly. He put wet hands to his face and tried to cool its fire. His body was agony now, each movement a gigantic effort.

Stone took his hands away, to see Paxbolón lift the gourd to his lips, fill his mouth with its liquid, rinse his gums, then spit onto the pavement. Wildly, comprehending his mistake, Stone watched the others do the same. None swallowed, none allowed water to enter their stomachs, all cleansed their mouths and no more. Stone felt the weight in his belly and knew what Paxbolón had achieved. He turned to Tutul Katun and saw the prince make a small grim bow in his brother's direction.

Paxbolón acknowledged the compliment and smiled. There was clear contempt on his handsome features. The water was taken away, and the ball thrown in once more.

As soon as he tried to move, Stone realized fully the damage he'd done. His body was heavy, the water like lead. Breathing was even more difficult, and his legs seemed to be without motion. He wanted to vomit but could not. He wished to be rid of this burden as he'd wanted to be rid of his thirst, but it would be with him for the remainder of this deadly game.

The ball came close to him, and he struggled for it, swung an elbow and missed. He landed, slipped on a wet patch of the court, and fell, the ball beneath him, knocking the air from his lungs. Another point was lost.

Slowly, he climbed back to his feet to hear the beginnings of derision in the voices of the crowd. Now they could not wait for Paxbolón to win. The Pale One was big, he had some courage, but he was tiring rapidly, and he was stupid. The trick with the water would never have happened to one of their own. They began now to call him Red Face and Water Belly. His death was merely a matter of time.

Limping, Stone returned to the key line, watching for play to begin. Gasping, he waited to see what would happen next—another of Paxbolón's punishing deceits? It came a moment later.

The ball bounced, Stone and Paxbolón ran toward it. Paxbolón arrived first, caught the ball on his chest, and balanced it on his knee as Stone lumbered up to him. When the Pale One was only three feet away, he lifted the ball into the air, brought his elbow around swiftly, and aimed directly at Stone's face. As the black bullet came toward him, Stone jerked his head away. His hands came up instinctively, and he heard Ceel cry fault. The ball had been played by hand.

Paxbolón smiled and lifted his head to the crowd. Once more he'd made a fool of the invader. The crowd raised its voice in applause. Paxbolón returned his sneering gaze to Stone and spat on the ground at his feet.

Now there were eight markers on the side of Paxbolón, two on the post of Tutul Katun. Paxbolón spoke softly to Varón, who nodded: he knew where to place himself.

Ceel threw in the ball. Paxbolón pretended to leap for it but turned and ran to the far side of the court. Pushing Tutul Katun aside, Varón caught the ball neatly with his knee, held it, then flicked it over to Paxbolón. Stone began to stumble in the same direction; Varón went with him. As he came abreast of the Englishman, he rolled onto the roadway in front of him. Stone could not avoid the tattooed Maya; he fell awkwardly, his hands slamming to stone floor, his knees scraping the ground. In spite of the loose gloves and the knee protectors, the fall was agony.

As Stone lifted his weary head, Paxbolón's elbow struck the ball up to the ring. It rose gracefully, hit the ring, held an edge, hung a moment, then fell away. Varón took it with his hip and shot it over the heads of the spectators to win another point.

Stone climbed painfully to his feet and joined Tutul Katun at the key line. Both watched in dismay as the markers were once more moved. Paxbolón and Varón now had nine of the ten.

The crowd roared in approval. Their throats opened in excitement and delight. The ring shot had been well planned, it had almost succeeded. The way Varón had

come in behind to score was a superb piece of games-
manship.

Silently van Staal stood among them, saddened by the
spectacle below. His own death did not seem to concern
him now. He had lived with the idea long enough to
accept it. It would be painful, but it would be brief. The
sight of the figure of Stone on the court below was much
more difficult to bear. Death would be darkness; this
was pain in remorseless light.

Stone was bleeding from both elbows now, there was
a cut on his forehead, he moved with a constant limp.
The leather he wore was laden with sweat. His head
was loose with defeat. He was totally in the hands of his
merciless opponent. Paxbolón had only to lose a point to
keep the game alive as long as he wished.

"Christopher," van Staal shouted, seeking some small
pause. "Listen to me."

Stone lifted his head, blinking into the sun.

"Take off the clothing," van Staal called down. "Free
yourself." Swiftly van Staal turned to Ceel, who held
the ball aloft, ready to enter it again. "The Pale One,
want take clothes off," the Dutchman shouted.

Ceel looked up in surprise as the crowd began to laugh.

"Heavy," van Staal persisted. "He no move."

"That is not possible," Ceel replied. "It has never
been done before."

"That not, matter."

"Play," the crowd shouted, clapping with impatience.
There was the taste of blood in all their mouths. "Play."

"Wait—"

"He can remove his clothing later," someone shouted.
"When he is taken to Itzamná."

The crowd roared wildly again, delighted with the
comedy before the kill. Ceel held the ball impatiently.
Stone stared at van Staal, not understanding the laughter
or the shouting. The old king lifted his face inquiringly,
and the Dutchman turned to him.

"My lord"—van Staal bowed—"is reason why clothing be, on?"

Canek studied Round Skull's worried look and paused

thoughtfully. "I know of no reason why the clothing should not be removed," he replied finally. "If you think it will make any difference."

"Thank you, my lord. Would you, tell Ceel."

Canek nodded; he instructed the judge of his decision as the crowd shouted their amusement, and Bacal hissed impatiently.

"Christopher," van Staal shouted. "Take it off. Your armor, take it off." He raised his voice, curbing the desire to descend and assist. "You understand? Take the leather off. You'll be freer."

Stone shook his head; slowly it cleared. He stared up at the Dutchman with great and simple gratitude.

"They'll wait," van Staal cried. "Take your time. Get your wind back."

"Aye." Stone breathed deeply. "Aye."

He walked to one side of the court and began to remove the heavy leather clothing. Tutul Katun went to him and undid the straps that held the broad belt in place. Stone threw the garment from him. He removed the knee protectors and those that were bound about his ankles. He tossed the gloves after them and undid his leather skirt. The pause had restored him, his breathing was easier. He felt a sudden rush of unrestricted energy but knew it would not last.

"Be wary," van Staal called. "They will try to throw you harder now."

"That they will," Stone replied, but there was strength in his voice. "They will."

Van Staal watched Stone tighten the loincloth and go back to the center of the sun-drenched court; he saw the tall man's back straighten. By God, the Dutchman thought as he listened to the excited voices all around him, now you'll have a death.

As Stone returned to the key line his glance took in the ring. He'd forgotten its existence in the course of the heated play. It was not until Paxbolón attempted the shot that it came to mind at all. Now he stared at it and calculated. It seemed high and small and distant: a speck in the eye of the sun. He looked at it, then away, and stood by Tutul Katun.

Ceel held the ball aloft for all to see, then tossed it among the players.

Paxbolón made no attempt to touch it; he threw himself at Stone. Stone had been waiting. He stepped to one side, a foot outstretched. Paxbolón tripped across it, and Stone brought his other knee up, crashing into the prince's side. He spun to see Varón beside him. With a snarl of rage, Stone elbowed the tattooed player in the face and heard the snap of teeth. Varón staggered as Tutul Katun stopped the ball with his hip, assessed his shot, and knocked it away for a clear win.

As the markers were shifted, Stone caught Paxbolón's eye and saw the ferocity it held. He glanced at Varón and saw the same desire for his death. Sooner or later, one of the two would throw him to the pavement or strike his unprotected stomach with the ball. He breathed deeply and moved toward the key line, holding his anger; he needed its force.

The ball was entered again. Stone saw it high above him and leapt toward it, using all his remaining strength, going upward with an elbow ready. He felt someone grab his legs and kicked savagely. He heard a grunt as he took the ball, guiding it over the heads of the others.

He dodged between Paxbolón and Varón, who clutched his stomach; he saw Tutul Katun move with him as the ball bounced on the edge of the inclined surface, and he took it with a knee. He needed time, and he hoped that Tutul Katun would understand.

Stone shot the ball ahead of him, calculating the angle of its rebound on the sloping wall. He ran toward the ring, and the ball was ready for him. As he lifted an elbow and measured the distance, there was the sound of feet closing in on him. He prepared himself to strike as Paxbolón reached to take him by the hair. Then Tutul Katun threw himself at his brother, his knees and fists thrashing like timber. Paxbolón fell away, his face a mask of fury, and Stone put the ball through the ring.

It passed cleanly, without touching the sides.

From the moment Stone had prepared the shot, he knew it would succeed. As he aimed and brought his elbow forward, the hole in the center of the green-spotted stone seemed huge; as the ball left him, there was no doubt about its direction. It went through exactly as he had known it would.

Varón raced up and struck him in the side. Stone fell backward onto the shoulders of Paxbolón, spun downward across the sloping surface, slipped on the damp roadway at its base, and crashed into the guttered keyline, tearing his hip open to the bone.

He lay stunned, the pain in his hip intense. He moved to a sitting position and looked at the wound. A flap of flesh had been ripped away, and the gash was bleeding profusely. Stone passed his loincloth into the wound, easing the torn flesh into place, and staggered to his feet, realizing that there was not a sound to be heard in the stadium.

The crowd was numb with shock. Never had any of them seen such a struggle; none would have believed such an outcome possible. The markers counted for nothing now. The winning shot had been made by the Pale One, and the game was won, absolutely.

Tutul Katun walked to Stone and bowed low in admiration. With that the crowd came to its feet, shouting as it had not shouted before. The sound of trumpets was heard; shrill whistles split the air. All stood, even the old king, and applauded, giving all they had.

Painfully, Stone tried to locate van Staal. When he saw the Dutchman he waved a tired hand. "By god, Rolf," he called, his voice breaking. "We've won their poxy game."

Van Staal replied, but his voice was lost in the cheering that filled the air with its thickness. The name of Tutul Katun was raised, caught by many, shouted from side to side of the frantic stadium.

Tutul Katun lifted his head and stared at his people; his eyes were moist. Behind him stood Paxbolón; it was his duty to die now, and also his wish. He glanced at the Pale One, whose honor it would be to take his life, and he scorned what the invader had become: he was crippled, his face was exhausted, he swayed as he stood. Paxbolón straightened his back, his handsome head held high: in death he would have no equal.

Then the people began to sing, their voices lifted in deep and bittersweet plainsong. The trumpets became muted, and the drums were still. They sang an anthem of glory, a song for the victor, and their singing calmed their frenzy.

Canek looked down at his sons; his heart was full of pride. Paxbolón was a great warrior, all the gods would know it. An honored place would await him. Tutul Katun deserved the victory, his prize had been sorely earned. It mattered little that the Pale One had struck the ball through the ring. Had it not been for Tutul Katun, the invader would have lasted no time at all. His younger son had taken great risks, had shown great courage. These were the strengths he would need as a king. Slowly, Canek bowed to both his children.

The singing was dying, the court was becoming hushed. Christopher Stone held his bleeding hip and limped closer to van Staal. "What happens now?" he called upward, his voice thick with pain. "This wound, God's pox, I'm sore."

Van Staal rubbed a hand over his face uncertainly. "They've not finished with you yet," he said.

"What?" Stone blinked up into the sunlight. "The game is done."

"Not yet," van Staal replied. "Both the defeated are to die. By your hand."

As van Staal spoke, Ceel walked down the center of the bloodied court, an axe held out before him. The instrument he carried had a head of solid copper, around which the sun formed a halo of light; the handle was carved in the shape of a serpent. Head and haft were bound together with an intricate weaving of fine cords. It was a further weapon of beauty and blood. Ceel held the axe aloft. Bacal, with a movement of both grimy hands, blessed it.

In silence, Paxbolón stepped forward and knelt before

Stone. "You have won," he said slowly, his voice dry with ridicule. "Now it is your duty to kill me."

Stone needed no translation.

Paxbolón inclined his head in the direction of Canek. "Farewell, great father," he said softly. "We will meet in the sight of the gods."

"I will be there soon, my son."

"I will tell them that, my father."

"I believe they already know." There was the faintest trace of irony in Canek's voice. "Have my place well prepared."

"It shall be done."

Paxbolón stared up into Stone's haggard face. There was not a sound in the stadium. The city was numbed; even the sun seemed stilled in the heavens.

"I ask for my death," the tall prince said, and the words were a threat. "It is my right. You cannot deny it."

Stone's mouth was dry. His hip throbbed like fever. Ceel presented the axe. As Stone watched, his hand, as if it belonged to another, reached for the burnished tool of death and grasped the serpent handle. About him the silence penetrated; it sang in his ears like the wind.

Paxbolón's eyes were steady.

Stone lifted the axe and felt a bitter blackness fill him. The man before him darkened; dark bile was in his stomach. He raised his eyes to see lines of dark figures surrounding him on every side. Bacal was in the corner of his vision. The old king was black and heavy. The court had shadows in all its corners. There were more deaths present than he could accommodate. There was a savagery that seemed to blind. Slowly, the axe head fell until it hung on the end of his arm. With a clatter, he released the weapon onto the stonework. Blackness filled his eyes, his mouth, his wound. He turned away, unable to commit the murder.

For a moment, those watching refused to believe what they had seen. Then whispers sprang like the beginnings of a gale. A growl came from the mass.

Paxbolón waited, a smile of scorn on his handsome

face. "You need do it only once," he called to Stone. "My death will speak for Varón also. I ask that he be spared." While van Staal translated, Paxbolón turned his eyes to the king and saw his father nod. "It is agreed," the prince continued. "One blow is all that is necessary."

Stone shook his head. "I'll do nothing," he told van Staal with disgust. "I care not if he lives or dies."

Slowly, stumbling over the words, van Staal told the crowd what Stone had said.

"Then the duty falls to me." It was Tutul Katun who spoke. He stepped forward and picked up the axe. "I claim the right to act for the Pale One."

The expression on Paxbolón's face altered; he stared at his brother. "So, you cannot wait for your succession?" he said bitterly. The true meaning of his death was clearer now.

"What I do is for my people." The axe was light in Tutul Katun's hand. "You would have sold them to the men from the north."

"It will happen in the end," Paxbolón replied, his eyes not leaving his brother. "It is written, you know that."

"The writings speak of many years before our kingdom dies." Tutul Katun stared down. All the rumors he had heard were true. His brother's games of war were played in many ways. "Those of Tayasal have one lifetime, perhaps more."

"Sooner or later we will all be slaves."

"Not if I am able to avoid it." Tutul Katun lifted the axe. What he did now would show all the shape of the future. "I will not sell my people."

Paxbolón's eyes narrowed. "You should have become a priest," he said venomously.

"On the contrary," Tutul Katun replied evenly. "I will make an excellent king." With the axe in both hands, he made a sweeping blow that struck his brother between the eyes. "You will be happy in the East Paradise of the Sun," he said. "In the Temple of the Warriors."

Tutul Katun stepped over Paxbolón's body. With further blows he severed the head from the shoulders; he lifted it by the hair and walked around the ball court, displaying it to all who were present.

Slowly, the crowd began to applaud.

He did not hear the Frenchman enter. His mind was filled with the sound of the harsh breathing of the blackamoor chained to the wall as he brought the hot iron nearer the terror-struck eye.

D'Avila had not believed the black man; not for a moment had he accepted the absurd lie he'd been told about the English captain's death. Stone could not die, would not die, until *he* pressed the iron—perhaps this very iron—into the blue eye and heard the sear of burning flesh. As he'd hear the cutthroat's scream. *Then* he'd die. Then he'd deserve to die: when his injury and shame matched d'Avila's own.

He'd taken Cramer, as he'd taken Carson, up the slime-green steps from the dungeon and brought him to the cell where the brazier waited.

At first d'Avila had pretended to believe the black man's lies. He'd thrust the iron into the coals and listened to the fractured Spanish, nodding as if he believed. Then he'd turned, the iron out, and approached the black and sweating face, determined to force the truth.

As the iron came closer, Cramer had repeated the lie. There had been a sudden cry from Alvaréz—who nervously watched and pleaded—but that was all d'Avila had heard. He'd pushed the iron to within inches of the black man's face. Cramer had gasped, and d'Avila had not heard the Frenchman enter. He'd not heard, or seen, anything but the man before him until a hand had gripped his own to tear the iron from his grasp, until another's rage had flung him into a corner.

"*Merde*," Cazaux fumed. "*Merde,* you are a pest."

D'Avila scrambled to his feet, looking wildly about him. Cazaux was alone. Alvaréz stood uneasily. Cramer let out his breath, both eyes intact.

"You killed one, and you would kill another." The scar on Cazaux's face was crimson with rage. "*Mon Dieu*, you deserve to die."

"I—" D'Avila wiped his lips with the back of his hand. "I did no more than was done to me."

"That, you brought upon yourself." Cazaux raised the glowing iron. "You failure," he fumed. "You stinking failure."

"He lied," d'Avila burst out suddenly, the words tumbling. "The black man said that Stone was dead. That all had died, save one who brought the message. He said they'd perished, all the others. He lied. The black man lied to me."

Cazaux turned to Cramer. "Aye," the Negro said, his voice relieved. "I did." He managed to smile.

"Why?" Cazaux spoke in English.

"I'd thought to stop his madness. It's the cap'n he wants." Cramer came a little way out from the wall. "He's crazed to have him back."

"And the other?" Cazaux swung back to d'Avila. "You fool," Cazaux swung back to d'Avila. "What makes you think he's yours?" he demanded in Spanish.

"Who? What?" D'Avila's fingers scratched at the eye patch he wore. "I do not understand."

"Understand this." Cazaux raised the hot iron threateningly. "You touch another prisoner, and you'll lose the only eye you have." He watched the Spaniard twitch. "Understand me clearly," he continued coldly. "Alvaréz will keep me informed. Another attempt, merely an attempt, and I blind you *both*, completely."

"But—" d'Avila's voice rose. "By God, it is my right," he exclaimed. "He's mine. The English pirate's mine. I've waited. I've waited, and I've bargained. The mayor promised him to me. As soon as he returns. I have him in return for my vote. I voted, and he promised me the pirate. He's mine, I tell you. He's mine."

"*Merde*." Cazaux spat on the floor. "You Spaniards are such merchants."

"It was a bargain." D'Avila babbled the words. "It was fair."

"Quiet," Cazaux said savagely. "Or I blind you now."

D'Avila was silent. He looked at the iron. It was steady in the Frenchman's hand and not far-enough away. His eyes flickered to Alvaréz, who stood as remote as possible, his palms rubbing the cloth of his stomach. He glanced at Cramer, who smiled in return. They were all against him. They all would pay, no matter what they threatened. He had come to Campeche with a mission none would take away. He licked his lips and subsided. He would wait. In time he would contend with them all.

CHAPTER 14

LIKE MOLTEN HONEY THE EVENING SUN HUNG IN A QUILTED sky over the city of Tayasal. Then, almost without suggestion of movement, it dissolved behind the temple, filling the gruesome chamber with its all-invading light.

As its last rays turned from purple to black, Paxbolón, dressed in his jaguar tunic, was buried. His headdress had been placed on his severed head, which lay beside his body in a box of scented woods. Paxbolón's body rested on its haunches as though alert.

He was surrounded by those possessions he'd valued most in life. His short stabbing spear, with its cover of jaguar hide, accompanied him. A jade bead had been placed between his lips to keep his soul intact until the voyage to the Temple of the Warriors was complete. Copper bells and jade necklaces, earplugs of jade inlaid with gold, were arranged about him. Over his shoulders was a cloak of quetzal feathers, so gloriously worked it danced like life in the glow from the pine torches carried by the warriors attending the burial.

No slaves were killed to serve him on his journey. He had died alone and would continue so. His heart had gone to Itzamná.

Canek looked on as the simple dishes of corn and beans, meat and fruit, were placed in the burial pit

beside the coffin. All was in order now. As the first
earth began to fall, he lifted his eyes to see the lips of
Bacal moving in the torchlight.

"We will build an altar here," Canek said abruptly.
"It will represent the power of the Fighting Lord, and
the great battle he won against the invaders."

"Yes, my lord," Bacal whispered. "It will be done."

"He was a formidable man," Canek said thoughtfully.
"His name will live long in our memory."

"When the altar is made, I will bless it so," Bacal
hissed.

When the ceremony was over, Bacal made his dark
way to the stone-and-mortar house by the lake where
the invaders had camped and where copal still burned to
eliminate any memory of their presence. Tutz awaited
him with five other priests whose stench overrode even
the smell of copal throughout the building.

In the large, high-ceilinged hall, with its scenes of
ritual murder, Bacal addressed them all. "We have been
deprived by trickery," the thin priest said. "Too many
have been taken from us. He who Itzamná demanded
most has gained his freedom. It must not come to pass."

The others nodded. In their blackened faces their eyes
tightened with anger. All had slashed their ears. Blood
ran in black lines across their cheeks, it glistened in the
coils of their thick, impenetrable hair. Bacal had cut a
hole in his tongue to show the extent of his regret, and
through it he had drawn a cord of thorns. As pain seared
and blood dripped, he had asked forgiveness from Itzamná.

"Tonight," Bacal continued, "when much balche has
been drunk, I will call the temple warriors." About his
swollen tongue, his words sounded more serpentlike
than ever. "The Pale One and Round Skull must go to
Chac, god of water. He will wash their sins from our
city." His eyes flashed. "Am I understood?"

Tutz nodded. "It must be done," he said. He was a fat
man whose eyes were crossed as a sign of his holiness.
As a baby, a ball of wax had been hung from his forehead until the eyes became permanently displaced. "Great
offenses have been committed."

"We will see it done." Bacal wrapped his cloak about his frame. "Tonight there will be vengeance for all."

A murmur of agreement went round the room. The priests rocked on their heels. They knew there would be much whispering if the Pale One and Round Skull left with their lives. It would be said that the gods were not propitiated sufficiently. Bacal would become even more obsessed: in order to restore his supremacy he'd scour the city for hearts to offer to erase his shame.

Sons would be asked for, daughters taken. Slaves would be demanded, and those in debt would pay with their lives. It would be a harsh and bloody time for all.

"I will call the warriors when the time is right," Bacal whispered. "The gods will not be deprived."

The priests muttered and nodded and prepared to leave, knowing that if Bacal emerged from this day with honor, it would seem like a miracle to them all.

Guadalupe watched the last knife-edge of light that lay along the horizon shimmer and die. She turned her eyes to Grajales, seated on the far side of the campfire. He drank from a gourd, then offered her the water.

Guadalupe shook her head.

"We are making good time," Grajales said conversationally. "We travel much faster than when we came."

Guadalupe nodded.

"Soon we will be back in Campeche," Grajales continued evenly. He studied her in the firelight. She was calm, almost tranquil; the fear that had hurled her from her horse had gone as quickly as it had come. "Just the two of us," he added softly. "We are all that remains of the bold expedition."

"What will you tell them?" Guadalupe asked. "When we return?"

Grajales shrugged. "The truth," he said simply.

"They will not believe it." Guadalupe's voice was sure. She heard again the scream cutting across the lake water; she saw once more the stream of light ascend the temple steps. "No one will wish to hear that pagan idols are still worshiped. That the power of the Lord God in New Spain has had so little effect.''

Grajales looked at her anew as she stared into the firelight. Her almost Oriental eyes were level; the hollows of her face were deeply molded. She was beautiful, and she never ceased to surprise him with her observations.

"A lie is all they will accept," she went on surely. "If you tell them that they all died bravely, then they'll listen. If you say that they sailed to Tayasal and left us on the shore, you because of your wound, me because am a woman, then they'll believe you. But they'll not believe the other.''

Grajales nodded slowly. "What of the gold?'' he asked.

"Tell them it remains.'' Guadalupe lifted her head, her look distant. "They'll believe that also. One day they will send more soldiers. One day they'll succeed in destroying the entire city.''

"Is that . . .'' Grajales paused, a frown on his friendly face. "Is that what you'd wish?'' he asked.

Guadalupe nodded. "That is what I wish,'' she said.

"But, are they not your people? Your mother—?''

"My mother is a Maya.'' Guadalupe's tone was without rancor; her face was calm, her hands were still. "My father was Spanish. I am a mixture, a Mexican. I belong to neither side. I am what this country will become.'' She paused. "Already there are many such as me. Perhaps more than there are either Spanish or Maya.''

Again, Grajales looked at her; again, he was surprised by this beautiful woman. "You have become very changed,'' he said, but it was more of a question than anything else.

"My eyes have been opened, that is all,'' Guadalupe replied. "I loved Cristóbal for what he was, not for what he did. He was brave, but, like the rest, he was greedy.''

Grajales reached for the gourd, then put it down again. he seemed unsure of how to comment. "Do not become reproachful,'' he said finally, very softly.

"I am not reproachful,'' Guadalupe replied. She put

out her hands to the fire. "But, as you say, I have changed."

Grajales stared, then looked away. About them the dry savanna's heat was dying; a little wind stirred dust and leaves. He did not know what to think of the girl. He did not know how to touch her heart.

Christopher Stone grunted against the pain in his hip. He lay on the simple frame bed in the windowless cell behind the palace and could feel the fever spreading from the wound. He wondered when they would be gone from this island; he needed to be moving once again.

After the death of Paxbolón, they'd been returned to the cell and told to prepare themselves for the evening. Their clothes had awaited them, as had their weapons. Shirts and breeches had been freshly washed; they smelled faintly of the sun. Their leather boots had been oiled and the jerkins brushed. Van Staal's axe was clean in its holster. Stone's pistols in their bandolier were intact. A bottle of powder and a pouch of balls accompanied the weapons.

There had been water to wash in, food and cornwater to eat and drink. But the door had been closed behind them, and they heard, still, the voices of those who guarded it.

"God's pox," Stone had grunted. "What more do they want?"

"You are a hero now," van Staal had replied cautiously. "They wish to celebrate that fact."

"I wish to be gone."

"Aye, so do I," van Staal had replied, seeing the exhaustion and the pain on the Englishman's face, "but first, let me tend the injury."

Van Staal had cleaned the wound as best he could, then bound it tightly with strips of cotton torn from a blanket. When the task was done, Stone had put his weight on the leg, the effort wrenching the muscles in his neck.

"It'll hold," he'd grunted. "It'll get me away." He'd

examined his scraped knees and elbows, the cut on his forehead, the marks on his ribs and groin. They'd seemed slight, compared with the gash on his hip. "What's planned before we leave?" he'd asked.

"I do not know," van Staal had replied. "A ceremony to honor you." He'd looked away. "Wash now," he'd said, "and dress. Then rest until they come for us."

Stone had done so, then lain on the frame bed, waiting and dozing as the hot hurt spread. Van Staal had changed also; he too had lain on his simple bed, looking up at the ceiling, wondering what was to come, fearing the worst.

They were both asleep when the cell door opened and Ceel, surrounded by torchbearers, strode in. He wore an open cloak that fell to his feet. His hair was drawn back sharply into a long plait bound with square plates of jade. Jade encompassed his neck and his wrists. In the torchlight he was magnificent: a ghost of Paxbolón.

"We await you," he said, bowing low.

"What?" Stone lifted his head; his eyes were feverish, his mouth dry. For a moment he thought the dead had returned. He reached for his pistols. "Sweet Jesu—"

"No," Ceel called to van Staal. "This is not a celebration of war. Tonight, we come in peace."

"What games do they play?" Stone wanted to know. His head ached—in the torchlight everything appeared unreal. "I trust them not."

"We must accept what they say," van Staal replied. "We have no choice."

"I have a knife in my boot," Stone muttered, but even as he spoke the words he knew the threat was empty. He stood, and fire tore down his leg; each step would be agony. "God's blood," he said. "Let's be done."

They were taken out into the night.

The city was torchlit. Rows of slaves, holding long conical earthenware tubes in which pine pitch blazed, lined the way from the palace to the great plaza. At the base of the temple a dais had been erected on the spot where the cage that had held them when they'd first been captured had stood: the symbol of a separate ceremony.

In the center of the dais sat Canek, over his shoulders a light cotton mantle. To one side was Tutul Katun, beside him were cushions for Stone and van Staal. On the far side of the king were Bacal and the cross-eyed Tutz; they sat in semidarkness.

All bowed, without standing, as Stone and van Staal took their places. Stone eased himself onto the cushion with a painful grunt and sat with his injured leg stuck out stiffly before him.

Seeing him, Tutul Katun leaned toward van Staal and asked if anything could be done to reduce the Pale One's suffering.

"Ask him, has he rum?" Stone said grimly when told of the request.

When Tutul Katun was delivered the question, he turned to a servant and spoke rapidly in Maya. Stone looked inquiringly at van Staal, but the Dutchman only shrugged. Presently, a delicately carved gourd was brought containing a scented liquid.

"It is balche," Tutul Katun explained. "The wine of our people. It will ease the pain."

Stone sniffed the gourd and made a face, but somewhere among an odor of herbs and sweetness was the bite of alcohol. He took a mouthful of the mixture and swallowed grimly. "God's heart," he muttered, "what's it made from?"

"Honey," Tutul Katun explained when van Staal spoke, "and the bark of certain trees." He looked about him. "There will be much consumed tonight."

"Aye," Stone grunted when passed the comment. "I'll drink my share. Enough of it will numb my sore."

As Stone raised the gourd to his lips again, there was the sudden blast of trumpets. Tutul Katun held up a hand. "Now the Pale One will be honored," he said quietly. "We think highly of those who have struck the ball through the greenstone ring. There are so few of us who have done it." He stared steadily ahead.

"You—?" Van Staal's head came around; something cold passed through his body. "You, also—?"

Tutul Katun nodded.

"Did, did Paxbolón know?"

"Perhaps not," Tutul Katun replied softly. "My brother was always more concerned with his own prowess than that of any other."

"Damn your blood," van Staal whispered in English. "In your way you're as bad as he."

Tutul Katun was no longer listening. "Look," he said, leaning forward intently. "This is the dance of the man-woman."

From out of the crowd, a line of twenty men emerged. In their center was a taller man whose face was painted white. His body moved from side to side in an exaggerated imitation of the walk of a woman. He sauntered forward, and the others encircled him; all carried rattles. The sound of their clatter joined the trumpets and the drums.

Stone stared at the dancers and sipped from the gourd. When it was empty, the servant appeared with another. Stone took a further mouthful and shuddered. "They make a vile brew," he muttered, "but, by God, the hurt has eased." He wiped his lips with the back of his hand and laughed, a little mirthlessly. "For all its taste, 'tis working."

Van Staal was about to reply when the trumpets and the drums and the sound of rattles ceased. Then a dwarf rose from behind the dancers. Carried on the shoulders of warriors, he began to play a sweet melody on a flute made from a human thigh bone.

Four masked dancers, one wearing the image of a snake, another an owl, a third a turtle, and the fourth a frog, approached the man-woman, each taking a limb. They held him motionless as the others from the circle came forward, loosened their loincloths, and made motions of sexual intercourse. As each took his turn, the man-woman cried out in a voice that was neither male nor female, but a mixture of both. He sighed, his eyelids fluttered, he groaned and whispered. As the last of them came to him, he gave a loud and penetrating shout. On this signal, all in the crowd began to embrace in a turmoil of copulatory movement.

"God's blood," said Stone thickly. "D'you see that, Rolf? They fornicate like animals."

" 'Tis a dance," van Staal replied, watching Stone carefully, noting how affected he'd become. " 'Tis part of the ceremony."

"Ceremony? My arse-gut it's a ceremony. 'Tis the first time I've heard it called that."

" 'Tis pretense."

"The hell it is." Stone pointed to a couple. "If he's not got his mutton well home, I'm—" He paused and shook his head. "What's in this?" he muttered, staring at the gourd. "What have they given me?"

"Do our customs surprise the Pale One?" asked Tutul Katun, who watched Stone carefully, seeing the reddened face, the dilated pupils. "Does he not realize that for three days all in Tayasal have been away from their women?"

"He, he understand," van Staal replied slowly.

"Or that the dance of the man-woman, and what is happening now, are only introductions to what is yet to come?"

Van Staal swallowed. "He understand," he repeated, "but Pale One has much pain. And wine—"

"That is good," said Tutul Katun understandingly. "For now he will need to forget his pain."

"Why?"

Tutul Katun held up a hand. "Wait, Round Skull. In a moment you will see," he said firmly. He turned his eyes to the crowd below, which was settling, preparing now to witness.

Then, once again, the trumpets lifted, and a procession began from the far side of the plaza. At its head was a girl of fifteen years. She was exquisitely dressed and delicately shaped, her forehead sloped and her nose fine; her hands and feet were tiny. She was Ix Mai, third daughter of Tutz; she had been chosen by Tutul Katun in a moment of delicate irony. As she approached the

man to whom she was to be given, she could barely
contain her fear.

"Sweet Jesu," Stone said when he caught sight of
her, "she's pretty." He gulped again from the gourd.

"She is for you, Christopher," van Staal said gently.
"She is the reason you are here."

"What?" Stone's eyes grew round, they protruded
from the gauntness of his face, red-veined and wild.
"What's that you say?"

"What, what the others bring is also yours," van
Staal said carefully. "Look, that is your reward."

Stone peered below. White-robed women, surrounding Ix Mai, carried feathered cloaks and mantles, necklaces of jade and chalcedony, ear plugs and pendants,
bracelets and anklets that glittered with the yellow of
beaded gold. Stone stared, then reached for the gourd
again.

Canek now turned to van Staal. "With this we honor
a great warrior," he said, studying them both briefly.
They held little interest for him now. It was almost time
he left this ceremony. "Take these gifts with our blessing," he added. "We wish you well."

"Thank you, my lord," van Staal replied.

"You will bear them with you when you go." Canek
eased his bulk on his huge cushion, and a gleam of
curiosity came into his eye. "But first," he added, "the
Pale One must take the girl."

Van Staal swallowed. "I no, understand," he stammered, knowing exactly what the old king meant.

'It is his duty to take her," Canek said simply, enjoying the expression on Round Skull's face. "Those who
win their lives as he did must pass their seed to a
virgin."

"I, ah . . . ." Van Staal nodded uncomfortably, "I
understand."

"Then tell him." Canek smiled broadly. "Tell him to
do it now."

"Now?" Van Staal glanced at Stone. His head had
drooped again, his eyes were fixed on the girl. "You
mean, here?"

Canek nodded with growing enjoyment. "It is an act we all should witness," he replied.

"I, ah, do not think he can."

"Can?" Canek laughed a little. "He looks like a man who could to me."

"I, ah—" Van Staal wiped sweat from his forehead. The old king's good humor was menacing. "He is—"

"Look at her." Canek pointed to Ix Mai. "Would not her prettiness stir any man?"

Van Staal stared at the girl; she lifted her eyes to him. For a moment they examined each other, and in that moment van Staal witnessed her terror. She was like a child being led to an unknown destination, a richly decorated sacrifice about to be slaughtered.

"Examine her," Canek urged heartily, his face creasing with mirth. "Tell the Pale One to feel the firmness of her flesh, then let me be told he cannot."

Stone's head came around to van Staal. "What in God's name's happening?" he asked. "What's all this talk?"

" 'Tis as I thought," van Staal explained slowly. "The gifts and the girl are yours."

"By god, 'tis a fine sense of humor they have," Stone said with sudden and bitter clarity. " 'Tis all the gold we've seen. The girl's far prettier than any they sent before. And all of it useless. I'll trade it all for a canoe and a pair of horses."

"There are no horses here. And we'll be fortunate to get a canoe." Van Staal breathed deeply. In the crowd was the beginning of restlessness; beside him he felt the demanding gaze of the king. "We'll get nothing if you don't take the girl now."

"She'd be useless," Stone replied; once more his voice was heavy. "We can carry none of this."

"That is"—van Staal cleared his throat—"that is not what is meant."

"What?" Stone's red eyes widened. "What'd you say?"

Van Staal told him.

"In Christ's name, no." Stone's angry shout filled the

plaza. "Before them, like a dog? They can drink their vomit before I'll touch her." He tried to rise, but pain bound him. His face went white, and lines formed about his lips. Clumsily, he reached for the balche gourd and drained it. Brown liquid ran down his chin. "I'll have no part of it," he muttered.

Tutul Katun leaned forward; his eyes were critical. "What is this the Pale One says?" he asked, his voice hardening. "Does he not like the girl we have chosen for him?"

"He, he like her," van Staal replied as calmly as he could. "But, he is, he is different."

"Different?" Tutul Katun's tone was carefully under control; he would permit no mockery. "You take a woman the way we do, is that not so?"

Van Staal nodded and licked his lips.

"Why, then, does he hesitate?"

"It is," van Staal began, fumbling for words, "for us it is, private." He put a hand over his heart in a gesture of sincerity. "The Pale One is great lord. What he does, with women, is personal."

"Does he have a small member?" Canek asked with loud amusement. He would go soon and cared little now about witnessing the Pale One mount the frightened girl. The painted boy, whose hands contained such skill, awaited him at the palace, warming the oil. It amused him to tease the invaders, but that was all. "Is he unable to make it grow while others look?" he asked, and laughed again.

Those who heard the words of the king laughed also. The plaza filled with jokes about the Pale One's penis and the size of the girl. The dwarf, with the flute made from a human thigh, began to play, and his haunting hollow notes eased the tension in the crowd. More balche was drunk. More of the water, with the dust of dried mushrooms added, was passed about. The moment of restlessness was turned to mirth; all waited to see what would happen when the daughter of Tutz was presented to the mad invader from the north.

"Well?" Canek continued, prodding van Staal. "Does

the Pale One's member not get large? Or is there something about it we should not see?''

"My lord," Van Staal began. He was sweating freely now; it was an effort to keep his voice even. "In private, custom of us. And, should be respected." He strove to make himself understood. "Is our, way. Respected."

There was a second or two of uneasy silence. Then Tutul Katun leaned forward; recognizing Round Skull's struggle, he could see that there was no mockery intended, only an attempt to avoid a spectacle. "You are correct to ask that your customs be respected," he said, allowing an opening. "But you are no longer among your own people." He spoke easily, encouraging Round Skull to continue.

"I know," van Staal replied, "but your customs say the Pale One, give seed to girl, no?"

Tutul Katun nodded, watching Round Skull with interest.

"Then, could it be done when, Pale One ready? So, the, the best—"

"So that the best of him goes to the girl?" Tutul Katun smiled briefly. "Is that what you would say?"

"Yes, my lord."

"You are no fool," Tutul Katun said with some respect. "But that would mean you must take the girl with you." He paused significantly. "Or remain until the Pale One is prepared to do what he must."

Van Staal breathed deeply. "We take girl," he said with a great sense of relief.

Tutul Katun nodded. The crowd was calm enough to accept the departure. His people were quiet and would listen to his explanation. He knew that the sooner the Pale One left Tayasal, the better. It was good that he be gone. Even if the invader had remained in death, his spirit would have carried too much power.

Van Staal wrapped his arms about himself. "May we go, now, my lord?" he asked. The words came out like a prayer.

"You may go, Round Skull," Tutul Katun said, his

tone quiet but firm. "But there is one matter that must be clearly understood."

"What, what is, my lord?"

"When the girl is with the seed of the Pale One, she must return to Tayasal."

"What, what if she come back without seed?"

"She would be put to death at once," Tutul Katun replied. His eyes were level, he was telling Round Skull no more than he must. "It is part of the price the Pale One pays for his freedom."

"Then," van Staal said slowly; again the cold went through him, "then, if not take girl—?"

"You would both have remained until the seed was sown." Tutul Katun's voice was deceptively simple. "Come," he said, "I will tell my people what has been decided, then you must be gone."

Van Staal felt a strange responsibility move him. He looked down into the eyes of the frightened girl. She stared up in horror at the barbarian who was to open her; she stared in terror, making no attempt to conceal it. She listened to what Tutul Katun had to say, and then she closed her eyes.

She did not know where she was going or what her fate would be. It will begin as pain and end in pleasure, they had told her as she was prepared for the ceremony. But none had spoken of this monster who sat drooling beside the prince, none had said a word of the animal to whom she would be given.

She closed her eyes and waited, trembling like a bird. As he watched her, van Staal thought she would fall.

CHAPTER 15

THEY WALKED THE DECK, ARM IN ARM, THE STARS SO CLOSE they seemed within reach. All about was the dark lapping of the sea. Angela's skin was velvet and warmer by far than the mild evening air that enveloped them. She was his midnight sun.

Cazaux paused to kiss the hollow of her throat. He felt the course of blood; his hand came up for comfort. They walked another turning. But he did not speak, and his tread was heavy.

"What is it?" she whispered, knowing she must begin. "What troubles you?"

Cazaux stopped to stare at her. She was magnificent in the delicate light, her face a kaleidoscope of shadow and pattern as she stood before him so still and calm.

"Speak of it," she urged, her voice lower than a whisper. "I will understand."

"It is," Cazaux began, hesitated. "Why do you ask?"

"Because I must." Angela lifted a hand and touched the scar. "Because what we do now we do together."

Cazaux drew his breath and held her. She would never cease to amaze him. "There is," he began again, surrendering. "There is a madman among us," he continued, and shrugged as if to question. "Madman, exactly? I do not know, but he acts insanely."

"And do you not know what to do with him?"

Cazaux shook his head.

"*You*, who have led? You, who have pirated." Angela had known from the beginning where the future lay. At times she was sure she knew more of survival than any of them. Even when he'd left her, when she'd discovered that Jean-Marc had sailed without a word, and she'd fainted in shock and disbelief, she'd known it was only a matter of time before he came back to her. She'd been as certain of it as she'd been of the warmth of his flesh. Of course, she'd used the condition, she'd made the most of the state to calculate more fully the life that lay ahead, the future as she would make it. She'd been deeply grateful for the support the dear blackamoor had given, but, he too, was just another who needed to be guided in the direction he really wanted to go. Now, she looked at Cazaux fondly. "*You* do not know what to do?"

"It is not simple," Cazaux replied. "On a ship you are your master. Here there are others. Anyway, this case is different. We have achieved a truce here in Campeche that this madman would destroy." He shrugged again. "I wish to succeed," he added as if that explained everything.

Angela smiled. "You sound like Papá," she said wryly.

Cazaux shrugged uncomfortably.

Angela's fingers touched the hair that curled over Cazaux's collar. "If he were a dog, what you you do?" she asked, and felt the power of her words lift the cords of his neck.

Cazaux stared. "I would kill him, of course," he said, simply.

Angela smiled; it was her only response.

"*Mon Dieu*," breathed Cazaux "Who would have believed your strength."

"Uf, I am just a fool, ask anyone," Angela replied with a laugh that floated over the water like an evening breeze. "But, if the dog is to be destroyed?" She widened her wonderful eyes, and they caught the stars. "It might be wise if, well, if Papá were to believe the idea his own. Is that not so? Perhaps also the responsibility."

"The responsibility?" Cazaux asked carefully.

"Of course. After all, he is the authority," Angela replied easily. "What is more, it would give him something positive to occupy his thoughts."

Cazaux reached for her and held her as the frigate rocked, as the stars were echoed in her eyes as on the surface of the sea. There was the sound of the ship, the tang of salt, and her presence. Wood creak and a knowledge he would never be alone filled him with wonder. Kill d'Avila or no, that would be decided later. But now she was on his side, and that, quite simply, was a miracle.

Ix Mai knew now that she must remain with the Pale One until the seed was sown. Then she must return to her father's house, where she would be cared for until the child was born. After that she could marry whomever she chose. She would be famous, she would be unique; she could select from the many who would want her. But only if she were able to overcome her terror of the barbarian who staggered ahead of her in the narrow street leading down toward the lake.

No one had told her what he was like. She had not seen him in the cage at the foot of the temple; she had not been permitted to attend the ball game. Her first sight of him had been as he'd peered down from the dais, his red-rimmed eyes filling her with cold and trembling dread.

Now, he moved behind the lord Tutul Katun like a huge awkward brute, dragging one leg, leaning on the shoulders of Round Skull, who looked like a monkey himself, whose hair was shorn as was sometimes done to prisoners, and her fear clamped her throat. Ix Mai clutched the woven cotton handbag that contained all her possessions and decided she would bear no child sired by this monster. She would kill herself first and knew of many ways to do so.

From where he waited, in the house of Tutz, Bacal heard them coming. There were four priests with him, and five temple warriors stood ready, each with a club or stabbing spear in their hands. Those who now approached this house were few. Bacal's forces were more than enough.

"They, they will have their weapons," Tutz, who stood beside him, said uneasily. It was as if he'd known what Bacal was thinking. "That axe, and those pistols." The fat priest with the crossed eyes shuddered.

"The Pale One is weak, and his head affected by balche," Bacal whispered harshly.

"Even s-so," Tutz stammered. "They are formidable."

"There will be no need for force," Bacal said, his voice like a snake's. "Lord Tutul Katun knows, as well as any, that this city must be cleansed of its filth."

"Yes," Tutz replied uncertainly. "He must."

Christopher Stone limped down the street in agony. Each step he took was like the scraping of glass against flesh. He hung on to van Staal like a cripple; without the Dutchman he could not move. The wound was afire with fever now, soon it would grip his entire body. He must lie somewhere, find shelter until the burning in his blood was done.

"Where are we?" he asked. His mind seemed more clouded than ever. "How far—?"

"We are in the street where we sheltered," van Staal replied. "The water is close."

"Thank God," Stone began. Then his head came up; he sniffed the air. "The warlock," he cried, pulling van Staal to a halt. "By God, he's here."

"What?" Van Staal peered but saw nothing in the darkness. "Come on, you're—"

"He's here," Stone shouted. "I scent the poxy priest."

From his position in the fore of the tiny procession, Tutul Katun turned at the sudden shout, wondering what had caused it. He glanced at Ceel, the only warrior to accompany him, and saw that he, too, was puzzled. Tutul Katun looked for the girl and could just make out her trembling form behind the Pale One, who stood with his head back, his eyes rolling, in the moonlight.

"What is this?" Tutul Katun called. "What troubles the Pale One?"

"He"—van Staal cleared his throat—"he say he smell the priest."

"Bacal?" Tutul Katun took a step toward them. "Is he sure?"

Van Staal nodded.

"He's here." Stone staggered; the fire in his hip was like a signal. "I smell him." The rot of the priest's garments, the vileness of his bloody face, were close and pressing. "He stinks as he waits."

"It is the balche." Ceel approached van Staal. "His mind is confused. Bring him, the beach with the canoe is near."

Ix Mai watched, unable to move with fear. The Pale One stared like a beast. His eyes were wild. He stood stiff-legged, his head back, seeing visions lost to the rest of them. He was like one who had eaten peyotl fruit, and she wondered how much had been added to his balche. She watched, her heart threatening to burst, as Lord Tutul Katun stepped closer to the crazed invader, and suddenly the street was filled with light.

From four doorways emerged temple warriors, each with a pine torch in one hand, a weapon in the other. They surrounded Stone as he shouted, as the tall black figure of Bacal appeared, his eyes mere slits in his face.

"Release him," Bacal growled in his low, harsh voice. "Release the Pale One to me."

"There?" Stone reeled and clawed. "He's here?"

Tutul Katun stood unmoving, his eyes fixed on Bacal. He ignored the temple warriors, he no longer regarded Stone, his gaze was fixed unwavering on the figure of Bacal.

"In Christ's name, he stinks," Stone ranted. His hand reached for a pistol. "I'll—"

"Stop him." Tutul Katun spoke softly but sharply to van Staal, his look not leaving the priest. "Do not let him touch a weapon. For then they will say *I* was threatened."

Van Staal held Stone's hand, his eyes uncertain. "Wait, Christopher," he grunted. "There is more said than I comprehend."

"I'll kill him."

"Let's see first what Tutul Katun will do."

Slowly, his feathered headdress magnificent, his cloak a ripple of light, Tutul Katun went closer to Bacal. When he spoke his voice was easy, as if in quiet conversation. "I had thought you far more able than this," he said for the priest's ears alone.

Bacal blinked. "With all respect, my lord," he whispered, disarmed by the prince's calm, "the Pale One has failed in his duty to us all."

Tutul Katun nodded, as if in accord. "To what do you refer?" he asked.

"To the game, my lord. He would not take the head of Paxbolón."

"That is true," Tutul Katun agreed, as if suddenly remembering.

"Nor would he take the girl before us." The words were like drops of venom from Bacal's swollen tongue.

Again the young prince seemed to conform. "So, what do you suggest?" he asked.

Bacal's voice dropped to a low and fierce hiss. "He must die, and his companion with him," he said. "They must go to Chac, god of water. He will cleanse the city."

Tutul Katun nodded thoughtfully.

"In that case . . ." Bacal felt the tension in the street tighten like a bow string. "If you agree, may we take them for the gods?"

"Yes," Tutul Katun said quietly, "we will let the gods decide."

Bacal turned to the temple warriors. "I have spoken to Lord Tutul Katun," he grated, his voice lifting with triumph. "He is with us. Take the invaders now."

"One moment." Tutul Katun held up a restraining hand. "First, I must know how they will be delivered."

Bacal's searing eyes came round. "They will be cast into the lake water," he said, confused by the unnecessary question. He stared at the prince and past him, searching the darkness. Was he to be deprived? How? "You have spoken. Is that not so?"

"That is true," said Tutul Katun; yet he appeared to be waiting. "I have spoken."

"My lord," Bacal began.

"My lord . . ." A new voice entered, and Tutul Katun smiled briefly; he nodded as Ah Cuc continued. "We were delayed, but I believe we are in time." Ah Cuc stepped gracefully into the street and bowed low to Tutul Katun. With him were ten guards from the palace, armed with bows that had arrows fitted to the strings. They bent to the temple warriors and politely offered greetings. "How may I serve you?" Ah Cuc inquired.

Tutul Katun paused a moment. All was as it should be. Beside him, Bacal's breath burned the air.

"Are we to proceed to the canoe, my lord?" Ah Cuc asked quietly. "Or have other farewells been planned?"

"We go to the canoe," Tutul Katun replied. "However, Bacal now wishes to be present at the departure."

"My lord," Bacal seethed, "the god Chac—"

"Chac is on the water," Tutul Katun replied evenly. "Once the canoe puts out they will all be in his hands."

"My lord," Bacal persisted, biting the words, "we cannot deny—"

As easily as if they were on a palace terrace, Tutul Katun put his arm through the priest's; when he spoke his voice was low and controlled and deadly.

"You have already gone beyond your powers," the young prince said, his words once more for Bacal alone. "For only that I could have you destroyed. But, if you press me further, I shall have you put to death with little knives and your body thrown to the dogs. I shall have your family treated equally, and your name stripped from our records. Your house will be struck to the ground and your memory totally obliterated." He smiled quite gently, but his eyes were stone. "Do I make myself understood?"

Bacal listened in silence.

"And if I were to do all that," Tutul Katun continued in the same pleasant, incisive tone, "you would have no place in this world or the next. A condition that would not please you at all, am I right?"

Bacal's intake of breath was sharp; his gaze was bleak with impotence.

"Good," said Tutul Katun. "I'm glad we are agreed." He paused to turn to those who waited. "I have just informed Bacal of the generosity of the Pale One and Round Skull," he explained. "They have presented to the temple all the gifts we have given them. Of course, they must take the girl until the seed is sown. But the cloaks and the jewelry, and the mantles so richly woven by our people, have all remained." He bowed slightly. "Is that not a most noble gesture?"

The Maya who listened bowed in acknowledgment. Tutul Katun then went to van Staal. "Do not be afraid," the prince said quietly. "You will go from here now."

Van Staal stared uncertainly. Stone hung like a weight about his neck.

"Trust me," Tutul Katun added softly. "For I have given my word." He gazed levelly at Round Skull for a moment, then spoke again, loud enough for all to hear. "Come now," he said, "we will put the Pale One and Round Skull and Ix Mai on the water. We will place them in the hands of Chac."

The procession, enlarged, continued. Ceel called to the palace guards. They formed behind Tutul Katun and the invaders as they went down toward the shore. Ceel spoke Ix Mai's name, and she came fearfully from the shadows. She glanced once at her father as the priests and the temple warriors walked along behind, but Tutz turned hurriedly away.

Witnessing her distress, Ah Cuc fell into step beside her and whispered in her ear. Immediately, the girl's face came up, surprised and disbelieving.

"It is true," Ah Cuc assured her as they went down the narrow street. "I have seen him tender with a woman."

Ix Mai looked dubiously toward Stone, held upright by van Staal. He was quieter now that the tension had died, but he contained nothing she could consider tender. She tightened her grip on the cotton bag that contained her possessions. "I will kill myself before I let him touch me," she whispered.

"Now, that would be silly." Ah Cuc clucked his tongue. "You are the daughter of a priest, and the one chosen to bear the child of a great warrior, to bring us the gifts of his blood. When you return, your honor will be three times increased. All you must do is submit yourself until the seed is sown."

Ix Mai shuddered. "I will never permit it," she said.

"The woman is dead now," Ah Cuc continued as if Ix Mai had not spoken. "She was pretty, and he was very kind to her." He lifted his voice encouragingly. "You'll have no trouble returning safely, and with honor. You carry the prince's seal."

"He"—Ix Mai swallowed—"he was kind, you say?"

Ah Cuc nodded. "Do not be distressed by his appearance now. He's fevered and drunk much balche. When he's recovered he'll be more agreeable, I assure you."

"Then, then I will do it." Ix Mai pressed her hands to her chest. "I will do it. After all, you are right—I am the daughter of a priest. It is my duty to bring honor to our people."

"That's a good girl." Ah Cuc smiled. "Here we are at the beach." He touched her cold hand briefly. "Soon it will be over," he whispered, "and you will be back home among us."

Ix Mai nodded and closed her eyes.

The canoe contained gourds of water, dried meats, and flat Maya bread. Three blankets had been placed within it; two paddles lay across its thwarts.

Van Staal took Stone to the vessel. "Come along, Christopher," he urged. "Into the bow."

Stone's head came up: there was torchlight and shapes, the smell of the priest, the sound of water lapping on a hull. "We're going?" he asked, his voice dry as dust, crumbling with relief. "It's true?"

"Aye." Van Staal half lifted him aboard. "Away from here, now."

"Sweet Jesu." Stone crawled into the narrow bow. "Be thanked for that mercy." Van Staal covered him with a blanket. He held the canoe as Ix Mai climbed into it. She sat in the stern, her bag between her feet, small and still but no longer terrified. She'd considered Ah Cuc's advice and was now determined to remain with the invaders until what had to be done was over. Then she could return to Tayasal and live as a queen. She only hoped that the Pale One was active so she might come home as soon as possible. Van Staal began to push the canoe into deeper water, then turned to Tutul Katun. "My lord," he began.

"Say nothing." Tutul Katun spoke softly. "Say farewell. We shall not meet again."

"I, I thank you."

Tutul Katun shook his head. "I did what had to be done," he said simply. "We are the last of our people. All that remain of millions." The words were for himself as well as Round Skull. "Go now," he added, "and do not look back."

Van Staal bowed. "I understand, a little," he said clumsily.

Tutul Katun's eyes softened. "Of them all, perhaps you do," he said in a voice that was final.

Van Staal pushed the boat from the shore, then leapt lightly aboard and took a paddle. He heard, over the sound of the waves, a whisper. "You are with Chac now. Pray the water god receives you." But he did not look back.

The canoe nosed into the night.

PART THREE

THE
KINGDOM
OF
HOPE

CHAPTER 1

DON LUIS DE CÓRDOBA, MAYOR OF CAMPECHE, SHAVED
with a hand that was steadier than it had been for some
time. For days he'd been unable to shave at all, had
been forced to sit as still as possible while Manuel scraped
gray bristle from his cheeks. At night he'd lain awake
sweating, listening to every sound—his mind magnifying
the nocturnal noises, his throat aching for the harsh
comfort of brandy. Once he'd hidden his head beneath
the sheets and sobbed like a child, thinking he was going
to die.

He'd begun to drink heavily again after he'd traded
Stone's life for d'Avila's vote. He'd remained seated at
the walnut table long after d'Avila had left him; he'd
remained until the cognac bottle was empty, and then
he'd called for more.

He'd continued drinking for three days, seeking relief
in oblivion and finding nothing but the urge to pour more
liquor down his throat. He'd hoped that his brain would
cloud and that the miserable deal he'd made would be
erased from his memory, but it had not been so. He'd
found no release in spite of the fact that he'd told himself again and again that the English pirate meant little
to him, that the bargain they had made had been forced
upon them both. But nothing helped, neither alcohol nor

reason. He realized that he'd arrived at the end of some sort of peace.

During his three days' drinking he'd slept little, mainly in his chair. On the morning of the council meeting, he'd had Manuel prepare him as best he could. Once inside the Municipal Building, he'd managed to face the others. With d'Avila's condemning vote he'd concluded his business and had immediately returned to his mansion with its cool courtyard and its view of the sea. There he'd called for more cognac and continued to seek his escape.

Looking back, the mayor found it difficult to recall the details of the council meeting. In his mind it remained a nervous blur, interrupted by the sound of voices lifted in anger and complaint, the slap of hands on the table. He remembered, more vividly, the sweat that had stuck his clothing to his body, the wretched demand for alcohol on his tongue. Yet he had succeeded. He had an image of the votes being cast and of the pinched line of González's tiny mouth when he'd realized that he'd failed.

It seemed a long time ago now, Don Luis thought as the blade cut clean his red-veined cheek. It might have occurred to another, and in a manner of speaking, it had. He had altered considerably. Don Luis examined himself in the mirror. He appeared older, the flesh of his face hung looser, giving him an even more mournful look. Don Luis sighed. It did not really matter; what was important was the control he'd retained, in spite of what it had cost him to survive. He had fewer doubts now about the deal he had made with d'Avila—Angela had seen to that.

He'd awakened late one afternoon, sprawled in his chair at the dining table, to see Angela staring down at him with such distaste that for a moment it had frightened him. He'd opened his mouth to speak, but his tongue had remained stuck to the roof of his clotted mouth. He'd reached forward with a shaking hand only to knock the brandy bottle over on the table before him. Rapidly he'd snatched it up.

Angela watched the pitiful movements without speaking. Then she said, "I had to come," her voice sad but empty of comfort. "Manuel told me you were dying."

"I . . ." was all Don Luis managed to say.

"Killing yourself is what you're doing," Angela continued, wondering how far she could go, how much bullying he needed. "Until this moment I had not realized how weak a man you were."

Don Luis lifted the fallen bottle and poured a little brandy into his glass. Desperately he drank it, sucking the fire into his mouth.

"Stop this now." Angela raised her voice and watched his eyes come up to her: they showed a surprise that made her press further. "Stop now," she insisted. "If not for yourself, then for me."

"I . . ." The mayor swallowed; he hung his head to avoid his daughter's gaze. "I'm . . . I'm all right," he managed.

"You are far from all right," Angela persisted. "You are a wreck, and you're becoming a joke. González says you are finished. D'Avila is acting like a madman. If it weren't for Jean-Marc, there would be no authority in Campeche at all."

Don Luis blinked. "You, you know so much?" he whispered.

Angela ignored the question. "Stop what you're doing to yourself right now," she went on determinedly. "Stop feeling sorry for yourself. Things could be considerably worse."

"No," the mayor said, his voice trembling. "I . . . ah, you do not understand."

"I understand completely."

"No . . . no . . . first it was you," Don Luis mumbled, "after Cazaux left. I thought you were . . . you'd lost your mind. Then, then the blackamoor . . ." He hesitated, stumbling over his words. "Now I never see you anymore. On *La Petite*, always. Always on the ship. Never with me, never. And what I had to do with d'Avila—"

"*Don't you dare blame me.*" Angela's voice cut in

like iron. Even she wondered if she'd said too much as her father's stricken eyes came up again. "You're the one who must take all responsibility," she went on, pushing as far as she dared. "If not . . ." She paused and breathed deeply. "Then I will leave immediately."

"Leave?" Don Luis queried stupidly, his mouth agape. "Leave here?"

Angela nodded firmly. "I will persuade Jean-Marc to sail immediately. There will be no wedding. I will go as his *whore*. What is more, I'll see to it that he leaves behind all those who wish to stay. Then, Papá, you'll be left not ony without honor but with a great deal of lawlessness as well." She leaned forward emphatically. "Campeche will become a ruin, a pirate's town, a name to be reviled."

"No." Don Luis shook his head heavily, trying to empty it of his daughter's words. "You wouldn't. . . ."

"I would and I will," Angela replied. "You'll see for yourself. The choice is yours."

With that she'd walked away, hoping that her threat would bring some sense to the wreckage of what once had been the father she'd respected. It was the only way she knew of to try to bring him back. And she had succeeded, although the process had been slow and hard.

When he was alone once more, Don Luis had lifted the brandy bottle and stared at it for a long time. Then, with tears running down his raddled cheeks, he'd emptied it onto the table in front of him. For days, for nights, he'd struggled, fighting alone. Angela had not returned to him. Manuel had merely attended to his basic needs. And now, after a week of suffering, it seemed to him he was ready to face the world again, to resume what he knew to be his fine position in Campeche, to attend to everything—including his bargain with d'Avila, his betrayal of Stone.

Don Luis paused as he wiped the razor clean, a new thought striking him: he wondered if they were dead by now, those who had gone for the gold. Had died, the way so many others had died, in their search for the wealth of the Itzá. Don Luis shrugged. Their deaths would not dismay him; in many ways they would be a relief. He wondered if the Frenchman knew anything about them.

He rubbed a hand over his cheeks. Perhaps that was one of the reasons why Cazaux had requested this morning's meeting. Cazaux had spoken of a fiesta he'd been contemplating, and a cockfight had been referred to. Don Luis had no objection. In fact, he welcomed the idea—it was exactly what Campeche needed now: an event to lift its spirit, an occurrence to maintain the new momentum in which all citizens could join.

And there was the further matter Cazaux had mentioned, something to do with the English prisoners and a jailer who'd contacted him. Perhaps *that* would relate news of those who had journeyed to the interior. The mayor shrugged again and reached for his broadcloth doublet; he straightened his hose. Whatever it was, it would amount to little, he felt sure. Everything in Campeche was settling down again. Now that he was once more in control, the port, and its future, seemed to be assured.

Guadalupe Santoya and Grajales reined their horses on the savanna-covered plain. Beside them the sun went down: a red ball descending to the arms of cactus, sliced by the shimmering of its heat. They paused, seeking shelter for the night, watching little whorls of dust eddying in the evening air.

Even at this hour it was hot, hotter than it had been over a month ago, when they'd embarked on the search that had ended so bloodily.

Remembering it, Grajales spoke, his voice almost wistful. "In a few days we will be back," he said. "It is close now."

Guadalupe stared ahead. In the distance there was nothing but the coming darkness. "I do not wish to return," she said abruptly.

Grajales turned to her, seeing the deep sadness that marked her permanently now. He recalled the happiness, the shy smile, that had crossed her face when

she'd been with the tall pirate. None of them had understood it, none had seen where the pleasure lay in such a
man, but all had warmed to the spirit of the girl, to her
simple delight. That was gone now. The eyes were hard
and the mouth set. Grajales doubted if he would ever
see her smile again.

"There is nothing for me to go back to in Campeche,"
Guadalupe continued in the same flat tone. "I have no
reason to return."

"You have, you have your mother," Grajales said
uneasily. Her mood was unexpected. "She will be
waiting."

"She will think I'm dead by now." Guadalupe's voice
dropped to a whisper. "As I might as well be."

"No." Grajales's soft brown eyes were comforting.
"You cannot deny life just because someone you loved
has died."

"Why not?" Guadalupe faced him. "I know of no
better reason."

"But that, that would reduce the importance of what
has happened," Grajales said, choosing his words carefully. "The Inglés did not wish to die. If you were to, it
would seem without respect."

Guadalupe's eyes widened. "Do you think I will kill
myself?" she asked with sudden roughness.

Grajales shrugged uncertainly.

"Then you are a fool."

"Perhaps so." Grajales smiled. "I am not very clever,
as I am not very brave. But I wanted you to understand
that life is very precious." He glanced at his crippled
arm. "Even now," he added. "Even now."

Guadalupe turned quickly away. "Do not try to comfort me," she said bluntly, and spurred her horse to a
canter. Dust rose from its hooves.

Grajales shook his head and followed, wondering if he
would ever understand the workings of this woman's
mind. He caught up to her and rode beside; they continued steadily, without speaking. The sun went down, and
still they traveled, black silhouettes against a flaming

orange sky, twin shadows on horseback, riding the toughened grasses.

In the last of the light they saw a group of rocks rising from the plain. "There," Grajales called, breaking the silence. "We'll find nothing better tonight."

Guadalupe nodded and turned toward the outcrop, hearing an unexpected note in the drumming of the horse's hooves: a hollowness, an echo that came from below.

"What's that?" she called, lifting her head.

Sudden fear crossed Grajales's face. "It is the stone," he shouted, reining, pulling away. "It is thin. There are wells below. Get back from here."

Guadalupe tore at her horse's head. Standing in the stirrups, she drew the animal to a halt. Grajales struggled to do the same, fighting with knees and thighs, his useless arm flapping like cloth. He turned the horse and was returning to Guadalupe's side when the earth beneath him split like a plate, opened with a crash under the dusty hooves.

"*Dios mío*," Guadalupe cried, not believing what she saw. "Grajales!"

As she called, the ground swallowed horse and rider. Together they went down into darkness. The horse reared, its mane burning in the final twilight, tossing like the sea. Grajales's eyes turned in fear and despair as he disappeared from sight. There was a smothering of dust, a single cry, the muffled crashing of hooves. A numb and hollow echo of all that had occurred filled the wide and shadowed plain.

"*Grajales!*" Guadalupe screamed. She flung herself from her horse and ran carelessly toward the edge of the broken rock. "Grajales," she implored. "Do not leave me now."

She came to the crevasse, regardless of her safety. Rock crumbled beneath her feet; she fell to her knees. Yet she persisted, crawling to the lip of the hole, shouting down into blackness. Nothing replied. Only the return of her voice came back to her frightened ears, mockingly distant and faint. The rest was silence.

Guadalupe wept. She wept much more deeply than she had been able to weep for Cristóbal alone. Sobs racked her as she hung on the edge of the limestone layer. She allowed all her grief its force. She wept: a woman deprived of all that remained. She wept for them all. And, later, she made her decision.

Christopher Stone lay in a fever that was sapping life from his tall, gaunt body. After the canoe had landed, in spite of the dark, he had struggled from the lake, limping with the aid of a stick, leaning on van Staal, allowing no one to touch his wound.

As he'd forced himself over the hills that led from Tayasal, his agony had been apparent, but he'd said nothing of it. He'd begun the return journey with a grimness and a determination that was both mute and deranged. He wanted nothing but to be away; he would not even rest.

Then, late on the afternoon of the second day, he had stiffened, blood drained from his face, and he'd collapsed on the floor of the forest, clutching his hip.

Van Staal and Ix Mai had dragged him to the lee of an outcrop and begun to attend the wound. When van Staal removed the breeches and unbandaged the gash, he thought he would be ill at the sight of the dark, pus-filled hole that stank as though already dead.

"Dear Christ," he whispered, "the black gangrene has begun."

Crouching beside Round Skull, her face curiously unmoved by the hideousness of the injury, Ix Mai at first remained silent, as she had done since leaving Tayasal. Then, however, after examining the ugly wound for a few minutes, she muttered to herself and fell among the contents of her handbag to produce a small knife. Its blade glinting in the late afternoon light, she moved even closer to the Pale One.

Immediately van Staal gripped her tiny wrist. "What, what you do?" he asked uncertainly.

"Clean it," Ix Mai replied simply. "If the poison is not cut away, he will die."

Van Staal shook his head. "No cut it," he said, his eyes going from the festering gash to the girl's small, resolute face. "We, take blood. We cover it. But, no cut it." His brow was creased with indecision; he knew too little of either medicine or language.

Firmly, Ix Mai removed her hand from van Staal's. "Unless I clean it, and put on healing herbs, he will die." She spoke with authority; she looked at van Staal as if he were a fool. "Do you understand?" she added.

"What—" Van Staal swallowed, impressed by the change in her. She was no longer silent and remote. "What, herbs?" he asked.

"They will heal the sore. Once it's cleaned." Ix Mai's voice became firmer. "I have much knowledge of herbs. My father, Tutz the priest, is very skilled."

Van Staal turned his eyes back to the wound. It was as rotten as any he'd seen; it was worse than he knew how to treat. Stone lay on his side, one arm over his face, shivering with ague.

"Rolf," Stone whispered. "I'm burning. Get Alec," he muttered, naming Carson of the *Courage*. "He'll bleed me."

"Dear God," van Staal whispered. "The fever's in his brain."

"Do you want me to help or not?" Ix Mai asked impatiently. She held the small knife ready: its blade had been made from a shell, its handle of polished wood; it was beautiful and capable. "Or do you wish him to die?"

Van Staal rubbed a hand over his face. "Why, why you save him?" he asked.

"Do you understand nothing?" Ix Mai's look was scornful. "I must keep him alive. With his seed I can return to Tayasal. Without it I am worthless."

Van Staal breathed deeply. "Do it," he said brokenly, knowing that he had no choice.

Ix Mai nodded. "You must hold him, for there will be much pain," she said crisply.

"Aye." Van Staal gripped Stone in his bearlike arms. "I will."

With great deliberation, Ix Mai cut into the mass of red-black swollen tissue on Stone's hip. The knife went in cleanly, and poison burst, splashing from the wound to run over the pale skin in foul-smelling ribbons. Stone shouted in new agony and struggled in the Dutchman's grasp.

"Keep him still," Ix Mai instructed, her eyes on her work. "There is much to do, and the pain has not begun."

"Please," van Staal muttered, holding Stone with all his strength. "Please, hurry."

"I must take my time." Ix Mai's tiny hands worked skillfully. "There is a lot that has already died."

"Rolf? Alec?" Stone struggled; his voice pleaded. "What in God's name is being done?"

"Steady," van Staal whispered. "The rot's being taken away."

"My leg." Stone tried to sit upright. Van Staal wrestled him back. "My leg is being severed."

"No," van Staal comforted, sweating in anguish at the other's pain. "Your leg will heal."

"God's pox, it will." Stone's struggles grew weaker, his strength faded until, finally, he lay in van Staal's arms, breathing shallowly, his eyes half-closed. "My leg," he whimpered. "My leg's been taken."

Not once did Ix Mai look at the Pale One as she cleaned the wound. She cut away inflamed flesh, squeezed pus from tissue, her hands operating slowly and carefully until all the infection was gone and the great red and open gash bled freely.

Then she lifted her head. "Build a fire," she instructed van Staal. "I will go and seek the herbs."

Van Staal nodded; he released Stone and reached for a blanket. He was about to cover the Englishman when Ix Mai stopped him. "Do not touch the wound," she said firmly. "It is clean now, leave it as it is." She arranged the blanket over Stone's chest and glanced sharply at van Staal.

"But"—van Staal felt useless—"the air?"

"The air will do it good," Ix Mai said calmly. "See

that he does not move. I will not be long." She began to turn away, then paused. "Do not forget the fire," she said, as if speaking to a child.

Van Staal opened his mouth, then closed it again. He stared at the girl silently, new respect on his face, as she went to search for herbs. When she returned, a small fire burned between three stones, and the Pale One lay as she'd left him.

"Does he sleep?" she aasked.

Van Staal nodded.

"That is good." Ix Mai glanced down at the handful of herbs she'd gathered. "First I will prepare a poultice for the wound. Then an infusion for the Pale One to drink. Now, the hip is clean, but there is poison in his blood, and he will need help to fight it." She looked at Round Skull carefully. "Did you understand all that?"

"Yes." Van Staal licked his lips. "He will, live?" he asked.

"That depends on his strength."

"When, you know?"

"As the days go by we will both know," Ix Mai replied firmly, and bent over the fire. "Now, keep him steady, for when I heat the dressing and apply it, he will wake with pain."

Van Staal watched the girl prepare the poultice. She seemed so delicate, so competent. Beside her he felt like an oaf. He had the curious desire to reach out and hold her, to share something of her knowledge. He watched carefully every move she made, and she seemed not to see him at all.

Guadalupe Santoya did not know how long she remained, curled like an infant, nursing her grief. About her the world turned black. In the distance her horse nuzzled harsh grasses; from somewhere a coyote howled.

Later, when the moon had risen and the landscape lay ghostly on all sides, she crawled from the crevasse and its echoing silence, unsaddled the horse and haltered it, then took a blanket and lay on the cold, hard ground looking up at the carpet of stars.

She was vacant now, isolated beyond touch, but her decision was firm: she knew what she would do. In the morning she would resume her return to Campeche. She would go back to her mother's house, sit at the corner of the hearth, and watch Magdelena's hands soak corn and husk it and flatten the dough for bread. She would tell her mother everything that had passed but say nothing to any of the others. There was nothing she wanted anyone else to know.

She would remain with her mother, become part of Magdelena's life, and perhaps, some evenings, she would walk to the edge of the town, her face covered, her presence denied, and look toward the foothills that surrounded Campeche.

There, she might dream, dream of Cristóbal riding back, his head high, his wild eyes searching. She had forgiven his greed as she had forgiven his dying, but she needed the fragile hope.

It was insane, she realized as she watched the unmoving stars. It was the beginning of what she would become: empty, dry, and old. But she knew of no other way to absorb her grief. She was the last of them; she must have her separate ending.

She stared upward, unsleeping, as cold as a stone in the sea, more removed from touch than she would have believed possible.

CHAPTER 2

VAN STAAL WORKED UNTIL IT WAS ALMOST FULL DARK, CUT-
ting branches to form a shelter against the rock under
which Stone lay. He searched the hills for bracken to
place beneath the Englishman. When he thought Stone
was as comfortable as he could make him, he took the
gourds to a nearby stream and filled them with fresh
clear water.

He occupied himself steadily, trying not to think of
the man who lay, white and exhausted, scarcely seeming
to breathe. He returned to the fire to find Ix Mai placing
small earthenware vessels among the coals, preparing a
further infusion to be forced down the fevered throat.

She looked up, saw the gourds, nodded, and said
nothing. Later van Staal chewed a piece of flat, stale
Maya bread and ate a little fruit; then, curling in his
blanket, he tried to sleep. On the far side of the fire, Ix
Mai did the same.

Twice during the night Stone cried out fitfully, and
they both attended him. Van Staal held the struggling
Englishman while, in the little light from the fire, the girl
kept the huge wound alive by cutting away tissue that
had become reinfected. She replaced the poultice of
herbs on the gash and made sure that he drank the brew
of leaves and bark and the scrapings of roots.

When the second nocturnal operation was almost over, Stone raised himself from the ground, his arms stiff, his mouth open. "It rots," he shouted. "It stinks of death." Then he shuddered, his teeth chattering, and fell back, his entire body shaking. Van Staal wrapped him in all their blankets and held him for the rest of the night.

In the first light of dawn, while pinkish haze wreathed in layers about the trunks of the emerging trees, while the first birdcalls cleared the air of the forest, van Staal took Stone's pistols and went in search of game.

He found a white-lipped peccary nosing among leaf litter, snuffling for grubs. He shot it easily, cleaned and skinned the boar, and carried it back to the campsite, where he divided the meat into that which would be smoked above the fire and the rest, to be eaten now.

The task complete, he went once again to the shelter to discover Ix Mai wiping Stone's buttocks clean of a thin diarrhea that oozed. She handled the man as if he were a baby; she seemed unconcerned by her work.

"How—" van Staal began, then cleared his throat. "How is, he?"

"He is not dead," Ix Mai replied matter-of-factly. She glanced at van Staal's worried face, then away again. "That is a good sign."

"Will, he—?" van Staal began incompetently. "Will he get better?"

"If he survives the next two days, he will recover," Ix Mai replied impatiently. "Now, go and heat some more water." She looked up. "Is that clear?"

Van Staal nodded, paused uncertainly, then turned away.

Ix Mai's eyes went back to her task. Neither of them held any terror for her now. The Pale One lay beneath her fingers, there was nothing about him she did not know. His member was normal, his body no different from other men she had seen wrestling or at play. She was a little ashamed of her panic the night she had been led to him and was grateful that he had refused to open her then, for she would not have been able to endure it. Now she wished him well and hoped he would recover quickly so that she might return. And as for Round Skull, he had been quite helpful, she thought as she glanced at him bending over the coals.

When she returned to the fire Round Skull looked up from a pot in which he was cooking something: its contents smelled quite dreadful. "What is that?" she asked, turning her nose away.

"It is, food," van Staal replied.

Ix Mai shook her head impatiently. "Where did you learn to speak the language so badly?" she asked.

Van Staal's cheeks reddened slightly. "I, ah, was slave. Some Maya slaves too." Van Staal's color increased with the effort. "From them, I learn."

"You, a slave?" Ix Mai's eyes widened with surprise. She peered at Round Skull's forehead. "You do not carry the mark of a slave."

"I not, branded," van Staal replied almost apologetically. "The Spaniards branded, Indians."

"My people?"

"Yours, others."

"How did you escape?" Ix Mai eyed him, only half believing. "How did you get away?"

"I tell you . . ." Van Staal began, then looked across to where Stone lay as the Englishman moaned. "Is he all right?" he asked.

"For a little," Ix Mai replied confidently. "The poison is going from him." She indicated the sweat that covered the Pale One's body. "He will call if he is in pain."

Van Staal nodded at her assurance. "We eat now?" he asked, reaching for the pot he'd placed on the fire.

"Not the way it is," Ix Mai replied firmly. "But if I add something to it, it will not taste too bad."

"What thing?"

"Do not worry. Be patient, then we will eat, and you can tell me how you stopped being a slave."

After considerable thought, Don Luis went to a cabinet in a corner of his bedroom, opened the glass-paneled doors, reached into the camphor-scented interior, and took out a pistol, a beautifully worked piece.

He carried the weapon to a window. In its light he checked the flint: it was clean and sound. He returned to the cabinet for powder and shot, then spent some time loading and priming the gun. It seemed the least he could do.

Don Luis had been deeply dismayed by what Cazaux had told him of d'Avila's blinding of a prisoner. It was not so much that the Frenchman's words had affected the mayor's vision of the future, but the persuasion that the solution lay in his hands alone disturbed him more profoundly than he could admit.

It was not the obligation in itself that concerned him—authority was what he lived for; nor did the fact that d'Avila had gone beyond a reasonable boundary distress him unduly: after all, prisoners were prisoners.

What alarmed him—more than it should, considering his position, considering the number of years he had survived in this outpost of civilisation—was the numbing realization that never in his life before had he actually killed another human being.

Without the slightest hesitation, he had condemned to death those convicted of crimes. He'd sent squadrons on missions that he knew, even before the order was issued, would result in the destruction of many. He had instructed the garrison, in its defense of the town, to fire on corsarios who would have killed his citizens. Once, to his admitted distress, he'd witnessed the sinking of an English pirate vessel; had seen, with his own eyes, men torn by shot, drowning below him on the breakwater. But he had never, in cold blood, taken a weapon and, with either a movement of the finger or a thrust of the arm, ended a life.

Now he hefted the pistol and admired its workmanship, to reinforce his resolve. It was masterly handsome, of that there was no question. As to its deadliness, he had no doubt. But when it came to its use, his mind darkened. He had no references, nothing to rely on. He closed his hand around the silver-inlaid butt to find it contained no real comfort.

Yet he recognized that the deed was his responsibility, not only for the need to compound his own leadership, but because to eliminate d'Avila would be to expunge the bond between them. True, d'Avila's promised vote had already been cast—but the bargained pirate had not yet returned. And if d'Avila were no longer alive when Stone came back, the deal made over the walnut dining table, which had caused Don Luis so much anguish, would be irrelevant.

For over a week now the mayor had touched no alcohol. He insisted that an open bottle of brandy be placed before him at the end of each meal, but so far he'd consumed none of it. Daily he felt resolution grow and was determined that nothing would break it now—unless . . .

Don Luis closed his eyes and nodded. There was only one way of becoming absolutely certain that he would not be tempted to seek oblivion again. What was more, the act was entirely justifiable, would carry no particle of guilt. It was simply a further matter that had to be attended to to keep Campeche safe.

But the business must be dealt with quickly and quietly, and by himself. In spite of the fact that he realized he'd been manipulated by Cazaux, he knew that to be the truth. He *was* the final authority. And although he had a well-earned reputation for making propositions, he was also respected for his sense of responsibility. It was merely—and the thought pierced like a needle—the manner in which the killing might be done. And, also, when.

Conceivably, the night of the *palenque*, the cock fight, would be the time. It seemed suddenly appropriate that this was the other matter Cazaux had discussed. It would occur soon enough, and such a night would present an ideal occasion on which to be rid of someone as universally unpopular as the obsessed d'Avila. It would be a chance, expected.

Breathing deeply, the mayor slipped the pistol into the waistband of his breeches. Its presence was like a wound in his groin. He fingered its length: it was a weapon of many aspects. He sighed and prayed he would be able to employ it when the moment finally came. But the image of destruction remained blank, an undefined hollow in his mind, and he wondered exactly how far he would be prepared to go in order to achieve it.

One reality, however, was apparent: a fortnight ago he could not even have taken the pistol from its camphor-wood cabinet, the fact that it lay now in his waistband was a measure, however grim, of his progress.

As the sun began to lower and the shadows on the forest floor grew long and dappled, van Staal experienced, for the first time in months, a sense of something approaching contentment. He sat on a log, a bowl of food in his hand, and watched the delicate Maya girl give herself a portion. Beneath the shelter of cut branches, Stone slept with relative calm.

Van Staal began to eat heartily. Ix Mai had added wild tomatoes and green chilies to the meat he'd prepared, and it tasted extremely good.

A moment later he lifted his head. "Why you not eat?" he asked, his mouth full, noticing that she waited.

"You are difficult to understand at any time," Ix Mai replied crisply. "And not at all with food in your mouth."

Van Staal spluttered, swallowed, and repeated his question.

"It is our custom to wait until the men have eaten," Ix Mai answered. "But I am hungry and wish you would hurry."

"Eat," said van Staal. "You are not with custom now."

"I will always be with my customs. But you are right, there is no one here to see." She began lifting the food to her mouth with her tiny fingers. "It is good," she commented. "Do you not agree?"

Van Staal nodded, watching her pick her meat from the dish. "How old, you?" he asked when she glanced at him.

"I have fifteen of the Haab years," Ix Mai replied evenly. "They are the same as your own."

"You are, young."

"I am old to be a virgin," Ix Mai said seriously. "My sisters had thirteen Haab years each when they married."

Van Staal swallowed the mouthful he chewed before asking, "Why you not marry—?"

"Why did I not marry earlier?" Ix Mai completed the question. "Because I am the third daughter in a family in which none have died," she explained. "That is considered fortunate. I was kept for something special."

"Like—" Van Staal swallowed again. "This?"

"No one in Tayasal ever thought of this," Ix Mai said, her knowledge sound. "However, when you arrived at the lake, none thought you would ever cross the water. When you did, everyone was sure you would all be killed. In the ball game, no one imagined that the Pale One would strike the winning shot. So, there were three changes of fortune, and I was the third daughter of a fortunate family. That is why the lord Tutul Katun chose me to carry the seed."

Van Staal stared, openmouthed.

"Do you understand me?" Ix Mai asked.

Van Staal nodded.

"It would not seem so from the expression on your face," Ix Mai observed, returning to her food.

"I, ah, I think of numbers. They very, important?"

"Everything is written, and all is decided by numbers," Ix Mai said, stating a simple fact. "Is it not the same with your people?"

Van Staal shook his head.

"Never mind," Ix Mai said. They were all, obviously, fools who knew nothing. She put her bowl aside and wiped her fingers on the grass. "Now, tell me how you stopped being a slave."

Van Staal cleaned his hands as she had done. Then, haltingly, but the language coming more readily as he used it, he told her how he'd come to the West Indies almost thirty years earlier, and how he'd been captured by the Spanish, who'd used him as a slave in the salt

mines of Venezuela. There he'd met those who spoke
the Maya tongue and had learned a little in the years he
was captive.

One night, he explained, there had been a fire in the
slaves' quarters, and he'd escaped, shackled to two other
Dutchmen. They'd trekked for days through swamps to
the coast. The two he'd escaped with had died. The first
had grown so thin his feet had slipped through the irons,
the second had been with van Staal a long slow time.
Finally he'd cut the body free with a stone.

Once on the coast he'd stolen a small boat, which
he'd sailed, single-handed, from Marcaibo to Hispaniola, where he'd joined a colony of buccaneers and become one of the Brethren of the Coast. There he'd been
captured again by the Spanish; they'd taken him to
Jamaica, where he'd been due to be hanged, but the Pale
One had sailed in with the English fleet to capture the
colony and set him free. They'd been together ever
since, he and the Pale One. They had become like
brothers.

Ix Mai listened to the long, faltering narrative without
comment. From time to time she offered a word or two
when Round Skull stumbled. But when he'd finished she
nodded politely and said, "That is all very interesting.
But of course, it cannot be true." There was no doubt in
her voice.

"What?" Van Staal stared in amazement. "I have,
scars to show—"

"What you have is unimportant," Ix Mai said with a
small, dismissive movement of her hand. "But you cannot have been to the places you speak of because they
do not exist. The world is not like that at all."

Van Staal scratched his head perplexedly. "How you
know what world like?" he asked, frowning.

"It is written," Ix Mai replied as if speaking to an
idiot. "They sky is held up by four gods. Each has a
color. Red is for the east, white is for the north. In the
west the god is black, in the south, yellow. The earth
itself is the back of a great crocodile which rests in a
pool filled with water lilies."

Van Staal blinked.

"There is nothing beyond the back of the great crocodile who supports us," Ix Mai went on in the same patronizing voice. "So, you see, you cannot have been where you say."

"This," van Staal began, feeling completely inadequate, "this back, back of—?"

"A crocodile. Don't tell me you don't even know what a crocodile is?"

Van Staal shook his head.

"It is a great animal, with a back like a mountain." Ix Mai stared at him in exasperation. How could anyone live so long and remain so stupid? "It swims in the water," she added for good measure.

"A, fish?"

Ix Mai looked at Round Skull with open contempt. She stood, hitched up her skirt, got down onto her hands and knees, and gave a reasonable imitation of a crocodile. Van Staal watched a moment, then began to laugh.

"Now do you understand?" Ix Mai, remaining in the same position, asked crisply. "Now do you know what a crocodile is?"

"Yes." Van Staal could not keep the smile from his face. "Lizard of water?"

"Very good," Ix Mai said with a touch of sarcasm. "At least you know something." She began to regain her feet, but van Staal squatted beside her. "On voyage," he said slowly, touching her elbow, then moving his hand to where her hair hung loosely over her shoulders, "I go from here to here on crocodile."

"Mmmm." Ix Mai squatted opposite him and dusted her hands. "I suppose that might be possible."

Van Staal nodded; she seemed very close.

"Did you see any lilies in the water?" Ix Mai asked. She could feel where Round Skull had touched her.

Van Staal shook his head.

Ix Mai grunted dubiously. She studied Round Skull's face for a moment, then stood and moved away.

"And, Spaniards?" van Staal asked, following. "Where they come from?"

"I do not know about them," Ix Mai replied. "Some say they are gods, but I do not believe it. Although they are as cruel as gods." She paused thoughtfully. "What color was your hair?" she asked abruptly.

"What?"

"Your hair?" Ix Mai patted her head. "You do know what hair is, don't you?"

"Ah?" van Staal nodded. "Before it, gray?"

"Yes, when you had some?"

"It was red. A red color."

"It wasn't fair?"

Van Staal frowned. "When I, child, yes," he said, puzzled by the turn of conversation. "Why?"

Ix Mai did not answer the question. She stared at him for what seemed to be a long time. "Perhaps you would do," she said finally, almost to herself, then she turned away. "Now I must look at the Pale One," she added in a different tone. "After that, we will sleep."

Van Staal watched her go, realizing that he was smiling. He could not help himself; a broad, easy grin softened his features. He saw her bend over the figure of Stone, and he felt again the desire to hold her, to draw her to him.

He waited by the fire until she returned. "How is Pale One?" he asked, looking at her carefully.

"He sleeps." Ix Mai's voice was crisp again. "And no more poison has grown in the wound."

"Will, will he get well?"

"In the morning we will know." Ix Mai looked at Round Skull levelly. "He shivers, so I have left two blankets with him. We will have to share the other."

Van Staal nodded. "What," he began, then cleared his throat and started again. "What you mean, when say I would do?" he asked, his voice almost a whisper.

Ix Mai shook her head and began to lay the blanket on the ground. "Later we might speak of that further," she said briskly. "I have not decided yet."

"I—"

"No more, please." Ix Mai held up a hand. "I have never heard the language spoken so badly. And I have had more than enough for one day." She sat on the blanket and watched Round Skull approach. "You must not touch me," she said firmly. "I am promised to the Pale One still. Nothing of that has changed."

Van Staal lay beside the girl. He doubled the blanket to cover them both and felt her fit, like a spoon, into the shape of him. He laid an arm over her shoulders and held her gently. About, the sounds of the forest fluttered, the firelight died, and both were soon asleep.

CHAPTER 3

GUADALUPE SANTOYA COMPLETED THE JOURNEY ON FOOT.
For two days, after she'd unsaddled her horse and turned
the animal loose with a slap on its flank, for two days,
after she'd buried saddle and bridle beneath a pile of
rocks, she walked back toward Campeche.

Early on the evening of the second long march she
crossed the low hills that surrounded the town. There
she paused and stared down at the groups of pale buildings nestling on the shore. Even in the slanting light, a
glow could be seen coming from some of the windows,
and the castellated shape of the main fort was stark
against the mirroring sea. There was the smell of salt
and algae in the air.

The sight caused Guadalupe to put a hand to her
throat, to hold back the wonder and the pain she felt
rising within. She gazed at Campeche and breathed deeply;
then she shook her head, as if to restore herself, and
made her way to the little barrio of San Román, where
her mother's house stood with those of other Indians, on
the outskirts of the colony.

She came to the twisted streets, winding between
buildings of stone and sun-dried bricks, at the hour
when darkness began. In the shadows Guadalupe passed
a woman whom she knew, and a curious fear touched

her: she wanted neither to speak nor be spoken to, not yet, perhaps never.

But the woman only glanced at her, no more, and continued on her way. It was then that Guadalupe realized how much she had altered, in dress as well as in spirit. She wore, still, the long skirt of dark, coarse-woven cloth, the shift, and the shawl she'd taken from the house of Tutz, on the evening she'd last seen Cristóbal.

The clothing was dull now and faded, scrubbed thin in places. She'd grown so accustomed to it, it seemed she'd worn nothing else in all her eighteen years, and as if she had lived twice that time, or longer. She looked like someone who had been used by life cruelly and often.

As the woman who'd not recognized her disappeared in a turning of the street, Guadalupe sighed, and the sigh shook her. She was anonymous; she was her own. She continued until she came to her mother's house, and then she paused at the doorless entrance to peer in.

Nothing had changed. In one corner of the first room the small fire burned on its bed of stone. Beside it were two benches cut from the trunks of trees, polished by years of use: the movement of cloth against wood. Hanging on the walls were earthenware bowls and dishes. Before the fire was the metate: the rubbing stone her mother used daily to grind corn for the bread she made.

Guadalupe touched the string of tiny bells that swung by the entrance, and at the sound of their ringing, Magdelena's face appeared around the blanket that hung from a cord forming the two rooms of the swelling.

For long seconds Magdelena stared, then her mouth opened in shock. " 'Lupe?" she cried. "Holy Mother of God, is it you?" She ran to her daughter, pulling her close, tears spilling, repeating the name again and again. " 'Lupe, 'Lupe, my God, it is." She held Guadalupe and shook.

"Mother."

They clung to each other, not believing what they saw; they ran their fingers over each other's faces, as if

they needed to touch in order to accept. The sounds
they made were neither words nor utterances, merely
the issuing of wonder and relief.

"Where?" Magdelena began, but drew her daughter
even closer, her arms asking more questions than her lips
could form. "My God, 'Lupe, it is, I do not believe it."

"Mother—"

"Wait. No, say nothing." Magdelena held her daughter a while longer, then stepped back, peering in the
little light inside the house. She wiped away her tears.
"My God," she said in a different voice. "My God, you
are so thin."

Guadalupe nodded. "It has been bad," she whispered.

"Come." Magdelena reached for her child once more;
she led her to the fire. "Come. Sit there. I will make
chocolate for you. Here, do not say anything just now.
Stay there, and be quiet."

Guadalupe allowed herself to be led, knowing a deliv-
erance that almost broke her. She sat on the polished
wood and watched her mother's hands prepare the foam-
ing chocolate, seeing her mother's look come up to her
from time to time in simple disbelief; it was as bright
with gratitude. When Guadalupe felt the warmth of the
drink through the brown pottery mug, she closed her
eyes and whispered, "I, I do not know what I would
have done if you had not been here when I came." She
lifted the mug quickly and put it to her lips.

Magdelena smiled. "I will always be here, my daughter," she replied.

Guadalupe nodded, a form of peace enfolding her.
Magdelena's timeless face, her gray-streaked hair, the
smells, the familiar objects, all helped to strip away a
little of the horror she had lived through. Tears suddenly
filmed her eyes, but they were tears of relief rather than
loss.

"I will always be here," Magdelena said again, watching. Guadalupe had altered, within as well as without:
the fierce pride was gone, but an aspect of something
more enduring had replaced it. "Although," she added
quietly, "much has changed, here in Campeche."

Guadalupe lifted her head, as if remembering that there was more to life than this room contained.

"The French corsario has returned," Magdelena explained. "Although he seems to belong here now. The English, who remained when you left, are prisoners. There is talk of war, but I do not understand any of it."

"What do you say?" Guadalupe shook her head. This reality was too extreme for her to absorb immediately. The outside world had intruded too severely. "What, what of Capitán d'Avila?" she asked, searching for some contact.

Magdelena turned her face away. "His eye is blind," she said, as if that were all that was necessary.

"Is that all?"

Magdelena shook her head. "He is, he is strange," she said, her voice restrained. "He is never still. He talks to himself. He lives . . ." She paused. "They say he lives only to kill the pirate who took you with him. The one you tried to kill."

"Cristóbal?" There were no secrets in her utterance of the word.

Magdelena stared at her daughter. "Is that what he's become?" she whispered.

Guadalupe nodded.

"Oh, my daughter." Magdelena's hands came out. "Is he with you?" she asked, her eyes going to the doorway.

"He is dead," said Guadalupe in a voice that was also dead. "They are all dead. I am the only one to return."

"All? Dead?"

Guadalupe closed her eyes. "I am all that is left," she said. The smell of chocolate filled her nostrils. She stared down at the bubbles forming and bursting. "The others died"—she felt a breath catch in her throat—"died, so horribly."

Magdelena remained for a long time, looking at the memory that etched her daughter's face. She watched the trembling of Guadalupe's hand as she drank the chocolate. Then Magdelena took the cup from the unresisting fingers; she placed her arms about her daughter and began to rock her as she'd rocked her as a child.

"Do, do you wish to speak of it?" Magdelena asked after a while.

Guadalupe nodded against her mother's breast, and in a voice so low that at times it was inaudible, she began to tell her of the fearful journey, of the man she had loved and how she believed he had died.

Ix Mai came to him, fully dressed, her hair braided and wound like a turban about her head. Her cheeks had been reddened with a sweet-smelling ointment, and her eyes were downcast.

Earlier in the day, he'd seen her seated on a fallen tree, examining herself in a small mirror made of pyrite crystals mounted on polished wood. Arranged about her were tiny pots of paints and creams. For hours she had preened herself, and then she'd approached, her hands clasped before her, presenting herself for his inspection.

"Do you think me pretty?" Ix Mai asked.

"I, ah, yes," van Staal replied. He felt his heart begin to beat rapidly. "I do."

"And, do you find me pleasing?"

Van Staal nodded. "You, pleasing," he said. He had more difficulty than usual with the words. "Very."

"Then I ask that you open me and plant your seed." Ix Mai's eyes came up, unwavering. "For if I am pretty and you find me pleasing, the task should not be too burdensome."

"You . . ." Van Staal paused to clear his throat. "You know what you ask?"

Ix Mai nodded. "I have been instructed. I am told it is not complicated. I understand that it may be painful, but I will try to be brave. For you it will be pleasant. And when the seed has taken I will be able to return to my people."

"But—" Van Staal's big hands came out and gently cupped the girl's exquisite face. Her seriousness impressed him more than he would have thought possible. "You are for the Pale One. He is to, open."

"I shall say nothing of who prepared me." Ix Mai's tone was resolved. "You have said that your hair was fair as a child. You are both of a similar race. No one will ever think that the child is not the Pale One's."

"Why?" Van Staal swallowed; the urge to hug her was overwhelming. "Why not wait for Pale One? Soon, he better."

"I have thought of that," Ix Mai confessed, her hands clasped before her, her little feet neatly together in their deerhide sandals. "But he will be weak and may not plant enough seed. Also, because of his fever, his seed may be affected. And I do not wish to bring an unhealthy child into the world."

Van Staal nodded, too deeply touched to reply.

"Then, you will open me?" Ix Mai felt Round Skull's rough hands tremble. Within her was the beginning of a strange response. She had not thought that any of it would be as tender. "Will you do it?" she whispered.

"Yes." Van Staal pulled her close. She was tiny and precious; he had never felt as clumsy. "We—" He glanced at the shelter under which Stone slept. "We go to where—"

"I know of such a place," Ix Mai said happily. "It is close to here. It is where the moss grows at the roots of a ceiba. Such a tree is holy. That is where we will go."

Van Staal took Ix Mai's hand. She could have led him anywhere. He followed without question. "I am ready for the seed," Ix Mai said as they walked. "I have been instructed about the time and the numbers." She spoke almost conversationally. "But I would ask that you be gentle, for I am small and you, you seem, so big."

Van Staal nodded. He glanced down at her hand, which had disappeared in the hugeness of his fist. "I be, gentle," he managed to say.

"Even . . . even if it reduces your pleasure?"

Van Staal nodded again and said nothing. They came to the clearing Ix Mai had chosen, and unable to resist any longer, van Staal lifted the girl and held her against him. "I gentle," he whispered. "And, you very pleasing."

"That, that is as it should be." Ix Mai's voice wavered just a little. "Then, we can begin."

Ix Mai removed her long, embroidered skirt. She placed

it carefully to one side, folded on the mossy grass. Then she lifted the deep shift she wore until it was above her knees and knelt, waiting for Round Skull to do what had to be done. She watched as he kicked off his seaboots, removed his breeches, and stood before her, his unbleached linen shirt protruding in front of him. She swallowed and, from her handbag, produced a small pot whose top was covered with leather.

"I was given this," she said a little uncertainly. "It will make the planting easier."

As van Staal watched she opened the pot, removed a fingerful of whitish cream, leaned toward him, and lifted his shirt. Her eyes rounded with astonishment.

"What?" van Staal asked. "You not see before?"

"I have seen children's. And some paintings." Ix Mai could not look away. "And, of course, the Pale One's. But nothing this size."

"No—" Van Staal coughed. "No, be afraid. Use what you, have."

Uncertainly, Ix Mai rubbed the cream on Round Skull's penis; she felt it quiver. She glanced up to see pleasure soften his features. "Is that good?" she asked almost coyly.

Van Staal nodded. He knelt before her and gently pushed her onto her back. "Now, I open you," he whispered. "If hurt, tell me. I stop."

Ix Mai nodded and lifted her head to watch Round Skull direct the organ of his seed toward her opening. She became surprised by the warmth of it as it pressed against her. It had a warmth that seemed to spread from her opening up to her breasts; they began to tingle. She made herself as wide as possible. Round Skull had begun to hurt.

"I hurt you?" he asked, pausing.

Ix Mai shook her head and tried to open herself more. "But you are not all in me yet," she said.

"If slow, hurt less."

"It does not," Ix Mai began, then caught her breath as she felt something break within. "Oh, it does," she whispered. "Now, it hurts."

"Then, we stop."

"No." Ix Mai gripped his arms. "Do not, do not go away now."

"No." Van Staal was held by a tenderness that weakened him; he had never known anything as honest or as fresh. "I no go from you."

Ix Mai breathed deeply. "It, it does not hurt as much now," she said a moment later.

Van Staal felt the beginnings of a response he was not able to control. He pulled her onto him; he heard her cry as his hips thrust. He buried his head in the hollow of her shoulder as he burst and shuddered and was carried by a force he could not restrain nor wanted to. It swept over him and emptied. For a long time he lay on her, unmoving. Then he lifted his head and looked down at her, at the color that was not cosmetic in her cheeks, at the light in her eyes.

"Was I brave?" she asked very softly.

Van Staal nodded.

"And pleasing?"

"Yes, pleasing."

"Then you must do it again. For I am told it will hurt less, and that it might also be pleasing for me."

Van Staal smiled. "Soon, I do it," he said. "But first seed must, re-form."

Ix Mai smiled back. "I will wait," she said almost primly.

"Aye," said Cramer, "we's safe for a while." He scratched the stub of his missing ear and touched the scorched skin below an eye. "We'll not be blinded. Not while the Frenchman stays."

"You," Lambe, the red-haired gunner began uncertainly, "you're sure of what you say?"

Cramer nodded. It became more obvious to him every day that none could be sustained much longer on bread and mash and unfulfilled dreams. He'd fabricated and he'd promised, he'd played the games he knew. And he'd been dragged up the stairs by the enraged garrison commander and had a poker thrust at his eye. Then the

Frenchman'd come, showing an anger equal to the
Spaniard's own. And for the moment, they were safe.
Yet they needed more. There had been too many prom-
ises and not enough substance. Time escaped them daily,
measured its pace through the archer's window, and
God alone knew when it'd end.

"You?" Lambe licked his lips and continued. He was
healthier now, as most of them were, fed and clean and
no longer dying of the flux. "You've thought what might
be done?"

"Yes," Cramer said, "and no." He moved his legs,
and the sound of chains clattered hollowly through the
dungeon. Someone lifted a head; another coughed. It
was almost dawn. Pale light turned pink in the darkness
of the cell; it carried a tint of hope. "No," he said, "and
yes."

"What?" In spite of the reality that shuffled about
them, the conversation still had meaning, no matter how
worn its cloth. "Tell me, what?"

"Well," said Cramer, "we've still the jailer."

Lambe blinked. "But, he grows more impatient every
day."

"Aye," said Cramer the Black very slowly. "Aye, he
does, and all."

"Then?" Lambe could no longer help himself; his
eyes went around the lightening darkness to the others,
who were becoming involved. "What do we tell him?"

Cramer shrugged. The easy promises were empty now,
and yet he'd seen men die from lack of hope, seen them
curl with their faces to a wall and decay so swiftly that,
between one dawn and the next, only a husk remained.
So he shrugged again, caught Lambe's eye, and made a
final attempt.

"There's the fiesta," he said, bending closer. "The
one the jailer talks of."

Lambe waited. For the first time since he'd known
him, he thought the Negro mad.

"They'll all be there," Cramer continued. "You've
heard him say it yourself."

"But—" Incredulity wrapped itself about the gunner's

voice; he tried to turn it with a laugh. "You, you think they'll invite us to join them?"

"I thinks they'll be too busy to care what we do," Cramer replied levelly. "I thinks it's our only chance."

"For what?"

"To get from here, and go."

"In God's name, how?" Lambe lifted his hands, and the rattle of chains replied. "Are you going to ask for the keys?"

"No," said Cramer, hoping more than he dared, plunging headlong now he'd come so far. "But we'll take the jailer with us. We'll get the *Courage* and go."

Lambe's eyes reached out in the semilight, the semidarkness. "You're crazed," was all he could say.

Cramer shook his head. What did it matter anymore? If the dream was to survive, it must grow larger, fill until it was bigger than the dungeon, outreach the stone that held them. Cramer smiled, and for the moment that was enough.

"But how?" Lambe insisted as other ears listened. The conversation itself was sufficient to grasp. "In God's name, how would you begin?"

"We promises him the world," said Cramer simply. "We fills his head with visions." He spoke for himself as well as them all. "We tells him where there's wealth he's never dreamed of." His deep voice lifted, and its magic flowed. All were awake now, all listened. These were promises they understood; these were the reasons they themselves had sailed. They clung to what little they had: the richly spun music of the Negro's voice, its painted future, its honeyed hope. "We takes him with us," Cramer continued. "We, all of us, we sail away."

The light grew, and the air bloomed; even those who doubted listened to the lie: there was no thinkable alternative. Their blood flowed, and their eyes saw: life was all around them. So they let the Negro spin his web. It carried them into a future.

CHAPTER 4

CHRISTOPHER STONE AWOKE TO THE SOUND OF IX MAI'S laughter. It came from somewhere close in the forest, from somewhere in the leafy green through the delicate yellows of late afternoon sunlight. He lifted his head to listen and became aware of his hip.

Cautiously, he peered in the direction of the wound. It was covered with some sort of poultice; when he examined the injury itself, he was surprised to discover how clean it was. Although deep and raw and red about the edges, there was no pus in the gash, and the flesh was healing.

Stone lay back, trying to recall where he was and how he'd arrived, but it was beyond his power to resolve. "Dear God," he muttered. "What has been done?"

The girl's laughter came again; it lifted like the fluttering of birds. There was a shout from van Staal, and then there was silence. Presently Stone heard the sound of bushes parting; he looked up to see them approaching, holding hands. When they saw him, they separated and stared like guilty children.

Then van Staal lumbered forward. "Christopher," he shouted. "Thanks be to God, you're back with us again."

"Aye," said Stone in a weak but clear voice. "I am, even though I'd thought me dead."

"So had we." Van Staal crouched beside the bed. "She alone has saved you."

" 'Twas so?" asked Stone, his eyes going from face to face. Then he laughed weakly. "By God, she's now your doxy."

"Do not call her that." Van Staal's face hardened. "She has more good than you or I will ever know."

Stone swallowed and looked again at the girl. Ix Mai had not moved; her little feet were together, her hands were clasped before her. "Forgive me," Stone said roughly. " 'Twas crude of me."

Van Staal did not reply. Ix Mai watched carefully the expressions on their faces, wondering why the Pale One had laughed and why Round Skull had become so angry. She hoped it was not because she'd given Round Skull the right to plant the seed. She needed more and now enjoyed the games they played when they planted and wished none of it to stop. She waited patiently for the moment to pass, for the Pale One to begin to speak again.

"How long have I been ill?" he asked.

Van Staal cleared his throat. " 'Tis seven days since we left the island," he began. "For two you walked."

"God's heart, I remember some of that," Stone said.

"Then you fell. The wound had almost killed you." Van Staal's expression relaxed a little. " 'Twas then she saved you with her medicines. She cut the poison from your hip. She nursed you like a child." Van Staal stood. "Without her you'd have surely died."

Stone stared up at the Dutchman's determined face, then lay back in the blankets. Suddenly he felt exhausted. Van Staal went to Ix Mai and held her face between his hands; he looked down at her lovingly.

"The Pale One is angry with me," Ix Mai said. "And he laughs because I did not wait for his seed."

"No." Van Staal's voice was tender. "He laugh, because he is alive."

"You, you speak the truth?"

"I speak the truth."

Ix Mai's face lifted. "Why, then, did he look at me so strangely before he began to laugh?" she asked pointedly.

Van Staal smiled. "He not believe one so, pretty, also good with herbs," he told her easily.

A small smile appeared at the corner of Ix Mai's lips. "Is that really so?" she whispered happily.

Van Staal nodded. "Now, give food," he said. "Then he, he surprised you cook well, too."

Ix Mai's smile grew. "There are many things I do well. Is that not so?" she asked softly.

"Yes." Van Staal's hard hands pressed. "But not for Pale One."

"No?" The word was mischievous.

"No."

"That is just as well." Ix Mai's eyes were shining.

"For I would not wish to plant with him. After what I have learned with you."

She turned quickly and went to the fire. Van Staal waited a moment before he returned to Stone. He could not have described the tenderness he felt, the overpowering desire to protect. To look at her filled him with simple delight, and he wondered how much of it showed.

"You love her, am I right?" Stone asked a moment later.

Van Staal turned his head away. "I shall miss her when she's gone," he said.

"Must she go?"

"Aye, she must," van Staal grunted. "That is why she came."

"Could she not—?" Stone began, but van Staal cut him short.

"I've thought of it often," he said with a shake of the head, "but my life's not hers."

"Make it so," said Stone with sudden determination.

"No, when she's with child she must return." The Dutchman watched the girl bend over the fire, saw the shape of her beneath the garments; he felt her warmth and her passion and his own unselfish love. There was nothing he could give her that could possibly replace what awaited her in Tayasal. "When she goes back," he added, "she will be treated like a queen." His face brightened. "And my son will be a prince," he whispered.

Stone stared at van Staal, seeing the pride, the strength, the simple endurance. Then he turned his head away, aware of a deep, indefinable loss.

For days Guadalupe seemed to do nothing but sleep buried beneath a blanket that covered her head, lying unmoving hour after hour, restoring her body, regaining some order in her mind. She became faceless, unseen. Few in the barrio knew of her return.

Then she began to rise, late in the day, to dress and sit by the fire, watching her mother's hands at work. She wore her own garments now. For a time she'd been unable to discard the clothing from the house of Tutz, but gradually, piece by piece, she replaced it as she returned to the present, to the old past.

One afternoon Magdelena, looking up from the corn she was grinding to examine her daughter's face, saw that the flesh was returning to the hollows, that the emptiness was going from the eyrs.

"Will you go back?" she asked. There was no need to say where.

Guadalupe shook her head.

Magdelena went on with her work. "Then who will tell him?" she said after a pause. "Who will say that he waits for nothing?"

"He will not be told." Guadalupe breathed deeply. "None of them will be told. It is better that they know nothing."

"But, he gave his word," Magdelena said awkwardly. "You know that. His word on your return. Do you think it fair?" She lifted her eyes again, questioningly.

"None of it is fair," Guadalupe replied without anger, without force. "In time they will realize that something has occurred."

"You do not feel—"

"No," Guadalupe said in the same flat tone. "I feel nothing for them at all. Not any of them." The memory of the barn, however vivid it might once have been, did

not touch her now. Looking back on it in the light of
everything else that had happened, it seemed innocent
and insignificant: an act without value. The kindness
that had followed was no more proper than it should
have been. The eye was blind. The shame had turned to
an obsession whose focus was no longer alive. These
were matters that were not of her concern. He was not,
now, her protector. "I feel nothing," she repeated. "I
will do nothing. There is nothing to be done."

Magdelena stared, but there were no words she could
utter.

Guadalupe began her mission just before dark, starting
out one evening without a word to her mother, traveling
in the same obscuring light in which she had returned to
Campeche. She walked slowly, her head bowed, covered with a shawl, going toward the foothills that rose
behind the town. She left the Barrio de San Román,
allowing her footsteps to carry her to a small mound that
gave a view across the landscape. From it she stared at
the purple shapes dying into darkness.

It was absurd, she realized fully, a mindless voyage
offering neither comfort nor reward, yet she was incapable of not making it. As she was incapable of forgetting,
as she was incapable of dissolving the memory in her
heart.

Magdelena did not comment on the evening meander-
ings. She did not know where Guadalupe went; she did
not think it right to ask, even when the absences became
frequent. But wherever her daughter visited contained
an element of hope. The almond-shaped eyes were
brighter now—not much, but enough: they displayed the
only sign of promise she'd seen since her child's return.
So Magdelena said nothing. Each evening she would
wait until Guadalupe reappeared, then she'd prepare hot
chocolate and remain by her side while it was consumed.

One evening, however, warming her hands about the
steaming mug, Guadalupe smiled very slightly, then looked
away.

"What is it, 'Lupe?" Magdelena asked casually, trying

to place no importance on the words: it was the first real smile she had seen. "What is it?"

"I saw him." Guadalupe's voice was very light. "He was staring at the sea."

"Who?" Magdelena's mouth had dried.

"He . . ." Guadalupe paused and sipped a little chocolate. "He, who they say is mad."

"Oh." Magdelena's expression softened; her lips relaxed. "Did you," she began uncomfortably, "did you speak?"

Guadalupe shook her head. "He stared at the ships that belong to the corsarios. He did not know who I was."

"Did he see you?"

"Yes, and looked away again."

"Oh, 'Lupe, it is because you've . . ." Magdelena's voice faltered, seeking a softer word. "You've changed."

"It pleases me, Mother." There was something of pride in Guadalupe's voice once more. "It pleases me greatly that he no longer knows who I am. That means I am my own again."

Magdelena opened her mouth to speak but said nothing. She stared at her daughter, then away. Guadalupe had altered yet again, and she knew not how to respond.

"You must." Ix Mai lay on the grass, looking up at Round Skull. "It is what I have been told. You must keep me in seed."

"I no have any," van Staal said, smiling. "You have all my seed." He knelt beside her; both were naked. Somewhere Stone was sleeping.

"That is not so." Ix Mai's voice was sure. "A man like you has much."

"I give you all."

"I do not believe you." Ix Mai's hand was on his thigh. "I will prove there is much left inside you."

"How?" Van Staal watched her. "All seed gone."

"By making you big again and putting you where the seed must go." Ix Mai wet her fingers with spittle and began to rub Round Skull. She watched his seed organ lift, like a head of wheat, slowly from his thigh. "You see," she said delightedly, her hands beginning to knead. "You are getting big already. I know the seed is there."

"I"—van Staal touched her—"all seed gone."

"Shhh, do not speak." Ix Mai pushed him onto his back. "I will do the work." She placed one leg on either side of Round Skull and eased herself onto him. "It is so big," she said happily.

Van Staal closed his eyes.

"The first time I saw it I was afraid," Ix Mai said, pushing herself around it. "I was very afraid."

"You no, afraid now?"

"No." Ix Mai's movement grew more rapid. "It is, as they told me, so very good." Her head went back, her little body became taut, the cords in her neck stood out. Then she fell onto him, her warm breath burning his throat. "So good," she whispered, "so very good."

Van Staal's great arms came up and held her.

Leaning on a stick, Stone took his first steps painfully, awkwardly. He put his weight on his leg, and then a brief smile cross his gaunt features.

"I may walk with a limp," he said, pleased with his progress. "But walk, I will."

He moved from the rock beside which he'd lain, and they began their return. With his axe across his shoulders, Stone's pistols over his chest, van Staal led the way. Stone followed. Ix Mai came behind; she wore her shift and carried her long skirt and her cotton bag. Of them all, she was the most content.

At first they traveled slowly, but gradually their pace increased. Once beyond the hills that surrounded Lake Petén Itzá, they decided to circle the dry savanna, with its dust and waterless stretches, to head westward along the line of the river they'd crossed on their way to Tayasal.

Then, one morning, they left that waterway and marched over the plain to a line of hills. The journey took most of the day and was more difficult than any they'd attempted. When they camped beside a stream none of them had seen before, Stone was exhausted. Although his strength had increased and he used his stick less and less and the wound was scabbed and healing, the trek across the arid plain had drained him. He crawled into a blanket and was almost immediately asleep.

Ix Mai looked at him, then took Round Skull's hand. "Come," she said, "there may be honey in these trees."

"Honey?"

Ix Mai nodded. "It will restore the Pale One's strength," she said, and smiled shyly at Round Skull. "It is also very good for seed."

Van Staal allowed himself to be led along the bank. Late sunlight slanted through the trees, a flock of doves flew to their roost; peace flowed all about them. Ix Mai walked silently, her head on one side, listening. Suddenly she darted to an old mahogany stump and plunged her hand into its interior.

Immediately, bees swarmed out to cover her arm. When he saw what was happening, van Staal shouted in alarm. "Keep still, they bite." He reached out as if to cover her.

Ix Mai looked at him with such disdain he paused.

"They no bite?" he said uncertainly.

Ix Mai took a comb of honey from the hive. Bees buzzed about her, clung to her arms, stuck in her hair. She brushed them away carelessly. She went to the river bank and sat, broke off a piece of honeycomb, and handed it to Round Skull. "Eat it," she instructed, and took a piece for herself.

Van Staal stared, honey dripping from his fingers.

"Those bees," Ix Mai began patiently, "that's what they're called, *bees*, don't bite. They are the sort that cannot. And bite is not the word we use. *Sting* is what they do." She shook her head as if there were no saving this stupid man. "It is just as well you will not bring up my child," she added mischievously. "He would learn nothing from you at all."

The honeycomb stopped on its way to van Staal's lips.

"He will have to be taught everything by the man I

marry," Ix Mai went on happily. "And he will become a
great ball player, like his father." She could not prevent
a bubble of laughter escaping from her lips. "You have
been very kind to me." She looked up at Round Skull
and spoke softly. "And I am fond of you, but I am glad
that my son will be taught by those who are better
qualified."

"You, you have child?"

Ix Mai smiled, she nodded. "Yes," she said. "The
child has begun."

Van Staal fell to his knees beside her. He wanted to
touch her, but he was curiously afraid. He felt extraordinarily clumsy again.

"I have known for some days," Ix Mai went on. "I
have been waiting for the right moment to tell you. For I
am certain; I have been instructed about the signs."

Van Staal stared. He did not know what to do with
the honeycomb.

"But now is the right moment to tell you because
. . ." She looked away, suddenly touched by what she
was about to say. "Because you thought the bees would
harm me, and, and you did not want to see me hurt. You
are a kind man," she murmured. "It is a pity you are
not one of us." She turned and stared at Round Skull,
and wished that her eyes were not so full of tears. "Our
son will be very beautiful," she whispered.

They remained a long while, looking at each other as
the bees resettled and the river flowed. Neither spoke;
the silence between them was perfect.

Much later, as van Staal sat with Stone in the light of
the campfire, watching Ix Mai stir a cooking pot, he told
the Englishman that the girl was ready to return. He
spoke quietly, his voice easy. And in spite of the loss
that he knew must be ahead, he felt comforted: to Ix
Mai he would always belong.

"She will be safe?" Stone asked.

Van Staal nodded. "She carries the prince's seal. And
she is capable of surviving anywhere." There was pride
in his voice.

Stone said nothing more, but when Ix Mai came toward them with bowls of food held ready, he looked into her face and smiled.

Immediately Ix Mai turned to Round Skull. "What has made the Pale One happy?" she asked with some suspicion.

"I tell him you have child," van Staal replied. "He is pleased."

"It pleases him?" Ix Mai's forehead furrowed. "Even though the child is not his?"

"He pleased for you and me." Van Staal took his food and touched her hand. "He happy for us."

Ix Mai's expression softened. "That is good," she said simply, then returned to the fireside and ate alone.

The following morning van Staal awoke to see Ix Mai preparing. He lay silently watching her fold her skirt carefully, arrange her hair, and examine herself in her pyrite mirror. Then he said, very softly, "You go now?"

Ix Mai turned to him. "It is time," she replied.

"I, miss you."

"And I you." Ix Mai came quickly to the blankets they shared. "Even," she began bravely, "even if you are impossible to understand."

"When, food is in mouth."

Ix Mai nodded; she pressed her cheek against Round Skull's and stayed a moment. "But I must return to my people," she whispered.

"You, you know how to go?"

"Yes, I will return the way we came. I have remembered the journey, and I have made some signs." Round Skull opened his mouth, but Ix Mai silenced him. She reached into her cotton handbag and took out a heavy necklace of jade and turquoise, gold and jasper. "This is for you," she said softly. "So that you will remember me always."

Van Staal touched the necklace. "I no, need this to remember," he said, and had difficulty forming the words.

"You will not forget me?" There was enchantment in her voice. "Are you sure?"

"Never."

Ix Mai sighed with deep pleasure. She placed the

necklace about Round Skull's throat. "Take it anyway," she said, then turned her face to one side. She smiled, but he saw that the corner of her mouth trembled.

Van Staal took hold of the girl, held her and felt her agitation. He held her for a very long time. When the moment came, she reached up and brushed her lips against Round Skull's cheek. "Good-bye," was all she said.

"Good-bye," said van Staal, and watched her walk away, straight-backed, steadfast, looking ahead. "May God go with you," he whispered.

Later in the day, van Staal and Stone, he carrying the basket with the cooking pots, came to a spur by a bend of the river. They climbed it and looked over an expanse of grasses and thorny bushes. Away in the distance, gray and shadowed, seeming to float above the horizon, were the foothills that surrounded Campeche.

They were suddenly aware of how close they'd come to the coast. There were gulls in the sky, palms growing on the river bank. The town was a matter of a few days away.

Stone was the first to speak. "What awaits us there, I wonder," he said, a new note in his voice.

Van Staal glanced at the Englishman. He stood straighter now, looking ahead. "The ship awaits us," he replied. "We've forty men aboard her."

"If we have," Stone said grimly, "they're all expecting gold. And the Spaniards will be ready for their share."

"The Spaniards are imprisoned." Van Staal suddenly felt the future invading. Too much had occurred since their leaving; too many had lived and died. "Those who matter are in the fort."

"You assume that nothing's changed?" Stone thumped the ground with his stick. "You think that Cramer's held them off all this time?"

Van Staal filled his massive chest with air. He could no longer see into the distance; too much lay behind him.

"It will all have changed." Stone watched the sea birds wheel and turn. "God help us if it's been too drastic. We must come in quietly," he said, thinking aloud. "We must discover what we can. Then, with luck, we'll slip aboard and be away before anyone's the wiser. "We'll take what's ours and go."

As they turned to descend the spur, Stone caught the glint of gold beneath the Dutchman's shirt and inquired what he carried. "God's pox," he grunted when van Staal explained. " 'Tis the only gold we return with."

"Aye," van Staal replied firmly. "And I share it with none."

They walked on, toward Campeche.

CHAPTER 5

IT WAS DECIDED NOW, D'AVILA KNEW WHAT MUST BE DONE: the night of the fiesta would be the night of his reckoning.

Then, when even the jailers would be wagering on the birds, he'd return to the dungeon and blind them all. Kill them, if he had to. Only all their eyes would repay him now; Capitán Fernando d'Avila had been used as a pawn for too long.

As for those who controlled the town, they gorged him with contempt. The garrison, as such, no longer existed. It had been reduced to a few who ran the fort: loiterers slouching about the waterfront, ruffians waiting for gold. And the French patrolled the streets under the guise of an alliance. In the name of God, who did they think they were? He'd bargained with the mayor, he'd cast his promised vote, and now he'd been betrayed. There was talk of releasing the pirates from the *Courage* after the festivities, after the cockfight and the wedding and the gloss.

They'd *free* them, he'd heard the sinister whisperings. They'd split with them the treasure pirated from the town. Give them the English frigate and, captained by one called Cordier, set the scum loose upon the seas.

And that, he knew, would mean the pirate Stone, on his return, would also be given his liberty. Well, there were ways to deal with that: he'd make the law his own. The prisoners would *all* be blinded—it mattered not how many died. They'd all be left sightless, useless, deprived of light, and then the mayor and his French conspirator would discover the use of setting free *cripples* from the fort. By God, even for them to think of such an act was treason—and yet they called *him* mad.

As d'Avila was his name, he'd show them. He was neither decayed by climate nor lacking in experience. He would make his mark when they least expected it. Life and death had taught him to employ what was available: power was as you wielded it.

He steadied himself as he stood on the waterfront, gazing out at the ships that swung with such hideous grace. He put a hand to a bollard and held himself upright—his anger had, once again, threatened to sweep him away. By God, they'd learn. By God, they'd be shown. The night of the fiesta would give them something to celebrate that none envisaged. It would be a carnival to remember, for as long as their traitorous lives continued. It would teach them to keep their bargains—at least any they made with him.

She saw them coming: a pair of merchants with blankets and baskets and pots on their backs. One of them was limping and walked with a stick. The other was shorter and almost bald; he had a gray fringe about his ears like a friar.

They approached through the foothills in the late afternoon, appearing to know where they were going. For a moment they meant nothing more than they seemed: men walking, coming to Campeche to sell their wares at the fiesta, to attend the *palenque* in two days' time.

Then, something about the shorter one's skull, and the manner in which the taller of the two lifted his head as if peering forward, looking beyond what lay next, seized her throat. In that instant she put her hands over her eyes for fear the image was a cruel betrayal. A sudden longing shook her violently.

She removed her hands, and the figures remained.

She pushed her fingers into her mouth and pressed as a great cry burst from her, and she was running down the hillside, running wildly, her mouth open, shouting.

"Cristóbal," she called. "Oh, my God."

Stone started at the hysterical woman and heard her unbelieving cry. It scythed through him, bringing sweat to his face. For a moment he could not bear the pressure of it. He stood numb and stupefied, until he felt her shuddering reality.

"Cristóbal." Guadalupe sobbed. Distraught; at any instant he might vanish, and she'd be once more alone on the hillside. "Holy Mary, Mother of God," she prayed.

Stone held her, the astonishment on his face matched by that on van Staal's. He clasped the girl to him. He stared at the Dutchman, and they grinned at each other like fools. He clung to her, and she babbled a string of sounds of gratitude, of relief, of simple disbelief. He spoke without knowing what he said, feeling her tears wet his shirtfront, burying his words in her hair.

Then she lifted her head abruptly and stared. "Are there others?" she asked, as if aware of present danger.

"No," Stone whispered.

"None?"

"We are all."

"We must go from here," she said quickly, terrified of losing him again. "It is no longer safe. Nothing is safe. The French have returned. Your men are imprisoned." Her hands would not remain still; she touched him as if he might dissolve as suddenly as he'd appeared. "Come," she urged. "We will go to my mother's house. There you will be secure."

Stone stared at her, at her fear and her joy. "Where is Cazaux?" he asked very softly.

"I do not know. Before this, I did not wish to know." She gripped his hand. "I will ask in the barrio. Someone there will know. The Indians know everything."

Stone nodded; he began to follow. "All of us are Indians now," he said simply.

*   *   *

Jean-Marc Cazaux watched with distaste as the comb was cut from the young gamecock. Blood ran, the bird's eyes were fierce, as though with anger rather than pain. The Frenchman was forced to look away. It was a curious reaction; the sight of blood had never distressed him, yet watching the bird being carved to a shape that would enable it to survive a few minutes more when thrown into the ring turned his stomach in a way that was new.

"There," said Paco. Don Luis's handler was a tiny mestizo with curly black oiled hair. He put aside the bird he'd cropped and reached for another. "In two years' time they will be ready. Cut like this, there is nothing for the enemy to catch." With the pair of iron scissors he began to clip red wattles from the second fighting cock. "They'll be good birds when they're ready. Two kilos, maybe more."

Cazaux nodded and wiped his lips with the silk neckerchief he wore. He'd been interested in the preparation of the birds but had not expected such brutality. He watched as the shears continued their work, then he looked away.

"These," Paco said a little later, holding up a pair of silver spurs, sharp as razors, as finely made as any blade Cazaux had ever seen, "they are pretty, no? All the way from Spain. We use them only for the real fight." He pointed to the hollows that fitted over the cock's own spur; he fingered the fine leather thongs that would secure them in place. "They make nothing like them here."

"They are, elegant," Cazaux commented, thinking of Angela and her penetrating eyes. One of them dies, she'd said, and he knew now clearly why. "Very fine, the workmanship."

"Come, I will show you more," Paco said cheerfully. He smiled, and his whole face creased with pleasure. "We teach them to fight with this." He held a padded leather muff, its surface scarred by beaks and claws; he slipped it onto his arm and went into a circle formed with bales of straw. Another handler approached, a bird held ready. When Paco nodded, the cock was thrown. It came at the muff, neck feathers flared, wings beating like flails, to tear at the leather with its beak, to turn in the air and lash backward with both unspurred feet. The muff jerked on Paco's arm. The mestizo laughed. "Think what he will be like when the knives are in place," he said eagerly. "He is ready for the day after tomorrow. You will wager on him, no?"

Cazaux nodded, wondering whom he would oppose.

Another bird was thrown, again the muff was attacked. Paco was sweating with his efforts to counter the challenge, to encourage it, to keep out of its way. Even a slash from a feather wing would have brought blood to his face. "It is good they are not armed," he said with great enthusiasm. "Both *güeros,* blond birds." He laughed. "They will fight the *colorados,* the red ones from González, and those from the hacienda of d'Avila." He threw back his head. "That will be a matching, no? Who do you think will win?"

Cazaux shook his head. "I have little experience of any of this," he said carefully. "That is why Don Luis suggested that I speak with you."

"I have much experience." Paco bowed with false modesty. "I have learned from my father. Training the birds is my life."

"Is Don Luis, what you would call, enthusiastic about the sport?" Cazaux asked deliberately.

"Not as much as he should be, señor." Paco threw the leather muff to the other handler. He came out of the ring. "That is why I am glad you asked for this *palenque.* The birds were becoming fat."

"And that is not good for them, no?"

"Very bad for them, señor." Paco winked. "They need to be trained. They need a special diet. They need to fight, and they need to fight well. Otherwise they will be slaughtered by the birds of González. Or those of d'Avila. And that would not be good, señor. Do you not agree?"

"Yes," Cazaux replied. "I agree."

Paco bowed again. "What else may I show you?" he asked politely.

"Nothing more," said Cazaux. "I have seen enough." He would reinforce the garrison once d'Avila was dealt with. He would take great care as far as González, the treasurer, was concerned. None would return from the interior, he was almost certain now, and if they did, they would be worthless. There was promise here, in Campeche. He must nurture it as best he could. He would speak to Angela frequently; her insight was endless. "You have been more than helpful," he said courteously. "I look forward to the performance of the birds you have prepared."

"The night after tomorrow they fight, señor."

"I know," said Cazaux. "I am prepared for it."

Paco laughed; his head went back, and in the sunlight Cazaux noticed that he seemed to have gold in his teeth.

It was dark when Guadalupe led Stone and van Staal into the Barrio de San Román, the darkness falling with tropical swiftness, turning the sky from gold to indigo almost as they watched. They walked quickly through the village, their faces hidden, to the doorless entrance of the humble house of stone and palm thatch.

Magdelena looked up startled as the three figures, two of them unknown, stood before her. " 'Lupe," she began, then saw a sureness on her daughter's face she'd never known before. It was something she herself might have once possessed. " 'Lupe," she repeated. "It is he."

Making no attempt to conceal her joy, Guadalupe brought Stone forward. "This is my mother, Cristóbal," she whispered. "Her Spanish name is Magdelena."

"It gives me great pleasure," Stone said formally.

"No, my son, the pleasure is mine." Magdelena came closer. "And this is Round Skull?" she asked in Maya, looking at her daughter.

"His name is Rolf van Staal."

"Come, come all of you, closer to the fire. You must be hungry, and there is food. Cover the door," Magdelena

said to Guadalupe. "Put a blanket over it. Some will
have to know they're here, but there are others who
need not see."

Soon they were given bowls of fish stewed with green
peppers, tomatoes, and squash. While he ate, seated on
polished wood, one leg stuck out stiffly before him,
Stone spoke of what had occurred after Guadalupe's
departure from the house of Tutz. He told of the long
night waiting for her to return and the battle in the
streets the following day when all were either killed or
captured.

As Stone's clipped Spanish filled the room, he felt the
warmth about him rise, and he loosened his shirt and
noticed that van Staal did the same. He spoke in some
detail of the majesty of the Mayan court, of the rivalry
between the princes. He told them of the ball game and
how, with God's good fortune, they had won. But he
said nothing of the sacrifices, nor did he mention the
copper-headed axe with its handle of the serpent and the
moment of blackness when it had fallen from his hand.
He could not bring himself to speak of the line of murder
beyond which he had been unable to go.

"So they gave us a canoe," he said simply at the end.
"Rolf and I and the girl who cured me. We were all
allowed to leave."

"And this girl?" asked Guadalupe quietly. "What became of her?"

"She returned to her people," Stone answered. He
glanced across to van Staal to catch his eye and saw that
the Dutchman was smiling. "She went back to where
she belonged."

Guadalupe followed Cristóbal's gaze, her own eyes
curious. When she saw the smile that curved van Staal's
lips, she was content. She knew she would never meet
this girl of the Maya, this faceless person who was part
of her, but her gratitude went out to Ix Mai, who had
healed Cristóbal, who now brought such pleasure to the
features of the loyal Dutchman.

Later, when they were alone, when Magdelena and
van Staal had gone to the house of a neighbor, after

they'd talked and listened and discovered some of what had passed, Stone and Guadalupe made love on the slatted bed in the room behind the blanket.

As soon as they touched they were taken by a force, a demand, almost a desperation, which left them both exhausted. It gripped and flung them; it left them stranded like flying fish upon a deck, scarcely breathing, looking at each other with awe.

After a while Guadalupe reached out and laid her fingers on the rough, almost healed scar that covered Stone's hip, her face drawn in sympathy.

"I am fortunate," Stone said softly. "I would have died if it had not been for the girl."

"We, we are both fortunate." Guadalupe's voice was barely audible. Her hand went to the thin line her knife had left across Stone's ribs. "But you are marked," she whispered. "So very marked."

'We are both marked."

Guadalupe was unable to reply; he spoke the truth.

There would be more, they knew, before they were done. It seemed there was no escaping it. He had fought and lost, played and won; she'd returned certain of his dying. Now, hidden in the barrio, neither could envisage an easy release: there would be further markings. Christopher Stone lay awake a long time, listening to Guadalupe's gentle breathing, making plans to get the *Courage* back, and blood lapped at every design he made.

In the morning he took van Staal aside. Both agreed they must secure what remained of their crew from the dungeons beneath the fort and then attempt to regain the frigate. All must be done in speed, with silence, then they'd leave as fast as the wind would take them. But none of it was simple, and there could be no avoidance of death.

"Let us go tonight," Stone said finally, "to the fort and take what we can." He stroked his chin thoughtfully. "I've six pistols, and you've your axe. If we were to seem like Indians, in the dark it would work. Guadalupe is sure of getting us garments."

Van Staal nodded.

"We could approach the guard," Stone continued. "Selling fruit. Our heads down." He shrugged. " 'Tis barely possible, but it's the best thought I have."

"The Spaniards'll not be heavily armed," van Staal observed. "The French will have seen to that."

"You think Cazaux's men will be at the fort?"

"No, 'tis not work for them." Van Staal studied the hollows of Stone's eyes and saw defiance glimmer. For a moment he almost welcomed the fight that lay ahead. He knew of no alternative, so it might as well be brave. " 'Tis as you say," he murmured, "the only chance we have."

Guadalupe came to where they stood. "What do you speak of?" she asked. They'd used English with each other.

Stone turned to her and told her what was planned.

"Then I will come with you," she said. "It will seem more natural if a woman's there."

"No," Stone began, but got no further. Guadalupe put her fingers to his lips. "I will be with you when you go," she said simply, without a trace of doubt. "I will not risk the loss of you again."

Stone took her hand and held it.

The moon was mother-of-pearl, casting shadows across the Plaza Principal, from some corner of which a drunken voice was lifted, then a woman laughed. Stone, van Staal, and Guadalupe went past the church of Guadalupe, past the oaken door that bore the scar of Jacques's pike and memories for them all.

Both men wore heavy ponchos, broad-brimmed straw sombreros, and loose white cotton pantaloons. Guadalupe was shapeless in an unbelted shift that fell to her sandaled feet; her head was swathed in a long, striped shawl.

As they shuffled past the church in semidarkness, baskets of fruit on their shoulders, their heads bent, no one would have taken them for other than Indians. They went beneath an olive tree, at a corner of the church, and came out of its shadow to see soft light spilling from an archway in the wall of the fort.

"There." Guadalupe pointed to the light. "That's where the dungeons are." She glanced at Stone. "There will be a guard inside the entrance. That's what I've been told. And others, perhaps, elsewhere."

"Occupied with what?" Stone whispered.

"Drinking, playing cards. At times they bring in women."

Stone grunted and moved on into the revealing light. When they were a few yards from the archway, Alvaréz, his doublet undone, came into sight studiously picking his nose. As he saw them he sauntered closer. Indians with fruit, he thought at first. Or to sell the woman? He peered closely with greater interest, and then he smiled in utter disbelief. Whatever misfortune had befallen him lately, his luck was still reliable.

"So the blackamoor was not lying," he said, watching the astonishment on the faces that turned to him abruptly. "And just when I was beginning to lose faith." He crossed himself hurriedly. "You have come with the gold, yes?"

Stone stared, his mouth dry, his hand on a pistol grip, his mind stunned by the approach. The ease of the fat, untidy Spanish soldier bewildered him utterly.

"It is just as he said." Alvaréz shook his head in wonder. "The captain has his own plan, he told me. If you treat me well, I'll see you get your share." He wiped his finger thoughtfully on his doublet. "Even after, *Dios mío,* even after that madman started blinding them, he swore it was the truth. I must light a candle for him," he added almost humbly. "I must remember him in all my prayers."

"What?" Stone glanced at the others. They were as confused as he. "What do you speak of?" he asked, and his voice was unusually uncertain.

"But of course, you know nothing of this." Alvaréz shook his head at his own stupidity. "You will want to talk to the blackamoor yourself." He smiled welcomingly.

"Come, I will take you to him. He will tell you himself of the bargain."

"What bargain?"

"I gave them food and blankets," Alvaréz explained, stretching the truth only a little. "Put straw on the floor. Carried away those who died." He shrugged quite amiably. "For that, I was promised a little reward."

"I see." Stone let his breath out slowly, helplessly, convinced by the Spaniard's directness, disarmed by the confident words. "Then, then you'd better take us to him now."

"Of course." Alvaréz glanced toward the lighted archway. "But by another entrance. There are others inside. They have women and rum, but they are greedy." He sighed philosophically. "Everyone has become so greedy here."

They followed him along the wall of the fort to a small, square doorway; here the darkness was absolute. Alvaréz paused. "You have no lantern, señor. No? Then I will go for one." He disappeared into blackness.

They waited, unable to speak, hardly seeming to breathe. They waited until the silence about them was broken by the soft, tuneless whistling of Alvaréz's return. He swung a storm lantern before him; he appeared perfectly at ease.

"Are you alone still?" Stone asked.

"Of course, señor." Alvaréz shook his head sadly. "If I had as little faith as you, your men would have died long ago." He led them along a corridor that smelled of rot. He paused at the top of a flight of steps, their paving worn by footsteps. Water trickled over the stonework, and the corners were filled with green mold. "Be careful," he warned. "It is easy to fall."

Slowly they began down to the dungeon; a stench drifted up to greet them. "My God, how it stinks," Stone said disgustedly. "You said you'd helped these men."

"It is better than it was," Alvaréz replied, his tone professional. "And the food is a miracle compared to what they once were given."

"How many are left alive?"

"More than you would expect, señor. Six weeks in here is a lifetime anywhere else."

"Six weeks, God's heart," Stone began, when Alvaréz stopped.

"We are here," he said, and indicated a heavy door reinforced with iron. "Help me open this."

Stone and van Staal went to his aid, and together they swung the ironbound woodwork open. Foulness came out to them in a wave; a soft sound of chains and the breathing of men rose to their offended ears. In the swirling light from the lantern, the sight within was sickening.

Gaunt faces peered out of the reeking dark. Some stared with round, seemingly blinded eyes. Others turned from the lantern's brightness. All were pale and thin; there were sores on wrists and ankles where shackles had worn; clothing looked as if it had rotted to the flesh.

"God's blood," Stone roared, fully alive now, furious. "You told me they were well."

Alvaréz stared back blankly.

"You—" Stone began again, when Cramer's voice lifted from a corner of the cell.

"A pox on my soul," he said in simple relief. "If it isn't Cap'n Stone."

"Cramer." Stone seized the lantern and went in the direction of the voice. "You?"

"What's left of me." The Negro sounded drunk with shock: it was a dream beyond believing. "If I wasn't chained to the wall, I'd get up and kiss your hand."

"Could you stand?" Stone lifted the lantern. In spite of the hideousness of the dungeon, the men carried more meat than he'd first believed. "All of you? Can you walk from here?"

"Aye," said Lambe, the red-haired gunner. "We're better than we look."

"How many are you?" Stone spread the light, seeing hope and disbelief on all the faces. "Who's here?"

"We're less than twenty," Cramer said. "And would've been fewer still if it hadn't been for Alvaréz here."

Stone turned to the Spanish jailer. "Then he spoke the truth," he muttered to himself. His eyes went to van Staal. The Dutchman stood impassively. He'd spent his time in prisons; this did not seem too rank. Beside him, Guadalupe was motionless. She'd not seen men as reduced before. "Do you think they'll walk?" Stone asked van Staal, trying to adjust to the sight of what once had been his crew.

Van Staal shrugged. "Let's get them out and see," was his reply. He reached out a massive hand and took Alvaréz by the arm. "Give me the keys," he demanded in Spanish.

"With pleasure," Alvaréz replied. It was a relief they no longer spoke their coarse tongue. "But first"—he sounded quite apologetic—"first, you have to pay me."

"The hell we will," Stone grunted. "Take them," he said to van Staal.

"Now just a minute, Cap'n." Cramer spoke; he'd worked too hard and woven too often to see the opportunity shattered now. "You've got to pay for what you gets."

"What if we left him here, chained to the wall himself?" Stone spat on the floor. " 'Tis no more than he deserves."

Alvaréz cleared his throat as if to rid it of the English in the air. "Excuse me, señor, I do not understand your language. But if you were thinking of, perhaps, not paying me—" There was genuine regret in his voice. "Then I should tell you that some of my friends wait at the top of the steps." He removed his arm from van Staal's grasp. "If I do not come out first, none will get away." Alvaréz shrugged, hoping the lie would be accepted. He'd confess it in the morning, but for the moment he prayed it would pass unquestioned. "I do apologize for being suspicious, but I have made for myself a little security. I did it when I went for the lantern."

Stone blinked, again disarmed by the forthright simplicity. "Do you believe him?" he asked, turning to Cramer.

"It wouldn't matter if I didn't," Cramer replied. "We need him. There's some that won't go from here unless they's carried." He scratched the stub of his missing ear. "We'll need our friend a while longer. I'd give him what you've got."

"He expects gold?"

"Aye, he does."

"We have none. That's the truth of it. There was no gold to be had." Stone's voice was empty. "None."

A sudden charge of tension filled the cell. It sprang from every corner, stilling the movement of chains, binding them all with its intensity.

Then van Staal spoke. "Wait," he said, reaching beneath his poncho for the heavy necklace of gold and turquoise he'd been given by Ix Mai. "Take it," he said to Alvaréz, and his face was harder than any flint.

Alvaréz's greedy hands came out. "That is very pretty," he said gratefully, his face beaming. "That is very pretty indeed." He licked his lips with pleasure.

"Now let them go," said van Staal.

"Ah, señor." Alveréz lost his smile; his eyes were sad again. "For one piece of jewelry, however pretty, I cannot give you them all." He shrugged, hoping they would understand his responsibilities. "It would not be possible."

Stone swung the lantern closer, glaring at the Spanish jailer. Van Staal made a half step in Alvaréz's direction. But Cramer's voice stopped them both. "Keep him sweet," the Negro said gently. "We'll have use for him again before we're through. Ten of us," he called in Spanish. "How is that for what you got?"

Alvaréz nodded agreeably. "That seems equitable," he said politely. "Would you like to select them now?" His eyes went back to the necklace. Then he placed it about his throat and followed Stone, unshackling the prisoners as the fittest were chosen. "There," he said when it was done, "I will guard the rest for you, señor. I will keep them safe until—?" He raised a questioning eyebrow.

"Tomorrow," Stone said fiercely. "Tomorrow I'll be

back." He raised the lantern and spoke to those who waited. "I'll be back," he said. "In God's name, I will. Hold hard, it will not be much longer."

A murmur went about the cell. Voices lifted, and someone tried to laugh. It was a draining moment for all involved. Those who were leaving would face more blood. Those who remained shared a new, but untested, hope. Each group, in a way, envied the other.

Stone led out the ten he'd selected. He followed the jailer with the lantern to the top of the stairs and then beckoned the others away, knowing that nothing more would be achieved this night. Those with him could sleep in the barrio, Guadalupe had assured him of this. Then, tomorrow, after they were cleaned and armed, they'd make their attack.

When the fiesta was at its height, when all who mattered were absorbed by the feathered battle in the ring, they would attempt to board the *Courage*.

It was the only chance they had, Stone knew. It was, also, slim. He glanced at Guadalupe. She walked silently, her eyes on the shuffling prisoners: they found their steps awkward after being so long enchained. Her hand was at her mouth in pity and fear that someone might see them for what they were.

"See that they go quickly," she whispered to Stone. "Tell them to walk in pairs or alone. Pray to God that no one recognizes them."

Stone nodded and passed on the advice. Then he spoke to Guadalupe again.

"They will be stronger tomorrow," he said quietly. "What they have to do will make them so."

"What do you mean, what they *have* to do?"

"Fight," Stone said. "It is all they know."

"To fight?" It was the same everywhere. It seemed endless. She would never understand any of it, not really, no matter how frequently it touched her. "They will *fight* for the ship?"

"They will fight because they have to," Stone said simply. "They will fight to survive. And they will fight because they believe they're better men."

"Better than who?" Guadalupe's eyes came round, hard suddenly. "Who do they think they are?"

"Do not question it," Stone replied with surprising softness. "Pray only that it carries them. For if we survive tomorrow, it may spell the ending of it all."

"What do you mean?"

"I am not yet sure," Stone replied. He reached for and took her hand. "There is still too much to overcome."

They walked on, the questions unasked, unanswered, both wondering what future tomorrow would decide for all of them, in any way at all.

CHAPTER 6

Don Luis de Córdoba, mayor of Campeche, woke knowing that the time had come for the deed to be committed. Tonight the birds would be thrown into the sanded ring, tonight he would draw the pistol he carried at his waist. How the blood would spill, and what color would emerge the victor, remained unclear in his mind. But he was decided now; his destiny was within his reach.

The twin loves of his ambitious life—his daughter and the town—were again beneath the cover of his hand. One to be wed, the other sheltered. His action would determine both. Tonight he would reinforce himself to the best of his ability. He would dress in his finest broadcloth, a silken shirt, hose that glowed, and buckled shoes in which he'd see his image. And the pistol would be fitted in his waistband.

Yet he knew the trappings would not carry the act. That was his alone. Bare or gloved, it would be his finger that pulled the trigger.

He must lift the gun and fire. He could call on none, there was none to answer. He was himself, and solitary. He had examined the gun in all its masterly detail; he'd cleaned and primed it often. He slept with it beside him, and still it gave him nothing. His was the responsibility, it would measure what he was made of.

Don Luis de Córdoba, mayor again of Campeche, lifted his head and looked out at the day. It was clouded, it was heavy. Thin light came in through the window, nothing shone outside. It was a dismal day for measuring.

He climbed from his bed and called his majordomo. He needed sweet biscuit and hot coffee. He would ask to be shaved and tended to. He would take what pampering he could. For, later, when the birds were thrown, he would be absolutely and intolerably alone. Alone, with a pistol he knew he had to use.

Christopher Stone had spent half the night in the house of Magdelena, designing the attack. With him were Cramer and van Staal, their faces hard, their eyes thoughtful. They had insufficient weapons: Stone's pistols, van Staal's axe, a bottle of powder, and machetes collected from Indians in the barrio. With luck they would win more, but they had little enough to begin with. Their only advantage was surprise—and the fiesta, which they hoped would attract the attention of many.

They'd talked for hours, considering this, discarding that. Finally, the plan at that stage incomplete, exhausted by the night's totality, they decided to sleep. Sleep and time would aid them, they believed, although there would be an insufficiency of both.

Just before he left with Magdelena and van Staal to sleep in a neighboring dwelling, Cramer talked of the brutality of d'Avila and how Carson had died in agony, his eye burnt out. As Stone listened his lips thinned in anger, yet he could not turn his mind to vengeance. He had reached, he knew, a limit beyond which he could not bring himself to go. With him, once again, was the moment in the ball court. He stood again, staring down at the arrogant head of Paxbolón—which all expected him to take—and felt the copper axe fall from his unresisting fingers. There had been far too much blood already spilled by his competent hands. That there would be more, he was almost certain, but he hoped that none of it would be spilled in vengeance, merely to escape. D'Avila must die, he knew that also, but in terms of simple justice. That task would merely be another to be handled before they were finally free.

But when he'd turned from his conversation with the Negro, he'd caught Guadalupe's eye, and she'd demanded to know what it was that Cramer had discussed that had hardened Stone's face so bleakly.

In Spanish Stone told her, and her own face had filled with repugnance. There was no escape that she knew of. She was as destined as any of the others to live forever with the past. Quickly she turned her look away, afraid of disclosing her fears.

The following morning they began again, all of them now in the little house of Magdelena: the ten from the prison, the two who'd returned, and the women who were with them. By midafternoon they'd produced a scheme, using what they had, inventing what they could. It was frail, it would depend on fortune, but it was the only device they had.

When they seemed to be agreed, Guadalupe approached and asked what was intended. They explained it to her, and her eyes grew pensive. She wished to be rid of all the fighting and the fear and the greed. Last night when Cristóbal had told her what d'Avila had done, she'd been saddened and dismayed, had seen no quiet ending to any of the violence that had caught her in its maze. But now she realized the only hope they had was to succeed in what was planned. The only way to end the bloodshed was to act boldly out against it.

She took a deep breath. "What if there was a fire in the town?" she suggested quietly.

"A fire?" Stone asked. His head came up; all the others listened intently. "Tell me what you mean."

"If the barn at the hacienda of Capitán d'Avila were to burn," she said, firm now that she'd begun. "There would be many who would run to fight it."

"God's heart," Stone whispered.

"Aye," van Staal agreed. "That's just what's needed.

Voices were lifted, there was a flush of hope. They argued, one over the other, about how it might be done.

"I will go," Guadalupe continued as if she alone had spoken. "I, I know it well. None will notice me there."

"You'll not." Stone reached for the girl.

"I must." Guadalupe was determined. It would extinguish the past in part, if not completely. "There is no one else you can spare."

"By God, there is," Stone began, but Guadalupe cut him short.

"You need every man you have." There was defiance in her voice. "And I am suited to the task."

"You went once before, and I lost you." Stone's voice was low. "I'll not let you go alone."

"Then I will go with her," said Magdelena, her words as forceful as her daughter's. "Together we will be stronger."

"Sweet Jesu," said Stone, but that was all.

They rested, waiting for the night.

The day curled, the sky darkened, heavy cloud began to build along the horizon. In the hills behind Campeche, lightning flashed. Whatever else the night would bring, storms were on their way. By the time the spectators started to assemble in the small plaza behind the convent of San Francisco, the ceiling lay low and full, the air was close with the weight of rain. A wind blew down toward the shore, carrying the smells of earth, the scent of woodsmoke.

Those who gathered represented the whole town, the wealthy down to the very poor. Those with birds ranged from mulatto muleteers, a fighting cock under an arm, to Paco, the mayor's handler, his face creased with smiles in the torchlight. Those who had not been out of their houses for weeks came to the plaza. They convinced themselves that this was the end of two bleak months. The French corsario was to wed the daughter of the mayor, and the bond, they were sure, represented security for all.

None who loved the spectacle had been able to stay

away. It was in their nature to smile and dance, to celebrate and sing, to watch a man dress himself in splendor and battle with a bull, to witness two cocks fight to the death in their circle of bloodied sand. These performances took them from themselves, added zest to all their lives. The thought of rain did not deter them in the slightest.

Don Luis arrived to take his seat, a polished wooden bench, slightly raised above the others, by the barricade that encircled the sand-strewn court. Behind him stood Manuel, his striped jerkin immaculate. The sport was now ready to begin.

The ringmaster, a fat Creole with a thin cigar, looked questioningly across to the mayor. Don Luis, conscious of the empty spaces beside him that were reserved for Angela and Cazaux, hesitated a moment, then raised a finger as a signal to begin. The ringmaster called for the first pair, and the handlers quickly entered the fighting area.

"Whose birds are those?" Don Luis leaned toward his handler.

"The *colorado* is from Señor González." Paco indicated the thin treasurer seated on the far side of the ring. "The *güero* comes from the hacienda where I was born."

"Is Don Alejandro here?" The Mayor's eyes searched the crowd, looking for more than the owner of the fighting cock. "Have you seen him?"

"No, señor. His son has the birds."

Don Luis cleared his throat. "Have you seen the commander of the garrison?" he asked as casually as he could.

"Capitán d'Avila." Paco smiled. "No, there is no sign of him." He shrugged. "Perhaps he will not come." His words left a great deal unspoken.

"Perhaps not." Don Luis moved a leg to ease the pressure of the pistol in his groin. "But—" he began, when Paco raised his voice.

"Look, señor, the birds are almost ready. Do you wish to wager?"

Don Luis nodded. "I will bet against González." He

called over his shoulder to Manuel. "Lay a piece of eight for me," he said. "The best odds you can find. Hurry."

As the majordomo moved about the ring, excitement in the crowd became fervent. In the dense and odorous air, lit by torches, lanterns, and flashes of lightning, everyone seemed to be shouting at once. Money changed hands. Its color glinted as it bounced across the circle, and it was piled as wagers were agreed.

Then, just as suddenly, all was quiet. The handlers and the fighting cocks were alone in the ring. The birds, spurred and groomed, were incited to battle. They were displayed to their opponent, thrust at each other, and quickly withdrawn, enraged by proximity and teased to a peak: their eyes seemed aflame with torchlight, their beaks struck at air, they struggled in their handlers' grip. Blood was lifted now, and hatred ran.

From his position beside Don Luis, the ringmaster cast an eye over the audience, many deep now against the barricade: it was the moment. He raised his cigar-carrying hand and gave the signal to start. The game-cocks were thrown at each other.

They met before they touched the ground. Springing from their handlers' grasp, their wings took the heavy air. They clashed, their talons slashed, they fell away, feathers drifting, scattering sand. They leapt again, like coiled springs, the *colorado* going higher; it went up, over the head of the *güero,* scything downward with its spurs. Both birds fell and rested an instant, exhausted already by the pace and the intensity. They lay, chests heaving, wings spread on the sand.

There was blood now on the yellow sand floor, a sprinkling of black-red drops from the wing of the *güero.* At the sight of it the crowd began to shout anew. Odds were altered, new bets were laid, the chances of the birds revalued.

"*Güero,*" someone offered. "I will give twice the odds against the *güero.*"

"Take them." Don Luis instructed his majordomo. He stared across the ring to González and saw the tiny mouth curve in pleasure. The treasurer raised a hand, accepting the bet himself. "Agreed," called the mayor, and returned his gaze to the ring.

And then the *güero* struck. It ran, trailing a wing, toward its red opponent. It started slightly to the left, then swerved and leapt, its great yellow-blond feathers beating the dusty air until they shrieked with the effort. It came over the head of the *colorado* as the red bird reached to spring, and then it carved down with its armored feet. Both silver blades flashed in the light, struck downward, and caught the *colorado* across the throat, killing it as it stood. The red bird collapsed in a heap, its dead feet kicking sand. González's handler came into the ring and carried it away by the neck.

Don Luis lifted his eyes to stare at the treasurer. González's mouth was as tight as a blade as he reached to pay his gold. Don Luis searched further. There was still no sign of Angela and Cazaux; he could see nothing of d'Avila.

Alvaréz had attempted to give the impression of being disappointed, even betrayed. He, who was dutiful, had told the others who were supposed to remain at the fort that he'd expected more. But they'd laughed, as usual, saying that the prisoners were his responsibility. Then they'd gone to the *palenque*. All of them, to drink and wager and look for women, leaving him alone.

As soon as the last of them had disappeared, Alvaréz had taken the necklace from beneath his shirt and examined it once again. It was truly beautiful, a fitting reward for all he'd done. It had not been a simple task, keeping the prisoners alive, in spite of the help he'd received from the French—not with d'Avila about. Alvaréz shivered and looked again at his prize. There'd be more tonight, when the Inglés returned. He'd be given all he rightly deserved.

He was counting the beads of gold again when a voice shouted in his ear. "You," it cried, and the word filled him with terror.

Alvaréz jumped, dropped the necklace, bent, scooped

it up, thrust it beneath his doublet, and turned to stare into the blistering face of Capitán Fernando d'Avila, commander of the Garrison. "Señor," Alvaréz gasped, and thought he was going to faint.

"What is that?" D'Avila's eye was on the bulge the heavy necklace made.

"Nothing, señor. A plaything, señor." Alvaréz looked past the commander, hoping he'd disappear as he'd come. "How may I serve you, señor?"

"The prisoners." D'Avila would show them now. All would see what he was made of. "Take me to them, at once."

"*The prisoners,* señor?" Sweat leapt to the jailer's forehead. He looked about him, as if seeking help. "The, prisoners, did you say?"

"You heard me, you fool." Fingers scratched at the edges of the leather patch over d'Avila's blinded eye. "The prisoners."

"Yes, señor. No, señor." Alvaréz's throat was dry, his head trembled like a maniac's. "I cannot, señor. I am not permitted to, señor."

"You fool." D'Avila spat the words. They were, all of them, incompetent. Uncontrolled, unkempt, undisciplined. He pulled savagely at his short black beard. "I intend to deal with them now. All of them. Give me the keys at once."

"*All of them?*" Alvaréz's voice rose to a squeak. Less than half remained. He'd prayed, he'd performed his penances, he deserved much greater fortune. "No, señor." He coughed, he whispered; his head would not keep still. "Tomorrow, señor." He grasped at whatever came to mind. "Please, señor. Tonight, we have the fiesta."

"Now," d'Avila shouted. White flecks danced on his beard. He reached for the keys with a shaking hand. "Now, by God, or I'll kill you also."

Alvaréz passed d'Avila the keys with the thought that death might be preferable. He followed the capitán into the fort and, with eyes that did not see, was aware of him taking a lantern from a wall. Alvaréz followed d'Avila down the slime-green steps and helped him open the ironbound door, with blackness roaring in his ears. He remained outside the dungeon, his hand on the necklace, feeling death beside him, waiting for the shout. When it came he was too terrified to move.

Minutes later the sound of the cell door still ringing in his ears, not knowing how he'd arrived, Alvaréz stood again in the open air, the capitán spitting words in his face. In his hand d'Avila held the glittering necklace.

"They bought them with this?" the furious commander hissed, no longer shouting now; his words were as fine as steel. "You mongrel, you'll be burned."

"No, señor. My God, señor, what else could I do?" The jailer's jaws felt stiff; nothing about him functioned. "They were armed."

"Burned and ridden," d'Avila fumed, impotent again, defeated once more by pettiness and greed. The shock of discovering half the prisoners gone had enraged him beyond all action, frustrated him beyond competence. Half was not enough. This represented yet another fiasco in his chain of failures. By God, his bitterness burned. "You'll die as the rest of them will die," he spat at the terrified jailer.

"No, señor. Please, señor—"

"Unless . . ." d'Avila paused, his one eye flashing. "Unless you help me now."

"Yes, señor. What, señor? How may I possibly help you?"

"I need men," d'Avila said in a quieter tone, trying to think, trying to overcome the ferocity that threatened to destroy his reason. "I need men tonight."

"*Tonight*, señor?" Alvaréz could not get his mind to work. "Tonight? Is that what you mean?"

"That's when you said they'd be back."

"Did I, señor?" Alvaréz could not take his eyes from the necklace that hung in d'Avila's hand. It was the only reality that remained. "Then, tonight, señor. Men, señor? They have all gone to the cockfight."

D'Avila's lips lifted from his teeth. His face came

very close. "Go and get them," he said very slowly. "Go and get them now."

"I—" Alvaréz began, then shook his head, wondering why death had deserted him. He closed his eyes, hoping for further darkness. "I cannot, señor. I must remain, señor. I have to stay with the prisoners."

"I order it."

"I cannot."

D'Avila's hand was on his dagger. He should kill the shaking jailer now, but the act would be empty, would achieve nothing. D'Avila stared at the trembling fool and knew he would not move. He himself must go for those he needed, take them quietly, bribe them, if necessary, but have them here for the English pirate's return. It was the only way he'd have his revenge. The law was in his own determined hands. Now was the time to act.

"In that case," d'Avila muttered, "say nothing. Do you hear me, *say nothing*. Nothing to a soul. If the pirate arrives before I return, keep him here. I will be back as soon as possible."

Alvaréz nodded vigorously. Relief weakened his knees.

"Do you understand me?" d'Avila hissed.

"Yes, señor. I understand you, señor. I will say nothing." Alvaréz licked his lips. "May, I, señor," he began, and felt himself swaying, "may I have my plaything back?"

But Capitán Fernando d'Avila did not appear to hear. He turned and walked stiffly away, placing Ix Mai's necklace about his throat as he went.

Alvaréz watched him go with tears of fear and frustration in his eyes. "Your mother was mounted by lepers," he whispered when d'Avila was out of earshot. "She got on her back for beggars with sores. Oh, in the name of the Virgin, why did this happen to me?" He knew that his luck had finally betrayed him, and he couldn't imagine why.

Jean-Marc Cazaux and Angela threaded their way through the colorful crowd, outshining all they encountered: brightly tinted shawls and sashes, multihued dresses, gay sombreros. Angela wore a billowing gown of heavy gold silk; its skirt was belled, and its sleeves were puffed, bound with black lace. About her milky neck was a string of pearls; over her head, a black mantilla. Her lips were painted, her cheeks were rouged. She was rich, lavish, larger than life, and she walked through the crowd like a queen.

"Oh, Papá," she said as she took her seat by the mayor, "isn't this all so spectacular."

Don Luis smiled. His daughter had never appeared more radiant. He glanced at Cazaux. The Frenchman wore fresh green broadcloth, his pantaloons were red, and about his neck was a scarlet scarf.

As they settled beside Don Luis, Manuel bent forward. "The next bout is ready, Your Worship. Do you wish to wager?" he inquired.

"Yes," the mayor replied, his eyes still on Cazaux. "Do you?"

Cazaux bowed slightly. "I will bet against you, *mon père*," he said. "Which bird will you take?"

"I shall bet the *güero* again."

"Then I'll take the red bird." Cazaux took a gold coin from a pocket in his broadcloth doublet and handed it to Manuel.

"Ah, my love"—Angela raised a whimsical finger—"is it wise to bet against my father?"

Cazaux smiled. "It is an even bet," he replied. "There are no odds involved."

Don Luis grunted, then turned his eyes toward the ringmaster, who gave the signal to begin.

The fight was unspectacular; neither bird was inclined to attack. After being thrown together they landed on the sand, circling each other uneasily, their wingtips trailing, their heads craned cautiously. The handlers tried to encourage them by clapping their hands, shooing the birds forward, shouting in their ears, but all to no effect.

The crowd became impatient. They whistled; they hissed. Someone threw a sombrero into the ring, and both birds sprang from it, their neck feathers hooped in fear.

"The hat has more courage than the birds," a voice called jeeringly. "I put my money on it."

"I will give you three to one, the sombrero versus the *colorado*," another replied. "Or four to one, if you take the *güero*."

The crowd laughed. More voices were raised. The ringmaster collected the hat, called the birds' owners, and spoke briefly to them. They tried again. Each lifted his cock and thrust it at the other until both were straining to get away. Then they were flung at each other from so short a distance, they had no choice but to thrash out in fear. They hung a moment, a struggling bundle of ruffled feathers, then fell part, both bleeding, both limping, looking for ways to escape.

"No contest," cried the ringmaster. "All money to be returned."

"There." Angela was the only spectator applauding. "It is as it should be. Neither of you has won."

Cazaux bowed at the mayor again. Don Luis nodded, then turned away. From the corner of an eye he'd thought he'd seen d'Avila, and his mouth was suddenly dry. No, he whispered to himself. So soon? It's far, far too soon.

CHAPTER 7

THEY CAME UNNOTICED INTO THE COURTYARD OF THE HACI-
enda, walking slowly, talking: a pair of women, as
other women who'd remained to prepare the meal those
who had gone to the *palenque* would expect on their
return. Guadalupe carried an earthenware jug of oil:
Magdelena, a flint and tinder.

From the main building of the hacienda light spilled
through whitewashed window frames. It fell through the
doorways of brick and woodwork; it glowed with brightness in the damp and heavy air. A horse wrangler sauntered past, his spurs jingling. From somewhere came the
sound of a guitar.

"The barn," Guadalupe whispered, "it's over there."
She pointed to the far side of the courtyard.

Magdelena nodded. "I will be grateful when this is
done," she said, her voice stiff.

"Are you afraid, Mother?"

"I would be more afraid if you were here alone."

Guadalupe took her mother's arm. They came to the
barn, entered its dark interior, and no one appeared to
have seen them. They found a corner to light the fire
where hay spilled across the floor, where the tang of
casked beef was all about them. It was beneath the loft
where he first had taken her.

422

She recalled the heat of the afternoon, the windlessness, the faint scuffle of rats' feet. It had been quick, and he had not been inconsiderate. Later he'd bought her a blanket of bright colors and said he would be her protector. Apart from the blanket, he had given her food and cloth, but nothing of himself.

Now, putting the flame to the hay seemed no more than was necessary. The barn was the last of those links with her past. The moment the tinder caught and the oil-wet hay began to burn, the act of erasure started. As the little flames curled and grew, Guadalupe sensed release. She remained, looking at the rising burn, too long. It was not until her mother tugged her arm, and the first of the servants came out of the house, that she turned away at all.

"Come," Magdelena said urgently. "Soon they will be everywhere."

The flames thundered now. Figures ran and shouted. There was the sound of horses being led to safety; there was the smell of salt meat scorching. Yet still she stared, as others stared. Magdelena pulled her away.

"Come," Magdelena said again. "We will return to the barrio."

"No." Guadalupe felt empty now that the match had touched. "We will go to the waterfront."

"There will be fighting there."

"That is why we must go."

Magdelena stared at her daughter.

Further doors were being opened. A servant girl ran toward them, a bucket of water in her hand. "Take this," she shouted. "I will go for more."

"What?" Guadalupe's hand withdrew.

"Water," the girl shouted. "Take it quickly." She peered suddenly at Guadalupe's undecided face. "Are you not—?" she said, recognition beginning in her eyes.

"Give it to me." Magdelena took the bucket. "Hurry," she said to the girl. "Go for more."

"Yes." The girl nodded, peered, then ran back to the hacienda. "I'll get more."

"Mother." Guadalupe shook her head, confused and
yet decided. "We must—"

"Come, help me with this." Magdelena held out the
bucket, and together they took it to the fire, where
servants and grooms, saddle hands and yard boys, ran in
all directions, attempting to fight the blaze. As they
approached a man turned, his hand out for the water.
Magdelena passed it to him. "We will go for more," she
shouted.

"Hurry. This is very bad."

"Now." Magdelena took her daughter's arm. "Away,"
she whispered, and they disappeared into the darkness.

It was then that the swollen skies opened, and the first
heavy drops of rain began to fall.

The next matched pair in the sand-strewn ring was the
colorado from the estate of González and the *güero* that
belonged to the mayor. The ring had been freshly swept,
the ringmaster lit a new cigar, the handlers approached
from opposite sides.

Paco crooned as he stroked the yellow-blond feathers
of the cock he'd trained. González's handler, a man as
thin as his master, was equally comforting as he preened
the bronze-red back of the bird beneath his arm.

The crowd was active once again. Disappointed with
the failure of the previous fight, they began to bet in
larger sums. Voices rose, odds were shouted, coins
changed hands or were stacked before the gamblers. So
great was the noise that the first cry of "Fire!" was
scarcely heard.

At that moment Don Luis lifted his head, not because
of the warning, but because he'd seen the bustling figure
of the commander of the garrison once again. The sight
of the short frenetic dark-bearded man filled him with
dread. The moment had come, and still, he was unprepared. The pistol had grown comfortable against his
thigh—now was not the time to remove it. He watched
as d'Avila spoke to a soldier, and then the cry of "Fire!"
was shouted once again.

This time everyone reacted. All saw the dull glow of

flames in the eastern sky. Fists tightened about their
gold. The fire rose, a brief gust of wind showered sparks
in a curving arc, and the crowd about the sand-strewn
ring exploded in all directions. Some ran back to their
cloistered homes, regretting having left them; others went
toward the hacienda, offering aid.

Don Luis saw Paco, his hands about the *güero* like a
blanket, bear the bird away. It would not be matched,
this night, against González's. Don Luis looked again
for d'Avila, but the darksome figure had gone.

"Have you—" he began, turning to where Cazaux
had been, but there was no sign of the Frenchman,
either. He lifted his eyes to Angela; her face was deeply
thoughtful. It contained a seriousness not usually displayed. "He has gone to the ship," she said evenly. "I
told him it would be for the best."

"You—?"

"Go also," Angela continued in the same level voice.
"Don't concern yourself with me."

Don Luis opened his mouth but said nothing. He
stood, his hand on the silver-inlaid pistol butt, and then
he began to fight his way through the crowd, heading
toward the breakwater. That was when the rain began
to fall.

Christopher Stone sat in a longboat, southwest of the
breakwater. His eyes were on the riding lights of *La
Petite* and the *Courage*. The frigates hung on their anchor warps, their prows to the coastline, held by the
offshore breeze that was beginning to carry rain.

Lambe, the red-haired gunner, watched a tongue of
fire lick the air. "She's caught, Cap'n," he said. "And
she's caught well. She's exactly what we wanted."

"Aye," said Stone, turning to the glowing sky. "It's
time we were away."

"Push out, lads," Lambe called softly.

There was a muttering, a movement of the craft, as it
slid from the darkness of the breakwater. No one saw or
heard them now, although the waterfront was aswarm

with figures. All were looking the other way, their voices raised in confusion.

"Lay into her, lads," Lambe called again. "Keep her on the *Courage*, nice and easy."

The boat headed out over choppy seas. Stone sat in the stem, a pistol in one hand, a grappling hook in the other, his eyes on the shape of his ship in the darkness. It would happen now, he knew, or not at all.

D'Avila had been waiting in the shadow of the fort with twenty men, bribed, threatened, cajoled, none of them agreeable, when the flames burst skyward. So intent was he on his search for Stone that for a time he knew nothing of the blaze.

Then Alvaréz, the jailer, his voice more ingratiating than ever, said, "Have you seen the fire, señor?"

"What fire?" D'Avila did not turn his head. His gaze was fixed on the corner of the church, by the olive tree, where he'd been led to believe Stone would appear. Then his soldiers, with their pikes, would seize the scum from the *Courage*. "Do not distract me," he hissed.

"It is, just, señor . . ." Alvaréz paused. He'd felt all day that the Blessed Virgin must have been offended by something he'd thought or done, but now he believed he might suddenly have been reprieved. "The fire, señor," he began again. "I think you'd better look."

"What?" D'Avila swung to the jailer. "What is it you say?"

"I apologize, señor." Alveréz stared straight ahead, trying to keep the pleasure from his voice. "It is just that there is a fire, señor. And some of the men, señor, they thought it might be at your hacienda."

"In God's name." D'Avila thrust Alvaréz aside. He stretched to see where the flames were coming from. They were high now, dancing on the horizon, mocking him with their liveliness. He began to run past the assembled soldiers and on into the square, where the crowd had gathered, looking toward the east. "In God's sweet name," he sobbed. "It *is* my hacienda."

He had never known a moment as tormented or as

bleak. All he owned was burning. All he desired was still
at liberty. He felt tears in both his eyes, a thunderous
ache in his chest. He cried out, saying nothing—a shout
of rage and impotence, acknowleding further defeat. He
swung behind him to see the soldiers he'd assembled
beginning to drift away. He turned back toward his
property to watch the fire dance.

Rain was falling now, but it would not be enough.
D'Avila needed aid as he needed time. He knew he must
help fight the fire himself, whatever agony it cost to tear
himself away. Voices lifted in what seemed like laughter
as he ran on raggedly in the direction of the hacienda, to
protect the only surety he knew, to leave behind another
forfeited opportunity.

Alvaréz, the jailer, watched him go, wondering what
had become of the necklace.

Cramer the Black paddled the canoe steadily toward
La Petite. In the prow of the narrow vessel crouched
van Staal, sheltering a crude bomb on his lap from the
increasing rain. The firepiece had been made from the
bottle of powder carried from Tayasal: flints were mixed
with the charge; a short wick protruded through the
cork. In an open bowl, beneath his poncho, was a lighted
coal. The Dutchman sat uneasily, like a monk guarding a
holy relic, as the unstable craft slid through the roughen-
ing seas. From time to time he blew on the coal, keeping
its fire alive.

The longboat was out to where the waves chucked.
Stone, and the nine men with him, wiping rain from their
eyes, peered through the drifting darkness as they swung
to come in under the stern of the *Courage*. Somewhere,
between themselves and the shore, was the canoe with
Cramer and van Staal, but they saw no hint of it as they
pulled against the wind.

Yet they noted with gratitude that the fire still glowed.
Showers of sparks curled above the hacienda, flames
rose and fell. Ant figures scampered on the waterfront.
Occasional voices were carried to their ears.

The shape of the *Courage* loomed closer. The sea chopped and battered against her bow. "Ease her in," Stone called quietly. "As close under as you can."

"You heard him, lads." Lambe's voice lifted. "And for the Lord's sake keep her quiet. A gun on us now and we're done for."

A man grunted. An oar made a sudden splash. Breaths were sucked in swiftly. But slowly, gradually, each man straining, the longboat came under the stern to hang like a leaf in a pool of sheltered calm. Above them, men could be heard shouting in French. A figure appeared over a railing, a black silhouette against the fire-limed sky, then left as suddenly as it had arrived.

In the longboat, hands were white-knuckled on the oars, sweat crawled down bodies, no one dared speak for fear of betraying more than themselves. They waited for other figures to appear, for shouts and the shapes of guns, but nothing came. French voices rose and faded, but none in their direction.

"What," Lambe began, then wet his lips. "What can we do?" he whispered.

"Nothing," Stone replied in a voice that barely lifted. "We wait 'til we hear the blast from *La Petite*. When it goes, then do we."

The men breathed and held the longboat steady. They looked into each other's faces and away again, all of them desperate for the explosion that would hurl them out of the longboat below the stern that trembled with their anxiousness.

Don Luis de Córdoba stood on the breakwater staring out to sea. Shapes drifted. The frigates rode, lit by firelight, polished by the rain; voices were everywhere. Beside the mayor was Ernesto Juárez, a bald sea captain, master of the port.

"You saw Cazaux go?" Don Luis asked suddenly. "You're sure of that?"

"Yes, Your Worship," Juárez replied calmly, as if his professionalism were in question. "He took a square-

sailed pirogue that was waiting for him. His mate, Sartou,
was also aboard."

"And they went to *La Petite*?"

"Directly, Your Worship. The wind was with them all
the way."

"Did he say why?"

"No, Your Worship. Nor did I see any reason to
question him."

"No, no, of course not," the mayor muttered. The
action in the town had been withheld from him again.
Cazaux knew more than he'd been prepared to share,
and this fire was no accident. Don Luis was suddenly
certain that the events of the night were part of a design,
but he could not fathom its purpose. He wondered what
Cazaux knew. Angela? And d'Avila? What role was his?
The mayor clung to his determination. *Now,* he realized.
It would be now. Once more he felt for the pistol.
"Have you seen the commander of the garrison?" he
asked.

"No." The master of the port shook his head firmly.
"I have seen nothing of him this night." He raised his
eyebrows at the mayor. "But I imagine he's gone to his
hacienda," he went on, as if explaining the facts to
someone who did not understand. It was said that the
mayor no longer drank anything stronger than water
mixed with the juice of limes, but perhaps they were
mistaken. "After all," he pointed out, "it *is* his hacienda that is burning."

No, thought Don Luis, that would be too simple.
The fire was to divert. Here, the waterfront, *this* would
be the stage. He ignored the patronizing tone of the port
master and kept his eyes on the sea.

"Would you like me to send someone to verify whether
or not Capitán d'Avila is at his hacienda?" Ernesto
Juárez asked quietly. "It would take very little time."

"Stay where you are," the mayor replied crisply, and
felt Juárez stiffen angrily beside him. "Wait here until I
tell you what to do."

Don Luis strained to see more of the frigates but
could make out little in the dancing light. Once, he

thought he caught sight of the sail of Cazaux's pirogue, and perhaps another shape, but he was unsure as more rain gusted. The firelight came and went, and nothing was as it seemed as darkness shifted in and out of his vision.

"Mon capitaine," Sartou asked as he held the tiller against the thrust of the sea, "why should anything occur tonight?"

"Because I sense it." Hashish gave him extra perception. "Because there is too much unexplained."

Sartou blinked; he swung the tiller and hauled the sail. The wind was taking them away from *La Petite*. He tacked to come in on the ship.

"The town is alive with rumors," Cazaux continued. He held the mast and stared ahead, his scarlet neckerchief fluttering in the wind. "Don't tell me you've heard nothing?"

"Nothing." Sartou could see *La Petite* clearly now; it had never seemed so peaceful. "I would have thought all matters to be—" He shrugged. "Resolved." Sartou spat with the wind. He'd had plans for tonight, until he'd been told to be ready. He wondered if they'd wait. "Especially tonight . . . well, it is the fiesta."

"Precisely." Cazaux turned to stare at Sartou. "It would suit Captain Stone most perfectly."

"Stone?" Sartou belched with surprise. "I'd thought him dead."

"So had I, so had I," said Cazaux, covering his nose with a hand as Sartou's breath surrounded him. "Until the rumors in the barrio began. Until there was food left uneaten at the prison this morning. Until Angela spoke to her maid."

Sartou blinked again and wondered if the green liquid and the Spanish woman had turned his captain's head.

"There is too much unexplained," Cazaux went on, looking again to his frigate. "And the fire." He smiled, and his scar curved vividly. Angela had known immediately. "The fire was the final indication."

"Merde," Sartou said, reluctantly impressed. "Who would have thought the English would return like this?"

"Any who thinks as I do," Cazaux replied. "That is why I asked you to be ready."

"Even before the fire?"

"The fire made it certain." Cazaux smelled excitement in the dark and lively air. "Before it, I relied on my senses."

Wind and sea carried them, rain buffeted. The sail cracked. A spume of boiling sea carved a wake behind them as Sartou tacked again. The wind had veered, and the mate knew they'd need another leg before they could come in on their ship.

"Hurry," urged Cazaux, peering at the shifting images in the curling dark, larger and more significant than they should have been. "Stone will be well ahead of us by now."

"Just tell me how you wants it," Cramer whispered as the canoe slid in toward the rudder of *La Petite*.

"Steady," van Staal replied. "We'll set it above the bulge line. Even if the timbers don't spring, she'll not steer."

"Aye," said Cramer, speaking yet not wanting to be heard. "She'll be useless in these waters."

Like a snake in the water the canoe went under the cover of *La Petite*. Away from the wind and the gusting rain, all seemed suddenly still. No sound was heard from the frigate's crew. Only the steady, mournful groan of the steering came to Cramer as he worked the paddle, to van Staal as he reached for the bomb.

"Where?" Cramer's voice was almost silent.

"Starboard. Clear of the rudder."

There was a soft knocking as the canoe nosed into the body of *La Petite*. Van Staal's face came round, white and furious. Cramer swallowed, his lips moving in a curse. Van Staal looked back and examined the bomb: the wick had remained dry. From somewhere beneath his feet he took a hammer and an iron spike.

"Hold me steady. Quiet, do you hear?"

"Aye." Cramer's eyes were round. "I hears."

Cramer pressed the paddle into the swirling water to hold the canoe against the hull of *La Petite*. The great blade of the rudder rolled, creaking loud and solemn. Van Staal reached, probing the hull, his fingers seeking a join between timbers. He found one and placed the tip of the iron spike against it. He swung the hammer in a short hard blow. The spike went in; the sound of the hammer reverberated the length of the ship.

"Piss on me," Cramer whispered. "They'll hear it."

"Don't move. They'll think it a log."

"Oh, Christ, I hope so." Cramer heard his stomach churn. "I do hope so."

They waited, not moving, their eyes fixed in their heads. Above them a voice called, then another. The pale glow of a storm lantern moved up by the bow and away. Tension threatened to break them.

Then van Staal's breath came out in a long, low rush. "We're safe," he said.

"They're quiet," whispered Cramer, "but that don't mean we're safe."

Van Staal was no longer listening. Leaning over the running sea, he hung the powder-filled jar on the spike. Then he reached for the coal beneath his poncho and blew on it softly—it remained unresponsively black. He blew again, and again the coal refused to glow.

"God in heaven," he said, new fear chilling him. "Light, damn you, light."

"What is it?" Cramer called softly.

Van Staal did not reply. He touched the coal, and his fingers burned. He tought he would faint with relief. Quickly he rubbed away layers of ash, then blew again, harder, persistently, until a faint pale pink sliver of light began. He blew continuously, and the fire spot spread. He blew until his head was spinning, until the whole remnant of coal was red and glowing.

He turned to Cramer. "When it's touched we go to the bow," he said.

"Aye." Cramer shivered. "Aye, we do."

"Be ready. I'm putting it to the slow match now."

"Aye. I'm ready."

Van Staal lifted the fiery coal and pressed the light to the fuse. He waited until it began to splutter; he waited until he was sure it had caught. Then he shouted, "Go," and felt the canoe leap away.

Cramer thrust the narrow craft. The paddle bit. They sped beneath the guns of *La Petite* to where the painter was, while those aboard turned at the shout, took their eyes from the hacienda fire, and wondered at the cry.

Below, beneath the stemhead, van Staal reached for the anchor warp, a heavy knife in hand. He sawed; the fibers split and twisted. With a crack the rope parted, and the frigate rode away. Those on board turned and stared at one another in dumb confusion as they felt the movement of the ship begin.

"Go," van Staal shouted again, pointing to the *Courage*. "Go for all the life that's in you."

The blast, when it came, was sharp and seemed very close. A flash of red-orange flame sprang from the stern of *La Petite*. She bucked in the water, then hung, drifting with her steering jammed hard over. As water rushed in through the hole in her timbers, she began to slant like a broken fort: one set of guns pointing skyward, the other to the sea.

CHAPTER 8

"Up," shouted Stone as the red sound tolled toward them as the black cries lifted. "Now, we begin."

He swung the grappling hook he held. It rose in the darkness as those above ran to watch the shape of *La Petite* drift clumsily away. One of the hook's metal spikes bit into the *Courage*'s poop-deck railing—its length of knotted rope trailed down toward the water.

His seaboots against the carved stern, his hands on the rope knots, Christopher Stone began to climb. He came over the taffrail—and there was no one in sight. He signaled his men in the longboat to follow, and pistol in hand, he began to creep along the deck.

Jean-Marc Cazaux saw and heard the explosion as the pirogue turned again toward *La Petite*. "*Putain de merde*," he whispered, not believing its intensity.

"A bomb." Sartou's eyes started from his head. "In the stern."

"*Mon Dieu*," Cazaux shouted, turning to assist. "Quick, there is no time to lose."

"None," Sartou whispered, giving the small craft all the sail he could, knowing they'd never board the lumbering frigate. "We have no time at all."

* * *

Don Luis de Córdoba saw the flame, then heard the blast, as he stood beside Juárez on the breakwater. "Sainted Mother," he said, "which was that?"

"The French," the port master replied, some of his authority returned. He lifted his hat and wiped his baldness. "I should go out and investigate."

"Stay where you are," Don Luis said, his eyes not leaving the dark and tilting hulk. "I need you here."

Don Luis knew he too was rooted here. The deed would come to him so long as he remained. What occurred at sea was beyond his realm, but that was serving to draw the crowd. At the hacienda the fire was dying—here was where the spectacle was being played. D'Avila, wherever he was, would also be attracted. Then he, the mayor, would be waiting with all the determination he possessed.

"Does any of this make sense to you?" the mayor asked the port master.

Ernesto Juárez shook his head. "None," he admitted reluctantly.

Christopher Stone lay on the poop deck, looking along the length of his ship. Lambe crawled up beside him.

"How many are there, Cap'n?" asked the red-haired gunner.

"Four or five on the main deck," Stone grunted. "They watch *La Petite*. And there'll be more below, never fear."

The wind changed swiftly, and the chatter of men came up. Then a figure moved on the half deck below them: it went around the binnacle to check the loop on the wheel. Stone reached down quietly and slid the knife from his boot.

"When I seize him," Stone instructed, his voice barely heard, "attack. All of you, with all the noise you can make."

Lambe nodded. He glanced behind him: the others were now aboard, crouched silently in the dark. Stone waited until the French sailor turned from the wheel. He saw the man pause as if listening, then move toward a ladder leading up to where Stone lay. As the head came level with his own, Stone struck. He pulled the Frenchman to him and cut his throat from side to side. Blood sprang in fountains. The sailor growled, but that was all. Stone let him go, and the body fell back to the deck with a thud; the man had died not knowing what had caused it.

Then, with a shout, Lambe and the others leapt forward. They ran, stumbling in their haste, roaring like savages. Their strength was fired by the energy of the moment, the cries of their companions. The French, standing by the railing watching *La Petite*, turned when the rabble was almost upon them. They had barely time to reach for whatever weapons they carried before Stone's pirates closed, shouting like madmen, fighting to repay the long hard weeks in the dungeon, desperate to secure their own escape.

Capitán Fernando d'Avila came from the hacienda as soon as the explosion of *La Petite* shattered the night sky.

There had been infuriatingly little he'd been able to do about the fire in the barn. By the time he'd arrived it was at its peak, and servants were wetting the walls of the main dwelling to keep them from catching. By then the rain was beginning to assist.

Flames licked and sparks showered. All d'Avila had been able to do was watch ineptly. Final timbers crashed, the smell of casked meat and some memory of the girl burned his nostrils. He was impotent again.

Then he'd heard the explosion and had known why the fire had begun. It had led him here, as it was intended to lead him here. Furiously, he'd turned and run back to the waterfront, to see the darkling shape of *La Petite* carried away by the wind, to hear the shouts aboard the *Courage*, to know that Stone was once more attacking.

For a moment his roaring anger had blinded him completely. His hand had tugged at his dagger; he'd have plunged it into the nearest breast, thrashed out at any who were close. And then he'd caught sight of the mayor, standing on the breakwater, and d'Avila had hidden himself immediately. He wanted none of them to see him now. What was to be done, he must do alone.

So he remained, the dagger unsheathed, waiting for the opportunity to use it to arrive. *He is mine.* The thought went through his mind like fire. *I will have his life. If I can do no more than that, I will have his life.*

Four Frenchman now lay dead on the blood-wet deck, and a fifth member of their crew slumped against the fo'c'sle bulkhead, his hands gripped tightly over his skull. Above him, in his wiry fist, Percy Flanders held aloft an iron pin.

"Wait," Stone shouted. "Do not kill him."

"He killed d'Lesseps," the Cornishman growled.

"Do not kill him," Stone repeated, coming closer, looking about uncertainly. "Does anyone speak French?"

"D'Lesseps did."

"God's pox." Stone bent to the terrified sailor. "How many?" he asked slowly in stumbling French, pointing through the deck. "How many, below?"

The man looked up, new fear in his eyes. "I'm English," he whispered. "Goddard—"

"Then speak. What others are below?"

"Six." Goddard swallowed. "Seven, I'm not sure. Cordier, the bosun, is in charge but—" His hands came up again. "Please don't kill me sir."

Stone spat as Cordier leapt up onto the deck. With him were six more pirates from *La Petite*. The bearded Frenchman raised the pistol he held and shot the nearest of Stone's men, who fell to the deck without a sound, his face a bloody hole. Cordier turned, a second pistol in his grasp, as Lambe leapt upon him. The pistol exploded above Lambe's head; the pair rolled into the scuppers, tearing with hands and feet.

The rest of those from *La Petite* attacked in a rush. Shots were fired. Steel rang. Men fell. Regained their feet to fall again. As they thrashed, the English knew their short strength could not last.

Stone leveled his pistol at a Frenchman's face; he pulled the trigger and heard a useless snap. He threw the

weapon and leapt aside as the man's sword carved.
They closed, struggling to grip in any way they could.
The sword fell to the deck.

One of the Frenchman's hands came up. Stone saw
the gleam of a knife blade and clawed at the steel as
someone kicked his injured hip. His body arched. His
ears were filled with his own scream of agony. He fell,
the Frenchman with him. Once more the knife blade
glittered above him, once again his hands reached for
the weapon. He grasped it as the Frenchman tore it
away. There was the cold deadly slice of the cutting
edge; pain leapt along Stone's arms.

Hurt seared him, from his hip, from his hands, from
every part of his body; he felt his power draining. The
Frenchman raised the knife again, and Stone saw a
blackness rising. It became almost a release into which
he began to drift. His eyes were fixed on the risen blade,
stained with the blood of his hands. There was no strength
left in his arms. He saw the Frenchman's features twist
as the man realized the fight was his. He saw the fixed
head lift from the shoulders as the great blade of van
Staal's axe hacked it away. Blood sprayed down on him
in jets. Stone rolled onto his bloodied hands and knees
and vomited into the scuppers.

In the shadow of the church, Guadalupe waited, her
eyes fixed on the sea. She stared out to where the
Courage lay, from whence came flashes and the sound
of shots and the rasp of steel. She peered past the
shapes of figures lined along the waterfront. She remained aghast, gripping her mother's hand, as men cried
out and killed each other, as the drifting darkness swirled.
Once she imagined she caught sight of d'Avila out of the
corner of her eye, but when she turned to look, the
image had disappeared. Immediately she gazed back out
again, over the water, as her heart filled her frightened
throat.

Jean-Marc Cazaux saw the tilted hulk of his frigate
turn in the dancing seas. Gripped by the tide and the

spinning wind, it headed for shallow water running out from the fort. It staggered and it rolled, it rumbled onto the sands. Water washed over the slanted decks, and the masts leaned low to the waves.

"*Mon Dieu,*" he whispered. "She is gone."

Rain soaked his broadcloth jacket, the scarlet scarf was a wet wound at his throat. He turned toward the *Courage,* where the sound of fighting raged, and had no desire for any part of it. There was as little for him on the English craft as there now was on his own. He tasted defeat in the salty air.

"Back," he said to Sartou. "Back to the shore."

"*Oui, mon capitaine.*" Sartou felt the loss of *La Petite* like a fine mist spreading. He turned the pirogue and began beating back toward the dying flames from d'Avila's barn as they faded in the distance. "What will become of us?" he asked.

"We will see," Cazaux said. The hashish no longer rode his brain; he felt tired and strangely calm. "But do not worry, M'sieu Sartou, somehow we'll survive."

"Somehow, m'sieu?"

"Yes," Cazaux replied, wiping rain from his face. He knew a sense of curious relief, as if he'd come to the end of a journey. All he wished for now was the whiteness of Angela's skin, and sleep. The game was almost over. "Somehow we will survive. We always do, my friend, we always do."

Sartou made no comment. He pushed the tiller toward the sea; he tested the wind and waited.

The only pirate from *La Petite* who was still alive on the *Courage* was the Englishman who'd killed d'Lesseps. Goddard had not moved; he remained curled against the bulkhead, his hands protecting his terrified skull. The others lay dead or had leapt into the sea when van Staal and Cramer came over the stern on the knotted rope that hung from the grappling hook.

Of those from the *Courage* who'd first boarded, Lambe rested against the railing, holding a bleeding arm. At his feet, Percy Flanders lay gasping. Three more were sound; the rest, apart from Stone, had died.

Stone's hip was agony, his hands were fire, there was vomit in his throat. He limped to a hatch and squatted. With fingers that did not want to move, he took off his shirt, tore strips with his teeth, and began to bandage his hands. He looked up to see van Staal staring down in pity.

"Let's go from here," the Dutchman muttered.

"Aye," said Stone. "Let's go."

Cramer came out of the dark. "What does we now?" he asked quite simply.

"We go ashore, to bargain." Stone breathed deeply, his body filled with pain, his mind resigned. "We'll see what can be done."

He ripped another piece of cloth from the remnant of his shirt, knowing they had nothing at all to bargain with. He stared at his gashed fingers. They seemed to mock him with their wreckage. His only hope was that those in Campeche wanted the *Courage*, and all she represented, away from these shores.

A longboat bearing the English, and Goddard the prisoner, rowed awkwardly in from the chopping sea. Before leaving the *Courage*, Lambe and Percy Flanders had thrown the dead into the water, to be taken with the tide, but the decks still stank of blood and death, of failure and defeat. Now the survivors sat silently, their eyes to the shore.

Not a word was spoken as the longboat ground to a halt against the breakwater and the worn faces of those it carried came into the light of the lanterns from above. Don Luis felt only compassion: they were not as they had been. He was certain now that endings were close—what had begun here, on the breakwater, would be completed before the night was done. Now, he began to believe, was a time of charity. He felt for the pistol and wondered about its use.

Hands reached down. Christopher Stone climbed painfully onto the mole. Van Staal and Cramer went with him. The others waited, resigned to the actions of those about them.

"Are there more of you?" Don Luis asked when they came to him. He looked toward the *Courage.*

"Only the dead," Stone replied, his voice blade thin. "And the prisoners who remain in the fort."

"No more?"

"No more."

Don Luis stared at the pirate: the face was gaunter than he recalled, the bones pushed through the flesh. The unshirted body was marked and pale; the bandaged hands were pathetic. Even the eyes had altered: they were quiet now, no longer questing.

Don Luis cleared his throat. "The Spaniards," he began, "Señor Toledo, Teniente Reyes?" An age had passed, the question belonged elsewhere, yet he must ask it. "What of them?"

"Dead." Stone spat. "All dead."

Don Luis breathed deeply. "And the gold?" he asked.

"There was no gold."

"So it was . . ." Don Luis paused, curiously moved: the men before him had earned their peace. "It was for nothing?"

"Nothing? And nothing we found."

Don Luis nodded. An emptiness embraced them all. He felt the pressure of the pistol and knew it would never be used. He was no murderer; he was, after all, merely a merchant. "What do you want from us now?" he asked.

"Nothing," Stone replied, his eyes on his shrouded hands. "Only to go."

"Of course, whenever you wish."

Stone's head came up in gratitude as Guadalupe, silent, her face ashen, was thrust forward into the lamplight—d'Avila's dagger at her throat. For a wild, incredulous moment Stone believed he'd been betrayed. He swung to the mayor in anger, in exhaustion, and saw the same confused expression in Don Luis's eyes.

D'Avila had seen him land and waited. He'd seen the hated figure limp along the mole, and still he'd held his hand. He'd loathed too long, detested too unfailingly, for the sight to break him now. The dagger trembled, hot bile rose to his lips, but he remained, seeing the mayor disregard his promises, watching the cutthroat live.

And then he'd caught sight of the girl. She was moving forward slowly, relief etched on her face. And he'd known, in that instant, why he'd had to wait so long. It had been to have them both. They would die together, as they deserved to die—he who had shamed him, she who had deceived: the expression in her eyes contained nothing but love for the pirate.

D'Avila seized her arm and turned her. Her mouth had opened, she'd paled with shock. He twisted the arm behind her before she'd had time to act and had pushed her forward into the pool of light, the point of his dagger beneath her chin.

"Now, Inglés, now," he shouted. "I have come for you. It is time to answer."

Silence surrounded him, broken only by the lapping of the sea. No one moved; no one seemed to breathe. His entrance had been too sudden for anyone to act. Now he held them, mesmerized and captive.

"You," d'Avila shouted to the wasted Stone. "You, for her."

Stone closed his eyes. The endlessness appalled him. There were too many debts, too many demands. "Guadalupe," he whispered, and looked at her. She was stilled with apprehension.

"Come," d'Avila urged, his eye a beacon in his face. "Now, you will pay."

"If I . . . ." Stone paused, attempting to bargain with what remained. "If I come, you'll release her?"

"Yes," d'Avila lied. Later he would kill her, but none would know it now. "Yes, come. But quickly."

"She"—every word was an effort—"she would have died for you once," Stone said, seeing resignation in Guadalupe's eyes. "You know that."

"Now she will live because of you." The dagger moved in the lamplight. "Hurry, Inglés, I cannot wait to kill you."

Stone nodded and began to walk. Each step he took was excruciating. He would do what had to be done.

"Cristóbal," Guadalupe managed to call, her voice a croak, cut short by d'Avila, "don't—"

Stone made no reply. He walked, and others watched him. His movements seemed to paralyze their own. Don Luis could not have reached for the pistol if he'd wanted to. Cramer and van Staal stood as though frozen. Even Magdelena was absolutely still. Stone walked, his bandaged hands like offerings. His pain was clear for all to see; most watched in morbid fascination.

"Please," Guadalupe whispered.

"Quiet." D'Avila tightened his grip. "Come closer, Inglés." He could feel the thin blade slicing into flesh. "I have waited a very long time."

"Fall," van Staal called in the language. The short hard word carried like a ball. "Fall," he called in Maya.

Guadalupe could not believe it. She could not see the speaker, her eyes were fixed on Stone. But she heard the word in the language and knew it was meant for her ears alone.

"Now," called van Staal. "Fall, now. Away."

D'Avila heard nothing, his gaze not leaving the object of his vengeance. Limping closer, he could taste the reprisal in his mouth. Guadalupe threw herself to the ground. She twisted from his grip, breaking the last of the unburned ties, thrusting his arm with the dagger away, surprising him completely.

With all the strength of his powerful arms, van Staal threw his axe. It flew, turning, the twin blades slicing the air. He'd held it ready, waiting for the moment. He'd called, the girl had fallen away, then he'd flung his anger.

There was an expanded instant: a fraction of stopped time. D'Avila half reached for Guadalupe, half turned to Stone, thinking that they were both extraordinarily close when the axe blade took him in the breastbone. Blade broke bone. He was hurled away, the dagger still gripped in his upright hand, his beard still flecked with his outcry.

Immediately Guadalupe rose and went to Stone and held him.

Van Staal walked to the corpse of d'Avila and bent to retrieve the axe. He wiped the blade clean of the Spaniard's blood, then bent again. When he stood upright, the dull glint of gold dangled from his fingers. Van Staal replaced the necklace about his throat and smiled.

CHAPTER 9

MORNING SUNLIGHT BURNED THE SQUARE. SMALL GROUPS of Indians arranged their produce in the shade. The town was a blending of black shadow and whitewashed wall, of tile and waterfront, of the stilling of the sea.

It had been agreed during the past few days, while those from the *Courage* recovered as they could, while they prepared themselves to go, that they, who had come to conquer, would leave humbly, accepting the mercies they were offered.

They'd take the frigate and depart as soon as able. Most of the crew from *La Petite* would accompany them. Cordier, who'd dived over the side of the *Courage* to survive, would bosun; Marcou would sail instead of Carson; there would be room for Claude le Grand, the one-armed lad, as there was for Sartou. Stone would sail with a collection of men more diverse than the one he'd arrived with, yet the company would be no more mixed than many he'd captained.

The *Courage,* now, was clean. Magdelena, with a group of women from the barrio, had spent a day and more scrubbing the decks free of the stains of combat.

After the death of d'Avila, the remainder of Stone's pirates had been released from the fort. Stone, van Staal, and Guadalupe had gone immediately to find Alvaréz waiting. Without a word he'd handed them the keys.

Only when the chains were unlocked and the prisoners led away did the fat jailer say anything. Then he approached Guadalupe and spoke softly. "Forgive me, señorita, but there is something I would ask." His voice was humble.

Guadalupe turned and stared.

"There was a plaything," Alvaréz began, then swallowed. "Well, it was taken by Capitán d'Avila, and I . . ." He was forced to pause again beneath the girl's unrelenting glare. "I, merely wondered, señorita, if you knew what had become of it."

"The Dutchman has it." There was something savage in Guadalupe's voice. "If you want it, speak to him."

Alvaréz licked his lips. "The one with the axe?" he asked.

"He who killed the commander of the garrison." Guadalupe spoke clearly, biting every word. "It was given to him by a woman he loved. I think he would kill again to keep it, but you must ask him yourself."

"It was . . ." Alvaréz shrugged, knowing he had profaned again. "It was only a plaything."

"Then I suggest you find another."

On their return to the barrio, they found the house rich with the smell of tortillas and chocolate. Stone, who in spite of his pain had insisted on attending the freeing of his men, sank to a seat near the fire, his bandaged hands held out before him. His face was carved with weariness, but his eyes were level.

Guadalupe crouched beside him on the polished wood and held him tightly. "You will not go from me again," she said. "Nor I from you."

Stone sighed, a deep, shuddering expiration that shook him with its intensity.

"We will leave together," Guadalupe whispered. "We will stay together."

Stone turned to her, his eyes wet with unfamiliar tears. "Cristóbal," she began, but he silenced her.

"Shhh," he whispered. "Just hold me."

The following morning, the sun high, Stone dressed and went to arrange the departure. His breeches had been washed, his seaboots oiled; he wore an Indian cotton shirt and, in the new day, felt less as if he were broken beyond repair. He still walked with a limp, but he knew that the cuts on his hands would heal; their bandages were fresh.

Later he stood with Cazaux on the breakwater, their eyes on the bulk of *La Petite* lying on the sands.

"I'm told you would have released my men," Stone said, looking forward. "Sent them off in the *Courage*."

Cazaux nodded. "It was a prospect the mayor and I discussed," he replied without comment.

"With Cordier as captain and some purchase?"

Cazaux shrugged. "We thought you were dead," he said simply.

"You sent them food and blankets." Stone turned and stared at the elegant Frenchman, who was dressed in cloth that seemed new. "Why?"

Cazaux smiled, his scar curved. "That was due to the generosity of my wife-to-be," he said. He paused, then added, "She is a remarkable woman."

"She must be," Stone remarked dryly, "as you are a rogue."

"We all of us are rogues, my friend." Cazaux's voice was even, untroubled by the condemnation. "But some of us not so deeply in the heart."

Stone looked again at the Frenchman, accepting the penetrative remark. "Speaking as a rogue," he said, but without rancor, "what happened to our purchase?" His eyes went back to *La Petite*.

"It is on the frigate," Cazaux answered. "Whatever is left of her."

"It was not split among your crew?"

"A little only, to stop them murdering me in Tampa Bay." Cazaux shrugged eloquently. "But who knows what there will be out there now. It is a great irony, no? The manner of its going?"

Stone grunted. "We can attempt to salvage what there is," he said.

"Of course," Cazaux replied, but his voice carried no interest. To be honest, the purchase concerned him little now. "But you must take whatever there is," he added. "I will present my father-to-be with a handful of coins. It will be all that was located. You, and those who sail on the *Courage,* are welcome to the rest."

Stone smiled frankly. "You will succeed here," he said with open admiration.

One afternoon a servant came to the waterfront for Cramer the Black, who waited. The tall Negro accompanied the man to the house of the mayor, then went upstairs alone into what had been Angela's bedroom, where he remained for some time.

Little was heard from the closeted room on the upper floor, no significant sound drifted down from the balcony to the courtyard below and the servants who pretended not to listen. None of them was even certain that Angela was in the house. All they knew of the occasion was the instruction to fetch the blackamoor at the hour of the afternoon when the sun was beginning its downward slant and the shadows were starting to lengthen. It was the time when one knew little of the events of another. It was the hour of siesta.

However, a maid who sat in her tiny dormitory, some distance from Angela's boudoir, thought she heard soft voices singing and, once, the sound of laughter, but she was never sure. And when she went to her window to listen, all was silent in the house once more.

Later Cramer emerged alone from the upstairs room and shut the door behind him. He walked slowly down to the tilted courtyard, scratching the stub of his missing left ear. He went out of the house and away, and none of them ever saw him again. However, the servant girl who'd been unable to sleep said that when he left he'd been smiling, that his eyes were like those of a man in a dream.

On another occasion, during those last spinning days, Christopher Stone sat with Don Luis de Córdoba in the elaborate council chamber with its portrait of the long-dead king.

Stone spoke of the deaths, the disaster, and the defeat, of the splendor, of Tayasal, the rituals of its people, and the absence of gold. He said nothing of the manner in which Toledo and Azcaráte had died; he did not mention the wealth of blood.

"They all died bravely," he said finally. "And Toledo asked that a Mass be said for his soul."

Don Luis nodded solemnly. "I will see to it," he replied.

"I would include them all," Stone suggested.

"It will be done." Don Luis cleared his throat. "But there was no gold, you say?"

"It holds no value for them. They prefer the feathers of a long-tailed bird."

"Curious," Don Luis said contemplatively. He looked away. "I am told they practice sodomy and sacrifice human beings to their pagan idols." He coughed loudly. "You saw nothing of any of this?"

"Nothing." Stone had a vision of Ix Mai walking away, her back straight; in her belly was the seed of van Staal. "They are brutal, but so are we."

"They are heathen." The mayor was uncomfortable with the conversation. His kingdom was here, by the sea. This English pirate knew more of the interior than he would ever absorb. The mayor shrugged. "Their souls are doomed," he added without conviction.

"Then I suggest you include them in the Mass for your own dead." Stone leaned across the table to the mayor. "If your God has any real compassion, He will understand."

Don Luis turned to Stone. "My God is your God," he said, wondering at the resentment in the Englishman's words.

"That, I may reasonably doubt," said Stone.

Don Luis looked steadily at the gaunt features before him, at the eyes that would never be still. "I will be glad when you are gone," he said quite simply.

Early one afternoon, when the tide had laid bare the bones of *La Petite*, Stone and van Staal, Cazaux and

Cordier, went out to discover what could be salvaged from the wreckage on the sand bank.

The sight of the beached vessel depressed them all, those who had caused it as much as those who had trod her decks. Timbers had sprung with the force of the sea, ropes and canvas were twisted about broken spars, masts lay across the water. Seabirds were perched on the salt-caked woodwork; they rose flapping as the men rowed closer.

"Sweet Jesu," said Stone as he stepped onto the sand bar, "she is a sorry sight." He turned to Cazaux, who stared with curiosity and dismay: so much had been reduced so quickly. "Where should we begin?" Stone asked.

"Oh"—Cazaux tore his eyes away—"in the cabin of M'sieu Sartou."

Stone clumsily removed his boots and walked through the little running waves that spilled over the sand. Behind him the others followed. He climbed up onto the sloping deck and came to a cabin awash with the sea.

"Is this it?" Stone asked.

Cazaux nodded, his face marked with disbelief.

Stone kicked, and the cabin door fell inward with a splash. The interior was filled with seawater, in which floated pieces of furniture enwrapped with lengths of ruined cloth. Stone removed his shirt and lowered himself into water that swirled up to his chest. His feet touched what had once been the cabin wall, and he began to creep into the gloom.

He bent and moved his long arms through the debris, not knowing what he searched for. His bandaged hands made contact with a square object. He pulled it free and peered. It was a once polished box of scented woods. Stone pried open the lid to see the glint of pieces of eight.

"Here," he said, passing it up to van Staal. "We have made a beginning."

They swept the water-filled cabin for hours, locating silver plate and jewelry, gold coin, and strings of pearls. They did not find all that had been stored, but they encountered enough. The men who sailed with them would have something to buy and boast with.

They loaded the purchase onto the rowboat and were ready to leave when Cazaux made a final tour of his ship. They waited in the rising sea until he returned with a small, silver-bound crystal flask in hand: it contained a dark green liquid.

"It was all that was worth taking," the Frenchman said with a shrug, and wiped water from his face. "It will be a small comfort."

They left the remains of the frigate. Soon *La Petite* would break completely, her timbers would strip, and her ribs would show. The sea and the sand would slowly swallow her; in the end she'd be forgotten.

Some days later, the *Courage* was ready to leave Campeche. At noon, the hour of departure, the sky was a creamy layer of cloud, and excitement charged the ship. She was clean and now polished; ropes lay coiled, the decks had been sandstoned, fresh provisions were stored: she was ready to voyage once again.

Aboard, the crew moved easily. They found new life as they loosened canvas and checked the sheets. As their hands ran over known woodwork, as their feet walked again, experienced passageways, their blood lifted, and something new was born.

There were fifty-eight of them in all: the handful that remained of the *Courage*'s original crew; the rest were mostly from *La Petite*. Two Creoles from the garrison had asked to join, and both had been accepted. One was Alvaréz, still clinging to part of Cramer's dream.

When the moment came, Guadalupe held her mother and allowed her tears to flow. When Magdelena spoke, her voice was strong. "Go, my daughter," she said. "It is what I would do."

Guadalupe nodded. "One day we will return," she said, and wondered.

"Of course." Magdelena stood back and wiped her daughter's face, seeing herself as she might have been. "Go quickly, before I too begin to cry."

Guadalupe turned; she was the last to board.

The waterfront, the breakwater, all the shore, held more than any would have expected. The fort, the white-walled buildings, were a background to those who had come to see the *Courage* go. In their midst was Angela, resplendent in a full deep dress of scarlet silk; she lifted a milk-white hand and waved.

Van Staal raised his voice. Men moved, and canvas took the wind. The graceful craft turned from the town. Campeche receded into its ring of purple hills, became a shimmering collection of white-cut jewels in an earthen setting. Above, the sun burned like fire through glass.

"Where is it we're going?" Guadalupe asked, still staring at the space that was her mother. "What is this town that has changed its name?"

"New York," said Stone, his eyes ahead. He smiled a little. "It is distant from here. It is on an island. But it is new."

Guadalupe turned to him and saw the pleasure on his face. "Are you sure?" she asked, catching the lifting mood.

"I am certain," Stone said softly. "It is new." His smile grew. "What is more, I have a promise to make you."

Guadalupe stared up at him. "A promise?" she queried.

Stone nodded. "I promise that we will make love all the way to New York. We've had such little time to call our own."

Guadalupe's arms went about him; he had reduced the memories in her heart. "Cristóbal," she whispered. Then, her voice altering, she asked, "Will this journey be very long?"

"That depends on the wind," Stone replied.

"Then I will pray we do not get any wind," she told him. "None at all. No more. Never."

The *Courage* rolled gently as she took the sea. Ahead, the horizon was a clear bold line. Behind, Campeche remained intact. Beyond, Tayasal endured. Each belonged, in some part, to the other.